DEATH LORD ARCANIST

ASTRA ACADEMY BOOK IV

SHAMI STOVALL

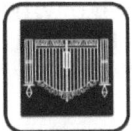

Published by
CS BOOKS, LLC

This is a work of fiction. Names, characters, places, and incidents either are the product of author imagination or are used fictitiously, and any resemblance to actual persons, living or dead, business establishments, events, or locales, is entirely fictional.

Cover Design: Darko Paganus

Editors: Nia Quinn, Celestian Rince

IF YOU WANT TO BE NOTIFIED WHEN SHAMI STOVALL'S NEXT BOOK RELEASES, PLEASE VISIT HER WEBSITE OR CONTACT HER DIRECTLY AT

s.adelle.s@gmail.com

Contents

To John, my soulmate.
To Justin Barnett, who is way too good to me and helped so much.
To Gail and Big John, my surrogate parents.
To Drew, my agent.
To Henry Copeland, for the beautiful leather map and book covers.
To Mary, Emily, Scott, James, Ryan & Dana, for all the jokes and input.
To my patrons over on Patreon, for naming the Academy.
To my Facebook group, for all the memes.
And finally, to everyone unnamed, thank you for everything.

A Recap Of Events

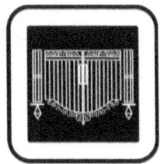

L ast time in the Astra Academy series, Gray Lexly suffered from a new kind of nightmare—dreams that were mixed with the memories of Death Lord Deimos. As Gray continued his studies at the prestigious Academy, the fragment of Death Lord Deimos's soul that was trapped within him gradually became more aware of Gray and his surroundings, even speaking to Gray through his subconscious.

It wasn't long before Gray and Deimos could communicate at all times, not just through dreams.

And while learning archery from the new Combat Arts professor, Gray displayed skills with a bow that he had never had before. Deimos's presence was fully seeping into Gray's body, giving Gray access to the Death Lord's skills and knowledge. And while it was helpful, it was also gravely concerning.

Unfortunately, Professor Helmith was still unwell after her battle with the Death Lord, and couldn't help him. Instead, Helmith's husband, Kristof, replaced her as a professor. But he didn't come to the Academy to help Gray—he specifically came to keep an eye on Gray. Kristof was concerned his wife's involvement in Gray's life would result in her death.

Gray attempted to be a model student, to prove Kristof wrong, but that all came to an end when Death Lord cultists kidnapped Gray's family and attempted to steal Deimos's soul fragment for themselves. They worshipped Death Lord Naiad, another arcanist in the abyssal hells who wanted Deimos dead.

During the struggle, Gray used more of Deimos's skills, and even some of his abyssal dragon magic. Nini also killed one of the cultists, adding to her reaper magic. Thankfully, Gray managed to save his family.

Once they returned to Astra Academy, they celebrated Phila's cotillion and bonded as a class. But Gray was worried about Deimos, and found himself concerned about his future.

Desperate to win Ashlyn's father's approval, so that Gray would be allowed to marry her, Gray decided to enter an Academy competition. Ashlyn's father would be in attendance, and since Gray had access to skills beyond his years, he thought the whole competition would be in the bag.

And while he did win, the resulting celebrations turned into a nightmare.

Death Lord Naiad managed to pull Gray, Knovak, Nini, and Ashlyn into the abyssal hells through Deimos's connection to Gray.

Once in the abyssal hells, Naiad attempted to kill them. Fortunately, Gray fended her off, but it was a tiring battle. Lost in the abyssal hells, Gray wasn't entirely sure how they would survive and return to the land of the living.

And now it's time to continue the story in *Death Lord Arcanist*.

Death Lord Deimos

CHAPTER 1

STRANDED IN THE ABYSS

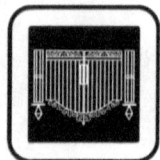

Although I wanted nothing more than to return to Astra Academy, somehow, I was trapped in the abyssal hells.

Thankfully, I wasn't alone. Twain, my mimic eldrin, was asleep in my arms, exhausted after our fight with Death Lord Naiad. And it wasn't just Twain who had joined me in this bizarre place. Ashlyn Kross, with her typhoon dragon eldrin, Ecrib; Nini Wanderlin, along with her reaper eldrin, Waste; and finally, Knovak Gentz, with his unicorn eldrin, Starling, had all been transported to the abyssal hells with me.

But *where* in the abyssal hells were we?

Everywhere I looked, I glimpsed strange sights. We all stood around a bizarre and freakish mire known as the *Wraithborne Orchard*. It was a swamp of dark water, where every ripple and wave formed the face of tortured individuals.

Under the water, making up most of the "ground," was a rocky surface of black and white stones. The black stones were nothing more than swirls and spirals, but the smaller white stones were carved into the shape of human faces, each with a different expression. Some sad, some delighted, some pinched in disgust.

Staring into the water only resulted in me staring at the many tiny faces.

It disturbed me.

The crimson "sky" had a gray haze of clouds, but we were actually underground. Roots—gigantic roots, for a tree fifty times larger than the treehouse—traveled from the ceiling down into the Wraithborne Orchard. Black waterfalls also cascaded from the ceiling, splashing in the horrid water around us.

Probably the most disturbing of all were the smaller roots growing off the larger ones. Each of the tiny roots was shaped like a human hand, and they grasped at anything that moved by.

Swaths of strange fireflies danced all around, and occasionally, the hands managed to grab one. The instant one did, the root hand receded into the tree, taking the firefly with it.

I never saw either again.

The chill in the air went straight to my bones. The place smelled of burnt incense and sea salt. Nothing about this place was welcoming.

And to make the situation even more tense, there was one last arcanist here with us.

Death Lord Deimos.

He stood in the ankle-deep waters not too far from us. Deimos's armor was shattered, exposing most of his body. He was taller than most, with a physique that matched his history of war and violence. He was muscled, and scarred, and when he moved, Deimos did so with purpose.

"Come," Deimos said to us. "Before we lose the option."

He slicked back his black hair with a quick motion of his hand. His eyes disturbed me. They were dark—nearly black with a hint of yellow in his irises. Deimos had a cutthroat and dangerous demeanor.

The Death Lord turned and sloshed through the water.

"We can't go with him," Knovak said.

I faced him. He was mostly unharmed, his fancy evening

clothes still intact. They were wet from the mire, and wrinkled, but otherwise fine. His plain sandy hair was disheveled, and he stood close to his unicorn, Starling. The little foal trembled.

"We can trust Deimos," I said.

Knovak shook his head. "He tried to kill you! *Multiple times.*"

"If he wanted to kill us now, he would've done so. C'mon. We don't have many other choices here."

I turned to Ashlyn and Nini.

For some reason, Nini refused to unmerge with her reaper. Waste was wrapped around her, his red cloak tight on her shoulders. Three chains hung from him, each holding a lit lantern. His scythe, once rusted and dull, was now as sharp as any masterfully crafted weapon and seemingly made from gold and silver with rubies in the shaft.

The lanterns...

They glowed yellow, but powerful blue magic oozed out from under Waste's cloak, disturbing and powerful both.

Nini didn't have her glasses, and her eyes searched my face for a long moment.

"We should trust Death Lord Deimos," Nini and Waste said together. She reached up and tucked her red hair into the hood of Waste's cloak. "Gray is right. If he wanted, he could kill us."

Nini glanced out across the disturbing mire.

Deimos waited next to his eldrin—a monstrous abyssal dragon.

It was a beast both terrifying and powerful. The dragon's wings were made of grafted souls, cobwebbed together and a bright, sickly blue, the same color of Waste's new magic. Human faces dotted the wings, their eyes circles, their mouths open as they softly moaned and cried.

Deimos's eldrin turned its massive head to face us. The monstrous dragon had six eyes, and they glanced around the Wraithborne Orchard independent of one another. It was difficult to know if the creature was fascinated by us, or the strange roots in the area, since it stared at both at the same time.

Abyssal dragons had rotted scales and muscles that oozed mucus. But Deimos's eldrin was in worse shape. One of its front legs had been sliced off just before the elbow. A nub of bone jutted out of the dragon's rotted flesh, and blue ooze dripped from the wound. As I watched, the ooze hardened and formed muscle around the bone, adding to the arm.

It appeared the dragon was slowly regrowing its limb, one tortured strand of flesh at a time.

"Are you sure we can trust him, Gray?" Ashlyn asked.

She shivered.

Unlike Knovak, who had near-pristine clothing, Ashlyn had fought against corpses, and their claws had torn her beautiful sapphire gown. Crimson stains and finger-length tears spotted her outfit. Her gown had no sleeves, and her bare shoulders were pale.

Ashlyn, even as scruffy as she was, remained beautiful.

However, I couldn't allow her to get cold in the middle of the abyssal hells.

I removed my school robe and wrapped it around her. She met my gaze as she gently tugged my clothing tightly around her body.

"Thank you," Ashlyn whispered.

"Don't mention it." I gestured to Deimos. "Trust me. We need to follow the Death Lord. You and Knovak shouldn't be here."

I wanted to tell her, "*You're both dying*," but I kept that to myself. Knovak shook, and his eyes were wide. He wouldn't take the news well, and I couldn't drag a hysterical man around through the abyssal hells while we were trying to avoid a Death Lord.

"If you trust him, I will, too." Ashlyn stepped closer to me. "Let's go."

Her eldrin, Ecrib, splashed through the mire. His blue scales seemed dull in this environment, even though they were typically vibrant. He lowered his head and sniffed the water.

"This place smells of the salt water found in the midnight depths," Ecrib said. He lifted his draconic head and the fins along his back twitched. "So much salt. And death. The bodies of fish and countless whales contaminate this place."

Knovak's unicorn whinnied and lifted his legs as though he wanted to fly out of the swamp and never look back.

"Knock it off," I snapped. "C'mon."

I placed my hand on Ashlyn's shoulder. Together, we made our way through the Wraithborne Orchard. Nini followed close behind, her reaper merged with her no matter what. Knovak and his unicorn were much slower, but they eventually picked up their pace when I neared the Death Lord and his dragon.

Deimos regarded me with a cold glare and then jutted his chin in the direction we needed to go. Deimos didn't walk—his dragon lowered its head, and Deimos took hold. His eldrin lifted him out of the water and carried him along.

Despite missing a limb, the abyssal dragon managed to walk just fine. Its soul-covered wings remained spread, creating an eerie canopy over us as we traveled.

The roots of the massive tree were so gnarled and thick, I wondered what kind of plant they even originated from. It was no tree I had ever seen in my life, that I knew for certain.

Ashlyn leaned on my arm.

We walked without conversing. In a normal swamp, the cries of birds and the chirp of crickets would be common. Here, the moans of anguish and the sharp snaps of something being broken were all I could detect outside our splashes through the water.

Deimos's dragon turned around a root, where a small island awaited us. The rotting dragon dragged itself up onto the dirt and then lowered its head. Its six eyes gazed, flitting in all directions.

Deimos slid off the creature, but held on to its shoulder for support.

"Is this the spot?" I asked.

It was just an island of dirt next to a giant root.

No plants.

No animals.

No gate.

Nothing.

Why were we here?

"The waters of this orchard steal your strength," Deimos stated. "We'll wait here for a moment. Then, we'll swim to our destination." He pointed with a finger to a root off in the distance. "Once we're in the water, Naiad will abandon her pursuit."

Nini, Knovak, and Ashlyn all walked onto the small island. I joined them, but I wasn't sure what we were supposed to do while we waited. If Knovak and Ashlyn only had so much time to live, wasn't waiting here just killing them? Wouldn't it be better to push forward as fast as possible?

Then Deimos collapsed to one knee, blood spilling from two injuries along his ribs. He grabbed at his wounds, his fingers practically sliding into his flesh, but it didn't stop the blood flow. A stream of scarlet marked his ruined armor and then fell to the ground, quickly seeping into the dirt.

I set Twain down and hurried over to Deimos. "Are you okay?" I reached out to examine his injuries.

Deimos tensed and snarled. "*Touch me, and your life is forfeit.*"

I stood straight and withdrew my hand.

The others leapt to the far edge of the small barren island, their eyes wide. Even Ecrib, the mighty typhoon dragon, was shaken. And why wouldn't they be? Deimos's eldrin seemed just as upset. It lifted its disgusting head and peeled back its cracked lips to showcase the many fangs in its undead mouth.

After a long, strained moment, I leaned forward and placed my hands on my knees. "I don't know if you're aware, but you're bleeding," I sarcastically whispered. "And sure, you're immortal, but it's really demoralizing to see you like this."

Deimos met my gaze with the iciest glare. "I'd rather the foul winds of the abyssal hells carry my ashes over this orchard than listen to your blighted jokes."

"Harsh," I quipped. "But noted." I inched a little closer. "Then why don't you let me help you, so we don't have to watch you bleed out like a stuck pig?"

Deimos didn't reply. He closed his eyes and took a deep breath.

A fragment of his soul still resided in me, and his thoughts occasionally crept into my own. He felt worried. Something about his soul. He was damaged. Death Lord Naiad had attempted to graft his soul to her eldrin, and in the process, she had damaged him at a fundamental level. He wasn't healing as quickly as he should be.

I touched my collarbone and felt under my tattered shirt. Vivigöl, Silencer of the Damned, the weapon made of abyssal coral, was around my neck and shoulders in the shape of jewelry. Since it had absorbed some of my mimic magic, it had the ability to transform, and I contemplated removing it.

"Would having Vivigöl make you feel better?" I asked.

Deimos slowly opened his eyes, his expression filled with contempt. "If you condescend to me, child, I will—"

"I'm being serious," I interjected. "Maybe it would make you feel better to have your weapon back?"

Deimos exhaled. Then he closed his eyes again, his hand red with his own blood. His injuries continued to gush vital fluid.

"Hold on to it," he commanded. "We may need you to wield it against Naiad. Or one of the others."

"The others?" I whispered.

"Death Lord Kallikore or Umbriel... They are both aware I've come here."

"How do they know?" I was genuinely curious.

"Death Lords seldom travel to the *first abyss*..."

I stood straight and glanced around. The first abyss? Nasbit had once told me about the many layers of the abyssal hells, and I struggled for a moment to remember what he had said. There were five layers, and the first was for all souls. It was a place of reincarnation. At least, from what I could recall.

"Is there something I can do to help?" I motioned to his wounds. "Twain can transform into an abyssal dragon. I could use its magic to fix this."

"Feh." Deimos almost laughed, but he stifled it with a growl. "You're still a student who has yet to master your magic. I have little faith you can mend my damaged soul."

"You're a skilled arcanist, aren't you?" Again, I inched a little closer, until I was near enough to reach out and help. "You can guide my hand. You've transferred your skills to me before, right? This'll be easy."

Deimos tightened his grip on his injuries, his own fingers seemingly agitating the wounds. The more blood that wept from his ribs, the more splashed onto the dirt, creating a blackish mud.

His abyssal dragon lowered its head, its fangs close, its putrid breath hot on my back.

I refused to inhale while Deimos deliberated.

We needed Deimos. If he became incapacitated—or was killed by another Death Lord—there was no way we were navigating out of the abyssal hells by ourselves. So, it was either help him get better, or a slow death in the land of the dead. I wasn't going to choose the latter.

Chapter 2

Eat Nothing

Deimos closed his eyes. "Very well. Have your mimic transform into an abyssal dragon."

With a nod, I turned around. Twain was still asleep. He was the smallest creature here—just a tiny orange kitten, rolled into a loaf as he slept. He had no tail, just a nub, and his ears were larger than a normal house cat's. He had the ears of a lynx, with tufts of fur at the tips. I called him a kitten, but he was a little bigger than when I had met him, and I wondered how large he would eventually grow.

I walked over and scooped him into my arms. Twain purred as he opened his strangely colored eyes. One was gray, and the other was rosy pink. I patted his head.

"I know you're tired, but do you think you can transform for just a short while?" I scratched behind one of his ears. "I'm going to attempt to help Deimos."

Twain closed his eyes and yawned. "I think... just for a little bit."

"Thanks. You're the best."

He dismissively waved a paw. "Oh. Stop." When I said nothing else, he twitched his whiskers, opened his eyes in a playful glare, and ended his purring. "But actually, keep going. I need more praise."

"You're the best mimic in the abyssal hells," I said.

Although he was the *only* mimic in the abyssal hells, he seemed to accept that as praise enough. Twain resumed his purring. I placed him back on the dirt and then mystically sensed the thread of magic that led to Deimos's abyssal dragon. When I tugged it, Twain's body shimmered.

I stepped away as he grew larger and larger, his body taking on the massive form of the dragon—including missing an arm. The wings were identical, complete with tortured faces, and I wondered what it meant to "duplicate" the souls like this. Were they real? No. Obviously. But still... it made me wonder.

The arcanist mark on my forehead was usually blank. Everyone else had a picture of their eldrin wrapped around the points of their stars, but mine was empty. Except for when Twain transformed—my mark burned as the image of the abyssal dragon appeared etched into my skin.

Our tiny island of dirt wasn't large enough for everyone. Deimos's dragon lowered itself back into the brackish waters, its rotting flesh becoming bloated.

Knovak, Ashlyn, and Nini watched from afar, all of them at the edge of our land.

With the power of the mighty abyssal dragon, I returned to Deimos's side. The man remained on one knee, his hand still gripped tight on his injury. He stared at the ground, his eyes unfocused. When I approached, he tensed and shot me a glare.

"Present your hand," he commanded.

I held it out.

Deimos grabbed it, his palm cold and sweaty. Although I wanted to ask him what I should be doing, I said nothing, opting to wait instead. He closed his eyes and exhaled. His thoughts drifted to the forefront of my own.

Soul manipulation...

Abyssal dragon arcanists could manipulate the souls of others. And since a person's soul was the heart of their magic—really, the heart of all magic was souls—the abyssal dragons had the ability to warp them.

Deimos's soul...

It didn't feel right. Not only was it missing a piece, but Naiad's assault on his being had left him exhausted. With Deimos's guidance, I attempted to use my magic to help. Manipulating something I couldn't see was more difficult, however. I closed my eyes, trying to imagine my work.

Deimos's soul was like a rag that had been twisted one too many times. Untwisting it required most of my concentration. I couldn't do this quickly. Deimos's thoughts told me souls were fragile. If I messed this up, I could damage him.

Or worse—rip his soul straight from his body.

As a matter of fact, Deimos's heart beat harder than before. His anxiety permeated his thoughts and emotions. He was afraid. Not of me failing, but that I would betray him, and attempt to use the abyssal magic to remove his soul and graft it to Twain...

Which was the only way to kill a Death Lord, really.

"You need to stop worrying," I whispered. "It's making everything difficult."

"I'm not worried, *child*."

"You're a terrible liar."

After a few moments of untwisting, I was halfway through the process. Unfortunately, my magic waned. I glanced over my shoulder and caught sight of Twain's dragon form. He huffed and collapsed to the dirt, rumbling the little island. A second later, he untransformed, becoming a small orange kitten once again.

I pulled my hand away from Deimos's.

I had helped him a little, but not fully repaired his injuries.

Deimos exhaled. When he removed his hand from his injury,

the flesh began to mend itself. The blood flow slowed, and with his teeth gritted, he managed to stand.

He was taller than me—which I hated, for some reason—but I tried not to let it influence my thoughts. The fragment of Deimos's soul in my mind allowed him to sense some of my emotions as well.

Deimos glowered down at me, but said nothing.

"Normally, people say *thank you* after someone does something nice for them," I said, my tone sardonic. "You can try it now, if you want."

"The only reason I'm in this situation is because of you," Deimos darkly stated. "If I had entered the realm of the living when my twin brother, Zahn, completed his Gate of Crossing, none of this would've happened. Furthermore, if a fragment of my soul hadn't been sealed away in the realm of your dreams, I wouldn't have gotten caught by Death Lord Naiad, and I never would've been injured."

With a nervous shrug, I said, "Can you really know that for certain, though?"

"The intelligent course of action would be to kill you and take back my weapon and soul." Deimos tightened one hand into a fist and then released. "But I will concede you came to my defense when Naiad attacked, despite not needing to interfere. And now... when I was at my weakest... you never faltered in your aid."

"And we really don't want to fight here." I motioned to Twain. "I mean, we're evenly matched, and it would be rough."

"Your mimic is spent," Deimos said. "It would be a short and pathetic fight."

"R-Right," I muttered.

Deimos smirked. "You need to stop worrying. It's making everything difficult."

That actually got me to smile and choke out a laugh. "Oh, you got jokes now, Dee? That's definitely an improvement over threatening to kill me every other sentence." I pointed at him. "Look, let's just agree we're not going to murder each other, and get out of here as quickly as possible."

Deimos didn't agree or disagree. He simply faced the location of the massive root he had pointed at earlier. With a simple gesture of his bloody hand, he garnered everyone's attention. "The Wraithborne Orchard takes its souls into the roots. We need to enter one, and ascend."

His statement left everyone silent for a long while.

"Enter one?" Ashlyn eventually asked. "How?"

"Are they hollow?" Knovak rubbed his arms, his teeth chattering.

"They are," Deimos stated.

No one had any other questions after that. What were we supposed to ask? *Why?* Seemed like it wasn't relevant at the moment.

I grabbed Twain and held him close to my chest. He purred, but otherwise offered no other interactions. Then we all walked to the edge of the dirt island. Deimos entered the knee-deep waters before everyone else. His blood stained the dark liquid until an opaque cloud slung around the shore.

"We'll need to swim," Deimos said. He glanced over his shoulder, his expression cold. "I assume you children know how that's done?"

Everyone slowly nodded.

"Good." Deimos walked a few feet out. "Follow me."

"Wait," Ashlyn said as she held up her hand.

Death Lord Deimos stopped, but he didn't turn to look at her. Due to our connection, I knew he was already irritated. He didn't much care for interruptions.

"My typhoon dragon magic can help us." Ashlyn motioned for everyone to gather close. "I can augment people so they can breathe underwater. That way, there's no chance of misfortune."

"Thank you," Nini and Waste whispered as one.

Knovak stepped close. Ashlyn touched his arm and augmented him first. Once he had the dragon's ability to breathe water, he stepped away, his stomach grumbling.

"Are there fish in the water?" Knovak glanced over at Deimos. "Or something we can find and cook?"

A group of fireflies danced down the dirt island right after Knovak asked his question. The tiny creatures swirled about, first circling Knovak, and then heading for the base of a root. As if asking for our collective attention, they bobbed by the bark.

It was only then I spotted something growing out of the roots. They were grape-sized berries, each glowing a pale blue. They grew right where the water touched the root, half-submerged, half-above the water's surface. The little glowing grapes blended well with the environment, but as the fireflies danced, I realized there were more around on *every* root.

"Are those insects helping us?" Knovak asked. He walked across the dirt island, heading straight for the grapes. "Oh, thank the good stars. I thought everything here would be unrelentingly evil."

"*Stop*," Deimos growled.

Knovak stopped dead in his tracks, his face paling.

The Death Lord sloshed the water as he turned on his heel. "Eat *nothing* here. Do you understand me? *Nothing*. No matter how tasty it may appear—or how many things may tempt you. Consume *nothing*."

Knovak wrung his hands. "Is... is something wrong with the fruit?"

"It isn't fruit, *simpleton*." Deimos once again turned on his heel, his back to us. "Everything in the abyssal hells, from the water to the plants, to the architecture, is a product of death—fragments of souls, bones, and blood. The abyssal hells have nothing else, no matter what it may disguise itself as."

His statement sent an icy silence through the group.

Everything here... was made of souls and gore? Even the glowing berries?

"What about the fireflies?" Ashlyn whispered. "Are they souls, too?"

Deimos nodded once.

Knovak leapt back into the company of the group, his skin covered in goosebumps. He practically rubbed shoulders with me in an attempt to distance himself from the glowing berries. "But... but why would the fireflies try to tempt me? What do they have to gain?"

Deimos growled something under his breath. His irritation was reaching an all-time high, but he calmed himself a moment later, probably because we would need to know this information if we were going to survive.

"If you consume anything here, your magic will become twisted—infested with the souls of others who desperately want your body. If your *eldrin* consumes anything here, it will grow in size and power. It will become an *elder creature*... And it will lose itself to the lust for power."

As if my stomach wanted to tempt me as well, it knotted with hunger. I rubbed my gut, trying not to think about it. We would be out of here soon, after all. We would be fine.

"What if..." Nini and Waste hesitated a moment before asking, "If we ate one another? Since we aren't part of the abyssal hells, will the consequences be the same?"

"That's a morbid question," I said, completely sardonic. "Have anything you want to share with the group, Nini?"

Her face brightened red as she shook her head. "I... I was just curious."

"You may eat each other if you want," Deimos said, no mirth in his voice. He was as deadly serious as when he had given us the warning. "I care not. However, if you want to escape, you'll stay close to me—and do exactly as I say."

The others nodded.

Ashlyn then augmented the rest of us, her magic soothing. I met her gaze, and her eyes told me she was frightened, but determined to get home. I appreciated that. Unlike Knovak, who I would need to watch, I could count on Ashlyn to have my back.

I needed that kind of support in a moment like this.

CHAPTER 3

THE ROOTS

Death Lord Deimos sloshed forward, away from the barren island. His dragon hobbled after him, walking oddly due to its healing limb. The beast's soul-grafted wings moaned and writhed, creating an eerie chorus of suffering in the otherwise silent abyssal hells.

Nini hurried after him, her demeanor different than before. She seemed... more comfortable around the Death Lord, and I briefly wondered if it was because she was still merged with Waste. That reaper of hers loved death, and perhaps this was his true home.

"What should *I* do?" Starling asked.

The little unicorn foal trembled at the edge of the island. He pointed with his horn, gesturing to the water. His thin little legs, frail body, and glistening mane were not really suited for swimming. He was large enough—about three feet at the shoulder—to make this all difficult. Carrying a unicorn foal while trying to swim through normal water would be rough, and apparently these depths sapped strength.

"I'll carry you," Ecrib growled. He stomped over to the unicorn and then scooped Starling up in his arms.

"You can swim like this?" Starling kicked his legs, his hooves glittering.

"I'm a typhoon dragon. I can swim under any conditions."

Ecrib cradled the unicorn close as he stomped out into the water. It wasn't yet deep enough for swimming, but the dragon continued to carry the foal regardless. Knovak walked alongside Ecrib, staying close to his eldrin, despite his own obvious fear.

With Twain still in my arms, I stepped out into the water. Ashlyn followed, and for a few minutes we kept pace with Deimos, but eventually Ashlyn's outfit slowed her down. It was her long flowing gown. The hem was soaked and kept getting caught on the strange stone faces. Pointy noses and sharp chins would hook the hem of her dress's train, and Ashlyn would be yanked back for a moment, and a slight tear would appear.

"Ugh," Ashlyn said as she yanked her clothing off another rock.

I grabbed her upper arm. "Take Twain. I'll fix this."

She lifted an eyebrow, skeptical but trusting. Ashlyn took Twain from me, and I grabbed Vivigöl from my body. The golden weapon *click-click-clicked* as it transformed from ornate jewelry to a keen sword with a guard made of six flared spikes. Vivigöl transformed into whatever object I needed in the moment, but it couldn't change its mass. I had wanted a small knife, but a sword was the best it could achieve.

I stepped forward. "May I?" I asked as I gestured to Ashlyn's dress.

She still wore my robes, and she tugged them tightly over her shoulders. "That's fine."

I knelt and sliced through the tattered blue fabric with Vivigöl. I slowly cut away at the dress, removing the lower half to give Ashlyn more room to maneuver. Although the weapon was quite sharp, she didn't flinch away when I cut close to her legs. Once finished, I tossed the ruined cloth into the water and stood.

Her dress now fell halfway down her thighs—short and frilled outward. Still dirty, and torn, and probably spotted with blood, but it was a little too difficult to tell. The lighting in the abyssal hells wasn't... natural. Everything felt like a bizarre mix of twilight and haze.

My robes hung longer than her dress now, and I was tempted to cut those as well, but Ashlyn removed them and then swaddled Twain.

"What're you doing?" I asked.

"I'll carry him," she said. With a confident smile, she added, "I'm a typhoon dragon arcanist. I can swim under any conditions. *You'll* need your strength."

Ashlyn used the sleeves of the robes to fashion a sling over one shoulder, and then tied Twain tightly to her chest, like a mother would keep a child.

"*Don't stray from me,*" Deimos shouted, his voice distant.

I turned around and spotted him by the far root in the orchard, almost out of view due to the lingering haze. Nini and Knovak were close to him, both staring at me with wide eyes.

"Coming," I called back.

Ashlyn and I splashed our way over. With her legs free, Ashlyn had better mobility, but the stone faces beneath our feet were still uneven. Running was out of the question.

With her face slightly pink, she shot me a sidelong glance. "Staring is improper," she said under her breath.

"I can look at disgusting plants and mire water, *or* I could look at a beautiful woman," I said, my tone both sarcastic and questioning, as though I were puzzled over which would be better.

Ashlyn didn't reply, but the slight twitch of her lips betrayed her approval of my comment.

When we reached Deimos, he glowered at me. Then he pointed to a dark patch of water. "Here. We swim down, and then up into the root. The *Fingers of Rebirth* shouldn't reach for you, since you're all still alive, but they might if you panic."

Knovak ran a hand down his paling face. "W-What are the *Fingers of Rebirth?*"

Death Lord Deimos motioned with a jut of his chin to the creepy hands sticking out of the roots. They grabbed at fireflies like snakes snatched at their prey.

"They will touch you," Deimos said, "but you mustn't worry. If you panic, they will think you're close to death, and they will strike."

"You probably would've gotten better results if you hadn't told us any of that," I said, trying to hold back the sarcasm.

Nini held her golden scythe close. "I'll swim ahead and cut them all down. My magic is so much stronger now..."

Deimos shook his head. "No. The Fingers of Rebirth harbor no malice. They are part of an elegant cycle—they're ancient and necessary. Only harm them if you must free yourself. Leave the rest to their sacred duties."

No one replied to that. When I glanced at the hands, I shuddered. Were they ancient? Yes. Were they necessary? Perhaps. But were they *elegant?* Oh, definitely not. Their gnarled fingers and grasping motions were straight out of my nightmares.

Deimos didn't offer any more explanations. He leapt into the water and dove.

His dragon followed him. The massive beast slammed into the darkest point of the water and disappeared beneath the surface, the soul wings moaning the whole time.

Ecrib went next. He slid into the water as elegantly as a dragon could. With Ashlyn's augmentation, Starling could breathe even while submerged, but the little unicorn still held his breath as Ecrib plunged them both under the surface.

Knovak and Nini went afterward.

When it was just me and Ashlyn, she glanced over, as if

silently asking for reassurance. I transformed Vivigöl back into a piece of jewelry that wrapped around my neck and shoulders, and then I gave her a playful shrug.

"Better than staying here," I said, grinning.

That seemed to ease her anxiety. Ashlyn nodded once and then dove. I went with her, my own heart racing. Swimming wasn't a problem for me. I had lived on an island, after all. Swimming was *everyone's* favorite pastime. But this wasn't a beautiful beach I was familiar with. This was the *abyssal hells*, and apparently there were hands and arms ready to grab me if I lost my composure.

Not a pleasant thought.

The water was dark, and I couldn't really open my eyes. The moans and whispers of Deimos's dragon were clearer now, and the haunting melody of suffering actually served a purpose—I followed the sound.

There were more stone-face rocks, and I clung to them as I pulled my body downward, going deeper and deeper. This was some sort of tunnel. It was a wide tunnel, thankfully, but a tunnel nonetheless.

And it was perhaps twenty feet straight down? My ears were starting to hurt.

Was Twain okay? I couldn't see.

The tunnel turned, and we were no longer going down, just straight. Breathing was fine, thanks to Ashlyn's magic, but I suspected she couldn't maintain this long. How far did we have to go?

My thoughts became dark.

Then the Fingers of Rebirth started grabbing at my legs. They clawed at my trousers, the wood cutting through portions of the fabric and leaving splinters in my skin. I tried to think of something *other than* the fact that I was in the realm of souls and dead people, but it was difficult. The horror of being lost in the abyssal hells was all too real.

And then more hands grabbed me.

One ripped off my boot.

My arms felt tired.

All those tiny facts started to pile up.

My heart beat harder, like it wanted to slam out of my chest and leave me to the Fingers of Rebirth.

But then Ashlyn grabbed my arm. Had she known I was in trouble? I knew her grip—her long slender fingers, and the calluses she hid on her palms. She tightened her grip on my wrist, and swam upward, helping me get away from the grasping hands that lined the bottom of the tunnel.

And Ashlyn was right. No one swam like a typhoon dragon arcanist.

She manipulated the water around us and shot away from the fingers. We sped through the rock-face tunnel, angled upward, and then headed for the surface. I was basically dragged along. I kicked my feet to help, but I didn't think it was necessary.

When we broke the surface of the water, I gulped down a breath. I didn't need it, but I appreciated it. Ashlyn threw her head back, her long blonde hair halfway slapping me in the face as she did so.

I laughed, and she bit her lip, holding back her own chuckle. She lifted Twain's head, even though his body was still swaddled in robes. He looked like a drowned cat, his orange fur so stuck to his body his head was a fraction the size it normally was.

"I hate water," Twain whispered.

Then we all glanced upward.

The inside of the root...

Was beautiful beyond reason.

CHAPTER 4

REINCARNATION

The inside of the root was its own wonderland of beauty.

The walls were black with sparkling speckles of blue. Bioluminescent leaves and mushrooms grew out of the roots, larger than any I had seen before. I felt like I was the size of an ant, their massive forms towering over me, forming a mystical jungle of magic.

Everything glowed. Everything.

The leaves were a soft green. The mushrooms a pastel orange. Flowers the size of chairs had an inner white light that shone through each petal.

And all the plants grew upward—far, far upward. It was like the root had no end. It just went up *forever*. It was a tower of plant life, complete with vines, moss, and even ferns.

Why? I didn't understand.

I had always imagined the abyssal hells as creepy and corpse-filled. Out in the mire, when I had fought Death Lord Naiad —*that* was the landscape I always pictured in my thoughts. Shallow waters, gore, insects, and a haze of bloodred that never left the "skies."

But this was different. It felt warm, and inviting, and the plants were so bright, I almost couldn't look away.

Ashlyn swam me and Twain over to a mushroom cap. It was above the water, and wide enough for all three of us to climb on top of. It glowed with the same dull orange as all the other mushrooms, and I stared at it for a long while, brushing my palm across the matte surface.

"What is this place?" I whispered.

"This is the heart of the Wraithborne Orchard," Death Lord Deimos stated.

I snapped my attention upward.

Deimos stood on a large blue vine that was growing out of the root's wall. His abyssal dragon was perched on another root just below him, the beast's soul-grafted wings blending in with the glowing environment.

It took me a moment of searching to spot both Nini and Knovak. Nini and her reaper were on a large green leaf, close to Deimos's position. She kept her scythe close, but her eyes remained on the Death Lord himself.

Knovak, Starling, and Ecrib sat on a mushroom cap, similar to me and Ashlyn. Knovak dried his unicorn off, and whispered words of encouragement. The little foal trembled the entire time, even as Ecrib patted his back.

"We need to climb our way to the top," Deimos stated. He motioned to the root's impressive length, and I almost asked how all this could fit under the ocean, but I thought better of it.

I seriously doubted this root was actually under the ocean. The entire abyssal hells were like the dreamscape—a place that existed, but perhaps not physically. Obviously, we were here, but it had dream-like qualities that betrayed its magical nature.

"Can we have a moment?" Knovak asked, his voice unsteady. "I'm not feeling well..."

Deimos didn't reply.

He didn't start climbing, either, so I assumed he didn't mind if we took a break. Besides, he had said Naiad wouldn't pursue us here.

"People are reborn into plants?" Nini asked. She glanced at the glowing mushrooms, and then at the leaves. "Do plants have souls? I mean... what happens... when someone is reborn as a tree?"

Deimos huffed. He crossed his arms and then motioned to the leaves with a tilt of his head. "Surely you have seen strange vegetation in the living realm? Trees with strange powers? Mushrooms that light fire? These *magical plants* carry with them a piece of someone once alive."

Starling's ears perked straight up. "W-What? Oh, no..." He shook his head. "You mean... even the midnight berries? The ones that glow?"

Deimos nodded once.

"But I ate so many of them! I was eating people's *souls*?"

That comment caused the Death Lord to chuckle. He shook his head. "Anything with magic holds a fragment of someone's soul. That is one of the great truths of life. But consuming magic in the realm of the living does nothing. It simply sends the souls back to the abyssal hells, where they can be reincarnated again."

"Why?" I asked as I wrung out my shirt.

It seemed like a sad existence. I was going to die and become a weird mushroom? And then, once someone ate me, I'd be reborn again? Only maybe as a magical loaf of bread or something similar?

Deimos shot me an icy glare. "Do they teach you nothing in your academy? The cycle of reincarnation is sacred."

"Pretend I know nothing." I poured water out of my only boot. "Why do I want to be reincarnated?"

The inside of the magical root was quite silent. Water dripped from the leaves, falling into the pool of water at the bottom, but otherwise there were no other sounds. Nini, Knovak, and Ashlyn remained quiet, each of them with a curious expression. They obviously wanted to know the answer to my question as well.

"When you perish, the parts of your soul that were fulfilled move on," Deimos said. He turned his attention to the vine under his feet. His gaze softened. "If you were a proud parent, the part of your soul that wanted children would be satisfied, for example. So, after you die, that part of you *wouldn't* travel to the abyssal hells. It would go to the stars, never to return."

Knovak ran a hand through his wet hair. "What about the parts of you that are dissatisfied?"

"Every part of you left unfulfilled is sent to the abyssal hells. All your resentment, unfinished deeds, and passions unquenched are given a new life—one where you will try to satisfy at least *one more* part of your soul. Perhaps part of you longs for a garden, or to be one with nature... Your soul would be guided here, to live with the forest."

Nini perked up. "And the part of you that loved nature would find purpose?"

"Correct," Deimos stated.

"And then, once someone ate the mushroom, a part of your soul would go to the stars? And you would keep living lives until all your soul found purpose?"

Once again, Deimos nodded.

He seemed bored with this entire conversation, like it was knowledge that everyone should know—like how the sky was blue, or how we all needed oxygen to live. But the information was new to me. No one had taught me about the specifics of reincarnation.

"Do you... help the souls find a new life?" Nini asked, her voice quiet but hopeful.

Deimos's abyssal dragon exhaled a breath that reeked of blood. Then it spoke. "Of course, child. A Death Lord whispers to the lost souls and sends them on their way. Souls steeped in vile resentment are sent deeper and deeper, to the blackness that consumes all. They are unworthy of finding purpose. Some souls will only be fulfilled by destruction."

That had been my next question.

Did murderers and cutthroats get to find their ultimate purpose? Apparently not. They were sent to the deepest parts of the abyssal hells, so they couldn't fulfill every aspect of their twisted desires.

"Death Lord Naiad and Umbriel both stopped guiding souls centuries ago," Deimos muttered. "And Kallikore only cares about feeding his eldrin creatures. I, alone, have been maintaining the flow of souls through the hells."

While the waters left me weak, I wasn't completely useless. I forced myself to stand and take a deep breath.

But then Deimos's words sank into my thoughts.

"Really?" I glanced up at him. "You've been continuing to guide souls?"

He nodded.

"Why?"

"Because if I don't, the entire balance of the world will be lost." Deimos's expression hardened once again, his body tense. "We must open the abyssal hells, find more individuals to bond with abyssal dragons, and set everything back in order. Before it's too late."

"You'll form an army once you're in the realm of the living?" Nini asked.

Death Lord Deimos grabbed a vine above him. He hoisted himself upward, and then stepped onto a large leaf. "Once I'm with my brother, I will claim a swath of territory. That's what is owed to me, for serving my time as a Death Lord in the abyssal hells. Once I am a ruler, I will form a massive army to fight against those lackwits."

"Who are the *lackwits*?" I sarcastically asked.

"Naiad, Umbriel, and Kallikore."

"Right."

Deimos continued upward. His dragon followed, but in a different fashion. The mighty beast slammed his claws into the walls of the root and hefted his whole body through the vegetation that grew all around us.

"What about Starling?" Knovak asked.

Having a horse body at a time like this was most inconvenient.

"I'll help him," Nini stated.

The chains of her reaper reached out like hands. Starling trembled and neighed, his eyes giant with fear. I thought the little unicorn was going to sprint away and throw himself into the water, but instead, Knovak placed a hand on his head, and Starling closed his eyes.

Nini grabbed Starling with her chains. They wrapped around his body and lifted him, the lanterns dancing with inner fire. Starling kept his eyes tightly shut.

"It looks like we have a lot of climbing ahead of us," Ashlyn whispered as she got to her feet. With one hand, she patted Twain's head, and with the other, she grabbed hold of mine. "Do you think you'll make it?"

"I'm a little tired, but that doesn't mean you have to carry me, too," I quipped.

Ashlyn couldn't hold back a smile. "Good. Because I was going to suggest we make a race of it."

"Heh. Always a competition with you." I walked over to the wall of the root and touched the black "bark" speckled with sparkling blue. "I'll have you know I was the best climber on my entire home island."

Ashlyn plunged into the water. When she surfaced, she swam over to the blue vines. With a display of athleticism, she yanked herself straight up and then sat on the edge of the vine. "What was that?" She sarcastically cupped her ear. "I couldn't hear you over the sound of me pulling into the lead."

I huffed as I reached up for another mushroom cap. The

fungus was both squishy and firm enough to hold my weight. I grabbed the edge and struggled to lift myself all the way. The strange waters of the abyssal hells had sapped *a lot* of my strength, but I refused to look weak in front of Ashlyn.

After I managed to roll myself onto the mushroom like a beached whale onto the sand, I sat up and turned my attention to the others.

Nini hurried after Deimos. She was already several stories above us, and showing no signs of slowing. Why? Was it because she was merged with Waste? Her reaper was so much stronger now...

Ecrib carried Knovak up onto the leaves, pursuing his arcanist.

And of course, Ashlyn was using the vines to her advantage.

At this rate, I would fall far behind. Which meant I needed a new tactic. I couldn't be outdone, after all.

CHAPTER 5

THE CLIMB

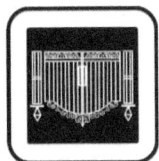

I grabbed the cap of another giant mushroom and hoisted myself, my arms shaking. Ashlyn continued upward, Twain in her makeshift sling. After a deep breath, I inched over to a collection of small mushroom caps and used them as stepping stones up the side of the root's interior.

One, two, three...

It was easier with these tinier mushrooms. I made great time, and distance, until I came to another collection of large orange shrooms. After a deep breath, and a grunt, I pulled myself higher, already regretting all my decisions.

I should've also asked Nini to carry me, dignity be damned.

Ashlyn glanced over from the opposite side of the inner root, perched on a glowing blue vine, the light illuminating her from below, and giving her a hauntingly beautiful expression. "Slowing already?" she playfully asked.

I straightened my posture and waved away her comment. "Never."

She giggled—which was cute—and then continued on her way.

I let out a long sigh, wondering how far we would need to

travel. Another cluster of smaller mushrooms weren't too far from me, and I walked over to step up onto them, but the first one *snapped* under my weight. I flailed, grabbed a larger mushroom, and almost tumbled off the cap.

I made the foolish mistake of glancing down.

My heart leapt up into my throat, and my stomach twisted itself into knots.

I hated heights. The thought of falling twenty feet back into the creepy water with the Fingers of Rebirth all but made me vomit. It took me a few seconds of calming breaths to even regain my focus.

Why was I so afraid? What was wrong with me?

And according to the Mother of Shapeshifters, if I was ever going to have Twain become a true form mimic, I would need to "defeat the most ancient shapeshifter—fear." So, I had to overcome this. I just wasn't sure how.

"Gray?"

I gulped down a breath and glanced over. Ashlyn had climbed around the inner root and landed on one of the nearby mushrooms. She was barefoot, and slowly scooted across an orange cap as she made her way over to me.

"Are you okay?" she asked, her eyebrows knitted. "What happened?"

I forced a chuckle and shrugged. "I'm fine. Totally fine."

"Your white-knuckle grip says otherwise," Ashlyn quipped.

She was right. I held myself tightly to the mushroom growing out of the side of the root, my feet planted firmly on the cap under me.

Ashlyn, once by my side, touched my shoulder. "I thought you said you were the best climber on your island."

"Well, in case you haven't cracked the case of *Gray is very afraid of heights*, let me be the first to tell you my claim was a lie."

With calm and gentle movements, she took hold of my wrist

and guided me away from the mushroom wall. Then Ashlyn pointed to the path she had taken over, and the many vines that grew out of the wall, leading upward. With her help, she took me on a path across a few more caps, and then up a larger vine with handhold indents.

Ashlyn climbed the glowing blue vine first, and I waited for her to finish. Not because I was afraid, but because I had cut her dress rather short, and I didn't want to accidentally glance up and catch an eyeful of... her. That didn't stop my imagination, but I had the common sense not to act out stupid fantasies. If I was going to be her husband, I had to embody the part.

A dashing nobleman.

I almost laughed. It didn't really sound like me.

"Gray? Are you coming?"

I grabbed the vine, and forced myself not to look down. "Yup."

"What were you thinking about?" Ashlyn asked.

I scaled the last of the vine, and crawled onto a gigantic fern leaf. It grew out of one wall and into another, creating a hammock-like plateau I was capable of standing on.

This place was bizarre.

"I'm not thinking of much," I said, eyeing our surroundings.

"You had an odd smirk on your face."

With a single laugh, I shook my head. "Oh. That." I offered her a smile. "I was thinking you were beautiful, but trying not to stare. Sorry."

Ashlyn patted Twain's orange head. He purred, but kept his eyes shut, his little body tucked away in the sling. Ashlyn didn't say anything else after my comment—she just motioned to another set of vines that led to an even bigger fern above us.

To my surprise, Knovak, Starling, Ecrib, Nini, and Deimos were all waiting there, as though Ashlyn and I had fallen so far behind, they were now worried. I rushed over to the vines and pulled myself up, my strength gradually returning. This root's visuals delighted me—I just wished it didn't require swimming through nightmarish water to get into here.

I climbed onto the second humongous fern leaf and rolled across its glowing emerald surface. Ashlyn followed soon after, and when her weight was added to the foliage, the whole leaf shook, bouncing people and creatures around.

"Whoa," Knovak said with a laugh.

Even Ecrib smiled and enjoyed the slight amount of bouncing.

Everyone did—except for Deimos, who stood at the very edge of the fern leaf, his hand pressed heavily against the root wall, his expression one of irritation.

"You all didn't need to stop for us." I motioned to Ashlyn and then myself. "We're capable grownups, thank you very much."

Knovak pulled his unicorn eldrin close. "We didn't stop for you two. We stopped because of Starling. He hasn't been feeling well."

The little unicorn softly neighed. He didn't look sick to me, but his legs trembled, and his ears hung low. Was he afraid? I would believe that. This place, while mystical and beautiful, still had a moderate hint of menace.

"We should rest for just a moment," Nini and Waste said as one.

Since everyone else was sitting, I carefully parked myself near Ecrib and leaned back on my arms. "Where's the abyssal dragon? What's his name?"

Deimos turned to glower at me. "My eldrin has gone ahead to search for the exact location. And his name is *Hektor*, but common arcanists and their ilk should never address him by his name without his permission."

"Hektor?" Ashlyn asked. She walked over and then sat next to me, so close we touched. "That's the cutest name ever. My nephew is named Hektor."

Deimos... didn't have a response to that. He turned away, his unnaturally yellow eyes fixed in mild confusion. I suspected it had been thousands of years since this man had really interacted with anyone who wasn't a fellow Death Lord trapped in a freakish underwater hellscape.

While Knovak stroked the mane of his eldrin, I relaxed a bit. Ashlyn did as well. She pressed her shoulder against mine, and even rested her hand on my knee. Which wasn't fair—if I did any of that, someone here would yell foul play. She was engaged, after all.

But no one said anything when she did it.

I wasn't about to say anything, either. I held back a smile as I glanced over at her. In a silent conversation, which we conducted with only subtle looks and raised eyebrows, I asked if she was okay with this level of public display. To which Ashlyn just squeezed my knee with a strong grip and then relaxed.

She wasn't concerned about the others.

"We're definitely going to make it out of here, r-right?" Knovak asked.

I nodded, and then half-shrugged as I turned my attention to Deimos. "Right, Dee?"

He didn't dignify that question with a response.

"We'll make it out of the hells," Nini and Waste said. She held her gaudy weapon close to her body. "I miss Sorin. I want nothing more than to see him." When Nini turned her gaze to Ashlyn and me, I almost felt guilty.

In order to take the focus off me—and Ashlyn—I asked, "So, Deimos, when you were a normal arcanist like the rest of us chumps, did you ever court a nice young lord or lady?" I lifted an eyebrow. "Or anyone, really?"

This question also seemed to intrigue everyone here. They shifted around to face Death Lord Deimos, their eyes bright with curiosity.

"The city I grew up in was known for its hedonism,"

Deimos stated matter-of-factly. "We were looked down upon and thought of as degenerates." He cracked his knuckles, his gaze unfocused as he clearly mulled over ancient memories. "My mere status as street urchin, and then a slave soldier, and finally a usurper, prevented me from ever having anything close to a normal relationship."

"You were looked down upon?" Knovak smoothed his hair, his attention momentarily darting to his eldrin. Then he asked, "Have you kissed anyone, at least?"

Deimos laughed. Like, really laughed.

It came out of nowhere, like even *he* couldn't believe he had been asked such a question. It took him a few seconds to calm himself, his laughter turning into something dark right at the end.

"Ah, I see I have misled you," Deimos said. "When I said I had abstained from *normal relationships*, I wasn't claiming to have been chaste."

That intrigued me, but I was also hesitant to continue the conversation. Deimos was the type of person who didn't mind sharing all the details—and I was pretty sure I didn't want the nitty-gritty. But I was curious...

"So, did you fancy anyone?" I asked.

But despite his normal openness, Deimos didn't answer this question. He remained unusually silent on the matter.

Knovak, obviously invested in getting the answers, asked, "Did you attend any parties?"

"In my day, we went to *rapture houses*," Deimos drawled, his tone now one of disinterest, like this conversation was boring him. "We often had competitions to see which of us could pleasure the most individuals before we finally finished ourselves." He shrugged with one shoulder. "That was the closest we came to *having a party*."

This was the type of nitty-gritty I definitely wanted to avoid.

The less I heard about these rapture houses, the better. Even Ashlyn seemed a little uncomfortable, her cheeks pink.

Knovak lifted both his eyebrows. "W-Well? What was the highest number of people?"

"*Knovak*," I hissed. "Don't ask that. What's wrong with you?"

"Eighteen," Deimos replied—again, with very little interest.

Knovak balked and waved a hand. "*Eighteen?* No. You're lying. That's impossible."

"These people in the rapture houses," Nini began, her voice breathy, "were they beautiful?"

"*No, stop that*," I snapped. I waved my hand around, getting everyone's attention. "Stop asking him questions! He'll answer them, and sometimes with way too much detail. I heard about *baby graves* one time because I asked too many things. Stop. Asking him. About this."

Ecrib craned his head over and snorted on me. "*You* started this conversation," he said.

"And I regret doing that—are you happy now?"

Deimos grumbled something. Then he snapped his fingers twice, regaining everyone's attention. "My brother's schemes won't wait. If you're done recouping, we should move."

The others got to their feet, the fern jiggling as we all stood at once. Ashlyn "fell" a bit onto me, and when I caught her gaze, I knew it was all a sham. I wrapped my hand around her waist to "help her," and she steadied herself, taking much longer to do so than normal.

I smirked, and she coyly smiled back.

Death Lord Deimos, in a feat of athleticism, pulled himself up onto another glowing blue vine, and then leapt onto the highest fern leaf. Above him, the vegetation was shifting, and becoming more tree-like. Giant star leaves created a canopy above. That was our destination, apparently.

"C'mon," I whispered to Ashlyn. "We better stick close, just in case we need to help each other up these perilous plants."

Chapter 6

The Elder Toad

Nini stepped closer to Knovak and his unicorn, her chains reaching out for Starling. But Knovak moved into the way and held up an arm.

"*No*," he snapped. "I think... I think your chains are what's making Starling unwell."

Nini's eyes widened, her gaze searching Knovak's. For a long moment, they said nothing to each other, and everyone waited with bated breath. Was Nini's new reaper form somehow hurting the little unicorn, just through proximity?

"You're right," Nini whispered. Her attention fell to the glowing fern leaf beneath our feet. "I'm sorry. I hadn't even thought about it. I shouldn't touch anyone here."

That was disturbing, to say the least. Nini's death powers were obviously quite strong. I wondered what Sorin would say, once we got back to him.

Ecrib growled, his scales flaring as he stared down at Starling. "So, what're we going to do about the horse?"

"Hey!" Knovak wrapped his arms around Starling's neck. "Don't talk to him like that."

"He doesn't have thumbs. And just like horses, he can't *climb*."

Which was a point. How would we take Starling up if Nini couldn't carry him with her chains? The only real solution seemed to be for one of the dragons to do it, and since Hektor was already much further up, that left Ecrib.

The typhoon dragon must've come to the same realization at the same time I did, because his scales flattened as he muttered, "Very well. I'll do it."

With careful movements, so as not to hurt Starling, Ecrib picked up the unicorn with his claws. Then he held Starling close to his scaled chest. The little foal trembled, but otherwise didn't protest.

"Be gentle," Knovak said.

Ecrib snorted in response.

With that taken care of, Nini went up first, followed by Knovak, who glanced over his shoulder every two seconds to watch as Ecrib went up behind him. Ashlyn and I went next, with Twain still tucked comfortably in her makeshift sling.

I helped Ashlyn climb onto a large leaf, and once her feet were firmly planted on a thick branch, she turned around and offered her hand to guide me. We did this a few times, one branch-and-leaf combo after another. The star-shaped foliage glowed golden, and this part of the root's interior seemed more fantastical than anything we had seen before.

Once up another ten feet, Ashlyn pulled me onto a narrow branch that was almost too small for the both of us. We stood close, practically squished together, and I had to brace myself on the root wall in order not to tumble off. Ashlyn was close, her breath on my face, her gaze meeting mine.

She grabbed my shoulders to steady herself.

The others were climbing faster than us—even Ecrib, with his extra burden—leaving me and Ashlyn quite alone. She leaned forward, inching our faces ever closer.

"This isn't like you," I whispered with a smile. "Is something about the abyssal hells causing you to abandon all regard for everyone else's opinion?"

Ashlyn slowly pushed herself away. She kept her hands on my shoulders, but held me at arm's length.

"What if we don't make it out of here?" she asked, her tone hard.

"We'll make it."

"But what if we don't? Will I... Will I really be the woman who lived her whole life not doing anything she wanted? Not even *one thing* for myself?"

I saw her point. But at the same time, I hated that she just wanted to complete a few things because she thought we would die here. Hadn't she heard me? I'd get us out of this. We had Death Lord Deimos on our side, after all. I mean... he was a *lord of the abyssal hells*. We'd make it.

Of course we would make it.

Of course.

I motioned to the leaves above us. "C'mon. We'll make it." I held up a finger. "And we're going to be together once we get out. You'll slap your ex-fiancé, and we'll have a glorious wedding. And probably like one to two dozen children."

That last statement caught Ashlyn off guard. She smiled and stifled a laugh, her cold demeanor softening, even in this strange environment where no one was entirely confident.

When Ashlyn met my gaze again, it was with a little more fear in her eyes. "I hope you're right."

We helped each other up to another layer of glowing golden leaves. These ones were thicker than the rest, and more densely packed. I couldn't see the water at the base of the inner root anymore.

And in this new layer, I spotted something concerning.

Bluish apples.

They hung from the branches in groups of three, each one

ripe and fat and glowing with the same sickly pale blue that radiated from the wings of the abyssal dragon. They hung everywhere, near the base of every leaf, their skin practically glistening with dew.

Ashlyn and I hoisted ourselves onto a gigantic leaf and carefully walked forward.

The appearance of the fruit must've taken *everyone* by surprise, because Nini, Knovak, and Ecrib were on this layer of leaves as well, their eyes turned upward to the apples. For some reason, seeing them made me hungry. I hadn't felt a single rumble from my stomach until my eyes fell upon the fruit, and now my need to eat dominated my thoughts.

That couldn't be a coincidence.

I moved closer to Knovak. "Are you thinking what I am?" I whispered.

He half-shrugged. "I don't know. *Eighteen people* just seems outrageously preposterous. Do you know how long that would take?"

I shot him a sideways glance. "Not that, *ya dunce*. I'm talking about the apples." I pointed to them. "Do you think they're making you hungry? Like... magically?"

"O-Oh. Well, obviously." Knovak rolled his eyes. "But you heard what the Death Lord said. We aren't supposed to eat them."

Ecrib placed the unicorn down and sniffed one of the apples. He snorted afterward, and then frowned, his fangs bared. "They don't have a proper scent."

The cluster of leaves above us rustled. At first, I figured it was Deimos, coming to yell at us for taking so long, but then I saw a flash of black and blue, and I knew it wasn't him. Something was walking across the leaves. It had to be about ten feet above, and it stopped on a leaf close to the root wall.

Then a head poked down beneath the foliage.

A toad head.

It was a large mystical creature, one with a bright neon-blue underbelly and glossy, ebony skin on top. Its eyes were huge, and the pupils within were fragmented. It didn't have one pupil per eye—it had four or five, and they moved about, unnatural and freakish.

It was an ogata toad.

Baby ogata toads were no larger than a house cat, but this thing was bigger than an adult man. Its finger stuck to the leaf, and to the wall of the root, with all the suction of a gecko.

Everyone stared, breaths held.

I...

I hadn't been expecting to see a mystical creature here.

"*Oh,*" the toad said, its pitch heightening in delight. "I thought my nose had deceived me. Humans? *Here?* That's never happened before."

When the toad spoke—and especially when it smiled—I noticed something horrifyingly strange. It had fangs. Ogata toads didn't have freakishly sharp teeth. This toad appeared as though it had stolen its maw from a dragon.

No one said anything.

I suspected, like me, no one knew what to say.

The toad darkly chortled. With a toad hand the size of my head, it reached out, grabbed a blue apple, and then brought the fruit to its large mouth. The ogata toad took a bite of the apple, its fangs tearing through the fruit right down the middle.

And the apple screamed.

It wasn't loud. It was like a scream made underwater. I *heard it*, but only barely.

My skin crawled. My heart felt like a hammer beating me from within. And yet, despite that, my stomach still grumbled with unmet demands.

With a second bite, the ogata toad finished the apple. It licked its fingers with its long, toad tongue, and then blinked its eyes out of sync.

"Why am I so lucky today?" the toad asked. "What has brought a *whole gaggle* of humans to my home in the Wraithborne Orchard? Has the Twilight Gate finally opened again? Strange... I thought I would've felt it opening."

The toad's elation eased some of my worry. It was happy to see us?

I forced a chuckle and stepped forward a single pace. "Uh, hello. My name is Gray Lexly."

"Hm? Is it?" The toad tilted its head to one side, and then the other.

"We were following our—"

"I don't care," the toad said, cutting me off. It smiled, showing its fangs. "I'm so sorry. I must've given you the impression I wanted to chat. That couldn't be further from the truth. I was talking to *myself*, which is far better company than that of filthy human interlopers."

The toad still sounded happy, but now its words took on a sinister undertone. The mystical creature reached for another apple. When it plucked it from the branch, it laughed once.

"We're just passing through," Ashlyn said. "We didn't want to talk to you, either."

"Leaving?" The toad took a bite of its apple.

This one screamed, too. Longer than the last. More twisted, yet still muted. When the toad chewed, its teeth crushing the fruit almost sounded like the splintering of bone.

Then the toad finished the other apple. With a smile—one marked with flecks of blue apple—it shook its head. "No, no, no. You can't leave. This is my lucky day! I haven't seen a human in years. *Centuries*. Maybe longer..."

Ecrib flared his fins and scales. He moved in front of Ashlyn, his tail swinging side to side. "You won't tell us what to do, monster."

"Monster?" The toad scrunched up its eyes in a pained look of both amusement and irritation. "I'm no monster. Look at these humans. *They're* the monsters. Disgusting, despicable *parasites.*"

Ecrib growled, his own fangs shown to the world. He had no answer, probably because he was confused. I knew I was.

"We're not parasites," I said, unable to keep my bewilderment out of my words. "Why would you even think that?"

"What? Are you serious?" The ogata toad laughed, its mirth half a croak. "You have so much to learn, my friend! Please, let me enlighten you. Then, once you've been shown the light, you will see you've been brainwashed and enslaved by the humans. A tragic and terrible fate."

"You're insane," Ecrib growled.

The toad crept down the root wall, its sticky fingers *popping* whenever it walked. Halfway down, and with its head angled so it could stare at us, the beast smiled wider than ever.

"Humans are worthless. It's in their nature—a real truth they can't escape."

Starling whinnied and shook his head, his mane fluttering. "All I hear is puffery. There's no substance to your claims. Begone, monster. My arcanist is plenty capable."

"*Your arcanist is only capable because of you!*"

The toad had shouted the last words, its mirth still there, but anger was quickly replacing that.

With a strong exhale of its breath, the toad inflated part of its neck. When it spoke again, it was much louder than before.

"*Humans have no magic.*" The toad motioned to us, its fangs flashing. "There is a natural order to the world. Animals with claws and fangs eat flesh. Animals with hooves and flat teeth eat grass. One devours the others in a perfect cycle. And what are we? *We are mystical creatures*—we only grow when we consume *souls.*"

This was all common knowledge.

"But that's why mystical creatures bond to humans,"

Knovak said matter-of-factly. "S-So mystical creatures can consume souls."

They didn't really "consume souls." They ate small portions of their arcanist's soul.

That was what we were taught, but it made sense to me. If you pricked your finger, droplets of blood would bead out. This small amount of blood loss wouldn't kill someone. That was what it was like when someone bonded to a mystical creature—the eldrin would consume droplets of the person's soul.

Never enough to kill them, and only enough to grow.

It was a beautiful and delicate balance.

It was also why no one ever bonded with more than one mystical creature. One cut wouldn't kill you, but *two* was too many. You would "bleed out," so to speak, and the creatures really would consume the person's soul.

The ogata toad maintained its wicked smile. "That's why humans are disgusting. They have no magic—so they steal it from us. And they promise *pittance* in return. Do you see me? Do you see how strong and large I've become? I didn't need a human's *pity*."

The toad lashed out its long tongue and struck an apple. The sticky tongue ripped the fruit from the branch as the toad sucked it back into its mouth. With one devastating *chomp*, the apple was consumed.

"*I* made myself stronger. I didn't need a pathetic human to control me—to chain me down." The toad turned its gaze to me. "Humans are the ultimate prey. No magic. No claws. No fangs. And they are *vile*. They start wars. They destroy nature. They hurt each other and derive pleasure from their sadistic nature. *They were meant to be consumed*, like a fly that falls into a spider's web."

When Deimos had told me about elder creatures, I had thought they would be mindless killing machines, like a monster from an old children's story. This was far worse—I didn't like where this creature was going with its logic, and how much it seemed to delight in informing us.

The toad croaked another laugh. Then it leapt off the root wall and hit the leaf canopy in front of us. When the toad stood on its hind legs, like a person, to its full height, the beast was more than seven feet tall. Its body was thin and wiry, its neon-blue belly glowing like the plants.

And its fangs were on full display.

"Come now," the toad said. "You must see it. If you never bonded with a human, they would be defenseless. They have enslaved you. *Tricked you*. You were always meant to eat them. That is the real natural order."

The creature reached an arm up and plucked off a trio of apples.

Rather than eating them, the toad threw them across the leaves.

"Free yourselves," the toad said with a laugh. "Grow powerful and join me! And not *just* me! Join *all* the creatures in the abyssal hells! We're a family. Your *real* family. Not these humans—not the fleshbags that hold pathetic souls."

The toad kicked one over to Ecrib.

"Eat," it commanded. "*So we can enjoy the feast of humans that comes afterward.*"

Chapter 7

Resentment

Ecrib stepped forward, his body tensed, his claws extended. I had never seen him so enraged. He always defended Ashlyn, more than anyone else, but this was a whole new level of anger.

"My arcanist has more worth and integrity in a single strand of her hair than you do in your whole disgusting body," Ecrib practically roared. He had never seemed so much like a dragon before.

The toad lowered himself, until its legs were fully folded and prepared to jump. The monster shook its head. "Ah, you're just a brainwashed house pet. Let me do the honor of freeing you from these taskmasters."

Ecrib was already prepared. The typhoon dragon opened his maw and unleashed a bolt of lightning straight from the depths of his throat. The *crack* of his power was stronger than ever—and for some reason, the glowing plants seemed to react to his magic. Everything got *brighter* for the brief second his evocation flashed across the inner root.

Normally, Ecrib's lightning evocation was quite difficult to dodge, but the ogata toad leapt out of the way, freakishly fast and rather prepared for violence. The toad hit the leaves above, stuck to the glowing foliage, and then used the gigantic leaves as a springboard for its next move.

The toad shot its body at Ecrib and slammed into the dragon with fearsome power. The two crashed into the root wall with the toad firmly on top. In a quick display of magical mastery, the toad vomited venom.

Ogata toads were deadly—everyone knew that. Their venom was legendary for melting skin. True form ogata toads could even do permanent damage, or so the tales go. Damage so thorough, it prevented normal arcanist healing.

The monster toad aimed for Ecrib's face, as though to clean the dragon's skull of all flesh.

Ashlyn evoked lightning just as the toad spat its venom. The bolt slammed into the toad, and its venom only half splashed over Ecrib. The typhoon dragon roared, and the toad spasmed slightly as the powerful lightning coursed through it.

Ecrib's scales on the left side of his face sizzled as they burned up under the purplish venom. The acidic magic of the toad was so powerful, all Ecrib could do was scratch at his face, attempting to clear it all away before it burned straight to his eye.

But once the ogata toad had its bearings, the monster whipped around and leapt for Ashlyn. I pushed her out of the way, almost on instinct. Maybe I didn't want her to get hurt—maybe I didn't want Twain to get hurt. All I knew was my body moved long before I was aware of what I was doing.

I shoved her away, and the toad collided with me. All the wind was knocked from my lungs as the monster slammed me against the far root wall. My vision blackened, and I thought I would barf. That didn't happen, but my thoughts did remain jumbled.

The ogata toad smiled wide with its fangs, but on instinct, I reached for Vivigöl. Deimos's soul fragment was still with me, and when I needed to rely on his combat skill, all that knowledge went straight to my muscles. I didn't have to *think* about what I was going to do—my limbs practically acted of their own accord.

Vivigöl *clicked* into the shape of a golden sword, and I slashed.

The toad was way too fast.

It cringed at the sight of Vivigöl, and leapt away long before I managed to strike. Nini swung her scythe, but again, that was useless. The ogata toad was much too fast. It jumped around us with the speed of ten rocs and the fatal venom of a basilisk.

The toad slammed into Nini's gut and sent her tumbling away.

The only individuals who hadn't moved, or even attempted to join the fight, were Starling and Knovak. They trembled and whispered to each other, ignoring the conflict.

Ashlyn's body crackled with electricity. She glared at the toad as it flung itself through the glowing leaves, its laughter now filling the interior of the root.

"How weak you all are!" it shouted in delight. "Don't you know? Elder creatures are *far* more powerful than any house pet an arcanist has!"

The ogata toad vomited purplish venom. It splattered across the glowing leaves, burning holes through our "platforms." The root shook, and each leaf that was hit, and burned, eventually dulled. The glow of the leaves vanished, leaving the area a little darker than before.

Despite my shaky legs, I had to roll to avoid the worst of the venom. The sizzling of the plant matter caused my skin to crawl.

Knovak wrapped his arms around his eldrin's neck, but neither moved. The venom, somehow, never touched them. I almost wondered if the toad hadn't even bothered to aim any at the pair, considering they hadn't done anything yet.

Nini and Ecrib both pressed themselves up against the wall of the root. The venom splashed Nini's reaper coat, and burned slightly through the fabric. She gritted her teeth, her face twisting in pain. Did she feel damage to the cloak? Like it was part of her?

"Face me, coward!" Ashlyn yelled. She protectively shielded Twain, who still rested in her sling. "*I'm ready.*"

The ogata toad let out croaking laughter as it dove from the leaves above. It flew at Ashlyn, its mouth wide open, its fangs poised to gouge her flesh.

Ashlyn, in a fascinating display of quick footwork, stepped just slightly out of the way. The toad slammed into the leaf, and it practically folded under the impact. The foliage dipped low, and while the toad was clinging to the leaf, Ashlyn unleashed a bolt of lightning. She struck the ogata toad, and the monster yelled. Its sticky fingers released the leaf, and it fell.

But Ashlyn was about to tumble down after. Once again, I leapt for her. I slid across a leaf on my belly and reached out my hand just in time. Ashlyn grabbed my wrist, but when I tried to pull her up, the leaf wobbled.

Vivigöl *click-clicked* and transformed into a chain whip. I lashed it toward the leaves above us just as Ashlyn and I were about to fall.

I had no skill with a whip. None whatsoever. I never even thought they were practical weapons. I thought they were mere tools for herding animals or spurring horses into motion.

But Deimos...

He must've trained with a whip for ages, because when I called on *his* skill to use a whip, I managed to lash the weapon around a leaf so thoroughly, I was able to use it to pull both myself and Ashlyn into an upright position.

I almost couldn't believe it.

"Gray," Ashlyn whispered as she pulled herself closer. She tied her arms around my neck. "Are you okay?"

I held her. "Yeah. You?"

"What was that thing?"

The toad exploded upward through the leaves. Ashlyn

tensed as the leaves beneath us shook. I held on to Vivigöl, keeping us from slipping or sliding.

The toad hit the root wall and hissed like a snake. Its eyes, wild and angry, flashed over to me.

"Human scum... You're too weak to kill me! I'm an elder creature. I'm fueled by the souls of hundreds—empowered by you human cattle."

Almost as shocking as the toad's return was the beam of raw magic that blasted down the root. It was a pillar of destructive energy that seared down through the vegetation like a finger of the sun. It scorched the ogata toad, cutting through its amphibian body in an instant. The death of the toad was sudden, and without mercy, as its head and chest were incinerated first. The rest of it flopped down with the raw magic, tumbling toward the water once again.

I glanced up, my heart pounding, and caught sight of Deimos and his abyssal dragon. They were a good forty feet above us, and had likely been watching the fight from their perch. The glow of the leaves hid the dragon well—its soul-grafted wings blending into the environment.

As a matter of fact, the many leaves that had lost their glow when the ogata toad damaged them regained their illumination when Deimos's beam of raw magic was near. It was like... the Death Lord's magic was somehow helping this place.

"Took you long enough," I quipped.

"I didn't do that to help *you*," Deimos called down. "It's my job, as Death Lord, to protect the cycle of reincarnation. Those elder creatures are a damn plague. More and more of them show themselves... It's disgusting."

"Are they breeding?" Nini and Waste asked together. She used her reaper chains to heft her whole body upward, slowly making her way to Deimos's side.

"Of course they are," Deimos replied, his voice low and his tone disgusted. "They mature by consuming souls, and then they mate and create more... Soon they will swarm this place, and add to Kallikore's army. The problems only mount and mount within this place, and I am the sole Death Lord who does a damn thing about it."

"What can be done about it?" When Nini reached his side, she was beaming up at him. What had gotten into her? Why was she so obsessed with the Death Lord?

I suspected it was Waste. He was a creature of death, after all...

Deimos said nothing. I thought I heard him snort something before tapping his dragon. The massive beast climbed the root walls, leaving the rest of us to climb on our own.

That was fine. I could climb. But when I glanced down to see if the leaves were sturdy again, I regretted my decision. My stomach flipped.

Ashlyn tightened her grip on my neck. I tore my eyes away from the long fall to look at her.

"Keep your attention up here," she whispered. It seemed sultrier than anything she had said to me before.

I nodded once. "All right."

With all my strength, I yanked us up the whip chain. Just a foot or two, nothing major—enough to get our feet planted on solid leaves. Ashlyn found her footing and then checked on Twain. She patted his orange head. My eldrin groaned, and I wondered if he was sick. Why was he sleeping through all this commotion?

I glanced over at Ecrib. The left half of the dragon's face looked like a smudge on a painting.

The dragon met my gaze with his good right eye. "Don't worry about me," he growled. "I can handle myself." Ecrib ran a claw over his injury. "No elder creature will kill me so easily."

"Good to know." Then I turned my attention to Knovak.

Knovak was still kneeling next to his unicorn, embroiled in a hushed argument. When I walked over, I managed to catch a glimpse of the end of it.

"But the ogata toad was right," Starling said with a snort. "People *are* terrible. They're so awful to you. Always mocking you, and calling you names."

"Don't listen to that monster," Knovak snapped.

"But you went to bed crying so many times!"

"Are you two okay?" I asked, alerting them to my proximity.

Knovak leapt to his feet, but his unicorn stayed knelt, one of the bizarre blue apples between his front legs. After a long sigh, Knovak met my gaze. "We're fine. Thank you for fighting that toad."

I motioned to the two of them. "You both just sat here? Why?"

Starling swished his tail. The unicorn said nothing.

Knovak shook his head. "I'm sorry. I just... I didn't think I could do anything. Ashlyn is a dragon arcanist, and Nini has all this power. I figured they could deal with the monster while I tried to talk down Starling."

"See?" Starling whispered. "Even *you* think I'm weak... I just..."

"*Shh,*" Knovak hissed. "We're done talking about it. Everything is fine. The toad was insane. Obviously. He spoke gibberish." Knovak leaned down, grabbed the apple away from Starling, and then threw it as hard as he could toward a hole in the leaves.

I watched the fruit sail away.

Had Starling been thinking of eating it?

I eyed Knovak. The man didn't meet my scrutinizing gaze. "Everything is fine," he said. "Let's just get out of here."

CHAPTER 8

CONVICTION

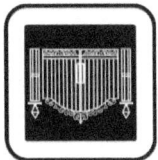

We continued our climb.

Why did it feel like forever?

The star-shaped leaves gradually became a different color the higher we went. At first, they were gold, but by the time we were nearing the top, they were white. And I knew we were nearing the end because the walls of the root narrowed. The hollowed root was smaller here, tapering off like the point of a tail.

The abyssal hells had such a strange configuration.

It reminded me of dreams.

And what did Professor Helmith always say about dreams? That was when people were closest to death.

I grabbed a giant leaf, one the size of a whole two-masted boat, and yanked myself up. Ashlyn joined me a moment later, and I scooted closer to her. Twain remained asleep, even as I patted his head. Twain's long ears twitched, but otherwise he didn't move.

Nini, Death Lord Deimos, and his abyssal dragon were already here.

There was nowhere else to go. No more leaves. No more

mushrooms. No branches or footholds or vines. The root continued upward, black and bleak, with blue speckles on the walls, but there was no way to climb without sticking to the wall.

All around us, flecks of white sailed upward, like snowfall in reverse.

The motes of light glittered as they sailed toward the infinite ceiling, drifting at a leisurely pace. When I tried to touch one, my fingers passed straight through the light as though it didn't exist. Despite that, a tingle ran down my spine.

Something about these motes of light was familiar.

And powerful.

They drifted ever higher, until they vanished from my sight.

Ecrib climbed up next, one clawed foot around Starling. The little unicorn acted like a corpse the whole time. He didn't move or help with the ascent—he was just deadweight. Knovak made the climb himself, his worried expression turned toward his eldrin at all times.

The leaves under us were so large, and sturdy, they held all our weight without moving. It was almost as if they were petrified—glowing rocks rather than vegetation.

Deimos stood at the far end with his eldrin, the white glow of the leaf beneath his feet illuminating him in an eerie way.

"What're we doing here?" I asked him.

The man turned to face me. "Waiting."

"Is... Is this it?" I motioned to the reverse snow. "Is this what we're looking for?"

"These are the souls that are being reincarnated." Deimos motioned to the area above us—the area with no vegetation. "All the souls that travel through the Wraithborne Orchard return to the realm of the living through this road."

"Some road," Ashlyn sarcastically quipped.

Once again, I tried to touch one of the motes. Just as before, I was unable to make contact. "These are souls?" I whispered.

Deimos growled. "Parts of souls. Unsatisfied lives. Now they will know peace in nature." When the Death Lord held out his hand, a dozen of the lights swirled around, as if drawn to his palm. "This spot in the orchard is filled with magic. My brother believes he can use that to bring me forth into the realm of the living."

His abyssal dragon snorted. For some reason, Hektor seemed skeptical, but it was hard to tell when his six eyes constantly flitted about.

"Ya know, while we were climbing, I had a thought," Knovak said. He walked closer to Deimos, but stopped a good twenty feet away, as though he didn't want to be within arm's length of the man. "You said the mystical creatures were breeding?"

Deimos glared at him. "I did."

"I know this is going to sound crazy, but, uh, why didn't the Death Lords have children while they were here?" Knovak shrugged. "I mean, there were several Death Lords—some men, some women—and you were all adults, so..."

"Life cannot be conceived in the abyssal hells," Deimos stated matter-of-factly.

"But you just said mystical creatures were having children."

"*They have no souls.*" Deimos's tone bordered on anger, but he reined it in with a deep inhale. After a calming exhale, he continued. "Humans are unique. Special. Only they have a soul, which grows and becomes ever stronger—and only in the realm of the living. Babes cannot be conceived here."

I walked over, now curious. Ashlyn joined me, and then her eldrin followed suit, until we were all in a close huddle. Well, everyone except for Knovak and Starling, who both kept their distance.

"Wait," I said, holding up my hands. "Let me get this straight. If *Ashlyn and I* were to, uh—"

Ashlyn shot me a glare, her lips pressed in a tight line.

Obviously, she felt this hypothetical situation was inappropriate to speak aloud. It wasn't very proper at all.

"—I mean, what if *Nini and I* were—"

Somehow, Ashlyn glared even harder. Nini also snapped her attention to me, deeply frowning.

I forced a chuckle. "Okay, okay. What I really mean is, what if *Nini and Knovak* were to share the same bed. Would they—"

"I would *never* be with Knovak," Nini said, her tone so icy and absolute, it sounded as though she would take her own life before so much as offering Knovak a kiss blown from her palm.

"*Hey*," Knovak snapped.

Nini pulled her reaper's cloak tight, her chains rattling. With her gaze downcast, and her voice as cold as before, she said, "You're not... the type of person I would ever be with."

"Why not?"

Nini didn't reply.

Starling swished his tail and then clopped his hooves on the stone-like leaf. "It's because she thinks you're weak."

I thought that reasoning was silly, but when Nini glanced away, as silent as the grave, I suddenly wondered if Starling was correct. I shook my head. No, that couldn't be right. Well, perhaps. Sorin was strong—in a gentle way. And he was gifted at knightmare magic. Maybe...

"Hmpf!" Starling stomped his front hooves. "I knew it! I told you, my arcanist. I told you. These people don't respect you. They all flock around the Lexly twins, and everyone knows they're a pair of petty liars."

I shot the unicorn a genuine glare. "What was that?"

"You lie all the time," Knovak stated.

I took a breath, ready to tell him off, but Knovak beat me to the punch.

"*You lied to Death Lord Naiad.*" Knovak pointed at me. "You do it all the time!"

When I glanced over at Ashlyn and Nini, they both

sheepishly looked away. Ashlyn even muttered, "You do tend to exaggerate. A lot. And sometimes for no reason."

And while they were right—sometimes I did compulsively lie—I wasn't upset by that. I was more upset that Starling would imply that *Sorin* was a liar.

"You take back what you said about my brother." I glowered at the unicorn. "I don't care what you call me, but I'm not going to let you speak poorly of Sorin."

Starling turned his nose up. Then he clopped all the way around in a half circle, until his rump faced me. "Fine. But my point stands. Everyone in the Academy *loves you,* but they treat *my* arcanist poorly. Why, I wonder? I know why. It's because you're a cheat, and a liar, and a lowborn."

"Gray saved your life!" Ashlyn stomped over, fully injecting herself in the conversation. If she had fur, her hackles would be raised. "I saw it happen just earlier today! He saved you from Death Lord Naiad. You didn't even thank him—now you're going to stand there and mock him? Call him names? *You're the only lowborn here.*"

Her shouting finally roused my eldrin. Twain opened his eyes, his gaze unfocused as he glanced around, his whiskers twitching. "Huh?"

The abyssal dragon wrapped his gruesome tail around us and then slammed it into the middle of our group. The rumble of his power shook the root, but it didn't crack or even disturb the glowing leaf beneath us.

"*Enough,*" Hektor growled, his voice haunted by dozens of distant voices. His rotted scales shifted along his disgusting body as he positioned his head closer, his breath stinking of death. "You disrespect this place with your bickering."

Deimos glanced between the lot of us, his posture stiff and his anger building. I always *felt* his true emotions, due to my unusual connection with the man, and I hated whenever he grew deeply upset.

"Your relatives could be amongst you," Deimos said. "What would they think, if they were to see you in this moment?"

Ashlyn, Starling, and Knovak backed away from each other, but they didn't seem completely convinced. All of them remained tense, and no one acknowledged the others. Nini, however, gripped her scythe and then glanced at the motes of light. She held her breath, her lip twitching. But only for a moment.

"So, my question," I said, trying to imitate a happy tone, "was how do you know for sure children can't be born here? I mean, humans haven't visited the abyssal hells in millennia. Maybe kids *can* be born here."

Knovak brushed his sandy-brown hair back with a hand. "Gray has a point."

"No, he doesn't, *fool*," Deimos barked. "The Death Lords *are* humans, even if you've forgotten that. And trust me—with centuries of nothing, and the landscape of the hells a mire of misery, we *attempted* to build a civilization of humans, only to be reminded of our limitations time and time again."

Ashlyn slowly faced him. "You and the other Death Lords? Tried? To have families?"

"There weren't many of us," Deimos said, sarcastic through and through. "And in the beginning, we were cordial to one another. Technically, I've been with all my fellow Death Lords in all possible ways, but as the years just dragged on, our enthusiasm for one another blossomed into contempt. Now, it seems we will all kill each other—that's what isolation has done to us."

Ah.

That was grim.

Deimos's situation reminded me of a prison. The Death Lords were the only inmates—the only people—for thousands of years. They once cared for one another? Naiad had killed so many... It was hard to believe there was a time in which they all felt they were friends.

This place was twisted in more ways than one.

It wasn't how it was supposed to be. Perhaps Deimos was right—someone had to set things right.

"So, we're just waiting here?" Knovak asked.

Deimos crossed his arms over his bare chest. "My brother will come through. We just need to be patient."

Starling snorted. "I'm hungry."

"Nibble on your tongue."

I didn't feel hungry. Now all I felt was curiosity. Ashlyn must've felt it too, because her gaze was distant. When Twain started to squirm, she pulled my eldrin out of the sling and handed him over. I cradled my mimic. Twain smiled up at me, awake and alert.

"Deimos," I whispered.

The Death Lord faced me. He said nothing—he just waited.

"I've made up my mind. I want to help you." I motioned to our surroundings. "With all this. I mean, maybe not help you build an army and kill everyone who stands in your way—but help you make things right. With the abyssal hells."

"Feh." Deimos shook his head. "If you're not willing to do what it takes, step aside, boy."

"Hey." I pointed at him. "I fought Death Lord Naiad to save you. I have what it takes to help."

The Death Lord gritted his teeth as he coldly stared in my direction. "The only reason I'm still here is because I refuse to relent. I *will* win. You know why?"

"Why?" I asked, sardonic.

"Because a hero *needs to win every time*—a villain only needs to win once. That's the truth. That's why darkness prospers more in the world than kindness. The moment I fail will be the moment the world is plunged into darkness. I don't care what it costs; I don't care what it takes from me—I will do whatever is necessary to win. If you don't have that kind of conviction, then stop pretending you're my ally. I only want arcanists I can truly rely on."

His words stung.

Why couldn't there be a solution that *didn't* involve razing a whole nation? Deimos might have conviction, but he didn't seem like the type to make complex plans.

Then it struck me—that was why he relied so much on Zahn. His twin brother was the brains of their operation. Deimos was the power.

Perhaps I would need to speak to Zahn. Maybe I could help him, and convince him there were other solutions.

After all, the other Death Lords were the real problem, weren't they? Once we handled Naiad, Kallikore, and Umbriel, things would be back to the way they should be. We didn't need an army—we just needed a way to deal with those three abyssal dragon arcanists.

"Gray?" Twain whispered. He shifted his ears to point at the rot walls. "Do you... Do you hear that?"

"Hear what?"

I held my breath. Then I heard something strange. The beating of wings?

Heat flooded the root. When I drew breath, my throat hurt, and panic consumed my thoughts. Something was nearby. Something powerful—and with the force and power of a volcano.

Deimos knew it, too.

He reached for his abyssal dragon, his yellow eyes wide with disbelief.

"It's Kallikore," he whispered. "And he brought his phoenix dragon."

CHAPTER 9

THE FURY OF XUANDI

The walls of the root burned from the outside in. Spots of fire bloomed across the bizarre black-and-blue root walls, the heat radiating inward. I stepped back, wondering what we were going to do about another Death Lord.

"I thought you said Naiad wouldn't chase us here?" I asked. "Why is Kallikore after us?"

Deimos steadied himself, his expression hardening into something murderous. He cracked his knuckles. "That fiend has lost all his respect for the abyssal hells. He pays no sacred location its dues. Now he means to sully this place with his monster? He's a disgrace. I'll be the one to end him."

"What're we going to do?" Knovak asked.

"*You* will do nothing. My brother will find a way to bring us to the living realm any moment. Wait for him. *I* will deal with Kallikore."

Knovak stepped forward. "I... I want to help. I haven't really done anything this whole time. I want to make up for that. I want—"

"*Sit down, child,*" Deimos barked. "You lack the power

needed for this fight. Pray the rest of us handle everything, lest you become a snack for the phoenix dragon."

At that moment, I wished both of them hadn't said anything. Clearly, Knovak thought less of himself. Did Deimos have to remind him he was the weakest arcanist here? And why would Knovak volunteer to fight *now*? Was he just embarrassed he hadn't done a damn thing since we arrived in the abyssal hells?

Either way, I agreed with Deimos. If we were about to escape, I wished Knovak would just be quiet and hold on. Everything would all be over soon.

At least, I hoped—because the outside of the root was torn open by massive talons.

Foul air rushed into the root from the outside, along with red-hot embers and the stink of smoke. The gargantuan root was ripped asunder, creating a window to the crimson skies of the first abyss.

I shielded my eyes from the heat and the embers. Twain puffed his fur while in my arms, his anger escaping him as a half-growl, half-hiss.

Outside the root, clawing its way inside, was a dragon.

No.

It wasn't a normal dragon. That would've implied certain features. This was unique—bizarre—and completely new to me. Professor Helmith had never mentioned any *phoenix dragons* in our studies, and I honestly hadn't even known such a thing existed.

But now I had seen one, and I developed a new phobia.

The monster was huge. Its mouth could fit a whole team of horses, even with its double-row of fangs, like it once had two maws that were merged together. Fangs over fangs over fangs, some of them golden, like Vivigöl. Did it have abyssal coral for teeth?

The beast's wings were a strange mix of red feathers and

yellow leathery skin. Its body was equally as disturbing. Scales and feathers everywhere. They were all some shade of scarlet, each with heat and menace imbued into their being.

The dragon's claws resembled talons, and its mouth was somehow reptilian and beak-like at the same time.

Its eyes... They were a disgusting yellow, the pupils fragmented, just like the elder ogata toad. I hated looking at the beast, especially because each exhale from its massive mouth brought another wave of heat.

And to top it all off, the dragon had a mane of souls—sickly blue phantoms just like on the abyssal dragons. The whole phoenix dragon pulsed with this forbidden energy, adding to its intimidation, and no doubt its magical power.

After a long grunt, the dragon opened the hole in the root even wider, to allow for its whole body. The reverse snowfall of souls awaiting reincarnation floated out of the root.

They just... floated away.

Whispers and screams echoed throughout the area as the heat seemingly burned them up. I watched as a few *popped* out of existence, and I briefly wondered if they had been destroyed.

"*What're you doing?*" Deimos roared. "You're disrupting the very flow of the world! To do this is insanity!" He angrily motioned with his arm, his sights on the tiny motes of light that blinked out of existence.

"I am Xuandi, the last phoenix dragon, future emperor of our new world," the dragon said, his voice so deep, so powerful, it was immediately burned into my thoughts. When the beast lowered his head, I hugged Twain tight. "And you already fouled this place when you brought human filth to tramp upon its beauty."

Deimos forced a single chuckle, his expression somehow manic and amused. "I am lord here, *not you*." He held up his hand.

In an instant, the bright blast of his raw magic evocation lit up the root. Hektor, his abyssal dragon, opened his mouth and blasted at the phoenix as well, the two powerful attacks catching the phoenix dragon by surprise. They burned holes through the scarlet scales and feathers, but their beams weren't forceful enough to shake Xuandi from the outside of the root.

The magic ripped through the dragon, leaving two holes through his shoulder, each of which gushed rivers of blood. The phoenix dragon yelled out, and flames sparked in the depths of his massive gullet.

But then Nini leapt forward, her scythe in hand, her cloak billowing and her chains clattering.

I honestly was surprised by her bold move to the front. We were about to be incinerated by the fire of the phoenix dragon, yet she leapt for it?

But the instant the dragon spotted Nini—and saw her for what she was—Xuandi turned his head and unleashed his inferno on the outside of the root. He didn't dare attack, because when someone killed a reaper, they were hit by the *King's Revenge*, an innate magical power that instantly slayed whoever dealt the killing blow.

If Xuandi had burned Nini alive, her reaper magic would've killed him in turn.

The phoenix dragon growled, flashing his hundreds of fangs. To my horror, the two holes in his shoulder were sealing themselves before my very eyes. Was the dragon really that strong? Or was it because this was an *elder* phoenix dragon?

"Humans are nothing more than lice on the scalp of the world," Xuandi said, his voice shaking the Wraithborne Orchard. "Your souls are ours for the taking."

Xuandi's talon-claws flashed brightly, suddenly becoming white-hot and sizzling the air. With a fierce strike, the phoenix dragon cleaved through the root, the stone leaf beneath our feet, and then deeper into the vegetation. His talons almost caught

Knovak and his unicorn, but the two barely managed to leap out of the way.

Instead of staying on the stone leaf, they tumbled through the rent in our platform and tumbled downward.

Ecrib grabbed Ashlyn, and then with his finned tail, he grabbed me by the waist.

But I had had enough of this.

I slapped myself on the cheek, mentally told myself I was going to handle all my accursed problems, and turned to Twain. My eldrin silently agreed, his expression one of determination.

I searched for the magical threads in the area, and the instant I found Xuandi's, I tugged on it. Twain's body bubbled, and instead of holding him in my arms, I threw him upward. His orange fur exploded outward into scarlet feathers and scales, his paws became taloned feet, and his shape shifted into a massive dragon.

My arcanist mark burned as it took the shape of the rare phoenix dragon.

But...

Twain was smaller than Xuandi. His fangs were a singular row of impressive canines, but there was no abyssal coral.

And most importantly, Twain didn't have a mane of souls. He had the crest of feathers common on large birds, and his scales were mighty and impressive, but he didn't exactly resemble Xuandi.

As Twain finished his transformation, he twirled in the air and lashed his tail at Xuandi, striking the monster in the side of the head. Then Twain landed on the torn hole in the root, his weight shaking everything, and tearing the hole wider.

More light motes escaped.

"*Don't destroy this place!*" Deimos shouted, somehow angry at me for this catastrophe.

"Do you have any better options?" I yelled back.

Twain lifted his claw, but Xuandi was faster.

And so much stronger.

The elder phoenix dragon sliced into Twain's torso, almost gutting him in a single blow. Twain roared, and the whole root wobbled, as though it would collapse.

Nini unleashed her evocation—raw fear. It washed over Twain and Xuandi, and the two dragons shuddered under her magic. Nini's attack must've reminded Ashlyn that she could still theoretically do something, so she and Ecrib also evoked their magic. Bolts of lightning lit up the root, the crackle of their power small compared to Xuandi.

Their attacks struck the elder phoenix dragon, and did very little.

I took a deep breath. Obviously, phoenix dragons could evoke flame. What did they manipulate? Augment? What else could I do? Xuandi would be immune to fire.

Death Lord Deimos grabbed hold of Hektor. Then—as I watched—some of the souls on Hektor's wings faded. They were consumed by the dragon to feed their magic.

How did I know?

Because I felt it, too. Deimos's soul fragment trapped within me let some of his empowering magic bleed into me and Twain. Deimos had consumed some of the grafted souls to increase his strength and speed. I felt it—my heart beat stronger, my limbs felt more limber.

Twain clawed at Xuandi's face, now emboldened by the abyssal dragon magic. He roared as he clamped his fangs down on Xuandi's neck.

The elder phoenix dragon leaned backward and released his hold on the root. He plummeted downward, toward the mire waters, with Twain still on his body.

"*No!*" I ran for the gaping hole in the root, but the stone flooring finally shattered. I gasped as weightlessness washed over me.

I fell.

There was nothing to grab onto, no way for me to fly—my stomach lurched as I just hurtled downward.

But before I went far, Deimos and Hektor practically slammed into me. Hektor caught me with his claws, his blood-soaked breath hot on my body. Death Lord Deimos commanded his eldrin up, and Hektor flew us back to the rent in the root, faster than any dragon had the right to be.

Then Hektor tossed me back onto the shattered stone leaf, his six eyes focused on the many light motes disappearing.

Xuandi didn't care *at all* that he had destroyed the Wraithborne Orchard, but it seemed like it was all Deimos really cared about. He frantically thought of ways to fix this, his memories seeping into my mind, telling me he was panicked.

I glanced around, concerned for Ashlyn.

She was still here with Ecrib. Both had backed up into the wall of the root. Ashlyn stared at me in terror, and I nodded, hoping to reassure her just a little.

Nini used her chains to lift her body to the edge of the hole in the root. Her rattling chains were basically extra limbs, like those of an octopus, that stretched out and took her places. The lanterns swung about, the fire within dancing.

"What will we do?" Nini asked.

Not me—she turned her attention to Deimos.

"Kallikore is near," Deimos growled, his gaze still on the small souls that were disappearing. "Come with me, agent of death. Be my weapon—we'll make short work of the elder monster."

I stepped closer.

Deimos turned to face me. "Wait here. My brother will arrive. *He will*. Any second... When he does, tell me."

"But—" I began.

"*You said you wanted to be my ally?*" Deimos shouted. "Then. Be. My. Ally." He clenched his hands into fists, his bones cracking from the force of his grip.

Twain… was fighting Xuandi. And I wasn't with him.

"I will return your eldrin," Deimos said. He grabbed tightly on to the neck of his dragon. "Wait here."

Nini used her chains to grip the dragon as well. Then Hektor took off, launching into the unknown beyond the root.

Where was Zahn?

I rubbed my arcanist mark, my thoughts on Twain.

But then I remembered Knovak, and I panicked.

Chapter 10

The Bug-Bloat Bog

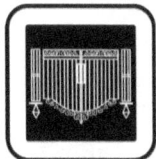

I couldn't wait for Zahn, not when my eldrin was somewhere else. And I couldn't leave the abyssal hells, not when the people I inadvertently brought here were lost. I had to do something.

"Gray?"

I glanced over at Ashlyn. She had spoken my name with an edge of hesitancy, and I knew she knew exactly what I was thinking. It made me half smile. I thought Sorin was the only one who understood me enough to guess my thoughts in advance.

"Wait here," I told her.

"I'm going to come with you." Ashlyn kept her hand on the root wall, the cracked leaf beneath our feet slowly dulling, the glow fading with each passing moment.

But the little light motes kept floating upward, the reverse snowfall beautiful but sad. They wafted out of the root and just disappeared. If Deimos couldn't fix this, who could? I didn't know.

"Someone has to wait for Zahn," I muttered. "And I need to find Twain, Knovak, and Starling."

Ashlyn motioned to her eldrin. "I'm a dragon arcanist. Let me handle it."

I pointed to the phoenix dragon intertwined with my arcanist mark. My sarcastic response actually got her to huff back a tense laugh. This was a terrible situation, but at least I could still get her to relax.

"I got this," I confidently stated.

Because I didn't want her to get hurt. Under no circumstances could that happen. She was only here because of me—same as Knovak. I had to make sure they would get out okay. It was fine if I didn't make it, so long as the others were okay.

Ashlyn would eventually die here. I could, in theory, live here until Zahn concocted another plan. That was fine. Everything would be fine.

I just couldn't stop. I had to keep going.

"Be careful," Ashlyn whispered.

Ecrib snorted, lightning flashing. "You better come back."

I nodded once, even though I wasn't entirely sure I would.

After a deep breath, I grabbed the edge of the broken stone leaf and lowered myself to the layers below. I had to get down the root as quickly as possible. Obviously, falling would be the fastest, but I also didn't want to die in the process. Plus, whenever I thought of falling, my guts twisted into a knot so tight I almost couldn't breathe. I'd have to climb—just quickly.

I lowered myself from one glowing golden leaf to the next, careful to maintain my grip on each stem, vine, and branch. The phoenix dragon magic coursing through my body felt like an oven. My chest grew warmer and warmer as I went, like the fire inside me wanted to escape.

It was an odd sensation—one I had never experienced.

When I touched one of the blue vines, I left a handprint afterward, my flesh so hot, it literally seared the foliage. When I glanced at my palm, the creases were glowing with power. I clenched my hand into a fist, and took a deep breath.

Heat...

Power...

Then, the root shook. Harder and harder, up to the intensity of an earthquake. I held onto the vines as tightly as possible, even though my hands were burning into them.

The root... tore open. Like a blanket being pulled in too many directions. The walls split open, and hushed wails echoed up around me. It was as if the Wraithborne Orchard cried out in pain.

The tears in the root were so wide, I could see outside it. In the scarlet skies, flashes of fire and raw magic lit up the orchard. Was their fight destroying this whole area? I gritted my teeth, and despite the rumble that shook the root, I continued downward.

"What's this?" someone with a squeaky voice asked.

"Death Lords and humans... in the first abyss?" another voice, this one icier than the first, replied. "Fascinating."

I slid down a blue vine and landed on a glowing green hammock leaf. When I whirled around, careful not to lose my balance and fall over, I noticed two more of the elder ogata toads. They slipped into the root through the near holes in the side, and they clung to the walls like geckos, hurrying inside like rats escaping the rain.

When one turned its eyes to me, the whole creature practically lit up with glee.

The toad flashed its unnatural fangs.

With the temperature inside me still rising, I held out my hand, my palm pointed in the beast's direction.

"Humans shouldn't be here," the elder ogata toad said with a hiss. "You're nothing more than—"

"Yeah, I don't care," I said, cutting it off.

Then a *roar* of fire erupted from my palm when I pushed the fire in my blood through my body. I just wanted to evoke *some* magic, but it was like a floodgate had been opened, and I just couldn't stop what came rushing out. A torrent of flames blasted through the root, catching one of the stupid elder toads before it could leap away. The poor deranged monster was crisped within seconds as the inferno of phoenix dragon magic scorched everything.

Even me.

I recoiled, my back slamming against the root wall. The whole place shuddered as the combat raged on outside.

My palm was bright red, a layer of skin cooked clean off. I took in a ragged breath, stunned it was even possible to burn myself with the magic. Were phoenix dragons not immune to their own fire? Or had I done something wrong? No evocation felt like the phoenix dragon's—it was like it was building in me, and then dying to escape. What creature was like that?

Embers and smoke filled with the inner root, and I realized I was now partially responsible for destroying part of the Wraithborne Orchard. I couldn't use this powerful evocation again—not if I wanted to keep my hand and this root in one piece.

But then the second elder ogata toad leapt through the black clouds of smoke and lunged straight for me.

Deimos's combat instincts kicked in. I barely stepped aside, allowing the toad to slam into the root wall feet-first. That monster had tried to crush me with its powerful legs, and instead, it damaged the root. With its eyes flashing, the beast opened its mouth, preparing to puke up its deadly acid.

I thought—it was a mere guess—that I could manipulate fire. Phoenixes manipulated fire, after all. It was a logical assumption. So when I waved my hand, hoping to take the tiny flames lingering in the area and use them against the toad, I wasn't expecting the ogata toad to shrivel.

Its whole body—from its webbed toes to its fanged mouth —shriveled like a grape left out in the sun for multiple days.

The toad screamed and staggered away, weaker than ever.

And then I felt *better*. So much better. My palm, which had been burning seconds ago, now felt cooled and relieved. I glanced down, only to find my skin perfectly fine—no injuries.

After a deep breath, I realized I was more awake, more alert, and more confident. Something about this bizarre exchange had revitalized me.

In that moment of realization, I was shaken.

What had I done with the phoenix dragon magic? Had I manipulated energy? Or life force? Or something similar?

The shriveled ogata toad wasn't dead. It hissed and grabbed at its wrinkled head, its eyes bloodshot, its strange pupils searching the area. When I didn't attack it a second time, the monster growled, obviously intent on continuing this fight.

In a split-second decision, I reached for the magical thread of the abyssal dragon. My arcanist mark burned as the symbol for the phoenix dragon shifted into the one for the abyssal dragon. I was granted the powers of the Death Lords, and as the elder ogata toad flew at me another time, I evoked raw magic and blasted the beast away.

Normally, using magic of older and more powerful creatures took a toll on me. My mimic was young, so it was difficult to wield such magics, but after the phoenix dragon's rejuvenation, I felt *good*.

No.

Better than good.

So alive. The raw magic didn't hurt, my muscles didn't ache, and I felt like I could swim my way out of the abyssal hells and still have energy left over to run in a marathon.

As I glanced around, my heart racing, I noticed the root was both burnt and mending itself. The raw magic I had evoked seemed to feed into the plants, and they were bright again. The embers were snuffed out by a chill wind that seemed to come from the glowing plants themselves, and it occurred to me that perhaps...

This place was more alive than I had thought.

After another deep breath, I slid down another vine and came to the section of orange mushrooms. This was near the bottom.

"Gray!"

The dark and gravelly voice took me by surprise. I turned my attention upward, to a hole in the root a good thirty feet above me, and spotted an abyssal dragon. Despite the fact he looked identical to Deimos's, I knew it was Twain.

"You're okay?" I called up to him.

The dragon slid into the root, practically falling forward. As he plummeted, the body shimmered and shifted until Twain reverted to his kitten form. I stepped forward, both arms raised, and caught my eldrin as gently as I could.

He landed with a *mew!*

Then I cradled him close, happy he had come back to me.

Then the rumbling and quaking stopped. Had Deimos and the phoenix dragon stopped fighting? I couldn't see or hear them. My heart continued to race, and I hoped Deimos and Nini would both come back to meet with Zahn.

What if they had been killed?

I shook away the thought. I'd know if Deimos died. His soul fragment would somehow convey that information. They were fine. Totally fine.

I hoped.

"What happened?" I asked as I hugged Twain. The orange glow of the mushroom cap illuminated us both.

"Deimos sent me back." Twain relaxed in my arms, his body so weak, his ears drooping in visible exhaustion. "He said I needed to stay with you. Just in case. I'm sorry if I didn't do the right thing."

"No, no. This is fine." I kept him pressed up against me as I slid down to another mushroom. "We just have to get Knovak now, and then we can leave."

"Where is he?"

"I... I don't know."

When we reached the bottom of this bizarre root, my heart sank into my gut. I didn't see Knovak or his unicorn anywhere. Unfortunately, there were holes in the root here, too. I spotted the murky mire out one side, and landscape I was unfamiliar with on the other. There were trees and dirt and spiderwebs—a new location in the abyssal hells that was both strange and terrifying.

Would Knovak have left the safety of the root? Would he return to the watery mire, or would he hide in the tangle of trees not too far from our location?

Starling hated the water, and couldn't swim...

"We need to hurry," I whispered to Twain. "We're going to grab Knovak and bring him back with us, okay?"

Twain barely moved in my arms. He had already given me so much already—fighting both Naiad and Xuandi now. How much longer could he go?

I crawled out of the hole at the base of the root and slammed my bare feet down on dark dirt. Ahead of me was a short path that led to twisted trees seemingly made of the blackness the inner root was made of. Mist swirled around the area, glowing with magic as though it were dreams and nightmares painted in the same brushstroke.

Then some of the fog parted, beckoning me forward with a clear path.

The webs covered the leaves on the trees, creating a cotton-like appearance that both disturbed and intrigued me. As I walked closer, I spotted spiders scuttling throughout the matted tangle of webs.

They weren't normal spiders the size of my fingernail—they were spiders the size of my fist. Their bulbous bodies and elongated legs made them seem nightmarish and somehow hostile.

As I passed the first tree, one spider actually raced to the edge of the webs and stretched out its little fangs. I flinched away with a sneer, disgusted by the creature. It didn't speak, nor did it pursue me. The spider retreated into the webs and continued scuttling about.

Fireflies danced in the mists, and as I watched, spiders managed to lunge from the webs and grab them.

"What's going on?" Twain whispered.

Deimos's knowledge trickled into my thoughts, but only briefly. "Those are... the Fingers of Rebirth."

"I thought the fingers were weird root hands," Twain said.

"They're different here... They're spiders." I paid more attention to the trees and their trunks, looking for more insects. Sure enough, I spotted worms and centipedes, each burrowing into the crust of the trees, eating them from the inside out. "You know how the Wraithborne Orchard reincarnated people into plants?"

Twain nodded once.

"I think this place reincarnates souls into insects."

Twain's ears twitched, and then his orange fur puffed. "Ew." Then he gasped. "Wait! There are magical insects. I've seen them. Like, uh, *star moths!*"

"Yeah," I muttered as I stepped forward. It grew darker the further I walked into this bizarre spider's lair.

"What's this place called?"

"I don't know." Deimos's thoughts were distracted, and his knowledge wasn't flowing as freely.

"Oh." Twain clung to my arm, his eyes wide as he watched the spiders and bugs skitter around the trees. "I'm going to call it... *The Bug-Bloated Bog.*"

With a chuckle, I said, "I somehow doubt that's its name."

Flowers blossomed at the base of the trees the longer I

walked on. Not only that, but clusters of grapes were there, too. They glistened with dew, ready to eat. I tried not to glance at them, because my stomach rumbled immediately afterward.

Clusters of bees, obviously drawing from ancient power coursing through the abyssal hells, glowed with an otherworldly luminescence, just like the mushrooms and vines in the root. The mystical bees flew from one blossoming flower to the next, and I wondered what was happening here.

"Gray... Look." Twain gestured to the path.

I turned my attention to the dirt.

Unicorn tracks.

CHAPTER 11

THE TALE OF DEATH LORD KALLIKORE

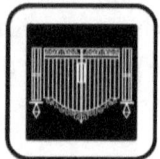

The trees grew in thick clusters. They were smaller than the roots of the Wraithborne Orchard, and more twisted. Their bark created furrows that writhed with life. Ants, centipedes, and beetles squirmed in the shadowed grooves. It made the whole *bog* feel alive.

The unicorn tracks were easy to follow... until they weren't.

Thick shadows blanketed the area. Only the glowing grapes and insects gave us light, and they were too infrequent—or they moved too quickly—to use as a guide.

I held Twain in my arms, and he purred whenever I glanced down to check on him.

Thankfully, I still had Vivigöl on me. If something happened, I would have a means to fight. I suspected Twain didn't have much more in him, and I couldn't rely on his transformation alone to get me out of a tight spot.

"How did Knovak and Starling make it through this mess?" I asked. The spiderwebs hanging from the tree branches grew thicker and more prevalent. I had to swat them away every couple of feet, and they clung to my arms, causing shivers to run down my spine.

"He can see in the dark," Twain whispered.

"No, he can't." I huffed and shook my head. "Unicorn arcanists can't see in the dark."

"No. But remember when we went to Phila's cotillion? She gave us all magical gifts. Knovak's trinket allows him to see through darkness."

I nodded once, my thoughts swirling around that happy event. Phila *had* given Knovak a means to see through darkness. He was using it now? To navigate the bog? On the other hand, all I saw were unicorn tracks, so perhaps Starling was out looking for a lost Knovak.

Another thought occurred to me as the darkness thickened all around me. What if these unicorn tracks didn't belong to Starling? What if they belonged to an elder unicorn?

I knelt and examined them further. They were smaller, the size of a foal's, and I reassured myself they belonged to Knovak's eldrin.

But still...

Elder creatures were everywhere, apparently. I had to stay on guard for anything. I reached up, grabbed Vivigöl still around my neck, and gently removed it. The weapon *click-click-clicked* as it transformed into a golden sword, one with a long blade and six flared spikes on the guard. It felt lightweight in my hand, and the blade pulsed with an eerie inner life.

Vivigöl didn't reject me, because of Deimos's soul fragment locked away in my being.

"We should be careful," I whispered to Twain as I took a step forward.

"You're not being careful enough when you're this loud," someone else said—definitely not Twain.

The gruff and completely unexpected voice startled me enough that I almost leapt out of my skin. I whirled on my heel, blade in hand, Twain crushed against my chest as I held him tighter than ever.

But it was too dark. The dancing fireflies, glowing grapes, and bioluminescent insects didn't give me enough light to see who had spoken. All I saw were the deep shadows between the trees, and the creepy darkness that surrounded the webbing.

"I... can't breathe..." Twain managed to choke out.

I loosened my grip on him, my eyes frantically searching the area. "Who's there?" I called out. "Show yourself."

A rustle from a nearby group of trees alerted me to the general whereabouts of our guest. I faced that direction, but I still couldn't see anyone. My gaze landed on the darkness pooled between two twisted trunks, and I just assumed whoever had spoken was there.

"I haven't seen another human in a long time," the voice said. Masculine, confident, but rusty. Had he not spoken in a while? "Are the gates open? I felt... something... maybe a year ago? A new gate had opened for only a couple minutes. Then it was closed again."

I held my breath as my thoughts returned to the basement of Astra Academy. Technically, the Gate of Crossing that led into the abyssal hells *had* been open for a few minutes. The sun and the moon had appeared in the sky at the same time, signifying the wondrous event.

I relaxed—but only slightly. "There was a gate. But it was destroyed."

"Ah. I see..." A twig snapped, and then I heard the crunch of bugs underfoot. Someone squished a handful of insects all at once. "How did you get here? Let me guess—the Followers of Umbriel?"

"No." His comment actually got me to chuckle. I lowered my weapon, but I took a step away, wanting to give myself more distance, in case this strange individual attacked. "It's complicated, but I was dragged into the abyssal hells because of Death Lord Naiad."

"Right. All the Death Lords have active followers ever since that gate was opened. Everyone is desperate to either escape the abyssal hells... or get into them."

Twain twitched his ears. Then he narrowed his eyes. "Gray?" he whispered to me. "Can you feel his magical thread?"

I twirled Vivigöl around in my grip as I attempted to sense this person's magic. It seemed... nebulous. Ever changing. Familiar.

"Are you human?" I asked.

The individual didn't answer for a long minute.

"I was," he eventually replied. "But a while ago, I fought the Followers of Umbriel. They were attempting to send humans straight to the fifth abyss—effectively killing them forever—just to help their *favorite Death Lord*. I went to stop them, but during the confrontation, I... ended up here."

The other Death Lord had followers in the land of the living? Of course. I had met a few who followed Naiad. And obviously, Zahn, Deimos's brother, had been leading a cult of people who worshipped Deimos.

"My name is Gray Lexly," I said. Then I held up Twain. "This is my mimic."

Twain waved his little paw. "I'm Twain."

"You can call me Everett," the man in the darkness said.

A loud roar pierced the strange forest. It rumbled the trees and jostled the webbing. The giant spiders, fireflies, and insects all scuttled to the safety of the shadowy voids.

"Xuandi..." I shook my head, wondering if the elder phoenix dragon would return to the Wraithborne Orchard. "You should probably get out of here. Death Lord Kallikore and his monsters are on the rampage."

Everett laughed. It was short, and almost sarcastic. "I appreciate the concern, but I've been here for years. I don't need help avoiding the elder creatures and their lust for souls."

Years?

It made me wonder.

Although, I didn't have much time...

But I was still curious.

"Do you know why Kallikore is working with elder creatures?" I asked. "I mean, why don't the creatures hate him like they hate everyone else?"

"Because Xuandi has sway over the sanest of the elder creatures," Everett replied. "Xuandi entered the abyssal hells long before the Twilight Gate was sealed."

"Why?"

"Because after his arcanist was killed, Xuandi was so angry—so distraught—he ventured to the abyssal hells to retrieve his soul."

Twain kneaded my arms. "*Awww.*" He glanced up at me. "I'd do that for you, Gray. Definitely."

I couldn't stop myself from half-smiling. Only Sorin had ever said something that nice to me before. But I didn't want to get distracted by sentimentality. "I take it Xuandi didn't find his arcanist?"

"He did," Everett replied. "But then the Twilight Gate was sealed, and it was too late. Xuandi was trapped in the abyssal hells, along with the soul of his arcanist."

"But what happened after that?"

"Death Lord Kallikore, with his magic over souls, agreed to preserve Xuandi's arcanist until the day the gates reopened. But that day never came... In order to survive, Xuandi consumed the souls of humans, warping his body into the monster we know today. For years, the beast has grown hateful. First, over how humans treated his arcanist—who apparently was killed in a treacherous manner—and then later, for trapping him in the hells. Xuandi's rage has only festered."

"Oh." Twain frowned. "But he likes Kallikore because he's helping him?"

"From what I could gather." Everett chortled. "But there's more to Xuandi's loyalty. Kallikore has turned himself half into a mystical creature—and the elder creatures like that. It's why they don't hunger for his flesh."

"How do you know that?" I asked.

"Because I did the same thing."

My blood ran cold.

Everything in the abyssal hells felt... wrong. It wasn't the death or the souls—those were natural things—it was like there was an infection here that was getting out of control. Elder creatures? Tortured lives? Followers of Death Lords killing people? Deimos was right. The natural order of things was gone.

And that meant, if Ashlyn, Knovak, Nini and I didn't get out of here, terrible things were going to happen to us, some of which were worse than dying.

Another roar, and the rumble worsened. I really didn't have time for this.

I took another step back, but then I hesitated.

"I, uh, know a way out," I muttered. "Do you want to come with me?"

"Out of the abyssal hells?"

"Yes."

Everett chuckled again. "I doubt that will work, but even if it could... I don't think I'd be welcome in the realm of the living anymore. I'm not... well. And I've been helping to cull the elder creatures whenever I catch them alone, attempting to help lessen their numbers."

"Are you sure?" Twain asked.

Everett didn't reply.

"Well, thank you for the information," I said. "If, uh, we find a way to set things right, I'll look for you. And other people like you. To help them. Okay?"

The man in the darkness waited a time before replying. "That won't ever happen. But perhaps, if you manage to make it home, you can tell my family I love them? I miss them more than anything."

"It *will* happen. I'm helping Death Lord Deimos. We'll set things right. I swear."

"Deimos is practically fighting alone, and on the brink of losing. You're better off staying in the realm of the living. Away from all this."

When the dragon screeched a third time, I knew this had to end. And I didn't want to argue with the man in the darkness. I had already told him everything he needed to know—I was going to help. I had to.

I had to.

Who else was going to do it? No one. I felt Deimos's indignant rage whenever he talked about this—no one else saw it as a problem. If the gates stayed sealed, who cared what happened to the beasts and souls in the abyssal hells? It was like a dam—so long as it wasn't going to break, who cared?

But I had seen too much now. I *knew* there was a problem, just as Deimos had said.

"I have to go," I whispered.

"I hope you make it, kid."

I ran deeper into the forest, Twain in one arm, and Vivigöl held in my other hand. Knovak was here, and so was his unicorn. I just needed to find them, and then we needed to leave. I would return to the realm of the living, tell everyone what was going on, and find a solution to this mess.

Webs from the trees fluttered onto my face. The phantom tickle that lingered on my skin caused me to shiver. I rubbed my cheeks and tried to clear away everything as I hurried into the darkness.

"Starling, we need to go..."

Knovak's voice was distinct, even when he was muttering. I skidded to a stop and listened.

"Starling, *please*."

I stepped between a few trees, my heart hammering. Where was Knovak? Twain clung to me, his claws in my arm.

"Knovak?" I asked, my voice barely above a whisper. I stepped between two trees, and into a small grove of glowing insects. The sparkle of their bodies gave me enough illumination to see the scene in front of me.

Knovak stood next to his eldrin. The unicorn foal munched on a cluster of glowing grapes that grew at the base of the strange tree. *Munch, munch, munch.* Starling gobbled them down by the mouthful, and from the looks of things... he had eaten quite a bit already.

CHAPTER 12

ABYSSAL LEECHES

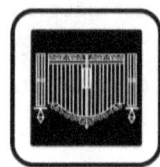

In my panic, I dropped Twain and Vivigöl, dashed over to Starling, wrapped my arms around the foal's torso, and yanked him away from the sinister soul fruits. Glowing blue juices stained his muzzle and some dripped to the ground. Whispers of agony remained on the wind, only vanishing once the unicorn licked his lips.

"*What're you doing?*" I shouted.

Knovak grabbed my shoulder and tore Starling from my grasp. Then he shoved me away before protectively standing in front of his eldrin.

The unicorn stomped and snorted. "The berries *wanted* to be eaten, and I *want* to be strong. And I will be strong. I can already feel it working."

I turned to Knovak, caught in a cycle of thoughts that all led to disbelief. "Are you insane?" I asked, still shouting. "Death Lord Deimos made it clear—*so damn clear*. You can't eat anything! What have you done?"

"I didn't eat anything," Knovak said, his volume rising to match mine. "And Starling only had a couple bites. He's fine!"

I grabbed Knovak's shirt and shoved him to the side. "Come here," I said to Starling. "You haven't changed yet—maybe we can make you vomit, or we can cut open a part of your stomach."

Knovak tackled me from the side, sending us both tumbling to the dirt. We struggled for a moment, simply because I hadn't expected him to attack me. Once I realized what was happening, I grabbed his shoulders, rolled on top of him, and then slammed his head on the ground, pinning him down.

What was wrong with him? Where was this coming from?

Knovak glared up at me, his eyes glassy. "I'm not going to let you hurt my eldrin," he yelled.

What was I supposed to say? "You've already hurt him far worse than what I could've done," I whispered.

When Knovak tried to shove me, I just stood up and stepped away. Starling leapt over his arcanist and nuzzled Knovak's face. Then the unicorn glowered in my direction, so much hate in his little foal eyes.

He still looked normal...

Maybe Starling hadn't eaten too much?

I hoped beyond hope that was the case.

"Why?" was all I could ask.

"I'm tired of being weak," Starling stated. "I don't want people to mock my arcanist. I'll be stronger now—you'll see. No one will make fun of us ever again."

I rubbed my chest, unsure what to do. Knovak stood and hugged his eldrin. The two kept their embrace for some time.

Taking Starling with us seemed risky to me. Then again, I didn't want to leave him. I honestly wasn't sure what to do.

"Deimos," I whispered to myself. "Can you hear me?"

But he didn't reply. He was the only one who I trusted to give me accurate advice in this situation, but he was probably too busy dealing with Death Lord Kallikore. That meant we were on our own, and I'd rather have Knovak and his unicorn close... We couldn't leave them.

"Let's go," I said, my voice shaky. "We need to hurry. We have to get out of here." Although I was still uncertain, I hurried over to Twain and my weapon.

Twain stared up at me with his two-colored eyes, his kitten brow furrowed. I scooped him up into my arms. "Will Starling be okay?" he whispered.

I patted his head and didn't answer. I didn't know.

Then I grabbed Vivigöl and headed for the strange path back to the Wraithborne Orchard. I stopped a few feet into the trek and turned around, making sure Knovak and Starling were going to follow. Thankfully, Knovak and his eldrin slowly made their way after me, and Starling wasn't monstrous or lashing out against us. He still looked like an adorable unicorn.

Maybe he hadn't eaten much of the fruits at all.

As we traveled through the trees, through the darkness of the forest bog, plowing through the spiderwebs, I no longer heard the roar of the phoenix dragon. In its place, I heard an eerie and familiar cawing.

Where had I heard that before?

It sounded like a high-pitched bird call, and done in short bursts. But then they stopped, and the forest became silent.

I stopped, terror coursing through me. Knovak and his unicorn almost ran into me. The woods were too dark to see into the shadows that surrounded us, but the fireflies dancing around allowed me to see the details of things close by.

"We should stay close together," I whispered, my grip on Vivigöl ironclad.

A quiet moment passed.

Maybe we were alone.

The trees rustled, and I glanced up. I really wished I had glanced up sooner.

A monstrous griffin loomed in the cobweb trees. It was a mass of muscle, its lion head fearsome, its maw filled with two sets of fangs, its mane putrid with sickly blue souls. The beast lunged before I could take in any more details.

"Gray!" Twain shouted.

I tossed Twain out of harm's way just as the monster slammed into me, its claws digging into my chest as its weight crushed downward. I hit the ground on my back, winded, my heart racing, my pain numbed. I never let go of Vivigöl—fighting instincts from Deimos told me that if I dropped my weapon, I'd be dead.

The elder griffin roared and brought his maw down to rip off my face. I stabbed the creature in the side of the neck before it could plant its fangs around my skull. Blood gushed from the injury, coating me in sticky heat. With gritted teeth, I willed Vivigöl to transform—while it was still inside the griffin monster.

Vivigöl forcibly clicked into the shape of a spiked wheel, the blade forming through the griffin's neck, head, and chest. I hadn't formed Vivigöl into a weapon I recognized—it was some sort of torture device from Deimos's memories. An actual wheel for flaying flesh. I didn't know why it was the only thing that came to mind when I was panicking.

The griffin twitched and collapsed, blood spewing from its slack jaw and the gash in its neck.

Knovak stepped closer. "G-Gray?"

Another screech chilled my blood. A *second* elder griffin lunged from the spiderweb trees, this one with the head of an eagle, and glowing blue souls attempting to claw their way out of the monster's beak mouth.

It, too, had fangs—and they were hauntingly large and curved, like nothing natural.

It was as if becoming an elder creature turned them into

monsters that only desired to eat humans. No matter what they had eaten before... now they wanted the flesh of mankind.

This eagle-headed griffin didn't go for me—it went for Knovak. It slammed him to the ground, but then he used his evocation. A blast of *pure force* knocked the elder griffin off his body. It *cracked* the air with its might, throwing the griffin upward, and even breaking the branches of the trees above Knovak in one mighty explosion.

The elder griffin hit one of the nearby trees and screamed. But then it quickly got up, its claws out, its fangs flashing. "*Human scum,*" it said, feminine and hate filled.

"Don't you speak about my arcanist that way!" Starling planted his feet and evoked another burst of powerful force from his unicorn horn. He blasted the elder griffin against the trunk of the tree.

That didn't kill the monster—so Starling charged forward, faster and stronger than I had ever seen him go. He slammed his horn straight into the elder griffin's chest, the blood splatter startling as it coated the unicorn foal, the tree, and the ground.

I managed to push the dead lion-headed griffin to the side, but the beast was so large and heavy, my legs were still trapped underneath. Twain leapt around me. He pushed the griffin's body from the side, though it was silly because he was just a kitten. Without transforming, Twain didn't have the strength to move the corpse.

"Knovak?" I asked.

He rushed to my side and grabbed some of the griffin's body. "I'll help you." He lifted, but it wasn't enough. Together, we struggled, but the creature remained partially on my legs.

Starling pulled his horn from the other griffin, and it slid to the ground, shallowly breathing, its coughs weak. Was it not dead? The monster didn't say anything else afterward.

Drenched in crimson from his horn to the tip of his muzzle,

Starling came prancing over as though he were king of the abyssal hells.

"Not so weak anymore," he said, his voice lower, darker.

As Knovak and I were getting the last of the griffin corpse off me, something inside the monster's body writhed. A wave of squirms, like a babe spilling from its mother's belly, rippled across the griffin's stomach. I felt the movement against my legs. It was an undulation of life.

Was the creature pregnant?

No. This griffin had a lion's head. It was male. It couldn't have—

A dozen squirming eels, each the size of a human finger, slid out of the griffin's mouth, pouring out onto me and the dirt. They hissed and spat, and flopped about like half-fish, half-snake monstrosities.

I didn't know how I managed it, but I jumped so hard and fast, I managed to untrap myself from under the corpse. I smacked away all the hissing eels. They were coated in fresh blood, and I sent splatters of scarlet everywhere, my heart hammering as I attempted to get every single one away from me.

"What are those?" Knovak shouted as he leapt away from the body, his face paling to a colorless sheet of white.

Starling and Twain both hurried away, their eyes wide.

The little eels, puke green with tiny tentacles, all writhed on the ground.

"Help us," one whispered. "*We're dying.*"

"Did you hear that?" Knovak stepped away, barely able to breathe. "What kind of nightmare land is this?"

"Help," another one pleaded, sweeter this time. "We need help."

I shook away some of my discomfort and decided the little creatures probably weren't going to kill me. They were too tiny. After a deep breath, and once I brushed off more of the griffin blood, I stepped closer.

"Don't touch them," came a voice from the trees.

Everett.

I turned, but the man remained shrouded in the darkness.

"You followed me?" I asked.

"Step away from them," Everett said. "I'll handle this."

Knovak and I both moved away, as did Starling and Twain. At first, I thought Everett would step out of the trees and squish the little creatures, but a moment later, a burst of intense flames roared out of the shadows.

It was a type of bright, blue fire that scorched the ground and heated everything. I had to shield my face—my eyeballs felt like they were drying out within just a few seconds.

The little eels screamed as the fire consumed them. They were short cries, at least. They were snuffed out in an instant.

Then the fire died off, and the darkness returned. The smell of charred flesh and smoke lingered, but it was quickly replaced by the stink of brackish waters. A few trees were even burnt, and a few embers remained, but the shadows were so thick, the light barely illuminated anything.

"Why did you kill them?" Knovak asked. "They were asking for help."

Starling stomped his hooves. "Disgusting. All the creatures here are right. Humans don't care."

"They were abyssal leeches," Everett said matter-of-factly. "They burrow into arcanists and steal from their souls. Normally, they only infest humans, but they can live in elder creatures as well, so those monsters have extra human souls on their bodies. If an abyssal leech burrows into you, it'll warp your soul, break your magic, or even kill you."

I ran a shaky hand down my chest. Had I managed to get all of them?

I hoped beyond hope I had.

Funny how much I was praying to unseen forces while I was here.

Twain ran to my feet. Then he gestured to the dead griffin. Vivigöl had transformed back into a trident, its natural form. I stumbled over to it, picked up the weapon, and held it close.

"We need to leave," I intoned.

From the depths of the darkness, Everett huffed. "I'll watch over you until you reach the Wraithborne Orchard. But we must hurry. The elder creatures know you're here..."

CHAPTER 13

REBIRTH

We raced through the spiderweb-covered trees, Everett in the branches, disturbing the spiders and knocking down leaves with each leap he made. Knovak and Starling ran beside me, neither growing tired. Unicorns and their arcanists always seemed to have a wellspring of stamina.

I carried Twain in my arms, and he occasionally mewed. He seemed so tired. And I was so hungry. It felt like we had been in the abyssal hells forever—with no rest, no nourishment, and no peace of mind.

We needed to make it out. Soon.

"We're almost out of the Silkshade Grove," Everett said through huffed breaths.

The *Silkshade Grove?* Was that the name of this insect-infested forest? That made sense. The name fit the gloom of this place perfectly.

Then we exited the forest and returned to the ankle-deep mire of the Wraithborne Orchard. The tall roots that reached up as high as I could see were a welcome sight. But as I glanced up, an elder ogata toad burst out of the water and flew at me with its fang-filled maw wide open.

I didn't even have time to drop Twain and ready Vivigöl.

But that didn't matter—a monster flew from the trees and collided with the elder toad in midair. It was larger than the ogata toad, but only slightly, but it was clearly faster and stronger.

The monster appeared to be human-shaped, but with the scales, wings, and feathers of Xuandi, the last phoenix dragon. Yellow leather wings, scarlet feathers that made a mane, toes and fingers with talons, and scales so red, they could've been dyed with fresh blood.

It was some sort of human-dragon fusion that looked so tortured and unnatural, I feared for it. The monster crunched down on the toad's neck. The elder creature screamed until its voice became a gurgled mess. When it tried to evoke its acid, the monster dragon-man evoked flames straight from its mouth, burning the toad down to its sinew.

The elder toad splashed into the mire water.

"What is that?" Knovak asked, his voice shaky.

Starling leapt in front of him, his fur standing on end, as if he were a wolf with his hackles raised. I had never seen a unicorn with such rage and bloodlust in its expression.

The monster stood on two legs, its dragon body oddly contorted to fit a humanoid shape. It had a tail it swished, and its wings tucked to its back. The freak of nature wore bangles on its arms, and a necklace with a pendant around its scaled neck.

"We need to hurry," the thing said.

It was Everett.

I held my breath. What had happened to make him like this? He had said he was part mystical creature, but I hadn't expected this. He stood almost eleven feet tall and was intimidating beyond belief.

He didn't look right. I wished... I knew how to help him.

Would this happen to Ashlyn and the others if they were forced to adapt to the abyssal hells? My urge to leave this place grew with each passing moment.

When Everett faced me, his eyes were shaky—unsteady, really. Like he couldn't focus on one thing too long.

"What're you waiting for?" he asked.

I shook my head. "R-Right. We need to go."

Knovak and Starling calmed down. They must've recognized Everett's voice as well, though they constantly shot him worried and suspicious glances. As a group, we sloshed through the water and headed to the cracked and shattered root that led to the point of rebirth in the orchard. I clambered through an opening and made my way back into the beautiful interior, where the plants glowed bright and colorful.

Everett, with his sharp talons, climbed the interior of the strange root, hauling his weight straight up the side. After a deep breath, I crawled onto the mushroom caps that were still intact, trying to hurry as quickly as possible.

When I glanced back, I expected to see Knovak struggling worse than me. He had to help Starling, didn't he? But that wasn't the case. Unlike before, when Starling needed Ecrib to carry his little foal body, the little unicorn was now *leaping* from one mushroom and gigantic leaf to the next. He resembled a deer as he bounded to and fro. When had Starling become that graceful?

My stomach twisted into knots.

It was the souls he had consumed, obviously. There was no pretending—the change was apparent. But Starling didn't look different... I still maintained hope he could puke up the grapes and be fine. We just needed to escape first. Then we would help him.

Everything would be okay.

It had to be.

A rumble shot through the root, threatening to steal my

balance. Despite my fear of heights, and my fatigue, I managed to stay upright. I suspected Deimos's combat skill had something to do with that—my feet practically moved on their own to keep me steady.

Twain squirmed in my arms as I awkwardly climbed higher.

"I can do it," he said.

I set him down, and my eldrin used his feline nimbleness to keep up with me as I climbed higher and higher. In my mind, I kept chanting that I was almost there, no matter the actual distance to my destination. With each breath, I tried to convince myself this whole nightmare was almost over.

The cracks in the roots allowed me to peek outward and see the Wraithborne Orchard. Far in the distance, Xuandi flew through the air, evoking a breath of flame onto the plants, fireflies, and roots below.

As I grabbed some vines, I glanced down to the mire water near the root. And I regretted my decision.

Another abyssal dragon was here, but this one had no wings. It was a freakish reptilian monster, its scales rotting, its body oozing fluids. Its back was a mangled mess of injuries, as though someone had torn the wings clean off its back and allowed the injury to just fester. Blood wept from the beast as it waded through the mire, its six eyes glancing in all directions, its tail lashing like an untamed whip.

Someone strode next to this tormented dragon, and in my heart, I knew his identity.

It was Death Lord Kallikore.

His armor, a macabre tapestry of bones and twisted metal, was almost identical to Deimos's, as though the Death Lords had a melancholy uniform. Kallikore was tall—perhaps taller than Deimos—but gaunt and wiry, as though starved and stretched. He had dark tanned skin and black hair that rivaled the night. His eyes, just like Deimos's, were tinged yellow, but Kallikore's glowed sickly pale.

But those features were mundane and were *nothing* compared to his wings.

Normally, Death Lords didn't have wings, at least none that I had met so far. But clearly, Kallikore was anything but normal.

It was obvious to me what Everett had meant when he said Kallikore was part mystical creature now. Death Lord Kallikore had torn the wings off his own eldrin and stitched them to his flesh, grafting himself a sinister and gory pair of wings. They were pale blue, and mostly made of the souls of humans, but there was enough dragon flesh and scales to see the skeletal structure underneath.

As I stared, my mouth slowly drifted open.

What kind of fresh insanity was this?

A hand slammed down onto my shoulder, talons cutting into my flesh and thoughts. I whirled around to find Everett—the dragon man—next to me.

"Quickly," he said, his tone desperate, his dragon eyes on the distant Kallikore. "If you have an escape, you best use it now."

With a shaky nod, I continued my trek upward. Twain, Knovak, and Starling were all higher than me, but their eagerness to flee didn't compare. I half stumbled as I climbed one vine, and then to another leaf. The whole root was torn and broken, and I had a much more difficult time climbing. Whenever I glanced out a tear in the root, I noticed Death Lord Kallikore and his abyssal dragon were closer than before.

Halfway up, Everett leapt down to my leaf. He growled just like a dragon, his scarlet scales flaring. "You're too slow." He scooped me up and then spread his wings. Before I could offer protest, Everett practically launched into the sky, one powerful flap of his dragon wings sending us hurtling upward.

I held onto his scaled arm, both surprised how human-like it was, and how animalistic it felt. The bangles around his wrists clacked as he moved.

We reached the top—with Ashlyn and Ecrib—in no time.

The rock-leaf platform was still shattered, but Ashlyn had remained in place, just as I had asked. She stared at me with wide eyes as Everett set me down. A moment later, Knovak, Twain, and Starling joined us.

Ashlyn hurried over. "Gray? Are you okay?" She lifted her hand, and lightning crackled across most of her body.

I stepped between her and Everett—I knew she thought he was an elder creature, but I was exhausted, and the words weren't coming to me. "He's a friend," was all I managed to blurt out.

Ashlyn cautiously lowered her hand. "What's going on? Did you find Deimos? Nini? How are we going to get out of here?"

I glanced up, at the pinnacle of the root. The little motes of light kept floating away, and I didn't see any hint of Zahn or how we were supposed to escape.

The root rumbled again, and the screeching roar of a dragon sent a shiver down my spine. I hurried to one of the tears in the root and glanced down. Death Lord Kallikore and his monster eldrin were scaling the outside of the root now, climbing up.

Were they... coming for us?

"Curse the abyssal hells," I said, meaning it literally.

"Do you truly have a way to escape?" Everett asked. He glanced around, his movements almost unnatural. "I see nothing but devastation."

"Deimos said his brother would get us from here." I motioned to my exact spot. "He told us to wait, and that Zahn wouldn't fail. I don't know what's taking him so long."

"Then perhaps... you just need time." Everett exhaled as he turned his dragon-like head to glance out the root's tear. He spread his wings, but I held out a hand before he could go.

"*Wait*," I said. "Are you sure you don't want to come with us?"

"I'm not the type of man to leave the front line," he calmly replied. "I'll delay Kallikore, and hopefully give you enough time to meet Deimos's brother. If not... I'll be back to help you with your... new reality."

I shook my head. "W-Wait. You said you wanted me to speak to your family, but you never gave me a surname or a city. Where am I supposed to—"

"Eh," Everett said with a groan. "I've forgotten how to interact with humans, it seems." He pulled the necklace over his head and then handed it to me with taloned hands. "All the information you need is here. Give this to my husband. He'll... He'll want it."

Not wanting to lose the pendant, I pulled it over my head. "All right."

Then the dragon man flew from the root, the powerful beat of his wings carrying him out until he had enough room to dive straight down. Toward Kallikore.

"Gray?" Ashlyn asked.

I turned around. My heart beat hard, and for some reason, I suspected the damaged root was why Zahn hadn't contacted us yet. How was I supposed to fix this, though? Xuandi had torn it up pretty badly.

My mind raced, and I mulled over most of the facts I knew about the abyssal hells and our current situation. Then it struck me—something Deimos had said, about everything in the hells being *souls*. Couldn't Death Lords affect souls?

I motioned Twain over. "Come here. Quick. I think we need to fix this."

"How?" Twain ran to my feet. "What're we going to do?"

"I need you to transform into an abyssal dragon. Just one more time. We have to... I don't know... Fix this. Somehow." I was panicking, and it was hindering my ability to coherently explain myself, but I didn't care.

"I'm a master at transforming," Twain said, determination in his tone.

Once upon a time, I had to initiate Twain's transformation,

but he had gotten better at doing it on his own—he had already done it several times in the past. As soon as Twain concentrated, he bubbled and shifted. My mimic eldrin shifted, his tiny orange body exploding outward into the hideous form of the rotting abyssal dragon. I had to step aside to avoid being knocked over.

Once the dragon was formed, and half covering our shattered platform, I touched the side of the root.

What was I doing?

I didn't know.

Manipulating the souls?

Yes. That was it. I was going to manipulate the souls in the root. I would attempt to fix this. I would mend the root, stop the light motes from escaping, and allow Zahn to find us. That was my plan.

Closing my eyes, I flooded the root with my magic. Although it was difficult—although I didn't really know what I was doing—the root felt *receptive* to my efforts. It took my magic, and easily allowed itself to be manipulated.

As I concentrated harder, I even heard whispered voices.

"*It hurts.*"

"*The dragon burned us.*"

"*Help us, Death Lord. Help us...*"

Death Lord? Did the souls think, because I had abyssal dragon magic, that I was one of the Death Lords?

I shook away the thought. Then I opened my eyes and glanced upward. The thick root walls were moving. Bit by bit, they flexed, and the edges of the tears reached out to each other, slowly at first, but with more of my efforts, faster. It was burning, and my head throbbed, and I knew Twain form couldn't last forever, so I focused on the holes near the very top of the root—the holes where the light motes were escaping.

I needed them...

To stay in the root...

"Gray, you need to hurry." Ashlyn stared out one of the

numerous holes. "I don't think your friend is going to last much longer."

Knovak rubbed his hands together. "If they reach us..."

Starling stood next to his arcanist, his head high. "I'll be here."

"We'll fight," Ecrib growled, his fangs shining.

This was taking it out of me, but I just kept pressing on. What else was I supposed to do? We were at our limit, and it was now or never.

"C'mon, Zahn," I muttered through clenched teeth. "Deimos seems to think you never fail... I hope to the good winds he's right..."

The holes near the top of the root stitched themselves like a wicker basket, but that was all I could do. My magic stopped. Twain transformed back into a cat, and I stumbled away from the root wall, my wrist burning, my chest hurting.

But the light motes weren't escaping anymore. They funneled back to the top of the root, like they had before.

"Is that it?" Knovak asked. "Are we saved now?"

We all stared up at the darkness—at the dots of light that slowly disappeared, like a reverse snowfall.

Nothing happened.

I was about to make a joke about how it was ironic we were dying in the hells themselves, but then a blast of white light rained down around us, the warmth almost unbearable.

"Gray!" Ashlyn shouted.

I grabbed Twain and ran for her, my hand outstretched. "Ashlyn!"

And then I felt... weightless.

CHAPTER 14

LORD OTO

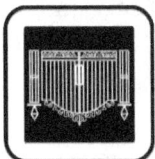

The weightless feeling only lasted half a second. Then I emerged from within a pumpkin. Yes—a pumpkin.

The gourd exploded in white pulp, orange flesh, dozens of seeds, and stringy goop. My shoulder ached as I hit some sort of hard surface during my emergence. With an unceremonious groan, I rolled over, my head pounding, my eyes adjusting to the new light.

Where was I?

It was a large room, ornate with a chandelier, wooden floors polished to a shine, and large woven tapestries to cover the tall walls. The ceiling was twelve feet above me, curved and painted to resemble a stormy night with thunderbirds sailing through the dark clouds.

I wiped the pumpkin juice off my face and immediately glanced around for the others. Twain was on the floor next to me, the stringy pumpkin innards wrapped around his cat-like body. He wasn't moving, and I panicked.

I gently picked up Twain, held him close, and ripped away the bits of pumpkin. My eldrin took a breath, and I relaxed a bit.

An arcanist's eldrin was like a part of their body—I wouldn't have been okay if Twain had been hurt.

"What in the abyssal hells just happened?"

The gruff and bizarre voice startled me. I had never heard this person before, and when I turned in their direction, I realized I had never met them before, either.

It was a short man. Notably short—perhaps not even five feet. He was lean and muscular, with a stiff stance that exuded his irritation.

He wore... clothing. So much clothing. The man sported a dark blue coat with similarly colored trousers, a black vest, an ivory shirt, a blue sash around the waist, another one on the shoulder, black ankle boots, a dark blue hat with a feather, a black cane, and leather gloves. Could he breathe under all of that? He was so small, he was practically just a pile of laundry.

The man also had a dozen medals pinned to his shoulder sash. Was he some sort of war hero?

The arcanist mark on his forehead was a seven-pointed star with a lustrous bird wrapped around the points. Was it a phoenix? The peacock tail reminded me of phoenixes.

"What is this?" the man growled. His teeth shone, and not all of them were white. Some of his teeth glittered with magic—they were enchanted with blue runes. Half the teeth on the top row. I had never seen that before. "Huh? *Zahn*? What's going on?"

Still baffled by the situation, I managed to take in the rest of my surroundings. This was a large room—big enough for me, Twain, Ashlyn, Knovak, Ecrib, and Starling to be sprawled out over a collection of sparkling pumpkins, mushrooms, and flowers. The others were unconscious, their faces peaceful in sleep.

Even Twain hadn't woken, though I felt him breathing.

Had we all burst out of the vegetation?

The only other people were the short man in his laundry outfit, and Professor Zahn.

Well, he wasn't a professor anymore—not after he tried to kill me inside Astra Academy.

He was standing closer to the fresh bunch of vegetables and plants, his expression grim. Unlike the short man, Zahn was notably tall and wiry. He wore long robes secured with black leather belts around the waist. Like the other man, Zahn wore dark blue—some sort of favored color here.

Zahn had darker brown hair that fell to his shoulders, darker tanned skin, and eyes that reminded me of Deimos. They weren't yellow, like Deimos's, but they were intense. He wore glasses—small spectacles, really—and glared at me through the tiny windows of glass.

He also had runes. A lot of runes. They were pink, blue, and gray and were wrapped around his hands, running the length of his knuckles and on his palms. The runes disappeared under his sleeves.

His arcanist mark matched mine.

A seven-pointed star with nothing in it. He was a mimic arcanist.

And then I spotted it—the mimic. It appeared to be a sleek and beautiful cat with pink fur, one gray eye, one orange-tan eye, and puffy paws that seemed larger than most. The mimic sat next to Zahn's feet, also glaring at me, the tip of its tail twitching.

"This wasn't supposed to happen," Zahn drawled, his tone a perfect blend of *annoyed* and *precise*. I had forgotten how much he sounded like someone who knew all the answers and hated that everyone around him was a complete rube.

The short man stepped forward, his black cane clicking on the wood floor with every other step. He stood close to Zahn, his lip curled upward in a sneer.

"You told me, and I quote—" the man held up a finger, "—

Don't worry, Lord Oto, you will have access to an abyssal dragon soon." Then the man pointed at me, Ashlyn, and Knovak. "What is this? What in the fresh manure is *this*? Children? Barely-of-age adults? *That's* what you summoned from the abyssal hells?"

Zahn fixed his small glasses on his long nose. "Something went wrong. Deimos should've been the only one capable of coming through."

"*I know something went wrong,*" the man sarcastically shouted. "I have two functioning eyes, you shabbaroon! You said a Death Lord and his abyssal dragon would be here, and instead, you squandered all my coin to pull off a disappointing magic trick."

Who was this person?

Lord Oto?

I had heard that name before... Someone in my class had mentioned him. Who?

Zahn closed his eyes so tightly, his whole expression seemed squished. He thought for a long moment, then exhaled. "I just need to try again. Deimos must've been nearby... He must've... triggered something on the other side... And these children... somehow..." He used his thumb and his pointer finger to rub both his eyes.

He was clearly struggling to understand what had happened.

Although I was weak, and still sitting on the floor in a mess of vegetable juice, I forced a cough to gain both of their attention.

"Deimos was in trouble," I said. I hacked up a pumpkin seed and spat it onto the floor. With a frown, I continued, "Death Lord Naiad was trying to graft his soul."

"*What?*" Zahn yelled, his voice echoing all around this vast and empty ballroom. He stepped closer, his body tense. "How could you possibly know that?"

I tapped my chest, though it hurt. I wanted nothing more than to go to sleep. "I have a fragment of Deimos's soul. And when Naiad was trying to rip his soul from his body, it pulled me, and the people around me, straight into the abyssal hells."

That information didn't sit well.

Zahn stared at me, his intense and intelligent eyes searching my gaze. Lord Oto just glared from his position close to the wall. He radiated contempt. I doubted he wanted to hear any of this.

"We were trapped there," I said. I held Twain close. "All of us. But Deimos told us about your plan. We had to, I don't know, get someplace within the Wraithborne Orchard so you could summon us. Teleport us. Whatever you just did."

"Eh?" Lord Oto scratched at his ear. When he sneered, his glowing rune-covered teeth seemed sinister, somehow. "The Death Lord was helping you unlicked cubs? Why?"

"I'm going to help set things right in the abyssal hells."

I made the statement as earnestly as possible, but it only occurred to me *after* I finished speaking that perhaps I sounded insane. They hadn't been there when I told Deimos I wanted to help. They hadn't seen all the horrors of the abyssal hells—how everything was clearly *wrong*.

"W-Wait," I said as I held up a hand. "Listen. I saw everything. The Death Lords fighting each other, the hells being messed up. *I saw the elder creatures.* They're only supposed to be in the fourth abyss, but they were there in the *first* abyss, trying to eat us, and consuming human souls. A-And I saw someone else! A man who, like, was half mystical creature!"

I was rambling. I knew it the moment I started. This wasn't adding to my claim for sanity, that was for sure.

Lord Oto's sneer grew deeper, his eyes narrower. "Yeah, kid. It's the abyssal hells—it's not a field of rainbows and flowers." He shook his head and slammed his cane onto the wood floor with a *clack*. "Look, I've had enough of this." He shot a glare at Zahn. "If you want more coin to fund you and your Death Lord-worshipping buddies, you'll get me pieces of an abyssal dragon. I don't care how you do it—or how many pumpkins you have to turn into children—I just want my dragon parts. *Understand?*"

"I understand perfectly." Zahn slowly exhaled. "I just need a little more time. I think I still have everything I need to help my brother breach the barrier between the realms of the dead and the living."

"Uh-huh. That's great." Lord Oto turned and walked toward the far door. He didn't need the cane to walk, though it *clack-clacked* every other step as he slammed it on the ground to emphasize his irritation. "Like I said, just get me some abyssal dragon parts. I already have buyers—those dragon bits will make for some fun trinkets and artifacts."

Zahn glared at the back of the short man's head, his own rage barely in check.

Lord Oto stopped at the door. He turned around, his expression one of bewilderment. Zahn's expression became a mask—neutral and without a hint of his anger, like he was hiding it from Oto.

"Wait," Lord Oto muttered. "What're you going to do with a bunch of children?"

Zahn's arcanist mark shifted across his forehead. What was once blank became an image of a spider with a human face. The mimic by Zahn's feet shimmered and shifted, transforming before my eyes into something I hadn't seen in a long time.

It was a soul catcher.

A wooden puppet spider the size of a full-grown human. Its eight limbs, creepy mask face, and knife-like fingers were the stuff of my nightmares. Literally. For years, a soul catcher had been trying to kill me while I slept.

I held my breath, my heart flipping around in my chest.

"I'll handle this," Zahn said as he snapped his fingers. "I'll extract my brother's soul from this *boy*, and then I'll try this again. Deimos is no doubt waiting for me. I can't fail him. *I can't.*"

The soul catcher reached out one of its eight limbs. I tried to stand and run, but I was exhausted. The time in the abyssal hells had taken such a terrible toll. Even standing was outside my capabilities.

And when the soul catcher touched me, its dread magic forced me into a deep sleep.

CHAPTER 15

NOW ALLIES

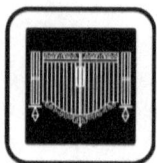

I awoke with a sore shoulder, my thoughts fuzzy. After I blinked, I awkwardly sat up and glanced around, quite familiar with my location.

It was a dream. No—a nightmare. The landscape was an infinite expanse of black rocks, each shiny, wet and glistening under the twinkle of a starry night. There was no sun or moon, yet I could see, a fact that reminded me dream logic was capable of anything.

One of my arms was held upward. With my free hand, I ran my fingers through my black hair. I was sitting next to a structure in this dreamscape—a cage made of stone, where some of the bars were cracked, and a few even missing. The shabby prison had exactly one occupant, and he was sitting on the floor, his back against the bars, his head hung.

It was Death Lord Deimos.

His soul fragment had been trapped in the realm of my dreams ever since Professor Helmith used her true form ethereal whelk magic to confine him to this place.

My arm was above my head, his arm also up, his clawed

fingers in my flesh. We had been intertwined for a while now... This irritated me.

With shaky legs, I stood.

Deimos's hand slipped off my arm, but blood remained. Not my blood—his. It was on my arm, at the bottom of his prison, outside and around the cage. Was he injured? I stumbled backward, trying to take everything in. I rubbed my arm, the phantom pain of his fingers still impaling my flesh.

Deimos didn't look well.

"Hello?" I asked. My voice echoed around the nothingness.

As I rubbed my face clear of any sweat, the click of boots on stone caught my attention. Zahn walked around the stone cage, coming into view, his gaze fixated on the cracked bars.

"What have you *done*?" he asked.

Before I could answer, his mimic-turned-soul-catcher scuttled over the top of the prison. Its wooden legs clicked along the black stone, its bizarre hands grasping at the tops of the bars, attempting to pry them open, but that had little to no effect.

A cold chill ran through me. I hated those soul catchers— especially since they could harm someone physically, even in the dreamscape. I closed my eyes and searched for the soul catcher's thread of magic, but when I tugged on it, nothing happened. Twain didn't transform. Was it because he was so tired? We had given it our all to escape the abyssal hells...

I opened my eyes and took a controlled breath.

"I didn't do that," I said. "Professor Helmith did."

Zahn clicked his tongue in disapproval. "I know Rylee was responsible. I can sense the ethereal whelk magic all throughout this, and I was informed ages ago you carried a small fraction of Deimos's power." He grazed his fingertips over the cage. "That's not what I'm talking about. What happened here? Why is the magic weaker? Why isn't Deimos answering me?"

My thoughts immediately went to the troubles brewing in the abyssal hells. I had left Deimos and Nini behind...

"He's busy," I said, my voice breathless. I shook my head. "Deimos was fighting Death Lord Kallikore and his elder phoenix dragon. I think whenever he can't focus on his astral projection, the fragment of his soul slumbers—if that makes sense."

Zahn yanked his hand away from the cage. When he turned to me, he met my gaze with an icy glare. "You were there? In the hells?"

I nodded once.

"And Deimos... was in trouble?"

"The other Death Lords were out to get him. Naiad attacked, and then Kallikore." I snapped my fingers as I remembered something. "He said the other Death Lords could sense he was in the first abyss."

Zahn's gaze fell to the wet rocks beneath his feet. He glowered at the ground for a long minute, his stare as intense as ever. Then he glanced over at the unconscious form of Deimos locked away in the prison.

"He should've escaped to the realm of the living..." Zahn whispered. "You've ruined everything with your meddling."

"*Me?* I wasn't the one who asked to be stalked by a dream monster." I motioned to the soul catcher. "I didn't want any part of this—but now that I'm here, I'm going to set things right."

"Feh."

With deliberate steps, I walked over to the cage. "It's true. I helped Deimos fight Naiad, and I've seen firsthand how bad things are in the abyssal hells. I told Deimos I would help. Ask him yourself."

We both turned to face Deimos. He didn't move. If anything, he didn't even look like he was breathing—he was more corpse than man, with his blood still seeping out around his prison. Again, I rubbed my arm where he had held me. It felt strange, like his blood had crept into my skin.

I nervously chuckled as I turned back to Zahn. "Well, ask him when he's feeling a little better."

"There won't be any *getting better*." Zahn sarcastically emphasized the last words. "Things have only ever gotten progressively worse. Now look at what you've done." He glanced up at the soul catcher. "Let's get this over with."

With my teeth gritted, I glanced up. The freakish spider marionette reached its knife-claws toward my face. I stumbled backward, but the creature pursued. On instinct, I grabbed Vivigöl. Even in this dream, the weapon was with me, one with my being or perhaps my subconscious. The instant I touched the golden weapon, it transformed into a trident with a *click-click-click*, the abyssal coral taking shape with rigid movements.

The soul catcher's face mask seemed incapable of movement. It didn't open its mouth, or even change its neutral expression. However, the soul catcher flinched back, which told me a lot. This mimic monster didn't like my new toy.

With Deimos's skill, I stabbed at the soul catcher, hoping to impale its disgusting mask face. The monster dodged aside—it was much faster in the dreamscape. Just like in all my nightmares, it scuttled with frightening haste, moving off the cage and then around me in a matter of a split second.

I swung a wide arc, and the sharp tines of the trident struck the soul catcher in one of its eight spider limbs. The monster screamed, somehow, even though its mouth didn't open, as the leg splintered like pure wood.

"*Twice!*" Zahn shouted. "Stop messing around."

The soul catcher growled. Then it used four of its seven remaining arms to attack. The knife-claws lashed out toward me, and while *I* had no idea how I would block four strikes at once, Deimos had the skill to handle such a predicament.

I expertly twirled the trident, knocking away three of the hands and catching the fourth with the trident's tines, damaging the soul catcher more.

The beast—Twice was her name?—scuttled away.

Then the environment shifted. The wet rocks melted into quicksand, and I sank into the ground all the way to my knees. It had all happened so fast, and when I thrashed about to free myself, it was impossible. All my struggling movements only made it worse.

The soul catcher lunged. Three of its claws went for me. I managed to knock away two, but the third sliced the side of my neck, my chin, and my cheek, the pain damn near blinding.

The monster had cut deep. Even in this dream, the sensation of hot blood disturbed me.

I shifted Vivigöl into a chain whip and cracked the tip of the weapon across the face mask. A gouge formed across the spider's face, splitting the neutral expression right from one eyehole to the other.

"*Zahn,*" Deimos said from the cage, his voice practically a growl.

The monster stopped attacking. Zahn whirled on his heel to face the cage.

"Brother?" Zahn asked. "Are you awake?"

"Leave the boy alone," was all Deimos managed to choke out.

Had he sensed the pain when I was injured? How else would he have known to focus on his soul fragment at this moment?

"I can free you." Zahn placed both his hands on the cracked bar. "Using the soul catcher magic, I can isolate your soul from the boy's. It'll only take a moment."

"And then what?"

Deimos remained in the cage, sitting on the ground. When he took a deep breath, it seemed to irritate him.

"Once the soul catcher releases me, my fragment will return to the hells. *Leave it with the boy.* I can see more of the living realm—and Gray is an ally."

Zahn exhaled as he shook his head. "The child will say

anything to free himself. He's deceptive. You can't trust a word he mutters."

"He fixed a portion of the Wraithborne Orchard. Helped me fight Naiad. Respected the rules of the abyssal hells... If his words are false, he'll regret them. But for now, he has done as he said. Leave him."

This didn't seem to sit well with Zahn. He gripped the bars of the cage, his posture tense.

When I glanced over at the soul catcher, I realized it was just waiting there, poised to attack again, but obviously waiting for the command.

"If your fragment can be trapped here in the boy's dreams, I can find a way to transfer you to another vessel," Zahn said, his tone desperate. "Please—let me remove you from this place."

"The risk is too great. Focus your efforts elsewhere. I need to rest at the Requiem Throne, but then I need to find a way out of the abyssal hells."

"But perhaps I can take your soul fragment. Wouldn't that be preferable? Deimos?"

But Deimos didn't answer. His head fell, and he returned to an almost stiff and still state.

The quicksand around my legs shifted. After a grunt, I lifted my leg and stepped out of the trap. With a huff, I brushed myself off and even tucked Vivigöl back around my neck and shoulders. It transformed into some sort of jewelry, ready and waiting for violence, if I needed it.

When Zahn turned back around, he wore a smile that looked like he had fished it out of the back of a dirty drawer.

"Well." That was all he said.

Well.

I half shrugged. "See? I told you. Deimos and I are good friends."

"*You are not good friends,*" Zahn hissed, his anger as intense as his gaze. But he quickly brushed back his hair and settled back into a calm demeanor. "You will wait here while I prepare things. I believe—*with your assistance*—I can get Deimos out of the abyssal hells if we use the Specter Sands, rather than the Wraithborne Orchard."

"What are the *Specter Sands*?" I asked.

Zahn took a deep breath, muttered something to himself, and then continued his monotone speech. "From the Wraithborne Orchard, souls are given new lives as plants. From the Specter Sands, souls are given new lives as minerals."

I caught my breath. "Y-You mean like glowstones?"

Deimos had said all magic was made of souls, basically. So glowstones—the little rocks that were always lit—were actually shining because of soul fragments inside them?

Zahn nodded, one of his eyebrows raised. "Ah. My brother must've informed you. Good. Saves me the time of explaining."

"You brought all those magical plants because you were using them as a gateway?" I thought back to the shimmering pumpkin we had all burst out of. "And now you're going to use magical rocks to get Deimos? Somehow?" I wasn't entirely sure how Zahn was planning any of this, but I was starting to understand his methodology.

"Something like that." Zahn motioned for his eldrin. The soul catcher scuttled over, and Zahn gently looked over the monster's injuries. "But you just need to stay put. I'll handle everything."

"Wait, if souls are made into plants within the Wraithborne Orchard, and they're made into minerals in the Specter Sands, or into insects in the Silkshade Grove... Where do they go to be people?"

Did people get reincarnated back into people?

Did that happen?

Zahn glanced over, irritation creeping into his expression. "Souls in the *Lament Valley* are used to make the bodies of mystical creatures. If a soul is to return to a human body, it must go through one of the Death Lords. Because you must understand—all the souls in the abyssal hells aren't whole. All the parts of your life you're proud of move on. It's only your regrets, resentments, and losses that are sent to the abyssal hells for another chance at life—a Death Lord will either find you unworthy, or send you back for another round."

"Right..."

I wasn't entirely sure how it all worked, but it was starting to make sense. The souls in the first abyss were waiting to be reborn as various things—minerals, plants, insects, other magical creatures—and the souls deeper in the hells were either going to oblivion, or given an even greater chance.

I rubbed my chin as I mulled it over.

Part of me wondered...

Where my mother had gone.

Deimos had said she was no longer in the abyssal hells. Where had she gone? It was a foolish question, because there was probably no way to know, but I was curious.

Zahn turned and started walking across the slick surface of the black stone. His eldrin followed after him, walking with injured limbs. I held out a hand.

"Wait."

Zahn turned.

I motioned to our surroundings. "What's going on? Why not just end this dream?"

"My brother needs time," Zahn drawled, completely uninterested. "So you can take a nap while he recuperates. Once he's done recovering, then I'll attempt to summon him again. Until then, goodbye, Gray Lexly."

He waved his hand, and the dream melted away, leaving me floating in a dark void.

That no-good lunatic.

As soon as Twain was ready, I'd just bust myself out of this trap he thought he had me in.

Chapter 16

The Cult Of Deimos

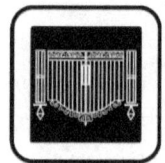

How long had I been sleeping?

I didn't know. It was difficult to tell when my dream was nothing but a dark void. What had Zahn done? Where was Deimos? It felt like... Deimos wasn't doing so well. Had he lost in the abyssal hells? Did he need help? I didn't have time to sleep—not when there were so many things to do.

Every so often, I felt around for the threads of magic, and I tugged on the one that led back to the soul catcher. Only mystical creatures with magics that could influence dreams would be able to break me free from this unresolved nap, and there weren't any ethereal whelks or celestial dragons nearby...

Those were the only three creatures I knew could affect dreams. Well, mimics as well, but only if another dream-manipulating creature was close. Altering someone's dreamscape was a rare ability.

Finally, my tugging resulted in *something*. I pulled on a thread of magic, and the mark on my forehead burned as it shifted and changed. The soul catcher's magic flooded me, filling my body with an unusual hunger. What was this sensation? I couldn't even articulate it. Instead, I focused on ending this dream.

I needed to wake.

With my teeth gritted, I tore apart the void, and my head hurt, as though a terrible headache bloomed from the back of my skull all the way to my eyes. The pain was enough that I lost my concentration. The thread of magic that allowed Twain to be a soul catcher faded from my mental grip.

That was okay—I sat up and took a deep breath.

I was now awake. Everything had worked as intended. And the moment the soul catcher magic drained from my body, the headache went with it.

After rubbing my face, I glanced around.

I almost wished I hadn't.

There were only three people in the room—me, and two others—but I was on a large, marble altar, one about the height of a table. The worst part was the fact I was buck naked.

Well, I had a white sheet over my loins, but calling it a *sheet* was being generous. It was more like a napkin, and it was trying its hardest to keep me decent.

My marble slab of an altar was cold, and so was most of my body, as though I had been inactive for far too long. I coughed, and my throat felt terrible, my lips cracked. What was going on?

The two other people in the room were odd, and that was me being generous a second time. One was a woman, her long hair dark, and mostly unkempt. She had dark rings around her eyes, either from makeup or lack of sleep, I wasn't sure which. The arcanist mark on her forehead had the image of a fish person wrapped around the seven points of her star.

She was... wearing a tight black dress with a large white cloak over it. Seven dashes were stitched into the collar of both her dress and the cloak.

"He's awake," she whispered.

The other person in the room was a man with short, red hair

and amber eyes that disturbed me. His pupils were so small, it was as if he saw the world through pinholes. His arcanist mark had a freakish sea serpent coiled throughout the star.

He, like the woman, wore black underneath white—he had a black tunic and dark trousers, and then wore his white cloak over his shoulders. The same bizarre seven marks were on his outfit as well.

"He *is* awake," the man said, more breathless and in awe than the woman. "This is... a wonderful event."

I held my napkin steady as I carefully swung my legs over the side of the cold altar. This room was small—maybe a bedroom? —but there was no other furniture. No chairs. No tables. No desks. There weren't any windows, either. Just a door.

And Twain wasn't here. Neither were the eldrin of the other two arcanists. The only source of light was the glowstone lamp hanging from the ceiling.

The glowstones...

I had more appreciation for them now. Before, I barely noticed them—barely cared they existed. Now they seemed extra magical, or perhaps just more beautiful.

The souls of those who had passed were still here, and still helping us.

I probably stared at the lamp for far too long.

"Ah, forgive us!" the man cried. "We were lost in your majestic presence." The man bowed deeply. When the woman didn't immediately bow, he grabbed her arm and tugged. She, too, bowed, both of them folded at the waist.

I glanced down at them.

"Who are you two?" I asked, trying not to sound dismissively sarcastic.

"I am Jacinto Ren," the man said as he stood straight.

The woman also stood, but she didn't meet my gaze. She kept her attention on the floor as she replied, "I'm Rosella Silvers, Death Lord. I'm so humbled to be in your presence."

Death Lord?

Not only did the souls in the abyssal hells mistake me for a Death Lord, but now random people were, too? How was this possible?

"We have waited our whole lives to serve you, Death Lord Deimos," Jacinto said with a second sweeping bow. Then he motioned to the door. "Please, we should hurry to your brother. He has long awaited your return. Longer than all of us!"

Ah.

They thought I was Death Lord *Deimos*. This was making more sense.

"You two were just standing around while I was sleeping?" I asked. I circled a finger through the air. "While I was just naked on this altar?"

Rosella stiffened her posture, but again, she didn't glance up. "We were told to watch over your vessel, Death Lord. Your brother indicated you might awake, and if you did, to inform him immediately."

"Wait." Jacinto stepped forward, his pinhole eyes focused on mine. "Are you just the vessel? Or are you truly our Death Lord?"

Vessel?

I hated that so much.

Then I waited half a second for Deimos to answer. He did that occasionally—he spoke with my mouth and my voice—but when he said nothing, I knew I was going to have to fake this. Which was fine, because I was really good at faking things, and I knew Deimos pretty well at this point.

I sat a little straighter, and hardened my gaze into something I had seen Deimos do.

"Do you maggots really think I waged three wars and waited multiple millennia only to awake *not* in control of this borrowed body?" I made the same kind of hissing growl of disapproval

Deimos often used. "*Feh*. If we were in the abyssal hells, you would be on your knees, begging for forgiveness."

"A-Ah, yes, I deeply apologize." Jacinto bowed twice more as he stepped away. "Please forgive me, Death Lord Deimos. I, uh, I'm unfamiliar with how one uses a vessel to communicate from the abyssal hells to the realm of the living."

I was pretty unfamiliar as well, but I wasn't going to say that.

With an arrogant huff, I motioned to my body. "I require *clothing*." I had to hold back a laugh after that. It was amusing to impersonate Deimos.

"At once!"

Jacinto dashed from the room. He opened and shut the door with such speed, I barely caught a glimpse of the hallway beyond. Where were we? Still in the same place as before? The same home with the large ballroom?

Rosella remained with me.

She slowly brought her green eyes up to meet mine. "I've waited a long time to meet you," she whispered.

I didn't know what to say, so I remained quiet.

Were Jacinto and Rosella part of that cult that worshipped Deimos? The ones who had attacked me before? The ones who had ruined Ashlyn's cotillion?

That was the only explanation. They were working with Zahn, after all. And Deimos's brother was probably the mastermind of that whole organization.

Rosella's face grew pink, and she shifted her attention back to the floor. "You probably already know everything..." She rubbed her arcanist mark, her fingers tracing the bizarre fish-person.

I had no idea what she was talking about. "I know a great many things," I cryptically replied.

Rosella quickly reached out and grabbed my hand.

I was about to jerk out of her grasp, but she got to her knees and knelt before me, pressing her forehead onto my knuckles.

"Death Lord Deimos, I have served faithfully for years in the hopes I might speak with you. I have something personal to ask. I... I will pay any price, or follow through with any task... but I need your help. Only the magic of a Death Lord will do."

I ripped my hand from her grip, my chest tight with awkward nervousness. "First, I will be dressed. *Then* I will hear your request."

Rosella clasped her hands together and held them close to her chest. With her gaze on the floor, she weakly nodded. "Yes. Forgive me. I'll... I'll help Jacinto find you an outfit."

She stood and fled the room, practically in one motion. I felt her embarrassment in the way she avoided looking at me at all costs. When the door shut behind her exit, I let out a long sigh.

"This isn't what I was expecting," I muttered to myself.

The silence that greeted me was unsettling. There weren't many times in my life I was truly alone. When I was younger, I had my twin brother. After I became an arcanist, I always had Twain. And once Deimos was stuck with me, I had his presence in the corner of my thoughts.

Now, to have no one...

I hated it.

After another exhale, I slid off the altar. I kept my napkin secured, but I wasn't sure what I was going to do. My legs trembled, and I had to take a moment to steady myself. How long had it been since I stood?

"Deimos?" I whispered.

No response.

I closed my eyes and focused. He was with me still—I felt a twinge of emotion that just wasn't mine.

"*Deimos.*"

"Your pleading is intrusive, boy," Deimos replied using my mouth and voice, though they were subtly different. He had a distinct way of speaking, his cadence strange.

I half chuckled. "You're there?"

"I'm resting," I whispered to myself—Deimos whispered to me, I should say. "I can't focus long. Why do you keep calling me?"

"Are you okay?" I asked.

"I need... time."

I ran a hand down my face and then shook my head. "Is Nini with you?"

"No."

My heart nearly stopped. When Deimos didn't elaborate, my imagination played terrible tricks with my emotions. What was I going to tell Sorin if Nini was dead? My brother wouldn't take that well.

"She hasn't perished," Deimos said through me, his tone dismissive. "She is wandering the second abyss. Perhaps she'll perish, but last I saw, she was still well."

Last he saw?

How long had it been since Deimos had last seen her?

I sighed, though I still didn't know what I was going to say to Sorin. Nini was lost in the second abyss? What a terrible fate.

I shook the thought away. Everything would be fine. We would get her. She was a reaper arcanist—she could live in the abyssal hells until we found a way to free her. Yes. That was the plan. Everything would turn out all right.

"Did you know you had a cult?" I asked, trying to switch the conversation to something upbeat.

"I have *followers*," Deimos replied through me, that same hiss of derision in his tone. "They have toiled long, searching for ways to open the abyssal hells."

"And you know them? Personally?"

"Zahn kept me appraised, but I never spoke with any of them. I trusted my brother to handle everything, including the management of those who would worship at my feet."

That was curious. And also odd. Why had Zahn told everyone I was just a vessel? Shouldn't he have told them I was my own person? I needed to speak with him. I also needed to find Ashlyn and Knovak so we could leave this place and get back to Astra Academy.

How long had we been away?

Surely everyone was worried.

The door slammed open, and I flinched.

"Here we are, Death Lord Deimos! An outfit befitting a king."

CHAPTER 17

THE HOME OF LORD OTO

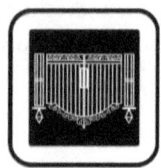

Jacinto rushed into the barren room and presented me with an outfit. I hesitated to call it "clothing" because that implied these garments were normal. No, this was some sort of ringmaster outfit. A pinstripe vest, a puffy white shirt, and black pants with bells on the hip. Three tiny bells, each missing a clacker.

What was this?

I snorted back a laugh. "I take it they were all out of sensible options?"

"This outfit is made from the silk of star moths," Jacinto said as he rubbed the material. "And the bells..."

When he handed the outfit over, I pinched the fabric between my fingers, surprised how soft and luxurious it was. The silk of star moths? Another magical creature—more souls who returned to experience life anew.

The bells were the faded gray of well-worn granite, and each the size of my thumb. I touched one, and a tingle ran through my fingertips.

"These are bells from the second abyss," Deimos said through me, his tone almost bored.

"Oh, yes, of course. I should've known a Death Lord would recognize them." Jacinto nodded and smiled. "Lord Zahn said they were a gift before the hells were sealed. I thought them appropriate for you."

I touched the bells a second time, half expecting them to ring, but they didn't.

"You need the bells... to navigate the second abyss," I mumbled, my thoughts entangling with Deimos's as I focused on the bells.

A labyrinth. The second abyss was a labyrinth. That was what Nasbit had told me, and the thoughts I gleaned from Deimos only confirmed it. A gigantic maze that trapped souls who lingered in the infinite corridors...

"I didn't know that," Jacinto said. He twiddled his thumbs. "I'll keep it in mind for when the gates are finally open."

The door opened a second time, and Rosella returned. The dark rings around her eyes reminded me of a raccoon, though her rush to present me with another piece of clothing was more akin to a skittish rabbit.

Rosella handed over a white cloak, similar to her own. It wasn't nearly as soft as the star moth silk, but it was as clean as ivory cloth could be, which was impressive.

But I was missing something more important than clothes.

"Where's my weapon?" I asked.

It hadn't occurred to me until then, but Vivigöl wasn't on me. I ran my fingers over my collarbone, my breathing strained. I was missing my eldrin, my friends, and now my only weapon? Nothing would feel right until I had everything back.

"Your brother had a difficult time removing your abyssal coral accessories," Jacinto said. He pointed to my neck. "With gloves and blankets around his arms, he pulled them from your vessel's body, and afterward, it *snapped* back into the shape of a trident. It's being stored in Lord Zahn's room."

"Right."

Although I wanted to avoid Zahn—and leave this place—it seemed I really would need to speak with him again. But I wanted Twain first.

Jacinto set the clothing on the altar and then proceeded to wrap the silk shirt around me. I moved away from him, careful to hold my little sheet. "What're you doing? I can dress myself."

"I figured such mundane tasks were beneath you," Jacinto said.

"I'm trying to keep this all under control." I motioned to the small sheet I held in front of me. Then I half shrugged in Rosella's direction. "You know. To stay classy in front of the fine lady."

Jacinto chuckled and waved away the comment. "You needn't worry about modesty, Death Lord. We've all seen your and your vessel's impressive silent flute and cullions."

If I were actually a Death Lord, this man would go straight to the fifth abyss. No reincarnation—no second chances—not after what was probably the single most awkward statement I had ever heard in my life.

I ran a hand down my hot face. "At least they're *impressive,*" I sarcastically quipped.

"It's a shame you're marred by all your vessel's disgusting scars."

I instinctively reached up to my chest and stomach. Long scars marked my flesh from my first fight with Death Lord Deimos. They had never healed properly, which was strange for an arcanist. Normally, wounds healed without a trace, but not after that specific fight.

"Once the gates are open, I'll have my own body," I said, still playing this game that I was Deimos.

When Jacinto attempted to throw the shirt around my shoulders a second time, I was done. I shot him a cold glare and motioned to the door.

"*Get out,*" I shouted. "I want to dress *alone.*"

"Of course. At once." Jacinto hurried away.

Rosella followed. And as soon as the door was shut, I exhaled, dropped my sheet, and quickly dressed myself.

I hated the clothing, but I didn't care. The silk felt like water given semi-solid form. It flowed over my skin, wrapping me in the most comfortable material I had ever experienced. The bells attached to the waist of the pants hung far apart from one another, so they didn't touch. They were otherwise silent, and I wondered what they would sound like in the abyssal hells.

No boots, though. No sandals or socks. Those two cult lunatics really hadn't thought this through.

Once I had the cloak secured over my shoulders, I headed for the door.

As a mimic arcanist, I sensed threads of magic nearby. Before I exited the room, I grabbed the door handle and closed my eyes to better focus.

I felt...

Deimos's magic thread, the one that led back to his abyssal dragon.

One for the soul catcher.

Several for sea creatures. A serpent. That humanoid creature. I couldn't quite name them.

Two manticores, which was a scary thing to sense.

A phoenix. No—this was different. A phoenix, but hotter.

A shadowy creature, far different from my brother's knightmare, but perhaps related.

Ashlyn's typhoon dragon. Knovak's unicorn.

And lastly, I felt the nebulous thread of Zahn's mimic. It was untransformed, and I sensed it for what it was. A shapeshifter.

There were a lot of arcanists here. What was this place?

I opened the door and stepped into the hallway. To my annoyance, Jacinto and Rosella were waiting for me. Both were rather short, now that I was standing and not worried about anything else. They held themselves with slightly hunched postures, and I wondered why.

The hallway was lavish; it looked like I was going out to a fancy dinner. Deep red carpets were underfoot, long curtains that stretched up to the tall ceilings, and exotic plants in ornate pots were placed by the walls. The place even smelled of incense, which was unusual.

"Where are we?" I asked.

"Lord Oto's compound," Jacinto replied, obviously eager to please with matter-of-fact answers.

Rosella said nothing. She waited, never looking directly into my eyes. It made me slightly uncomfortable, especially since I knew she had something to say to Deimos, and I could already tell I didn't want to hear any of it.

"Who is Lord Oto?" I asked.

"He's the blue phoenix arcanist who rules over the Sellix coast. He runs this town, and owns several mines." Jacinto rubbed his palms together. "Lord Oto is also our benefactor. Our brothers and sisters all reside here. He built us places to study and rest, and provides your brother with all the coin and resources he needs to reopen the abyssal hells."

Sorin?

No. I shook my head. Jacinto was referring to Zahn, obviously.

And Lord Oto provided Zahn with coin? Right. Oto had mentioned that when I awoke from that pumpkin. He was supplying Zahn with materials in order to get his hands on abyssal dragon parts.

Who was this Lord Oto, anyway? He believed Zahn when the man told him he could bring back a Death Lord?

I glanced around the hallway again, taking note of the gold inlaid in the plant pots, the silk of the curtains, and how detailed the crown molding was near the ceilings. And this was just a hallway.

Clearly, Lord Oto had coin to spare.

But I could worry about that later.

"This vessel is a mimic arcanist," I said, putting some *snideness* into my tone. "Where is it? Where is the mimic?"

"In the room with the others," Jacinto replied. "Shall we take you there?" He had an overly cheery disposition that didn't sit well with me. It bordered on fanatic.

I nodded once. "Take me there immediately."

Rosella and Jacinto bowed, and then Jacinto took the lead. When I walked by Rosella, she didn't walk alongside me, even though there was plenty of room in the hallway—instead, she walked behind me, never saying a word.

The hallway went on for an eternity before turning down another corridor. This one had large windows that gazed out into a luscious courtyard filled with fountains, flowers, and a man-made stream with tiny bridges that allowed for quaint walking paths. Half a dozen individuals, none of them arcanists, tended to the flora.

The sun was on a downward trajectory, which meant it was almost sunset.

"How does Lord Oto make his coin?" I casually asked as we walked by the floor-to-ceiling windows.

"He has gathered hundreds and hundreds of star shards," Jacinto replied as quick as a whip, always chipper. "*So many* star shards. And he even has a crew of people he uses to harvest occult ore. He has a vast wealth of raw magical resources."

"Don't star shards just fall from the sky randomly?" I thought back to my first few weeks at Astra Academy. One of our lessons involved finding star shards that had fallen around the campus. "How did Lord Oto gather hundreds of them? Was he just fortuitous?"

Jacinto shrugged and shook his head. "I don't know. I'm not privy to such matters." His smile widened. "But does it matter? Once the abyssal hells are open, more magic will flow into the world—our glorious globe of Vardin—and there will be so many star shards that the streets will be paved with mystic energies!"

The man held out his arms as he spoke, his eyes unfocused, as though he could see it all perfectly in his mind's eye.

We stopped right before we turned down another hall. Jacinto whirled on his heel to face me. I tensed, wondering if he realized I was just Gray Lexly, and not the Death Lord he so adored.

"I've wanted to ask you something," Jacinto whispered.

I lifted an eyebrow. "Right now?"

"Can I be granted the title of *Seven?* I think I've earned it."

It took a short moment for his words to settle in. Seven? A title? And he wanted me to grant it? I wasn't entirely sure what was going on...

"*Tsk*, Jacinto," Rosella hissed from behind me, her voice cold. "Asking him in the middle of this dank hallway? Have you forgotten yourself?"

Jacinto bowed deeper than before. "You're right. Forgive me. I was just so eager to have the title. No one has taken it since... well... since the doppelgänger arcanist failed in her mission."

Since I wasn't entirely certain what they were talking about, I decided not to comment. Better to remain silent than open my mouth and remove all doubt I was an imposter.

Rosella motioned to a nearby door. "Through there is where all the prisoners are being held. They're asleep, of course. Including the mimic."

Twain?

I needed to see him. Especially if I was going to have a chat with Zahn. I couldn't let him put me back to sleep again. We needed to leave this place, because I certainly wasn't going to wait until Deimos had recovered before I returned to Astra Academy. What did Sorin think? He probably had no idea where I was—not to mention Nini—and that would upset him.

I definitely needed to speak with him.

CHAPTER 18

CULT MENTALITY

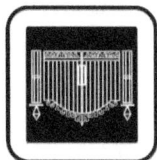

Rosella opened the door.

The room was a strange combination of creepy and comfy. There were a dozen beds, six each lined up against two of the walls, and it honestly reminded me of the dorms at Astra Academy. The beds were covered in fluffy blankets and half a dozen small pillows. Their wooden frames were carved to look like sea serpents at all points, including little scale detailing.

There were at least six people, all sleeping, their bodies barely moving. When I stepped into the room, I coughed loudly, hoping to wake some of them, but no one stirred.

"That won't wake them, Death Lord," Rosella said.

Two of the beds had been pushed together. Ashlyn and her typhoon dragon, Ecrib, were asleep on those beds, their blankets draped over them. They were magically compelled to sleep, obviously, since both were barely breathing and awkwardly placed against each other.

Fortunately for Ashlyn, they allowed *her* to keep her clothes.

Ecrib's body was curled protectively around most of

Ashlyn's sleeping form, his blue scales beautiful, even though there wasn't much light in the room.

I didn't spot Knovak, however, and my concern for him mounted.

One of the beds had a blanket with a lump under it, and in my heart, I knew it was Twain. I marched over, but before I could throw back the blanket, the lump moved. With my breath held, I placed my hand on it.

"Twain?" I whispered.

The lump hurried out from under the plush blanket. Twain's head poked up to greet me, his feline smile adorable, as always.

"Gray!" He leapt from the mattress to my shoulder in a single, graceful bound. I chuckled as he nuzzled up against the side of my neck, his purring constant and noisy.

Jacinto stormed over and smacked Twain from my shoulder. The mimic tumbled back onto the bed. I whirled on Jacinto, barely keeping my anger in check, but Jacinto's attention was solely on Twain.

"How dare you touch Death Lord Deimos!" Jacinto shouted. Then he bowed his head to me. "I must apologize. I have no idea why this mimic is awake. He should be slumbering, like the others."

Twain hissed and spit, his orange fur puffed. "Hey! How dare *you!*" He held up a paw, flexed his little fingers, and extended his tiny claws. "These were made for cutting, punk! Are you ready to have your face rearranged?"

I grabbed Twain and held him close to my chest. "Enough. I want the mimic. It's fine he's awake. Now let's go speak with my brother."

"Why would you want the mimic? Is the eldrin of your vessel still loyal to you?" Jacinto glared at Twain, his pinhole pupils disturbing. "It can't possibly be bound to your soul. You have an abyssal dragon."

Rosella knitted her eyebrows. "But his arcanist mark resembles the mimic's and not an abyssal dragon's..."

Their suspicion got me nervous. They were both deeply fanatic, that much was certain, and I feared they would attack if they thought I was an enemy. And what if they attacked the sleeping Ashlyn and her dragon? What if they had Knovak somewhere and they were hurting him because Starling had eaten those soul grapes?

I couldn't risk any of that.

"Mimics can be controlled by their arcanists," I said as I stroked Twain. "They can force them to transform—and I still retain that capability, thanks to my vessel. Besides, this creature knew what would happen. His old arcanist was quite aware of the transformation. So I'd like to keep the mimic close."

Twain glanced up at me, his little mouth in a tight frown.

When I met his gaze, I subtly lifted a brow.

My eldrin snorted and twitched an ear, his irritation waning. He knew it was me and not Deimos. Of all the people in the world, Twain had seen Deimos speak through me the most. My eldrin knew the difference between us.

"That's right," Twain said with an upbeat tone. "Gray knew he was giving up his body for Deimos. It's all according to plan."

Jacinto and Rosella exchanged silent looks. Their expressions to each other conveyed a lot, but in the end, they both bowed to me.

"Our apologies," Jacinto stated. When he stood straight, he smiled. "To your brother, then?"

I held up a hand and then pointed to all the people around the room. Besides Ashlyn, there were five others here, none of whom I recognized. At least four of them were arcanists, their marks clear as day on their foreheads.

"Who are these people?"

"Enemies," Jacinto said matter-of-factly. "They've been forced to sleep so they can't interfere with our plans."

One of the sleeping individuals looked like a frightening knight. His brow was settled into a permanent glower, even while he slumbered.

I nervously chuckled as I returned my attention to Jacinto and Rosella. "Why not kill them? I mean, I'm not suggesting you do that—I'm not ordering that, either—I'm just curious."

Rosella held her white cloak close. "Zahn said we might need their souls. He said we shouldn't waste them, so we're keeping them until a need arises."

"And that's your ultimate plan?" I glanced around. One of the sleeping individuals was a younger girl. "Killing these people?"

"Anything for our Death Lord." Jacinto bowed deeper than before.

His answer worried me the most. I knew they were like this. I had seen the insanity in the eyes of the cultists who had attacked Ashlyn's cotillion. But I hadn't been expecting this complete lack of empathy. It was a new level of disturbing. What had Zahn told them to gain such loyalty to a disturbing cause?

"Why would *you* be concerned with killing them?" Rosella took a single step away from me, her suspicion obviously more pronounced than before. "Death Lords take lives. That's the order of things."

"Death Lords are in charge of reincarnation," I whispered. Then I glared at her. "And I wasn't concerned about *death*—I was concerned about your plans and how you conduct them. There's a big difference." I added heat to my words, even though I wasn't really angry. What else would Deimos say?

Jacinto threw an arm up in front of Rosella, shielding her as he stepped between us. "Of course, Death Lord Deimos! Forgive us, please. Rosella and I never should have spoken out of turn."

After a long exhale, I decided it was best not to speak too much. Zahn had to be around here somewhere, but then it hit me. If they killed people for their own plans, did that mean they had killed Knovak?

"Where's the unicorn arcanist?" I asked.

Jacinto and Rosella exchanged another round of glances. Then Rosella motioned to the door. "He wasn't put to sleep. Zahn believed him special. He's been working for us."

"He has?" I balked.

Rosella nodded. "Do you know him, Death Lord?"

"Of course he does," Jacinto hissed. "That unicorn arcanist is obviously an agent of the abyssal hells. Don't ask stupid questions. You make us both look like fools."

An agent of the abyssal hells?

I motioned to the door. "Take me to him."

The two cult lunatics complied with my demand as though their lives depended on it. They rushed to the door, and Jacinto opened it for me as I approached. Twain stuck his tongue out at the man, and I just held him back, hoping he wouldn't do anything to agitate these people.

Who knew what they would do?

And where was the soul catcher? It was around here somewhere. I needed to avoid it at all costs. I didn't want to be put back into a forced sleep.

Once we were out of the room, Jacinto and Rosella led me down the hall, and then to a gateway that veered toward the tended courtyard. As soon as I stepped outside, I had to blink back the dry air. Were we near a desert? I coughed back the heat and continued down a stone walkway that led to a wooden bridge over a small stream.

When I glanced down, I realized the dirt was soft and fertile, and the stream ran with plenty of water. It was hot, but someone had taken great care to make sure this courtyard would not be affected by the weather.

"Right this way, Death Lord Deimos," Jacinto said louder than normal, his voice carrying.

The many gardeners tending to the flowers glanced up from their work. Those who caught sight of me stopped what they were doing and got to their knees. They pressed their foreheads to the ground, prostrating themselves to me.

That was awkward, but a part of me knew Deimos would like it.

"Carry on," I said in a haughty tone.

We made it to the other side of the courtyard, and Jacinto opened another door. "This is for magical training, Death Lord."

It was a vast room with marble floors, tall ceilings, and mirrors across the far wall. It was ornate and opulent—which didn't seem like the décor someone would want for magical training, but I said nothing.

Two large double doors were on the opposite side of the room, large enough for gigantic eldrin to fit through. That was a prudent decision, because a massive unicorn was here, one the size of a draft horse stallion. It was muscled and sleek, its ivory coat glittering.

But its eyes...

They were unsettling.

The beast turned its head and glared at me. It was only then I noticed its polished golden hooves looked sharp enough to slice a skull in two.

The horn was twisted and notably sharp at the tip. It seemed sinister, and curved just a tiny bit, as though meant to skewer someone good.

Another mystical creature was here—a bizarre fish person. It was green and scaled, but had webbed feet and hands. Its large eyes locked onto Rosella as soon as she entered behind me. With a smile only a mother could love, it scampered over to her. Its teeth were as thin and sharp as sewing needles, and nearly as golden as abyssal coral.

"My arcanist," it said with a joyful hiss, "you're here. You're finally here."

"Are you watching the unicorn arcanist?" Rosella asked as she glanced around.

"Of course, of course. There he is." The fish person pointed to the unicorn.

Knovak walked around the giant horse and stood next to it, one of his hands on its shoulder.

No...

It couldn't be...

Twain's huge ears perked up, and he softly mewed, his surprise just as thick as mine.

"Knovak?" I asked, breathless. "Is that... Starling?"

The massively muscled unicorn turned, its hooves stomping on the marble. "Who else did you think it was?" the unicorn asked, cold and threatening.

Starling had never sounded like that. This was...

A nightmare.

Knovak patted his eldrin. He didn't reply to me—his look said it all.

Starling had gobbled up the soul berries, which forced his little body to age. Normally, it would've taken a year or so for his unicorn to get this big, but now Starling was fully grown—and quite intimidating.

Was he an elder unicorn? Was there no chance to save him now?

How long had I been sleeping?

"Is something wrong, Death Lord?" Jacinto motioned to Knovak. "Isn't this the minion you wanted to see? The great elder arcanist, Knovak Gentz?"

Wow.

I didn't like where this was going.

Twain's ears went back and flat against his skull. I stepped forward, limiting the distance between me and Knovak. Now that I was closer, I realized his arcanist mark was different.

The seven-pointed star was drooping, like it had melted.

Did elder creatures bond to humans? No. They ate them. But Starling had bonded *before* he consumed the food in the abyssal hells, so this was a unique situation. I was surprised Starling hadn't eaten his own arcanist—or perhaps he wasn't *completely* an elder creature yet?

I hoped so.

"Hello, *minion*," I quipped. "I see you've grown up to be big and strong."

Knovak glowered at me. Then he sarcastically bowed at the waist. "Oh, Death Lord Deimos, it's so great you're *finally* awake and can tell us all what to do." When he stood straight, he frowned.

I stepped closer and lowered my voice to a whisper, so only he and his eldrin could hear. "Are you okay?"

"I was doing just fine without you, actually. I'm mastering all my new magic, and telling stories of the abyssal hells. Everyone respects me here—we didn't need you to wake just yet."

CHAPTER 19

PHOBOS

"**Y**ou're doing *just fine*?" I repeated, obvious amounts of sarcasm in my whisper. "Starling is fully grown. When did that happen? *Overnight?* How is that fine?"

"You've been sleeping for almost a week," Knovak said under his breath. "That's enough time for Starling. He's stronger now. More powerful than ever before."

Wait, what?

His statement caught me off guard. A whole week? I had been asleep that long? When I glanced down at Twain, my eldrin shrugged. He had been asleep as well, it seemed. Then it occurred to me the only ones *not* sleeping were, in fact, Knovak and Starling.

"You didn't try to wake me?" I asked, keeping my building temper out of the tone in my voice.

Knovak waved away my question. "You were fine. They all said so. And I needed time to get used to all my magic." He held out his hand. "Watch."

A burst of evocation left his palm, though I couldn't see it with my naked eye. It was a wave of force, which I had seen him evoke before, but not like this. His evocation slammed into three

145

wall-length mirrors on the other side of the ornate room. They shattered, the glass blasting out to the sides and hitting the hard marble floors a moment later, splintering further into sharp shards.

It was startling to see so much damage.

Part of the wall was cracked, and I felt the rumble of the whole room from the attack.

"Are you insane?" I glanced up, wondering if the ceiling was damaged. "You should use your magic outside."

Knovak only huffed in response.

Before I berated him a second time, the shattered bits of glass jiggled and then slid across the floor. They picked up speed and slammed back together, repairing themselves while everyone watched. Piece by piece, the glass was reassembled and then clinked up into the frames of the mirrors and became whole again.

Likewise, the wall hardened and the cracks vanished.

This room...

Was obviously imbued with magic. Or else there was another mystical creature nearby—or an arcanist—who could repair it. But when I felt for the magic threads, I didn't detect something with that kind of magic. It had to be the room.

So that was why he was training here—it would all fix itself, damn near immediately.

"I wasn't even trying then," Knovak said, standing a little straighter. "I could obliterate that wall with my magic, if I really wanted."

I nodded once. "Wow. *Knovak, the Destroyer of Buildings.* Very impressive."

He glared as he clenched his hands into fists. "Don't pretend you're not impressed. I know you're jealous. This is amazing. Everyone here says so."

"My arcanist is extraordinary," Starling growled. The unicorn nudged me away with his long and powerful muzzle.

"Now that I'm strong." When he exhaled, his rancid breath burned my nostrils.

Had Starling been that ashamed of being weak? That was why he had done this? Why he had committed such a heinous act as consuming souls?

I hoped Deimos would know how to fix this...

Jacinto rushed over and stepped between Starling and me. He glowered at the unicorn, and then at Knovak. "Do *not* touch the vessel." He had spoken each word through clenched teeth. "He carries the soul of our Death Lord and will remain *safe* until his true body joins us once again."

Rosella and her fish-person eldrin also hurried over. They went straight to me, examining my clothing and fretting over the wrinkles in my cloak. The slimy green-scaled creature was shorter —maybe three feet in height—and tugged at the hemline, investigating for damage, I assumed.

I pulled my clothing from its clawed grasp. "Uh, why don't you keep your hands—or your fins—to yourself?"

"My kappa's name is Rooks," Rosella quickly said. She motioned him away and then bowed her head. "I'll make sure he doesn't touch you again."

The fishman—a kappa, apparently, by the adorable name of *Rooks*—stared at me with his huge, round eyes, obvious sadness in his twisted, aquatic features. I almost felt bad for him, but an odd memory lingered at the edge of my thoughts. Professor Helmith had told me about kappas before. I couldn't remember much about the lesson, though.

I hadn't been interested, for some reason. Something about how they only bonded with women...

"Enough tours and sightseeing, yes?" Jacinto stepped close to me and smiled wide. "Why don't we head straight to your brother now? He'll be extremely disappointed if we dally too long."

"Right..." I gave Knovak one last look before I motioned to

the door we had come in through. "Lead the way. I'm sure I can speak to the unicorn arcanist later."

Knovak didn't reply with words. Instead, he gave me a bizarre glance. His mood seemed a mix of irritation and worry— I wasn't sure the word for such an emotion. Before I fully turned away from him, he frowned, like he wanted to say something else but either lost the moment or his courage.

I hoped he was okay.

He didn't seem like it, though.

And the way Starling snorted in my direction, and then licked his lips, made the hairs on my neck stand on end.

As we left the decadent training room, Jacinto walked in front of me, and Rosella behind. Her kappa hopped along behind her, his scales and webbed feet slapping the floor with each awkward step.

We made our way back through the lavish hallways, which were much cooler than the courtyard, and clearly kept colder through more use of imbuing. That had to be expensive. Every time magic was made permanent, star shards were used as the glue—was Lord Oto so wealthy that he could afford to make an indestructible room for training, and corridors with a slight icy chill to keep the desert heat at bay?

What else would he have?

All his personal rooms were probably the stuff of legend.

Then again, my mind wandered to the souls in the abyssal hells. Some of them would be reincarnated as a heating pad in a rich man's mansion. Was that really what they wanted?

I supposed it didn't matter, because any parts of the souls unfulfilled by life would return to the hells to get another chance at being something that would make them complete. If they continued going back and forth until every part of them found something satisfying in life—even if it meant being a chandelier for one cycle—did it really matter?

Some part of me wanted to pay more respect to magical items now that I knew the source of their power.

Like...

I should be more grateful, in general.

Some part of me had an entirely new outlook on life, it seemed. The world felt more *alive* than it had before. Magic was just *magic* before I had seen what happened in the abyssal hells. Now magic was...

Special.

"Your brother stays here, in the southern building," Jacinto said, as though he were giving me a tour. His voice jarred me from my contemplative thoughts. "It was built nearly ten years ago and has operated as our base of operations since then. Lord Oto and his family reside in the northern building, the farthest one from us."

"Right," I muttered.

Rosella quickened her step until she was walking next to me. "Is everything to your liking, Death Lord Deimos?" Rosella knitted her eyebrows. "You seem dissatisfied."

"No. I'm just... thinking." I glanced between them. "Are you two aware that the magic all around us is actually the fragments of souls? People who were reincarnated?"

"Of course," Jacinto replied, matter-of-factly. He waved an arm through the air as he spoke. "Why do you think we're here, doing all this? The flow of magic from the abyssal hells has been stifled! The world would be infinitely more magical if the gates were allowed to be opened and closed once more. That's why we fight, and struggle against the powers that would keep it closed."

"So, you both know?" I was a little shocked to hear that. "Everything?"

Rosella nodded. When she faced me, it was with a tepid smile. "Your brother gives us many lectures on the subject matter. Every week, we gather to discuss the magical significance of our plight, and why we must continue with our mission, for the betterment of the world—even if it means destroying the order of things now."

At least they weren't following Zahn without knowing what was going on.

Then again, I recalled the night Zahn opened that gate in the basement of Astra Academy... His doppelgänger buddy had been quite obsessed with seeing "true magic."

Now I had a better understanding of why.

"And you're both excited for this new future of magic?" I asked, trying not to sound suspicious.

Jacinto couldn't contain his smile. "I'm extremely excited to be on this righteous crusade. There is no greater calling in life than to bring forth the ultimate magic into the world."

That was extreme.

Rosella nodded. "We... We will see souls in the abyssal hells, won't we? Of specific people?" She met my gaze again and frowned. "I... I hope that day will be soon."

Before I could comment, Jacinto stopped in front of a well-crafted door. The image of a dragon was carved into a solid piece of wood that looked as though three men would've been needed to drag it inside.

"This is your brother's study." Jacinto motioned to the door. "Rosella and I will wait here. Take your time with your brother. If you need anything from us, you need but say the word."

I nodded to him, almost thankful to be out of their presence. I had felt uneasy since waking. Nothing about this place put me at ease, and the fact that Ashlyn was still asleep, Knovak was clearly having problems, and Nini wasn't with us, only added to my growing sense of urgency.

I needed to get out of this place.

After a deep exhale, I shoved the door open, careful to keep Twain close to me. He had said nothing the entire trip here, but when our gazes met, I knew he was okay. Twain twitched his ears and wiggled his whiskers, alert and ready should I need him.

There was no better eldrin in the universe, as far as I was concerned.

Then I stepped into Zahn's room, and it was like stepping into another world.

Although modest in size, there was an astonishing trove of trinkets and star shards. Shelves lined three of the walls, bending under the weight of the many items. The trinkets—maybe some were artifacts, I didn't know—came in every shape and size.

Daggers, tomes, gloves, a mirror, chests, and even a statue of a woman.

I knew they were magical items because of the mimic arcanist sense—each had a faint thread of magic. Could Twain transform into them? Probably. He had the ability to turn into objects, I remembered that much from my classes.

Though Twain had never wanted to be an item, for some reason.

My eldrin whipped his head around, his eyes wide as he took everything in.

Glowing orbs and crystals that radiated a kaleidoscope of colors sat at the top of one of the shelves, painting the ceiling in a rainbow. At the heart of this cramped room of magic was Zahn. He stood in front of a large oak desk, the chair shoved into the corner of the room and stacked high with books. He clearly had a grudge against sitting.

Placed on top of the desk was Vivigöl, Silencer of the Damned—*my* weapon.

Well, Deimos's weapon, but I couldn't help feeling like it was mine. It practically called to me, the golden tines of the wicked trident sharp enough to cut someone just for looking at it.

There really wasn't much else in the room. A small table, buried in papers and books, was the only other piece of furniture. This wasn't a room for sleeping or living—it was purely meant for some kind of magical research.

The door shut, but Zahn didn't turn around. He continued to study Deimos's trident, even going so far as to lean down close to it.

"I'm busy," he said, no emotion in his voice.

I walked across half the room, making sure not to step on any of the stray papers that littered the floor. "We need to talk."

Zahn instantly straightened his posture and whipped around, his mouth pressed into a tight line of irritation.

"*You*," he hissed. "What're you doing here? How are you awake? You should be *sleeping*."

Twain growled, his orange fur puffing up, even in my arms. "You can't keep a mimic arcanist down with magic. I *am* magic, thank you very much."

As if summoned by that proclamation, a pink cat leapt out from the jam-packed shelves and landed on the oak desk next to Zahn. After licking its paw, the cat huffed. "Have you forgotten who you're talking to?" The pink mimic had a haughty masculine voice that reeked of condescension. "You're just a baby. A master mimic arcanist stands before you now."

Zahn's arcanist mark matched my own. An empty seven-pointed star.

Unlike me, Zahn had runes on his skin—glowing marks of power that from his knuckles and palms up his arms until they disappeared under his sleeves.

"Look, I'm not going to just sit down and let you hold me—and my friends—captive." I was trying not to be sarcastic, but it was difficult. "Why don't we work together to do something productive? That's what Deimos wants, too."

"*Don't you dare speak on my brother's behalf*," Zahn said, his anger clear, even though he kept his volume low. He probably didn't want anyone outside this room to hear anything.

"Fine." I sighed. "Deimos? You want to tell your brother what's going on?"

Deimos really wasn't... feeling well.

Something was wrong, because his presence in my mind felt like someone being roused from a deep slumber. Sluggish. Partially unaware.

"You think my brother can hear us?" Zahn asked.

"I can hear you," Deimos said through me, his cadence slightly different than mine. It always felt weird. "But I need rest."

Zahn—who had barely been containing his rage, really—leapt to me and grabbed the front of my cloak. He jerked me close as he shouted, "*Don't you dare try to fool me!* My brother would never—"

"*Phobos*," Deimos growled, his consciousness more awake than before. "Calm yourself, brother."

I tugged my cloak from Zahn's grasp.

For some reason, Zahn looked shocked. Or perhaps "shocked" wasn't the right word. He seemed completely stunned.

For a long moment, neither of us said anything.

"I think you broke him," Twain whispered.

The pink mimic twitched his tail. "M-My arcanist?"

Zahn swallowed and then rubbed his face under his glasses. He backed away to the oak desk, never turning away from me. "No one knows my true name anymore... No one but Deimos." After a long exhale, he looked at me with renewed interest. "My brother really can speak through you."

CHAPTER 20

TRUE FORM ELDRIN

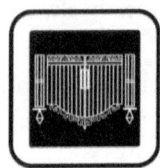

"I tried to tell you," I said. "Deimos and I are allies now, and I want to help restore the abyssal hells."

Zahn exhaled, his eyes slowly narrowing. He took another prolonged moment to speak, and I wondered why he was so resistant to this idea that I might be on his side. "I see," was all he said in response.

I walked closer, until I was next to his desk, and I placed Twain next to the pink mimic. The cat pressed its ears back on his skull and glared at my eldrin. They both eyed each other, neither speaking.

"So, what's the plan?" I crossed my arms over my chest. "Oh, and how do I wake my friend in the other room? Should I just use the soul catcher magic?"

Zahn ground his teeth as he turned around to face his desk. Vivigöl sat on the desk, glittering with dangerous beauty. He reached out like he might touch it, but then recoiled before he did.

"My *plan* is unchanged," Zahn said. "Souls travel between the living realm and the dead, even though the abyssal hells are sealed. They do so through the rebirth process. I suspected if

Deimos physically went to one of those locations in the abyssal hells, where the barrier between realms is weakest, I could use vast amounts of magic here to weaken the barrier enough for his physical body to transition."

Zahn spoke every word like they pained him.

"And that's why I sprang out of a magical pumpkin," I said. "Because I went to the weakest point in the Wraithborne Orchard." I snapped my fingers. "And now you want to try it in the Specter Sands, right?"

"Correct."

"So, that's it? Wait until Deimos recovers and then have him go to another spot where reincarnation happens?"

"Unless you know another way," Zahn sarcastically commented. He took in a deep breath, and calmed himself. "Will you be able to return to the first abyss, brother?"

"I need rest," Deimos said again through me. He seemed distant again, like he wasn't doing so well, and even speaking through me was difficult.

In an instant, Zahn's whole demeanor changed. He turned to me, concern written across his face. He grabbed my shoulders, and I tensed up as he stared into my eyes. "Are you truly well?" he whispered. "You told me Naiad and the others would never catch you. What happened? Why are you *this* hurt? What can I do to help you?"

Deimos stirred, but only long enough to reply, "I miscalculated. I didn't think Naiad would sense me in time. Perhaps her followers have sent word of our plans."

"But you will recover, yes?"

"I need time."

That was a suspicious way to respond. It made me worry. Perhaps Deimos wasn't telling us everything.

Then Zahn pulled me into an embrace. I had already been tense before, but now it was just awkward. I patted Zahn's back, unsure what to do.

He *really* missed Deimos.

"I'll keep trying everything here," Zahn murmured into my shoulder.

"Uh, I think Deimos is resting now," I said. His presence was further away than before, at least.

Zahn growled a curse as he released the hug and pushed me away. He then turned on his heel and rummaged through the overstuffed shelves full of books, trinkets, and crystals. I brushed myself off, mulling over his reactions.

"What should I do to help?" I asked.

"Just leave the logistics to me." Zahn had enough disdain it practically dripped onto the floor.

"When you were my professor at Astra Academy, you weren't nearly this condescending," I said. "Have you lost the ability to be a teacher since then? Or are you just having a bad day?"

Zahn slowly turned to glower at me. After he took another breath, he replied in a cool and calm manner. "I apologize. Let me be perfectly honest. I... hate you."

"What?" I pointed to my chest. "You hate *me*? You don't even know me."

"True. But that doesn't matter. If you had simply died in your sleep, like all the other twins I had found, I wouldn't be in this mess because I would have a fully functioning Gate of Crossing into the abyssal hells. Or if you hadn't fought back in the basement of Astra Academy, I could've recovered and I still would've had my gate. *Or*," his voice rose slightly, "if you hadn't trapped a piece of my brother's soul in your being, I wouldn't be making *yet another plan to solve this whole situation*."

"Well—" I began.

Zahn cut me off. "I've been attempting to help my brother for *thousands of years*." He ran a shaky hand through his hair, his anger barely contained this time. He had a desperate and furious look in his eyes that was difficult to describe. "If *you*—a *no one* from a *nowhere location*—hadn't destroyed my plans *three times over*, I wouldn't be here."

His restraint was legendary.

Clearly, Zahn wanted to strangle me.

This didn't bode well for us working together.

After a long minute where Zahn held his breath, he gradually turned back around to face the bookshelf. "My life's work is to help Deimos—to unseal the abyssal hells. Perhaps now you'll understand why I don't particularly enjoy working with you."

"Right." I nervously chuckled. "Well, how about I go wake my friend? I'll leave you alone to, uh, do whatever you're going to do here."

"That sounds amazing," Zahn sardonically stated.

"I'll probably head back to Astra Academy after that."

He shot me a cold glare over his shoulder. "Do not, under any circumstances, leave Lord Oto's compound. Do I make myself clear?"

I couldn't argue with the man. He wasn't in the right mindset. So, I just nodded once, and replied, "All right. But we'll need to talk about this later."

I didn't intend to stay here any longer than I needed. Hopefully, once Deimos had rested a bit, we could speak to Zahn without him losing his mind. Until then, I wanted to keep my options open—or at least speak with Headmaster Venrover or Professor Helmith.

"Good." Zahn returned to his work.

"Oh, by the way, the others think I'm Deimos. Like, actually *him* and not just a way to communicate with him, type of thing."

"Yes, well, that's because I told them you were a husk that held his soul." Zahn didn't even look at me as he said, "Just avoid them. Tell Jacinto you need to rest, and he will provide you a private room. *Stay there* until this evening. We can speak more then—after I've had time to analyze this situation from every angle."

I lifted an eyebrow. "What will that do?"

"I'll come up with some way for... someone like you... to help me."

Uh-huh.

I, one hundred percent, wasn't going to stay trapped in a random room until this evening. Lord Oto's compound was *huge*, and I needed to know more about him, and my environment.

"I'll head off to my room, then," I said. Then I motioned for Twain.

But my eldrin was too busy wrestling with Zahn's. Both the cats were tussling across the top of the desk, fighting like only cats could. The pink mimic was larger than Twain, and on top of him, softly growling. That was okay, because Twain had the cat's tail in his mouth, and his little fangs were chomping down hard.

"Hey," I said. "What're you two doing?"

Zahn scoffed. "*Twice.* Leave the other mimic alone. Come to me."

The cat ripped her tail away from Twain and then leapt over to Zahn's shoulder. "I was asserting my dominance."

Twain puffed up his orange fur. "What was that? Come say that to my face, coward!"

I grabbed my eldrin and petted his fur until it was less poofy. "Hey, whoa. There's no need to have a little mirror match."

Zahn's mimic, Twice, stuck out her tongue. My eldrin growled the cutest little kitten growl I had ever heard in my life. It wasn't helping the dominance game, though.

The glitter of Vivigöl's golden shaft caught my attention again. Intent on keeping it with me, I reached out and grabbed it.

Zahn practically whirled on his heel. "Don't touch that!"

But it was too late. I already had the weapon in hand. Vivigöl casually *click-click-clicked* into the shape of ornate jewelry in order to conform to my body. It was a useful form, especially since I could hide the weapon under my clothing.

The weapon shifted up my arm and around the base of my neck, all while Zahn and Twice watched with horror in their eyes.

"I'm fine," I said with a shrug.

"Abyssal coral absorbs souls and magic," Zahn said matter-of-factly, but also with a hint of anger. "Only arcanists immune to such dangerous soul-damaging magic can touch it."

I shrugged a second time. "Death Lords are immune."

"You. Aren't. A Death Lord."

With a half smile, I nodded. "But Deimos is—and his magic is with me. So don't worry about it. I'm just going to take Vivigöl with me. So I'm protected. Besides, what if someone comes looking to hurt Deimos? Now I can fight them off."

Zahn dwelled on those statements for a moment. It seemed his anger faded a bit.

Then he pointed at me. "Don't take it anywhere near the typhoon dragon or its arcanist."

That...

Surprised me.

I hadn't expected him to say that.

"Why?" I asked.

"Typhoon dragons can consume abyssal coral. When they do, they achieve their true form. I suspect your associate may want Vivigöl for her own purposes."

"Wait, really?" I asked.

I had learned about true forms in class. A true form eldrin was more powerful, and even had special abilities that were far stronger than anything they had before. Their magic was pure, or so our professors had claimed.

If Ecrib had to consume some abyssal coral... that meant

typhoon dragons had a *geas* requirement to achieve their true form. They were on a quest—to consume abyssal coral.

Which made sense, now that I thought about it. In order to bond with a typhoon dragon, you had to swim down and gather it an abyssal pearl. These were dragons of the depths, after all. Their magic probably stemmed from something related to the abyssal hells.

"I don't think Ashlyn knows about that requirement," I muttered. She hadn't been looking for the coral when we were in the hells together. "So, you don't need to worry. Plus, I wouldn't let her harm the weapon."

Abyssal coral just grew in the hells. I knew that much from Deimos's knowledge.

Perhaps, if we did open the gateway back to the abyssal hells, Ashlyn could effortlessly empower her eldrin. I would need to speak with her about it.

Zahn sighed and then returned his attention to the bookshelf. "And he can touch my brother's weapon?" he muttered under his breath, obviously to himself, even though I could hear. His final curse was a little too hushed, however.

Was he... jealous?

It sounded that way.

Of course, my mind was momentarily distracted by the thought of true form eldrin. I walked to the door, my eyes on Twain. I had to overcome fear itself to help my eldrin transform. Ashlyn just needed some abyssal coral. It seemed I had all the pieces in place to strengthen us.

I definitely needed to speak with her.

After opening the door, I stepped out into the hallway. Jacinto and Rosella were still there, but someone new was also in the hall.

And it caught me by surprise.

Raaza?

CHAPTER 21

TRAITOR

Wait, what was *Raaza* doing here?

We stared at each other for a prolonged moment, our disbelief mirroring each other's. Had he come to look for us? Was Raaza so concerned about our safety that he had left Astra Academy just to search the world over for us, and somehow stumbled upon our location through sheer dedication and tenacity?

"What're you doing here?" Raaza finally asked, shattering all my theories. "You... You disappeared from the Academy. No one has been able to find you. What's going on?"

He clearly hadn't come here for me.

"Silence," Jacinto growled. "This is merely a vessel for our *Death Lord*. The boy you know is long gone."

The color drained from Raaza's desert-tanned skin.

He didn't look well, even once he had all his color back. His face was scarred, his black hair was disheveled, and he smelled weird. Like rot. He wore a long cloak, but it wasn't the same bizarre white everyone in this cult was wearing. No, he wore one of brown and black, dusted with sand and ripped at the hems.

Normally, Raaza seemed rather competent. He was lean with muscle, and observant, but today clearly wasn't his day.

His kitsune eldrin, Miko, poked her head out from the folds of Raaza's cloak. She was a red fox with fiery features. Her eyes glittered with mischievous intelligence as she glanced up to meet my gaze. "This *isn't* Gray anymore?"

"Apparently, he's finally been taken by the Death Lord," Raaza intoned, his eyes fixed on mine.

I stared at him, trying to somehow indicate that was a lie, but he just huffed and glanced away.

"Sorry, Death Lord Deimos," Raaza said. "I was just here to report something to Zahn." He didn't offer me another glance as he entered Zahn's study. Once the door was shut, it was just me and the cultists again.

Rosella and Jacinto both turned to smile at me. It was a little too in sync. It came off as creepy.

"My apologies," Jacinto said with a bow. "Lord Oto hires many arcanists to come and go through this compound. You don't need to fret about their presence."

"What did Oto hire that arcanist for?" I asked.

And *how*? Why was Raaza even here? Shouldn't he be at the Academy?

"That man, Raaza, is our eyes and ears inside Astra Academy." Jacinto straightened his posture and smiled, his eyes still disturbing, especially when they drilled into me. "That's how we kept tabs on everything happening within her walls."

I held my breath as I thought about Ashlyn's cotillion. I had wondered how those cultist lunatics knew who I was, and where I was going to be. Had *Raaza* been the one to tell them? This whole time? It was him?

Knowing that enraged me.

"Zahn said you two would prepare a room for me to rest in," I muttered. I kept my gaze on the far wall, my anger more than I had expected. The more I thought about the situation, the angrier I became, however. "I need plenty of sleep. Taking over this vessel was exhausting."

Rosella and Jacinto exchanged glances. Then they nodded.

"At once," Rosella said. "We'll prepare everything."

I nodded once. "I'll wait here, with my brother. Come get me once it's all ready."

Lucky for me, Jacinto and Rosella both realized I was dismissing them. That was what I wanted—to be free of their presence. They turned and walked down the hallway, including Rooks, the creepy little kappa, and hurried for a far door.

I didn't really need to rest.

But now I wanted to wait for Raaza.

I stood in the middle of the hallway, tapping my foot. I mulled over everything that had happened in the Academy. My father and stepmother had been kidnapped at one point in order to get a hold of me—that was because of Raaza, too. He must've told these cultists all about my family and where they were from so they could use them against me.

How could he do all this?

"Are you okay?" Twain whispered.

I replied with a curt nod. Then I set him on the floor near my feet. "I just can't believe Raaza would betray us like that."

Normally, Deimos's thoughts bled into my own, sometimes coloring my feelings on a situation. But in this instance, it almost felt like the opposite. As if... my thoughts were bleeding into his. He hadn't been angry about the situation, but the longer I dwelled on it, the more agitated *he* became.

I wondered why.

Then Zahn's door opened again, and Raaza stepped into the hallway, his kitsune with him.

With all this excess anger swimming in my veins, I whirled around on my heel.

"Raaza," I said, not bothering to hide the disgust in my voice.

He clenched his jaw. "Yes, Death Lord Deimos?"

"You betrayed Astra Academy?" I shook my head. "Is that true?"

"Well..." He averted his gaze and then nodded. "I did it for you, obviously. I'm such a loyal servant to the cause."

Miko once again poked her head out of his robes. She offered a foxy smile. "We'd do whatever it takes to help the team! Long live the Death Lords." Then her ears twitched backward. She murmured to Raaza, "Do Death Lords *live*? Or are they already dead?"

I grabbed Raaza's cloak and twisted my fingers into the fabric. When I jerked him close, he tensed. "*You* told these people about what was going on inside Astra Academy?" I kept my voice low, but not calm. "*You* endangered everyone? For what? For Death Lord Deimos?"

"You're still Gray," Raaza muttered, realization dawning on him.

I shoved him. Surprisingly, he hit the hallway wall with a hard slam. Was I that strong? It felt like Deimos's magic was coursing through me. The thought of everyone at Ashlyn's cotillion circled my thoughts, reminding me they all could've died during the attack. The cultists who followed Deimos had used some sort of monstrous kraken to attack us. We *all* could've died.

Raaza had done that?

He held up a hand. "*Wait*. I can explain."

"You just did," I quipped.

Despite my joke, I did wait. What was he going to say? In a sardonic way, I couldn't wait to hear his explanation.

But it never came. Raaza just stared at me, his eyes searching mine, like he was torn on whether or not he *should* offer an explanation.

Miko leapt out of her arcanist's robes and stood in front of me, her fangs bared. "You better step away. We're not going to play nice."

"*I'm* not going to play nice," I said with a dark laugh. "It was you two who endangered my father and brother? My stepmother? Ashlyn? The rest of our classmates? For what? Coins? Star shards? Is that it? You *were* always talking about how you wanted more magic—is that what they offered you, huh? *Power?*"

Raaza narrowed his eyes into a glower. "You don't understand." Then he threw open his cloak and held out his hand. A flash of fake fire enveloped his palm. *Fox fire.* Kitsune arcanists could use their magic to create tangible illusions.

And Raaza created a short sword. It was a silver blade, with a thicker handle, curved to the tip. His ability to create larger and larger things was really coming along. Raaza had improved, and in more ways than one.

Raaza pointed the sword at me. "Stay back."

"Are you threatening me?" I asked. "You can't be serious."

Twain stood by my legs, his back arched. He hissed at Miko.

I grabbed Vivigöl from around the base of my neck, and the weapon easily slid off, as though it had been bored and needed a bit of violence. It clicked into a sword of its own, one with a golden blade, and six points to the guard. It was an elegant weapon, though long and gaudy.

"I didn't want to betray Astra Academy," Raaza said, his words quick while staying quiet. He was obviously trying to whisper, but he seemed almost as angry as I was. "*Back off.* I have more work to do. If I don't get back to the Academy soon, everyone will know."

"Oh, I'm going to make sure everyone knows, so you don't need to worry about getting back in time." I wanted nothing more than to report this straight to Headmaster Venrover. We would all be a lot safer if Raaza was locked away in a prison somewhere.

Then Raaza swung his sword.

On instinct, I blocked. It wasn't even difficult, and our weapons *clanged*, echoing throughout the empty hallway, Raaza's blade chipping. But Raaza hadn't swung his sword to attack me—he had swung it as a distraction.

More fox fire exploded from his other hand, forming into a powder. As I brought Vivigöl back to swing, Raaza threw the blackish ash-like substance at my face. A mist filled the hallway and burned my eyes. I grunted as I stumbled backward, caught off guard.

Raaza took off.

He just... ran. Down the hall. His kitsune chased after him.

I coughed back the mist and rubbed at my eyes as they filled with water. My vision returned in tiny amounts. "*Twain*," I growled. Then I sensed the magical threads around us and grabbed for one I was familiar with. My arcanist star shifted as my eldrin transformed.

"I won't let him escape," he said, his anger matching my own.

Twain leapt from the mist as a typhoon dragon, his blue scales glittering. He opened his fanged mouth, and lightning crackled from the depths of his gullet. In one powerful release of breath, he evoked a storm's worth of lightning, which flew down the corridor and hit Raaza in the back.

Raaza hit the floor face-first, his body twitching.

Miko puffed up in anger, whirled around to face us, and actually stood between Twain and her arcanist. With fire blazing around her paws, she yipped. Then she evoked fox fire across the floor and walls, creating more mist.

My eldrin flew into the smoky environment and then yelped. When he thrashed, he cleared away the dark mist, revealing the floor. Miko had covered the floor in fox fire nails, broken glass, and jagged rocks. When Twain had leapt toward her, he had landed on the booby trap with all four feet. Blood wept from his injuries, but he growled back the pain.

The wounds were mostly superficial, but they still added to my already growing anger.

Once the water in my eyes cleared, I held up my hand and evoked a blast of lightning. It struck Miko, and she cried out as she hit the floor. All her fox fire illusions vanished.

Raaza practically flew up from the floor. He wrapped his arms around his eldrin. "Miko!" Then he shielded her with his body, and cradled her close. "Miko? *Miko?*"

She twitched her ears and moved a bit, albeit weakly.

I thought someone would've come to see us by now, but when I glanced around, the hallway was still empty. Zahn had never exited his room, and I wondered if he just didn't care about anything else when he was working.

With a huff, I walked over toward Raaza.

He managed to stand, despite his shaky legs. He kept his eldrin in his arms even as he glared at me.

Twain, looming over him as a typhoon dragon, didn't seem to intimidate him.

"What're you doing?" I asked as I approached. "You want another scar on your face, is that it? Because I'm pretty sure this abyssal coral weapon can do that to you."

Raaza gritted his teeth as he took a step back. He hugged Miko, but he kept his eyes focused solely on me.

"My arcanist," Miko whispered. "Just tell them. They'll... they'll understand."

"Tell me what?" I demanded.

But Raaza didn't answer. His intense gaze finally fell to the floor, the corners of his lips twitching.

Why wasn't he talking to me? Was he just so ashamed of what he had done?

Good. He should be ashamed. That was the appropriate feeling.

"What's going on?" someone shouted.

I turned and spotted Jacinto and Rosella at the end of the hallway. They were staring with wide eyes. Finally, someone had arrived.

"I…" Raaza began.

CHAPTER 22

PLANS

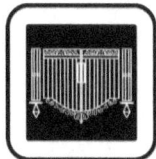

"This jackwagon attacked me," I said.

Jacinto and Rosella gave Raaza one brief glance. Then Jacinto leapt forward, waved his hand, and a blast of ice shot from his body and covered the hallway floor. The chilly crystals didn't touch me—they exploded across the floor around me and Twain, leaving a perfect circle for us to stand in. Instead, the ice traveled up Raaza's legs before he could move. The rime encased his limbs from the knees down, preventing him from lifting his feet and fleeing.

His eldrin, Miko, didn't move in his arms. She was still suffering from the blast of lightning, but clearly breathing and alive.

Rosella held out her hand. Yellowish acid dripped from the wrinkles of her palms. It splashed onto the frosty floor, disintegrating the ice and damaging the tile underneath. She didn't seem to care. She made a pathway straight to me, bowed slightly, and then motioned for me to exit the situation.

"I didn't attack him," Raaza shouted as he attempted to lift his legs. "It's the other way around!"

With a mere thought, I transformed Vivigöl back into an

accessory that wrapped around my body. "That isn't true. He slashed at me with his fake weapon. And he's a traitor."

Jacinto walked across the ice as though it were a normal floor —never slipping, never losing his balance. Was it his magic? Or did he just have wild amounts of practice?

"Even if our lord attacked you first, you're still in the wrong." Jacinto sneered. "Either way, you're coming with me."

"Wh-What're you going to do?" Raaza asked.

"Yeah, what *are* you going to do?" I asked.

"Whatever you wish." Jacinto half bowed his head. "The will of my Death Lord is my will in turn."

Which was unfortunate, because I wasn't entirely sure what I wanted to do. "I need to think about it," I said. "Just... hold him in custody. I'll think of something."

Raaza held out a hand. "Wait! I can't stay here! I need to go. People are depending on me."

I waved away his comments as I walked along the acid-crafted path made by Rosella. Twain shifted back into his mimic form and landed on my shoulder. I patted his little orange head and completely ignored Raaza's pleas as I followed Rosella away from the situation.

Jacinto stayed, but the rest of us went deeper into Lord Oto's mansion.

"*I can't stay here!*" Raaza's voice echoed throughout the corridor.

But then there was nothing. He had been silenced. Somehow. I preferred not to think about it. Perhaps after I spoke with Ashlyn, we could think of a fitting punishment.

"I apologize for taking so long to prepare the room," Rosella said. She offered me a forced smile. "We gathered some food and drink and prepared a meal for your quarters."

I shrugged. "Thanks. You didn't need to."

"I'm starving," Twain whispered into my ear. "Tell them they need to bring us even more food."

"You haven't even seen what they got us," I murmured under my breath.

"I don't care. It's not enough, I bet. And also, I want fish. Tell them Death Lords need seafood."

Before I had time to explain that all to Rosella, she stopped in front of a large door. After a deep bow, she opened the door and motioned me inside.

The splendor of my new room shocked me for a moment. Tapestries hung near the windows, and they were so fine they could be the envy of a king. Silvers, golds—the tapestries were beautiful, and glittered in the light of the glowstone chandeliers.

I had a four-poster bed that appeared to be carved from the finest oak. It was draped with a canopy of silk, and the blankets were plush with down feathers. These, too, were gold and silver, like whoever was in charge of decorating loved gaudy extravagance.

A grand fireplace dominated the opposite wall, its soot-blackened bricks a stark contrast to the otherwise meticulously whitewashed walls. The warmth the fireplace provided was beyond cozy, and I almost wondered if it, too, was magical.

Oh, and the writing desk was impressive! A massive, immovable piece of furniture with an inkwell permanently stained with the ink of a quill pen—it reminded me of the desk Zahn had.

By the time I spotted the table with all the food, I was already in awe. The food solidified that feeling. So much meat and bread and baked vegetables. No fish, though. Despite that, I was still having a great time. This whole room? For me? This was a room big enough for fifteen people. And the meal they had gathered up for me could've fed that many, too.

"Hopefully this room will be satisfactory for the time being. Lord Oto has promised to provide you accommodations befitting your station, but he has yet to do so." Rosella bowed again. Then she nervously straightened her posture. "Is there, uh, anything you need in the meantime?"

"Fish," I absentmindedly said as I continued to glance around.

Twain pawed at the air. "Yes! So much fish. And a variety of fish, yes? Baked fish. Grilled fish. *Marinated fish.*"

"R-Right." Rosella hesitantly backed away. "I'll go to the kitchen straight away, Death Lord Deimos." She exited the room and softly closed the door.

"Okay, here's the plan," I whispered to Twain. "We're going to eat, and then we're going to wake Ashlyn."

My eldrin nodded once. "Okay. And then what?"

"Well, hopefully escape." I gave the room another long stare. "Maybe after resting for a bit, though."

Rosella brought us fish. Her eldrin, Rooks, seemed to know which fish were the tastiest, and he placed them in a line on our table from most delicious to least delicious. Once those two were gone, I snuck out of my opulent quarters and returned to the bizarre room where people were sleeping.

There weren't guards or many people around. Lord Oto's whole compound was gigantic, and it seemed the cultist area wasn't as filled as it should've been. Was it because so many of them had died? Probably.

That was fortunate for me. I didn't want to have to explain myself to a bunch of lunatics.

Ashlyn and her eldrin, Ecrib, hadn't moved an inch since last I saw them. I crept to the side of their beds and vigorously shook them both.

Nothing.

Twain even leapt on top of Ecrib and kneaded his scales. That did nothing.

They were magically compelled to sleep, obviously, so I would need magic to wake them. Fortunately, the disgusting soul catcher was somewhere in Lord Oto's compound, since I felt its thread of magic. I tugged on it, and Twain morphed into a hideous spider puppet with eight spindly legs and a wooden face mask.

My arcanist mark burned as he transformed, but as soon as I had the soul catcher magic filling my system, I touched Ashlyn's shoulder.

Just like with ethereal whelks, I had the power to shape dreamscapes—or shatter them. After a deep breath, I ended her ceaseless dreaming and brought her back to the waking world.

Ashlyn slowly blinked her eyes open, her gaze gradually focusing until it was clear she was awake. "Gray?"

"That's me," I said. "You get enough beauty sleep? Because I need your help."

Ashlyn sat up. She rubbed her temple and glanced around with a raised eyebrow. "Where... are we?"

"We're currently in the heart of some false lord's compound in the nation of Sellix," I said in a casual but sardonic tone.

She snapped her attention to me. "Why?"

"Because said false lord has enough money to fund a small cult's worth of crazy people. In exchange for his money, the cult has promised him abyssal dragon parts for his trinket and artifact creation."

Twain, as a creepy soul catcher, touched Ecrib and woke the young typhoon dragon. Ashlyn's eldrin slowly lifted his head and then shook it with enough force that static cracks of lightning flared from his fangs.

"What lord are you talking about?" Ashlyn asked, her brow furrowed.

"Lord Oto."

Once she finally shook the last of the sleep from her mind, Ashlyn stood from her bed. Her legs trembled for a second, but then she pulled herself together. "So this Lord Oto man is helping Death Lord Deimos?"

"His brother, technically." I touched her arm. "C'mon. Let's go to my room. I'll explain everything there while we eat."

Twain shifted back into his cat form. He landed on the floor and then hurried to my feet. "Yes! Finally! We need to eat so much!"

Ashlyn, Twain, Ecrib, and I could all fit on my four-poster bed. The silk curtain canopy hung around us like an elegant tent, and it reminded me of the dorms back in Astra Academy. We had created a fort out of blankets, and this bed, with the canopy closed, was like having another little personal fort. Or a tent. A fancy tent.

We had food laid out on a blanket between us, like a bizarre picnic. It reminded me of when we went camping as a class.

Between bites of cheese-baked bread, I said, "And that's when I met *Raaza*. He's here. I bet you never would've guessed that."

"Technically, Astra Academy is nestled in a mountain range that borders the nation of Sellix," Ashlyn muttered. She nibbled on some dried pork. "It isn't that surprising he's here looking for us, especially considering the Gates of Crossing."

"I didn't say he was looking for us. He's actually working for Lord Oto as his little stooge." I pointed at her with my half-eaten bread. "Raaza has been sending information to the cultists about everything happening in the Academy."

Ashlyn handed some of the meat to her eldrin. Ecrib happily slurped it up from her hand, his long tongue practically prehensile.

"Raaza?" she whispered. "Why would he do that?"

"I don't know." I tried to hand Twain some more smoked

fish, but my eldrin was so bloated and ball-shaped, he couldn't move. Instead, I gobbled down the fish and turned back to Ashlyn. "He wouldn't really say, but I bet they just offered him tons of trinkets or something. He's always been a bit of a weirdo. Never talks much in class, always goes on about wanting lots of power. He's totally the kind of man who would turn against us for his own benefit."

"I never thought Raaza was that callous."

"Eh. What does it matter? The cultists have him now."

Ashlyn rested back on the many pillows. She stared up at the top of the canopy. "In our dorm back at the Academy, there's this plaque on the ceiling. It's... kinda hidden. There are words engraved on it that read: *Mercy. Without it, we cannot help others find redemption.*"

"There's a *plaque on the ceiling*?" I repeated in mild disbelief. "Why?"

"I don't know. I've just thought about the words a few times." She closed her eyes. "I sometimes imagine I get into an argument with my father about... about my life... and we get into a fight, and I somehow best him. But afterward, I let him go, and he forgives me, and we're... we're a happy family."

"What does this have to do with Raaza?"

Ashlyn opened her eyes again. "I don't know. I just... I think about the words a lot, and hearing you talk about Raaza made me think of them again. Maybe he needs help."

I gulped down some water. "Okay, so the ceiling gave you some advice, and now we're going to forgive Raaza? Am I understanding this correctly?"

Ashlyn narrowed her eyes into a sarcastic glare. "Okay. Tell me more about Lord Oto. You said you wanted to get out of here, but you were worried about all the arcanists."

"Well, actually..." I swallowed some bread as quickly as I could. "I *want* to team up with Zahn to help Deimos get into the realm of the living. However, I don't really like all his *buddies*, and I think Headmaster Venrover would be a better help."

"Uh-huh."

"So I want to escape here."

"Is Lord Oto intimidating?"

Twain burped. Then he rolled his sphere-shaped body over on the silky blankets. "That man doesn't look like he can fight. He doesn't even look like he can tear up pictures with babies on them."

I pointed to my eldrin. "Yeah, I'm not worried about Oto. I'm more worried about... getting into a fight with *everyone here*. Does that make sense? I think we should just... wait until tonight, slip out, tell Headmaster Venrover—and maybe Professor Helmith—everything that has happened, and then return to get Zahn."

Ashlyn sat all the way up. "All right. Let's do it."

CHAPTER 23

THE TWILIGHT GATE

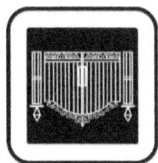

Waiting was the worst.

I hated waiting in all its forms. Lines. Opening times. The minutes before class officially started. Nothing was quite as boring.

So while we waited for this evening, I leaned on the windowsill of my room, and closed my eyes. I figured maybe I could focus on my magic, and sense out threads of magic even further away from my location—something useful to do with my time since I was forced to wait.

But as I concentrated, and honed my attention on my magic, I felt something else happening. It was as if... I could sense my whole being, and picture each piece of me. It was similar to a cake, when cut into slices but not yet torn apart. I was a whole cake. And I had slices. And I could use the slices.

What was this feeling?

"Gray? Are you okay?"

Ashlyn's voice startled me out of my focus. I glanced over my shoulder. She was still on the bed, her dragon curled around her like a scaly pillow, my eldrin comfortably in her lap. The three of them had been lounging for a while. Ashlyn seemed incapable of sleeping—she had done enough of that already—but that didn't stop them from relaxing.

They looked cozy. I half wished I could rest my head in Ashlyn's lap.

"I'm fine," I replied. "Just thinking."

"Don't hurt yourself," Twain said with a snicker.

I shot him a sarcastic glare. "Ya know, *you* bonded with me, which means I earned your approval. Maybe think of that when you make jokes."

He waved a paw through the air. "Pfft. You're just jealous of my savage wordplay."

I chuckled to myself as I turned away. The window overlooked Lord Oto's garden. It was peaceful, and easy for me to focus. I closed my eyes again and took a deep breath. What was that feeling I had before?

"It's your soul," Deimos whispered through me.

My eyes snapped open. I gripped the windowsill, a little confused by his presence. When I glanced back at Ashlyn, she was busy petting both Ecrib and Twain, muttering pleasant things to them. She had a beautiful smile. She clearly hadn't heard me talking to myself.

I glanced away a second time. In a quiet tone, I replied, "So you're an expert on mimic magic now?"

"You're not using *mimic magic*, child. You're tapping into my abyssal dragon abilities. Segmenting your soul like that is how an abyssal dragon arcanist astral projects."

That was interesting. I had been wondering about that. Deimos had used a piece of his soul to pass through one of the gate fragments—that was how he had gotten caught in my dreamscape. And why part of him was stuck with me now. Apparently, abyssal dragons could just slice up their souls and send a piece out into the world in order to view, or spy on, other things.

"Does astral projecting help you watch over the abyssal hells?" I asked.

"Yes," Deimos quickly replied. "It's how I can watch some of the other layers. I have a part of my soul in the first abyss at all times to watch the Twilight Gate."

The Twilight Gate...

The elder ogata toad had mentioned that when I was in the abyssal hells. So had Everett. They were all concerned with whether it was opened or not.

"What is the Twilight Gate?" I asked. "Like, who made it? Where did it come from? Where is it now? How was it sealed?"

Deimos's emotions—both irritation and a pedagogical urge—seeped into my thoughts. "Close your eyes. I'll show you."

Again, I glanced over to make sure Ashlyn and the others were okay. They were still on the bed, blissfully chatting. They were fine.

So I closed my eyes, just as Deimos had instructed. At first, I saw nothing, but then my consciousness... shifted focus. I no longer felt the windowsill held in my hands, or the hot Sellix breeze that wafted through the window. I couldn't feel my own breathing, or hear Ashlyn's whispers as she spoke to her eldrin.

Instead, I heard the splashing of shallow water. The distant roar of waterfalls.

The soft chime of bells.

Then, my eyes opened. Well, not my eyes—Deimos's eyes.

In a reversal of positions, *he* was the one with the body, and I was but an onlooker. Well, maybe this wasn't even his body. It was his astral projection—a tiny fragment of his soul that was present in this new landscape, with me as a backpack, tagging along.

His astral projection seemed like a physical manifestation of his body. Just like how he appeared in my dream, when Professor Helmith trapped him.

"This is bizarre," I said—through Deimos, using his mouth.

He growled some sort of curse under his breath. "Quiet. Simply observe."

Where were we?

Deimos stood before an odd, gargantuan structure. It was an upside-down gate built into a stone wall. The gate was over fifty feet tall, and at least a hundred feet wide. It was white, and glittered with an iridescent sheen. Through Deimos's thoughts, I understood the gate was made of *nacre*—the same substance as pearls.

This was the Twilight Gate.

It was a gateway that joined the realm of the living with the abyssal hells. It couldn't open or close. This wondrous and ancient structure blocked everything from entering or leaving— except for souls and the occasional trickle of water.

And water *did* trickle in.

The potent smell of sea salt was all I could detect as water leaked from the cracks of the Twilight Gate. Waterfalls showered down the stone walls the gate was built into, crashing to the stone floor and filling the space with a shallow pool of water that was no more than three inches deep.

What was this place?

The bars of the Twilight Gate were twisted into the grand stone walls, which seemingly stretched on for eternity. There was no "ceiling" here, just a mist of soul fragments that glowed a faint white, giving illumination to the otherwise dreary atmosphere.

It was as if we were in a gigantic room. Water for a floor. A wall of waterfalls on one side, and endless mist all around us.

The gate reminded me of the Astra Academy crest. One fourth of the school's crest was the same upside-down gate to represent the journey we would take to death. And here it was— in the flesh.

"This is the very top of the first abyss," Deimos stated. "This is where the Twilight Gate once stood as a barrier between worlds."

It was all... very impressive.

"Wow," I said through him.

He hissed something, his irritation growing. "*Quiet.*" Then Deimos exhaled and continued his explanation. "The Twilight Gate wasn't crafted by the hands of man, or even spawned from the magic of mystical creatures. It was here before any of that. Here before life on this world began. It is as old as the stars, and as mysterious as the blackness in the night sky."

"Who sealed it?"

When I spoke through him, I had his voice. It was odd— Deimos was a lot gruffer than me—and my words with his tone were amusing.

"Astros, once a god-arcanist, now dead, used his abyssal kraken magic to slay the Twilight Gate and prevent it from opening. In doing so, he earned the title *the Warden*, and set the world on a terrible path. He disrupted the flow of magic, and of life, and it will soon spiral out of control."

"Wait, the gate was once alive?"

Deimos clicked his tongue. Then he glanced up, staring at the top of the gate. "Yes. It was once alive, and every Death Lord felt its pulse. Now it's just a rotting corpse. A dead *thing* that sits in the rocks of the deepest crag in the ocean."

"So the Twilight Gate has a physical location?"

"It has a location, but just like your Gates of Crossing, it is just a magical gateway that takes souls—and people—to the lands of the abyssal hells. The Twilight Gate has always been in the darkest pit of the ocean, and it will remain that way for all time. Even if the ocean moved, the gate would move with it."

I wished I had something to write this all down with. Instead, I told myself I would commit it to memory. I had to tell the others about the Twilight Gate. It was important that we find a way to open it once more.

"Are there any other mysterious and powerful gateways?" I asked.

Deimos turned away from the gate, the roar of the waterfalls echoing in his ears. *Our* ears? Whatever. I could hear it all, too.

"There is one other gate similar to the Twilight Gate. It is located at the bottom of the abyssal hells—beyond the void that destroys all. It is known as the *Oblivion Gate*, and is supposedly where all magic goes to die."

"What do you mean *supposedly?*"

"I have never seen it for myself," Deimos muttered. The mists in the air swirled around us, stinking of salt. "Death Lord Umbriel is obsessed with the Oblivion Gate, and continues to search for ways to travel through the void in the fifth abyss in order to see the gate with her own eyes."

The splashing of water kept me focused on our surroundings, but something tickled my shoulder. I couldn't move Deimos's body—just like how he couldn't move mine. All I could do was faintly feel my real body in the realm of the living. Someone was touching me.

"How can we revive the Twilight Gate?" I asked.

"I don't know," Deimos growled. "If I did, I would've done it already."

Well, obviously he didn't know. He was a master of death, and combat, and souls. He didn't know anything about healing or revival.

But I bet Headmaster Venrover would know. And maybe even Professor Helmith. This was even *more* of a reason to visit them.

More tapping on my shoulder. It was distracting.

"I need to go," I said through Deimos.

"Nothing would make me happier. I prefer to contemplate my problems in *silence*."

Had Death Lord Deimos come to this spot in order to mull over the situation? I could understand that. This was a gigantic room devoid of all other life. There were no people, no mystical creatures—just hundreds of waterfalls, a beautiful gate, and a shallow amount of water that reflected the white mist all around us.

It was... lit. Not a lot of darkness. Like this was the middle of the day.

A magical place I had never seen before.

A beautiful place to dwell on problems.

And as soon as someone touched my shoulder for a third time, I left it. My consciousness left Deimos's astral projection, and I was snapped back into the room inside Lord Oto's compound.

"Huh?" I shook my head and rubbed my temple.

"Gray?"

Ashlyn stood next to me, her brow furrowed. Twain was in her arms, and Ecrib sat on the other side of me.

"Hey," I muttered. "What's going on?"

"You weren't answering me when I was speaking to you. I thought you were asleep."

"You looked asleep, but you started murmuring things," Twain added. He squinted at me.

Ashlyn pointed to the window. "It's night. Maybe we should get going."

Night? Already?

I nodded once. "All right. Let's get out of here. I have new information to tell Headmaster Venrover."

CHAPTER 24

MY BROTHER

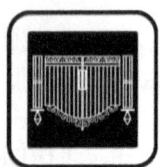

Ashlyn motioned to the window. I glanced outside and focused on the far wall that surrounded the compound. Lord Oto liked to keep everyone out—or everyone in, I wasn't sure—so we'd have to do some climbing, it seemed.

Right as I was about to slip outside, something occurred to me. Everett had given me a necklace, and I no longer had it. I touched my collarbone, happy I had Vivigöl, but fearful I had lost the personal item he had entrusted me with. Everett wanted me to reach out to his family, and unless I had the necklace and pendant, I wouldn't be able to prove I had seen him. Well, at least not easily.

"Wait." I stepped away from the window. "I need to get something."

"We can get supplies once we're out of here," Ashlyn said.

"It's not that. I'll be right back."

"*Gray*. We shouldn't stay here any longer than necessary. I need to get back to my father—and my family—to let them know I'm okay."

I waved my hand. "It's fine. It'll only take a moment."

She pressed her lips tightly together and didn't say another word. Her father was definitely going to be furious, but once he heard everything we had gone through, I was certain he would understand. We had survived the abyssal hells, after all. How was that *not* impressive?

"Fine," Ashlyn said. "But please make it quick."

In a display of sheer feline athleticism, Twain leapt from the bed to my shoulder. He clung to my cloak and purred. Of course I wasn't going to leave without him! I patted his head as I walked to the door. Hesitantly, and carefully, I opened it and glanced out.

The hallway was empty.

"No one's around," Twain whispered.

I slipped out of the room and closed the door. Then I hurried down the hall, though I slowed my pace when I realized I didn't know where I was going. A few cultists in white cloaks walked by. They were clearly in a hurry to get *somewhere*, but they bowed and offered me smiles as I went in the opposite direction.

I wondered where my original clothes were. They hadn't given them back to me when I asked to get dressed. All I had was the same bizarre white outfit everyone else had, even if mine was a tad bit fancier.

Hopefully they hadn't thrown my old clothes away—that would make retrieving the pendant far more difficult than I wanted.

The night sky beyond the windows was clear and bright, as though the moon wanted to be a second sun. That was fine by me—I wanted more light.

"So, uh, what're we looking for?" Twain twitched his whiskers. "Or did Deimos tell you some secret, and now we're going to do something crazy?"

"What? No. I just need—"

I turned the corner, to head down another hallway, when I

slammed into someone. I muttered apologies as I stumbled away, rubbing at my shoulder. "I'm in a hurry," I said.

Rosella stood in the hallway, her gaze searching mine. Her kappa eldrin, Rooks, was by her feet, but instead of being a scaly, slimy creepster, he was now dressed in a little vest with tiny matching pants.

That was odd.

Most people didn't dress their eldrin. If the mystical creature was humanoid in appearance, like erlkings, they tended to have their own clothes—they were really part of their body in some way. I had never given it much thought, because it wasn't a concern, but mystical creatures, while intelligent, seemed to favor nature over humans' focus on civilization and "decency."

"I'm so sorry, Death Lord Deimos," Rosella said with a bow of her head. "Forgive me. I should've been watching where I was going." When she stood straight, she smiled. "Does this mean you're rested and ready to speak with your brother? He's been waiting for you in the dining room for some time."

"Uh, not yet." I glanced over my shoulder, and then down the hallway.

When I sensed for magic around us, I felt the threads of several mystical creatures, more than I had before. Raaza's kitsune was near, and so was another manticore.

But none of them felt like they were in this hallway. They were all several floors above or below my current position.

I needed to learn to sense for arcanists and their mystical creatures more often. It was a useful tool at my disposal, but it was rarely my go-to method of scouting.

I shook away the distracting thoughts. "Rosella, when I arrived here at Lord Oto's compound, this vessel was wearing something unique." I patted the collar of my cloak. "It was wearing a necklace. Do you know where that is?"

Without missing a beat, Rosella reached deep within her cloak, and then produced Everett's necklace. In the low light of the hallway, I could tell the pendant was made of a darker metal, and it was engraved with both symbols and words. Unfortunately, the pendant was tarnished, and well-worn. It was difficult to make anything out, especially since I wasn't holding it.

"You kept this?" I asked as I reached for it.

Rosella held it away from me. "It bears the crest of the typhon beast—a symbol used by one of the old god-arcanists and his allies. Why would your vessel have something like this?"

"Why indeed?" Deimos asked through me, his mind more awake after I had visited the Twilight Gate.

I mulled over her question for only half a second before I held out my hand. "That isn't for you to know. *Give it to me.*"

That was probably what Deimos would've done. Right? He seemed only half-satisfied.

Rosella hesitated. With an unsteady hand, she placed the pendant in my palm. "R-Right, Death Lord. I apologize for asking too many questions."

I turned the pendant over in my fingers. Up close, the words read: *Dodger, Zelfree, Savior.* The picture was a multiheaded monster, like a hydra, just more intense. When I flipped the pendant over, there were faded words that seemed hand carved. They read: *A Promise Kept.*

"This creature here is a typhon beast?" I asked, pointing at the monster.

Rosella nodded.

Her little kappa straightened his vest and also nodded. "It's dead, though." His voice grated on my nerves.

I slipped the necklace back over my head. "That's fine. Dodger is the last name of a family, right? I know them." *It was Nasbit's last name.* I wasn't sure who the other two names referred to. "That's all I really needed, thanks." With that, I turned on my heel.

But Rosella leapt around me, her kappa keeping pace. She

held up a hand. "Wait. I must know—how long are souls in the abyssal hells before they move on? Please. Zahn only replies with cryptic statements. I must know. Is it too late? Is my son no longer in the abyssal hells?"

I half swallowed, my chest tight. She wanted to know about her dead son? Rosella seemed... young. She was an arcanist, though. She could have lived for centuries and kept her youthful appearance.

I didn't need to know.

"When did your son die?" I asked.

The kappa glanced up at me, his giant eyes squinted, his head tilting. But Rooks didn't say anything. All he offered was an incredulous stare.

Even Rosella acted uncomfortable with the way I asked the question. She rubbed her arms and then slowly shook her head. "He... died... four years ago. Four years, two months, twenty-one days, to be specific..."

Unfortunately, Deimos wasn't replying, even though he was awake and listening. This was his area of expertise, and while his thoughts occasionally bled into mine, this wasn't one of those moments.

"I was told that if you and your brother opened the abyssal hells, my reward would be to see him." Rosella took my hand, her palms sweaty. "Please. T-Tell me it isn't too late. Will I be able to speak to my son? I'd do anything to speak with him. Even if just for a few moments."

"The abyssal hells are complicated." I stepped around her. "But if you help me, I'll do everything in my power to reunite you with the parts of your son that can communicate." I patted her shoulder. "Now, I need to study this necklace. In my room. Alone."

Rosella hardened her gaze as I turned down the hallway.

Her eldrin took a couple steps toward me, but didn't give chase. I left them as I hurried down the hallway, my chest still aching. I didn't know why, but the thought of Rosella wanting to speak with her dead son agitated me.

"*Deimos*," I hissed under my breath.

"Mortals don't address me with such disrespect," Deimos said through me, his words curt. "Count yourself among the lucky. If I could stop you from calling my name, I would."

"Stop being grumpy," I said, playfully sarcastic.

Twain snickered. "Now he *really* wants you to stop calling his name."

"How long are souls in the abyssal hells before they head on?" I asked. "You heard all that with Rosella. Why didn't you answer her?"

"Because it depends," Deimos stated. "If they are to be reincarnated, it can take years. If they are shuffled down to the fifth abyss, it will be swift. A matter of hours or days."

I rubbed my chest as I walked. "You wouldn't throw children into the fifth abyss, would you?"

"Feh. Of course not. Only the souls of the vile and corrupt —those who have urges and yearnings not suited for reincarnation. Babes have none of those taints that make them unsuitable."

I took an easy breath. It seemed Rosella had a chance, then. I didn't know how old her son was when he died, but it seemed he would still be in the abyssal hells. Well, a part of him. I wasn't sure she could speak to him, though. Those motes of light in the Wraithborne Orchard didn't seem like they could speak much outside of vague whispers.

"Do you want to help Rosella?" Twain whispered.

"I..." Then I shrugged. "I don't know Rosella, but she makes me think of my own mother."

"Oh."

"So I guess... I want to help her. Yeah."

Obviously, it was too late for me to see my own mother.

Deimos had said her soul wasn't in the abyssal hells anymore... But maybe Rosella could speak with her son.

I would like that.

"You want to help her, too. Right, Deimos?" I had asked the question in a quiet voice, so my words wouldn't echo far down the long hallways that were the veins of Lord Oto's compound.

"She's a *kappa* arcanist," Deimos muttered through me. "I have reservations on this matter that I don't wish to discuss. However, in general, I am lenient with individuals who wish to see their parents, or their children. If I can, I will help."

I shrugged as I made it back to the door. "Good. I'm glad we're of one mind about this."

"We are *never* of one mind on *anything*."

He sounded irritated, but at the same time, rather resigned to this fate.

Once I made it back to the room, I quietly opened the door and slipped back inside. Ashlyn and Ecrib were by the window, ready to go. Ashlyn lit up when she saw me.

"That was fast," she said.

I pointed to the necklace. "Remember when we were in the abyssal hells? And there was this elder creature thing who helped us? He gave me this necklace, and asked me to relay a message to his family."

"So you took advice from a monster in the abyssal hells?" Ashlyn sarcastically lifted an eyebrow. "Am I hearing that correctly? The monster you found in the bushes?"

"It was the woods," I corrected. "The Silkshade Grove, to be precise." Then I pointed at her. "I don't appreciate that snark, young lady."

Ashlyn lowered my hand with her own. Then, smiling, she said, "You better get used to it, Gray Lexly."

With a chuckle, I headed to the window. "The necklace is my bush-monster buddy's, okay? I have to find his family and let them know he's okay." I stopped and half shrugged. "Well, I'll let them know he's alive. I doubt *okay* is the proper word for his state."

"He's beyond twisted," Deimos said through me, his deadpan voice sending a shiver down my spine.

Ashlyn heard the same statement and met my gaze for a long time. She said nothing, but I understood her glances more than anyone. She was concerned now, and if I was going to help the man, she would aid me in that task—to an extent.

I glanced outside.

We were a little way up from the ground below. Maybe a story and a half? An awkward height, but not impossible to jump.

Ashlyn walked around me, flashing me a confident smirk as she went.

She slipped out the window and landed in a beautiful garden bush with all the poise of a dancer. Then Ashlyn stepped out, no leaves or twigs on her clothing, her blonde hair still perfect. How did she do that?

"*Are you coming?*" she mouthed.

I scoffed and smiled.

Not to be outdone, I also leapt out the window. Twain dug his claws into my shoulder as I hit the bush, but instead of stepping out, I instinctively tumbled forward with my momentum. Twain didn't hang on through that, though.

I exited the shrub on my feet, and lunged forward like I was on the offense. Ashlyn flinched back, startled by my sudden emergence.

Twain puffed up like a rising bread loaf, his orange fur sticking in all directions. Then he calmed down, frowned at me, and then leapt back to my shoulder, clearly indignant.

I was covered in leaves, and hadn't landed as graceful as Ashlyn, but I figured I had still done an impressive job.

"*You like that?*" I mouthed to Ashlyn, trying to stay as quiet as possible.

She playfully rolled her eyes—but I also caught her genuinely smiling.

Then Ecrib went next. He practically crushed that shrub with his size. Fortunately, he was slender enough to retain some grace. Like Ashlyn, Ecrib slipped out of the foliage without many leaves on his blue scales.

Moonlight cascaded over the rest of the garden, highlighting the white flowers and illuminating the fountains. It was magnificent, and I wasn't even a person who liked gardens. Not too far from our location was the wall surrounding the compound, which was fortunate.

I glanced at Twain. "Are there any creatures nearby we can use to get out of here quicker?" I whispered.

He huffed. "I don't know. Like what?"

Again, I sensed the threads of magic.

An abyssal dragon. No—it could fly, but everyone and their sister would see it and know something was wrong. We'd get caught.

A soul catcher? No. That was creepy and wouldn't help us escape.

A sea serpent and a humanoid sea creature... both of which I didn't have names for. The sea serpent was Jacinto's eldrin, though. I knew that much. It had ice. That wouldn't help.

Three manticores...

A manticore had wings, and they were strong. *Really* strong. And they flew. We could use that. So I tugged on the magical thread.

Twain shifted on my shoulder. I grabbed him and quickly placed him on the ground as he bubbled outward, becoming larger and larger, but still retaining his feline form. Wings burst from his body, and so did a tail.

My arcanist mark burned as I assumed the role of a manticore arcanist.

Then Twain fully formed.

He was as fearsome as the darkest night, and I took a step backward just to admire everything he had become. Manticores had the body of a lion, complete with tawny fur and puffy dark manes. Their claws were massive, and leathery bat wings sprouted from their back. A black scorpion tail—gigantic and deadly—curled up and over the back of the beast, the stinger large enough to take a man's head off.

Twain had the face of a lion, but I saw through all that to his personality deep in his eyes. He preened a bit, holding his head up like he was proud of his new body.

"Intimidated?" Twain asked, his voice deep and guttural.

Ashlyn rubbed her chin. Then she walked all the way around him, glancing up and down his new body. "I think this is a good look for you, Twain."

Ecrib snorted. "He can't swim. I hate it."

Twain shot Ecrib a glare. "You're just jealous because *I* can fly."

"Heh. Creatures that grow tired in the air can always land. Creatures that grow tired in the water? They drown."

"The depths of the ocean are perilous, and those without a means to deal with them always perish," Deimos chimed in through me—like he was just having a great time with friends. I gritted my teeth, almost irritated he was part of this conversation.

"You're supposed to have *my* side," Twain growled.

I shrugged. "Deimos loves the water, what can I say." Then I pointed at Ecrib. "You know where swimming doesn't help?" I motioned to our surroundings. "A weird desert town. So, everyone, pack away your ego—I know that's gonna be hard for some of us—and let's head for the wall, okay?"

Everyone muttered agreements.

Unfortunately, Twain wasn't big enough to carry all of us. That was a shame, but also probably for the best. Ecrib didn't look like he wanted to be carried at the moment. He was frowning, and offering my eldrin a competitive glare.

I grabbed one of Twain's new wings, and I hoisted myself onto his muscular back. Not only was he strong, but yanking my weight upward was actually quite easy. My own strength had increased, and I smiled in appreciation.

"Twain and I will fly to the wall. Meet us over there?"

Ashlyn nodded.

With a few powerful wingbeats, Twain took to the air. The garden rustled beneath us as we flew over to the wall. It was a short flight, but epic nonetheless. The feeling of the wind rushing by my head never got old.

I didn't look down, though.

No. I hated being up high. I just kept my eyes closed the whole time, my heart rate accelerating.

"You shouldn't fear falling," Deimos said through me.

"Don't tell me what I can and can't be afraid of," I muttered under my breath. "*You* wouldn't understand. You apparently can't die. There's a lot more at stake for me, okay?"

Deimos responded with some sort of growl that rumbled through my chest. His feelings on the matter seemed scattered. Something about not wanting to be controlled by fear, but also about how I should be *harnessing it*. He was difficult to understand sometimes.

Once Twain hit the wall, his claws dug into the stone. Then he growled as he perched himself on the edge, his scorpion tail curling up and above me.

Ashlyn and Ecrib made their way slowly through the shrubs.

"Hello?"

The shout startled me.

I tensed as I glanced around.

"You, up there!"

It was the voice of a young girl, not a guard. Who was yelling at me? I glanced down—outside Oto's compound—and spotted

194

a ratty little street urchin staring up at me. Her white dress was dirty, her shoes were scuffed, and her skin marred by scrapes. But her hair... it practically glowed with an otherworldly luster under the stray beams of moonlight.

Her amber eyes were wet with tears.

"Can you help me?" she called out, staring right at me.

I pointed to myself.

"Please," the little girl said. "I need help. I can't find my brother. He has our mom's medicine, and he went to see Lord Oto, but he never returned."

The girl's beautiful black hair was loose, and with a shaky hand she pushed it out of her tear-stained face. How old was she? Ten?

I didn't know what to say.

"If my mom doesn't get her medicine, she'll die. Please—I need to find my brother!"

Chapter 25

For The Family

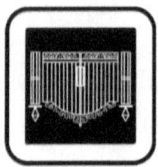

Ashlyn and Ecrib leapt up onto the wall next to Twain and me. I caught my breath, startled by their appearance, but relieved they were here.

"Please," the little girl called up. "I need help! Have you seen my brother?"

Ashlyn patted the scales of her dragon eldrin. She gave the girl an odd look. "Who is that?" she whispered.

"I don't know," I replied in a soft voice. "But she's obviously scared. And her mother needs medicine..." I exhaled and then called down, "What's your brother's name?"

"Raaza." The girl wiped tears from the corners of her eyes. "He hasn't r-returned. Can you please find him?"

Damn.

My heart sank into my gut. Raaza? Her brother was *Raaza*? Was that why he had been so eager to get out of the compound? Raaza had *medicine* on him? Why hadn't he just said something if that were the case? He could've told me, but instead, he had kept quiet.

I would've helped him if his mother was sick.

By the abyssal hells—*Death Lord Deimos* would've helped

him if he had a sad sob story about his mother. Why hadn't Raaza said something?

"I saw your brother," I called down to the girl. "But he's tied up at the moment."

My own joke almost made me laugh. Twain *did* laugh. He chuckled, his deep manticore voice almost making him sound sadistic. Ashlyn gave both me and Twain half a squint, indicating she didn't appreciate the joke.

"Our mom... She'll die..." The girl rubbed her face with the heels of her palms. "I... I don't know what to do. Please help. If Mom dies... I'll be all alone..."

Damn. Why was everyone's mother in danger? My chest hurt just thinking about it.

Anger and regret mixed in my veins in equal amounts. Ashlyn must've known everything I was thinking because she crossed her arms and hardened her gaze.

"*We could easily find Raaza,*" Ashlyn mouthed, no audible component to her words, yet I understood all the same.

"*I know,*" I replied in similar fashion.

"*You don't have to forgive him. We could just get the medicine from him and take it to his mother on his behalf.*"

That was a good point.

Ashlyn glanced down at the girl. "What's your name?"

"My name's Emma." She rubbed her wet cheeks.

"What kind of medicine does your mother need? Maybe there's a doctor in town."

Emma shook her head. "N-No one can help... Lord Oto is the only one who has the medicine Mom needs. Lord Oto says it's magical."

A part of me wanted to head over to Raaza's mother and heal her myself. But... what eldrin could heal illnesses? I slid off Twain and stared at his lion-like face. What nearby creatures could heal? If Twain could transform into one, we'd be set.

"Isn't Lord Oto a blue phoenix arcanist?" I crossed my arms. "We can just go heal Raaza's mother with that magic."

Ashlyn, still on the back of her eldrin, offered a disapproving glower. "Did you not pay attention in class? Blue phoenixes don't heal. They just burn things. And make magical items."

"They don't heal *at all*?" I balked.

She slowly shook her head, along with Ecrib, like I should've known this and they were both disappointed.

Perhaps I had slept through that portion of class. But if that was the case, there really weren't any nearby creatures that could heal. Manticores couldn't mend others—neither could sea serpents or kappas.

It seemed, if we wanted to help, we'd have to physically get whatever kind of medicine Raaza had on his person.

"Fine," I said through clenched teeth.

Then I turned my attention to the girl on the other side of the wall. Emma had dried her tears, but her brow was still furrowed, her expression still twisted in concern. "I'll go see if I can find your brother."

Emma nodded along with my words, her gaze becoming a tiny bit more hopeful. Although I wasn't particularly happy with Raaza, I hated the thought of someone's mother being in distress.

Ecrib snorted. "Let me guess—we're sneaking back across the garden?"

Twain, in his manticore form, snarled out a laugh. "I bet you wish you could fly now."

The two of them narrowed their eyes into challenging glares. I patted Twain on the side, pulled myself onto his back, and then motioned him to fly back to the compound. When I glanced over at Ashlyn, I was going to tell her just to wait for me, but it was obvious she didn't want to do that.

Ashlyn urged Ecrib back, and together, we crossed the garden. Did Ashlyn just want to stay close to my side?

I felt better knowing she did.

"There are few mystical creatures that can cure chronic ailments," Deimos said through me as I rode on Twain over the garden.

"What are *chronic ailments?*" I asked.

"Failing lungs. A weak heart. Diseases that eat you from the inside out. *Most* mystical creatures who heal, only heal *damage.* Cuts. Tears. Scrapes. They don't strengthen your dying heart, or turn back the clock on entropy and old age."

"What're you getting at?" I asked as Twain landed on the windowsill.

My eldrin carefully hopped down into the room.

Deimos's irritation was rising. When he spoke through me, it was with more bite in his words. "I'm saying your *medicine* might be a ruse. In fact, I suspect if this woman needs to continually take medicine, it's actually more a temporary relief to an ongoing pain that was never meant to be healed in the first place."

"Oh, you're a detective now."

Twain transformed back into his kitten form. When he turned to face me, his two-colored eyes were huge, and his smile even bigger. "I love being a detective."

"Look, we need to leave," I said, waving a hand down. "*Not* do things here. We're helping Raaza's mother, and then we're going."

Ashlyn and Ecrib climbed back inside. I was surprised how well they kept up with us. Then we crept over to my door. Ecrib hung back and sighed. He knew he was too big to go stomping around the compound.

The rest of us slipped into the hallway.

"For the record," Ashlyn whispered, "I think this is the right thing to do."

I held up a finger. "If we keep going back and forth through

Oto's house, we're definitely going to get caught by someone. One hundred percent, no doubt in my mind."

"Going back once to find Raaza isn't *that* risky. We can do it."

I huffed as we headed down the hallway. When we came to a T-intersection, Twain leapt onto my shoulder. I patted his head, trying to determine which way to go.

"What's the plan?" Twain whispered to me.

I closed my eyes and tapped the side of my head. "Magic."

The threads of magic were invisible gossamer strings connected to each creature. When I sensed them, they appeared in my imagination, like ghostly threads dangling in the air. They pointed in the direction of specific creatures, so I focused until I found one that led to a kitsune.

Raaza.

There he was. He was beneath us.

I glanced down one hall, and then the other. A stairway that led to the lower levels caught my eye. I pointed to it and then motioned with a jut of my chin. "There."

Ashlyn followed the point of my finger with her eyes. "How do you know?"

"I'm a mimic arcanist," I whispered. "The best kind of arcanist, because I can detect magic. And Raaza's magic is below us."

"Hardly *the best*." Ashlyn playfully threw back some of her golden hair. "Were you also sleeping through the class about god-arcanists?"

"Pfft." I waved my hand. "They all died or something after the war, right? I'm still here."

Deimos's irritation was present in my mind, but I ignored him, too.

"The god-arcanists didn't all die." Ashlyn shook her head. "We met the Warlord of Magic, remember? He was one. He's still alive."

"Right. But he's not a god-arcanist anymore. All the *god creatures* died, so their arcanists had to bond with new creatures, making them *normal* arcanists."

Ashlyn huffed. "Extremely talented normal arcanists."

"Good news—we're definitely not going to meet a former god-arcanist out in the willy-wags. This place probably isn't even on the map. No one visits the Nation of Sellix. We're fine, this is fine, everything is fine."

That made her chuckle, which was all I was going for. She rolled her eyes, and then we hurried to the stairs and headed downward. The entire way, I marveled at the plush rugs, the detailed paintings, and the many glowstone chandeliers Lord Oto seemed to collect.

When we reached the lower floors, I realized we had gone underground. There were no windows—just oil paintings of vast landscapes to make up for the fact you couldn't see the sky. The whole lower portion of the compound felt like a luxurious prison, if only because most of the doors had large and noticeable locks made of shiny brass.

It was also strange to me how no one was around. Ashlyn and I were sneaking, but it almost seemed unnecessary. Where was everyone?

Then again, why would they be patrolling? This was a walled compound with several powerful arcanists. Not only that, but they also thought they had a Death Lord on their side. In their minds, anyone who snuck into the compound would instantly regret it. So, it was probably silly for us to be skulking about—I only needed to avoid people because I didn't want them asking me too many questions.

And it wasn't like there were many people to avoid. How many people were here? Less than a dozen.

I stood a little straighter as I walked the long hall, my focus on the magical thread that led to the kitsune. We grew closer and closer until we came upon a door that looked exactly like the rest. It had a large brass handle, and a lock the size of my fist. When I grabbed the handle, I realized it wasn't locked, which amused me, but was only in line with all my theories.

No one here was worried about someone sneaking into the place.

The instant I glanced into the room, I realized why they weren't worried about Raaza leaving, either.

He was fast asleep on a plain white bed—the soul catcher magic wrapped around his mind and forcing him to slumber. Miko, his foxy kitsune, was curled up inside a brass cage set at the foot of the bed. The flames on her paws continued to flicker, and were reflected in the shiny metal bars.

I crept inside. Raaza was still dressed—and his clothing still dirty from our battle. There was no need to wake him. I hadn't forgiven him for what he had done, even if I was here to help his family.

With a sigh, I rummaged through his coat.

To my surprise, Raaza had a lot on him. Coins. Papers. A small book that seemed to be some sort of manual for crafting wooden objects. A key. And also, a small vial of sparkling orange liquid.

"This has to be it," I whispered.

Twain wiggled his nose as he sniffed the cork stopper at the top of the small vial. "Smells good." Then he turned to me. "We aren't going to wake him?"

"Why would I?"

Twain didn't reply after that. Which was good, because I didn't want to discuss it anymore. Instead, I took the vial of liquid, backed out of the room, and quietly shut the door. I flashed the vial to Ashlyn, who nodded and then gestured down the hallway.

This was going so smoothly. I took it as a good omen. Maybe all the luck in the world *wanted* me to succeed. I wished my brother were here—he would find it interesting.

Ashlyn held my arm as we rounded a corner, and I tried not to dwell on her touch. Ever since our time in the abyssal hells, I felt closer to her. Maybe it was all the danger we had been in. Or maybe she just looked more beautiful at night, when the moonlight gave her an otherworldly glow.

Something.

She glanced over at me as we climbed the stairs side-by-side. "Are you okay?"

"What? Yeah. Obviously."

"You've been quiet."

I gave her a sarcastic glance. "We *are* sneaking."

Ashlyn stifled another chuckle. When we made it back to the main hallway to my bedroom, I was still shocked we hadn't seen a single person.

Were they... all together somewhere? I was starting to worry, actually. Like perhaps we were missing some important detail.

Ashlyn and I slipped back into my room. Ecrib was there, poised to attack with his scales flared, and his fangs ready. Thankfully, he relaxed.

"You found the medicine?" he asked.

Twain nodded. "Thanks to my mimic magic."

"Heh."

None of us wanted to wait any longer. Twain transformed into a manticore, and we flew out of the room. Ashlyn and Ecrib crossed the garden with lightning speed. As we went, I examined the vial. The orange liquid was thicker than water. More like a syrup. What was it?

"Do you know what this is made out of, Deimos?" I asked.

He replied through me, though I could tell he didn't much care to. "I have no idea. I'm a master of souls, not snake oil. I stand by my assessment. It's likely not a real type of medicine."

Twain hit the wall and then used his scorpion tail to stop his momentum. Then I glanced over and found Emma just waiting, her eyes hopeful.

"I found Raaza," I called down. "He gave me your medicine." I held it up so the moonlight glinted off the orange liquid.

Emma's bright smile rivaled the sun. She clasped her hands together. "Thank you! Thank you." Then she stared for a long moment. "Where's my brother? He didn't come with you?"

"He's busy with Lord Oto's business."

"O-Oh." Emma nodded once. "Then... can you please come with me? To deliver the medicine?"

I was about to drop the vial down to her. Instead, I lifted an eyebrow. "Why do you need me?"

"There's a bounty hunter in town." The girl fidgeted with her dirty dress. "Raaza would've taken care of me, but without him..." Emma glanced around. The dark streets seemed shadier than before. When she returned her attention to me, her voice was quiet. "I'm scared."

A bounty hunter? Was there a criminal in town? I wondered who they would be after.

Twain growled. "I told you we should've woken Raaza."

Ashlyn and Ecrib finally leapt up the wall to me, Ecrib's claws digging into the stone as he hoisted himself into a sitting position. Then Ashlyn glanced between me and the girl.

"What's wrong?"

"We're going to deliver the vial ourselves," I muttered. "*Then* we'll get out of here and return to Astra Academy."

No more detours.

CHAPTER 26

ROT BLOSSOMS

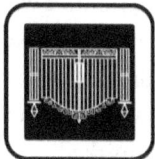

Manticore-Twain leapt from the wall, taking me with him. I held on to the long fur of his mane, trying not to look at the ground as we quickly approached it. Something about falling always made my stomach flip.

When Twain hit the ground, Emma flinched backward, her face twisted in fright.

She was small, even for a ten-year-old.

I patted Twain on the side and then slid off him. "Don't worry." I offered her a reassuring smile. "My eldrin isn't scary. He just likes to pretend."

Twain reverted to his cat form, his body shifting and shimmering until it twisted into the cute little kitten I had come to know and love. With his bobtail flicking, and giant ears, he trotted over to me, his nose in the air.

"I'm a professional pretender, thank you very much," Twain said with a fake snobbish tone.

Ashlyn and Ecrib leapt off the wall. The typhoon dragon landed with an elegant twist, and Ashlyn rolled into a standing position after her jump. She was so... athletic.

And she must've noticed me staring, but she gave me a playful smile afterward.

"This way. Hurry." Emma turned and hustled down the road. She never glanced over her shoulder to see if we were following, and I wondered if the bounty hunter was just that spooky. The town's denizens didn't want to be involved.

I quickened my step and followed Emma at a distance, my attention on our surroundings. Twain ran beside me, his padded feet as silent as any cat's. When he noticed me staring, he twitched his whiskers and smirked.

"I'm a big boy now," Twain said with a slight purr. "I can keep up!"

With a chuckle, I nodded.

We ran along the cobblestone road that led deeper into town. The place was a veritable paradise—if the paradise included *creative destitution*. The place was a hovel of half-ruined houses and broken roads. Beyond the town was a dirty beach and a broken harbor.

Ashlyn ran to my side and then matched my pace. She glanced around, her brow furrowed. "What is this?"

"Well," I said as I jogged, careful not to go faster than the little girl, "if you glance to your left, you'll see a collection of quaint shanties. And if you turn your attention to the right, you'll see some charmingly dilapidated fisherman huts."

Ashlyn snorted back a laugh and then squinted at me. "Are you ever *not* sarcastic? I meant, what town is this? Did you get the name?"

"This is Waxing City," Emma said over her shoulder. She had grown tired and slowed her gait to a simple walk. After a few deep breaths, she said, "But so many people moved away, Mom says it's not a city anymore."

It really wasn't.

Calling it a *town* would be generous.

As we turned down a street it occurred to me the *only* place here that looked to be in proper condition was Lord Oto's compound. The compound's stone walls were beautiful, and the trees growing in his courtyard reached up into the sky with leaf-covered branches.

There weren't many plants in Waxing City outside of Lord Oto's property. Most of the trees were dead, and the shrubs seemed to be actively dying.

Emma took us down one more broken cobblestone road before she stopped in front of a shack with a roof patched with what one could only hope was waterproof material. The walls were thin, and the windows stained with so much smoke residue, it was impossible to see through them.

Black flowers grew around the outside, and dozens of flies swarmed the petals. When I stepped closer to them, a scent of death went straight up my nostrils.

I flinched away, my teeth gritted. "What is that?"

"Those are *rot blossoms*," Deimos said through me.

Emma ran to the door of the stinky shack. She glanced at the smelly black flowers. "They keep the flies from getting inside," she muttered.

Sure enough, the stink of the flowers attracted flies, keeping them from flying into any buildings. They buzzed around the black petals in groups of ten to twenty, moving as though in a flock. They were like bizarre bees that occasionally landed on the rot blossoms and rolled through the pollen.

Twain snorted and sneezed three times in a row, obviously hating the smell as much as I was. He backed away from the dilapidated little home, his orange fur puffed. "I'll, uh, wait out here."

Ashlyn motioned for Ecrib to do the same. Then she walked to my side, her nose wrinkled in disgust. "Let's do this quickly," she whispered.

I nodded and then followed Emma, my gaze lingering on the bizarre flowers as I walked by. They were magical, that much was certain. Something about the scent put me on edge. It wasn't the *rot*, it was the intensity of the decay smell. It was as if a single rot blossom held three whole dead bodies inside its stem.

"Once, they only grew in the abyssal hells," Deimos said. "They were a gift from the first Death Lords to arcanists in the land of the living. Rot blossoms are sacred."

"They don't smell sacred," I muttered.

Emma held the door open, and Ashlyn and I stepped inside.

I glanced around and almost regretted it. The walls, artistically adorned with an array of holes and cracks, offered a rustic charm that only a lifetime of neglect could provide. The floor was made up of uneven wooden planks that creaked with my every step.

I didn't know why, but it sent a shiver up my spine.

The home was clearly one large kitchen space and two bedrooms. That was it. The table in the middle of the kitchen had seen better days, and the stains across the top told me they did their own butchering—but didn't have the tools for proper cleaning.

At least the inside didn't smell of death. There were no rot blossoms here.

"Wait," Ashlyn said as she also examined our surroundings. "Did Raaza live here?"

Emma stopped next to the grimy table. She nodded once. "We lived here together. But Raaza went to work for Lord Oto so he could pay for Mom's medicine. Lord Oto makes him do all sorts of things. And then he sent Raaza to Astra Academy."

"Sent to Astra Academy?"

Emma nodded.

I caught my breath, the reality of the situation slowly seeping into my thoughts.

Lord Oto had sent Raaza to Astra Academy?

"He's being manipulated," Deimos said through me. "Blackmailed."

Emma said nothing, but Ashlyn met my gaze, her expression shifting to realization.

Deimos was right. Raaza had been blackmailed into betraying Astra Academy. I should've seen this coming. Was *that* why Raaza hadn't talked to me? He was ashamed of what he had done? Even if it was to help his family... He probably hated himself for being beholden to someone like Lord Oto.

When I turned my attention to my surroundings this time, everything felt dirtier. Raaza had *lived* here. In this... dump. And then he had sold himself to Lord Oto for his family.

No wonder he was always talking about *power* and how to get stronger than ever. I'd want that too, if I were him.

Another part of me—the part of my heart that ached whenever I examined all my old and childish behaviors—remembered when I complained about living on my poor little island.

But the Isle of Haylin was *way* better than this. Sorin and I had grown up with our own rooms, in a house that was clean and had food, with a loving father, and even a stepmother who had been there for us.

Raaza and his sister...

Didn't have any of that.

Funny, how easy it was to take beautiful gifts for granted...

I grabbed my silk shirt and twisted my fingers into the fabric, my chest hurting at the mere thought.

Death Lord Deimos's thoughts bled into mine, mixing with all my realizations. He, too, had lived a hard and difficult life. He had made terrible choices, and one memory filtered into mine, like it was secretly mine all along.

A memory of... stealing food for Zahn, who had become ill. They had lived in a dark alleyway, with other children, where most were sent to work for soldiers who fought on the front lines. Deimos remembered every second of those dark days, keeping them close to his heart, hating the struggle, but allowing it to fuel him...

I wondered if Raaza did that, too.

Why hadn't Raaza just told me? I knew he couldn't tell me while we were attending the Academy together, but why didn't he say something in the hallway in Lord Oto's mansion?

But shame really did keep some people quiet. I never told people about my days as a mere candlemaker's son, because I thought they would look down on me for it.

"Where's your mother?" Ashlyn gently asked Emma, her tone comforting.

Emma motioned to the left room. Then she held a finger to her lips. We nodded and followed her to the bedroom as quietly as the squeaky floor would allow us.

Her mother's room was dark. Heavy curtains were pulled over all the windows, and a thick scent of musk and sweat hung on the air. I pulled the vial of orange liquid from my pocket and crept into the shadows.

While I entered, Ashlyn stayed behind, waiting in the doorway, her arms crossed.

Emma stopped near a bed.

The mattress was perfectly contoured to fit the form of the older woman resting on top of it. She was emaciated—a skeleton with skin stretched taut—with wispy hair and deep lines that started at the edges of her lips.

"Mom needs her medicine," Emma whispered. She held out her hand to take it from me.

I gave her the vial, my arm stiff. The little girl gently woke her mother with a few shakes of the woman's shoulders. When Raaza's mom opened her eyes, it was obvious she couldn't see more than an inch away from her face.

"Em?" the woman rasped.

"Good morning," Emma muttered. "Raaza got your medicine for you. Here it is."

"Oh, Raaza." The woman glanced over at me, her milky eyes never really focusing. "Thank you. What a good son you are. Thank you."

She thought *I* was her son. I said nothing.

Emma didn't reveal my true identity, either. She simply opened the vial and carefully poured the contents into her mother's mouth. With a forced smile, she rubbed her mother's arm. "You're gonna feel better now."

"I need... something to eat," her mother replied.

"Lord Oto's men will bring us more food tomorrow. We have to go to sleep now, so we aren't hungry for too long, okay?"

Raaza's mother closed her eyes. "Thank you," she murmured again.

I wondered how lucid she was.

Emma grabbed the sleeve of my cloak and took me from the room. Ashlyn stepped aside, and once we were all back in the disgusting kitchen, she closed the bedroom door.

With silent tears streaming down her face, Emma looked at me. "Thank you. But... But could you please find Raaza and tell him to visit? I... I want to see him. I don't have anyone else."

I had never felt so terrible in my life. Every word she spoke was like a knife straight into my chest. The only reason Raaza wasn't here was because I had him locked away in Lord Oto's compound.

He shouldn't have betrayed us. I stood by that statement.

But I didn't want him to suffer anymore. Clearly, Raaza had suffered for the majority of his life. What he needed was to turn things around—to tell Lord Oto where to shove all his blackmail. And if we could take Raaza's mother with us to Astra Academy, there was no doubt in my mind that Doc Tomas, the arcanist who ran the infirmary, could help her more than this orange syrup.

"You'd make for a soft Death Lord," Deimos whispered.

I shook my head and then glanced over at Emma. "I'll see what I can do about Raaza."

She sniffled, wiped her face, and then stiffened her quavering lip in order to give me a firm nod. "Thank you. For bringing the medicine."

"Don't worry about it."

I motioned for Ashlyn, and we exited Raaza's home. Once outside, my nose was assaulted by the fragrance of the rot blossoms. I almost gagged.

"These are sacred, huh?" I gritted my teeth. "I hate them."

"They only smell this way when someone nearby is close to death," Deimos said. "Otherwise, they have no fragrance."

Hm.

Well, now everything made sense.

Holding back my vomit, I walked with Ashlyn all the way over to Twain and Ecrib, who had taken up a position across the road, away from the stench. Our eldrin rushed to our side as we approached.

I turned to Ashlyn.

She was a master at reading my expression, because it only took her half a second to harden her gaze. "You want to go *back* to Lord Oto's compound? *Again*?"

"I know, it's risky," I said. "But we have to."

"We've gone back and forth twice now."

"One more time won't kill us." I gestured to the shack, and then to Raaza's sister. "You can't tell me this isn't the right thing to do."

Ashlyn inhaled, and then exhaled. "We can come back for them."

"It would make way more sense for us to grab Raaza, then come here to collect his mother and sister. Once we get to the Academy, they'll be safe, and Raaza won't have to listen to Lord Oto anymore."

Ashlyn ran a hand down her face as she sighed. She clearly

wanted to get home to speak with her father, but this was far more important. We needed to get back to Astra Academy, but I absolutely refused to leave any more people behind.

We had already lost Nini, after all. She was still trapped in the abyssal hells.

And Knovak...

Well, part of me wanted to collect him now, but another part of me didn't know what to do with him. He had a monster of an eldrin now. Should we force the elder unicorn to accompany us back to the Academy? Or should we leave him here to train?

I wasn't sure what to do.

"All right," Ashlyn said with a groan. "Let's go back. *But we need to be quick*." She swung her arms out, gesturing to everything. "I don't want to get trapped here. This is one of the worst places I've ever been."

"Don't worry," I said as we headed down the street. "Everything will be fine! Trust me."

CHAPTER 27

THE BOUNTY HUNTER

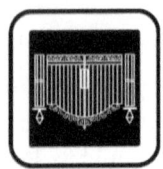

As we raced back to Lord Oto's compound, more of Deimos's memories filtered into my thoughts.

At first, I hadn't wanted to see them, but the more I saw, the more I understood.

Deimos really loved his mother—but she had been killed by Deimos's father. He never forgave the man. One memory that rolled through my thoughts was the night Deimos had gone to his father's palace. Deimos was an adult then. A warrior. He was there to be honored—to be brought back into his father's family —but once Deimos was officially accepted, he killed his father.

Decapitation.

There had been no forgiveness.

"If there was no mercy for my mother, then there was no mercy in my heart for that man," Deimos whispered through me.

Was he thinking back to all these memories? Was that why I was seeing all this?

And I also sensed his dislike for Waxing City.

In his memories, there were cities like this everywhere. No one was really in charge—just whoever had enough power to do whatever they wanted. Clearly, Waxing City wasn't answering to any higher authorities, so "Lord" Oto had seized control and now treated the other residents like they were his.

Was it his fault the city was in disrepair? No. It was the Nation of Sellix that was failing the people here. But that didn't mean Lord Oto wasn't making things worse. Everyone in town clearly had to work for him. Either that or starve.

And Death Lord Deimos *hated* that.

He hated anyone who tortured mothers or killed small children.

I felt the same way—either because his memories were now filtering into my own, or because I just generally hated anyone who picked on the less fortunate.

Once we reached the walls of Lord Oto's compound, Ashlyn turned to me. "Gray?"

"Yeah?" I whispered.

"You've been muttering to yourself a lot." She eyed me. "Are you speaking with Death Lord Deimos?"

"Uh, yeah, kinda." I shrugged. "I'm mostly just thinking."

"You look enraged."

I grazed my fingers over my face. "Do I? Sorry. I'm not feeling like myself lately."

She stared at me for a long minute. So did Ecrib. Were they concerned? I smiled and shook my head, hoping to dispel any lingering anger from my expression.

"Everything is good. Let's get Raaza and get out of here."

Once again, I transformed Twain into a manticore. He preened a bit, stretching his bat-like wings and even arching his back and curling his scorpion tail. Ecrib snorted a bit of lightning before scaling the wall with Ashlyn on his back.

"He's definitely jealous," Twain whispered with a smile, flashing his fangs.

I effortlessly pulled myself onto his back. Manticore arcanists had a lot of strength—Twain's new magic was flowing into me like water into an empty bowl. Enhanced stamina, increased fortitude—could I throw a boulder? I felt like I could throw a boulder.

Twain flew me over the wall and then across Oto's personal garden. Going back did seem silly, but this would be the final time, for sure. When we reached my room's open window, something felt different, though.

There was a new thread of magic nearby.

It was at the eastern side of the compound, near the front door. I hadn't... ever felt this thread of magic before. It was special and demanded my attention. Who was here? It intrigued me, though part of me suspected this wasn't good news.

As Ashlyn and Ecrib crawled through the window, I nervously grabbed her upper arm. "Someone is here," I whispered. "An arcanist. Someone... powerful."

"How can you tell?" she asked.

"I can feel their magic."

"Your mimic magic can detect the strength of someone's magic?"

I nodded.

Ashlyn stared into my eyes. Without saying a word, we had an entire conversation. She was worried. She wanted to leave now. But I narrowed my gaze, sticking with my original plan. We had to get Raaza out of here. Ashlyn didn't like taking that risk, but at the same time, an arrogant—perhaps *confident* was a better word—expression crossed her face.

We could do this.

I nodded once, and she replied in kind.

"You two sure are staring at each other for a long time," Twain said. "Are you gonna kiss or not?" he playfully added.

Ecrib growled before he said, "Now isn't the time for frivolity."

Ashlyn and I stepped away from each other, but her flushed

cheeks told me she liked the idea. So did I, to be frank, but Ecrib was probably wise. Now wasn't the time.

I ran to the door and then opened it a tiny amount. As though the universe wanted to lull me into a false sense of security, there still weren't any guards or servants around. The corridor was empty. We were free to go where we pleased.

"C'mon," I whispered.

Twain bubbled and shifted, transforming back into a stealthy cat. He bounded over to me, but halfway along, Ecrib scooped him up with his clawed hands. Then Ecrib placed Twain on top of his head, between the horns that sprouted from his skull.

"You sit here," Ecrib commanded.

Twain hung on, his nose twitching. "Your scales remind me of fish."

"I'm a *typhoon dragon*. Of course they're like fish."

"I love fish." Twain's pupils went large and circular.

Ecrib frowned but didn't say anything.

Once we were all by the door, I opened it wide and slipped into the empty hallway. Ashlyn stuck close to me as we headed back to the stairs and down to the subterranean level. We already knew where Raaza was—grabbing him and leaving would be a breeze.

Ecrib hurried along behind us, but he wasn't as fast when he was trying to stay quiet. Twain remained on his head, like a little orange hat. His big ears made it look like Ecrib actually had large fluffy ears—which was rather cute.

As Ashlyn and I exited the stairway, I glanced over. "Why is your eldrin holding mine? Weird, right?"

"As we were crossing the garden, I told Ecrib he needed to be better friends with Twain." Ashlyn eyed me. "I just thought it would make things easier in the long run."

Oh. I hadn't thought of that.

They were good friends already, weren't they? Or maybe

rivals, a little. Either way, they got along fine. Everything would work out.

"My mother has a theory about two arcanists' compatibility," Ashlyn said as we headed for Raaza's room. "My mother has told me for years that arcanists won't get along if their eldrin come from two different places."

"Places?" I asked, confused.

"If one eldrin lives in the ocean, and the other prefers the sky, then their arcanists won't be compatible." Ashlyn rolled her eyes. "It's just superstition. But just in case it's not..."

"My father believes in omens, so don't worry, I totally understand." When I smirked, I added, "And Twain can swim when he wants. I think you worry too much about this."

We slowed our walk and stood in front of Raaza's door. Ashlyn glowered at me.

"I bet you'd think about it more if it was all your parents ever talked to you about," she whispered. "Trust me. I've had countless speeches about who I should marry to bring into the Kross family—I sometimes dream about it."

"Well, if they're dreams about me, they're probably good ones, right?"

Ashlyn chuckled, but she didn't answer me. Instead, she shoved open the door and motioned for me to go inside. I did as she wanted. I went straight to Raaza's bed. His kitsune eldrin was asleep in her cage, but I went to him first. His breaths were even, and his chest rose and fell in a gentle rhythm. He was perfectly asleep.

So I slapped him. Hard. Across the cheek.

That was for betraying us.

"Raaza," I hissed into his ear. "*Get up.*"

But he wouldn't wake without the aid of magic, so I sighed and had Twain transform into the soul catcher once more. I used that creature's magic to break the hold on Raaza and his kitsune, though Miko didn't wake right away.

Raaza's cheek, on the other hand, was still red.

He stirred, but sluggishly. Raaza blinked back his grogginess and then stared up at me in utter bewilderment.

"Gray?" he croaked. "What're you doing in my house?"

"You don't remember us getting married?" I asked in a sarcastically sweet tone.

"*W-What*?" Raaza bolted out of bed, nearly panicked. He was about to say something else, but then he managed to get a good look at our surroundings. His expression shifted from confusion to despair. "We're still in Lord Oto's compound?"

"Yeah. Now come on—we have to go." I hurried over to the door and motioned for him to follow.

"What?" Raaza flailed an arm around, his face growing red. "*You sent me here!* This is all your fault. What're you even doing?"

"Listen, I made a mistake." I gestured to the door a second time. "This is my way of apologizing." I held up a finger. "And I just want to point out that what I did is way less terrible than what you did, so let's call everything even, okay?"

Raaza was clearly stunned into silence. This whole situation seemed difficult for him to grasp. He had been sleeping pretty hard.

But we didn't have time for that. I pointed to Miko. "Grab your eldrin. Let's go. I'm not going to tell you again."

The thread of magic, the one that led to the new arcanist, returned to my thoughts. That arcanist and their eldrin were getting closer. Their magic felt *wild*. Almost unstable.

Who was here?

"Oh, no..." Raaza whispered.

He patted his clothing. He sifted through his robes, then shirt, and then pants. He searched every pocket, his movements becoming more and more frantic. With wide eyes, he glanced around. His attention lingered on Miko, his eldrin, but he didn't focus on her long. Instead, he knelt and investigated under his bed.

"Where is it? *Where is it?*" He stood and then checked all his pockets a second time, his hands shaky.

"We need to go," I whispered.

Death Lord Deimos's thoughts turned dark. "I know who's here," he said.

"Who is it?" I asked—talking to myself.

"He's died before. His soul crossed through the Twilight Gate, but then it was snatched away. A *true form phoenix* resurrected him after his death…"

I smiled. "Wow. He died once already? Sounds like a sad sack."

Deimos darkly chuckled. "We'll see about that…"

"I can't leave yet," Raaza murmured. He searched the bed, completely ignoring my conversation with Deimos. "I can't leave without it. I can't."

"Without what? Your medicine?"

Raaza froze in place. When he turned to face me, he was paler than ever. "Do you… Do you have it?"

It amused me to watch him squirm, so I hemmed and hawed as though I couldn't remember what had happened to the medicine. I even rubbed my chin and muttered a *hmmm*, my every action driving Raaza closer to the angriest I had ever seen him.

He stormed over and grabbed the edges of my white cloak. With barely restrained rage, he asked, "Where is it?"

"*Gray,*" Ashlyn snapped from outside the room. "Stop messing with him."

I exhaled and then shrugged. "Fine." I pushed myself out of Raaza's grasp. "Your sister told me everything. I gave the vial of medicine to your mother—and now I think your whole family should get out of here, okay? Lord Oto is busy. It's night. If we manage to get to Astra Academy, he can't use your family against you anymore."

Raaza caught his breath.

He stared into my eyes, as if searching for a lie. I didn't look away—he could search all he wanted.

"But why?" Raaza asked. "I thought... you hated me."

I half shrugged. "I don't know. Deimos doesn't like the thought of your mother suffering, so I guess I don't, either."

"The Death Lord?" Raaza's confusion came back in full force.

"Yeah. He has mommy issues." I waved my hand around, ignoring the intense hatred that shot through Deimos's thoughts. "It's a long story. Let's talk about it once we're safe back at the Academy."

A chill ran through the room.

Then the crackle of lightning seemed to spark through the air.

I glanced over at Ashlyn. She stared up at the ceiling, some of her blonde hair standing on end due to all the static. Ecrib's scales flared, and his fins fanned out to their full length. Twain was extra puffed, his eyes narrowed in a glare.

"What's going on?" Ecrib glanced around. "Someone here... is using magic. The lightning... It's almost overpowering."

No.

It was suffocating.

"This is someone's aura," Ashlyn whispered.

"Aura?" I asked with a chuckle. We hadn't really covered that subject much in class yet.

"It's when an arcanist is so talented with their magic, they push it from their body and fill the area around them with an effect." Ashlyn rubbed her arms, all the hairs on her body practically standing on end. "Thunderbird arcanists are known to have a *thunderclap aura*. Lightning answers their calls and destroys the area around them... This feeling... It reminds me of that."

"So a thunderbird arcanist is nearby?" I asked.

Ecrib shook his head. "No. This isn't a thunderclap aura. It's different."

Raaza pulled his eldrin out of her cage and gently shook her awake. Then he jogged over to my side. He sheepishly stared at the floor. "Thank you for coming to get me. And for... helping my mother."

"Don't thank me till we're out of here," I muttered.

Then it hit me.

I knew who was here, and why this aura was in effect.

"It's the bounty hunter," I said, breathless. "The bounty hunter is here in Lord Oto's compound."

CHAPTER 28

THE SOURCE OF THE STORM

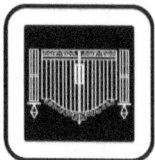

"The bounty hunter the little girl was complaining about?" Ecrib asked. He sneered enough to flash his fangs. "I doubt we have to worry about that. We've no bounties on our heads."

"Deimos says the bounty hunter once *died* and came back to life." I lifted both my eyebrows, trying to lighten the mood with some levity, but the others just stared at me as though I had given them the worst news of their life.

"Are you and Death Lord Deimos just... friends now?" Raaza rubbed his face with one hand. "Oh, by the good stars, I hope I'm still dreaming..." He hugged Miko close to his chest. She blinked her eyes several times, clearly groggy.

The crackle of power on the air made me wonder. Anyone flashing this amount of power was doing it for a reason—and that reason was intimidation.

"Do you think Headmaster Venrover sent a bounty hunter after all of us?" I motioned to the group. "Because we disappeared during an Academy function?"

Ashlyn rubbed her palms together. "That's a good theory." She walked over and patted her dragon eldrin until his scales calmed. "The bounty hunter would be here to make sure we safely returned. We've been gone for a while, but not too long to give up hope."

She was right. And now that we weren't in the abyssal hells, I was certain arcanists could use their magic to track us.

"Would the headmaster do that for a few missing students?" Raaza asked.

Ashlyn exhaled. "If he didn't, my father would have. At least for me. I could see him easily hiring a whole team of bounty hunters to find me."

"My arcanist?" Miko whispered. She opened her eyes fully, and the fire on her paws blazed a bit brighter.

"Everything is okay." Raaza patted his eldrin. "We're about to escape this place. Gray came back for us."

"But what about your mom? We haven't... We haven't given her the medicine yet." Miko yawned, her cute canine teeth a bright white that contrasted nicely with her red fox fur. "I'm awake! We can do it. I told you I'd support you no matter what!" She patted her cheeks with her forepaws.

"Gray took care of it."

Miko's eyes flew open. "H-He did?" When she glanced over, I offered a little wave.

Ashlyn yanked my arm, and I turned my full attention to her.

"We have to go." She hardened her gaze as she pulled me toward the door.

"Right," I muttered. The taste of electricity got worse. "But what if the bounty hunter *is* here for us? Should we go see him?"

"No. *Never.*"

Once we exited Raaza's room into the plain hallway, I jerked my arm from Ashlyn's grasp. "Why not? If he's here to take you to your father, wouldn't that make life easier? I'm sure he could take us all."

"Because if he was hired by my father—or by Headmaster

Venrover—and he drags me back, my father will take that to mean I was too weak to make it home myself. And I'm not *weak*. We can make it home without any of his help."

I half smiled as I nodded. "Hey, not only are we going to make it back to the Academy, but we're also going to show up with valuable information. Once everyone hears about the state of the abyssal hells, we'll be heroes."

"But that won't happen if the bounty hunter has to carry us like injured birds." Ashlyn pointed down the long hall. "Trust me. I know my father. That will be the exact term he uses."

Ecrib slid out of Raaza's room and walked alongside us. Twain was on his back again, his little orange body complementing the blue scales of the typhoon dragon.

"Should I turn into an injured bird?" Twain tilted his head. "Can I turn into normal animals? Hm. I don't think I can..."

"Just mystical creatures and magical items," I muttered. "And I don't want to be a *sad-sack bird arcanist*."

Once Raaza and his kitsune were with us, we hurried down the hallway. Then we took the stairs as fast as we could. Unfortunately, cracks of lightning sparked through the air, even as we headed for the ground floor.

When I reached for the handle of the door, a *zap* of raw power arched from the metal to my hand. I sucked in air and flinched away.

Ashlyn grabbed the handle. Even though lightning flared from the metal and struck her palm, nothing happened. She didn't look injured or even recoil from the spark.

"Are you okay?" I asked.

"Typhoon dragons and their arcanists are immune to lightning of any kind," she whispered. "Don't worry. I'll open all the doors."

"So chivalrous of you," I quipped.

"Anything for my man," Ashlyn playfully replied.

We stepped onto the first floor of Lord Oto's compound,

and I almost regretted it. Three people were there—and obviously waiting for us. Zahn, Jacinto, and Rosella occupied the hallway as though they had known we were coming and just needed to wait.

Zahn stood tall and straight, and his glasses were sparking with the lightning in the air. He took them off and shoved them into his pocket. The runes on his knuckles seemed to be shining a dull blue, and I had almost forgotten he had enchanted his body.

Jacinto and Rosella were tense, their white cloaks practically filled with static, but each seemed more than willing to fight, if that was what was needed.

Zahn stepped forward, his mimic on his shoulder. Twice's pink fur glittered, and her dual-colored eyes were narrowed in a glare.

"We have a problem," Zahn stated. "But *thankfully*, you are here to solve it, my brother. I hope you'll be quick about the matter as well."

"I hope you're not hoping too hard," I sarcastically said as I stepped closer to him.

Ashlyn and Raaza, with their eldrin, waited in the doorway, their gazes shifting from the cultists over to me. I gave them a slight wave of my hand, indicating I'd handle this. Although, I wasn't sure how I would do that, exactly.

Jacinto, with his tiny needle-point pupils, smiled. "A god-arcanist is here."

"A *former* god-arcanist," Zahn hissed at the other man. Then he turned his attention to me. "But he's still a true hero of the God-Arcanist's War. And he's come to snoop around the compound. He's convinced that students from Astra Academy are here."

Ashlyn wrung her hands, and remained silent.

"Why are the students awake?" Rosella asked, eyeing Raaza and Ashlyn.

I stepped between her and the others. "I needed to question them. Don't worry about it. They won't cause us any trouble. Isn't that right?" I flashed them a quick smirk.

Thankfully, both played along and just nodded.

"We need to kill the *former* god-arcanist," Jacinto said, ignoring all that. "It should be no problem for a Death Lord." He motioned to the hallway. "Quickly—while we still have the element of surprise. You should strike while the man is speaking with Lord Oto."

"Whoa, whoa." I held up both hands. "Why are we killing this guy? Just tell him to leave."

Zahn pressed his lips together in a fine line. "He knows you're here." When Zahn leaned in close, he spoke through gritted teeth. "The headmaster is bonded to a sphinx that has the capability to determine your location."

"O-Oh, right," I muttered.

Oops.

Zahn stood straight, and his mimic huffed.

"Surely we don't *have* to kill him," I said with a chuckle. "I mean, we could capture him. Or put him to sleep. You all seem to like to put people to sleep. It's an elegant solution, really."

"Shouldn't you take his soul and graft it to your abyssal dragon?" Jacinto asked.

That one question angered me. Well, not *me*. It upset Deimos. His thoughts flooded mine, and I spoke—his words— with venom. "It's a heinous crime against nature to disrespect the god-arcanists in such a way. Their souls, and their eldrin, are all honored in the *Spire of Gods*. I would never take one's soul for my own."

Deimos felt *very* passionately about this.

"Didn't this god-arcanist die once already?" I asked.

Zahn nodded, though both Rosella and Jacinto didn't seem to know what I was talking about.

Since I hadn't even been born yet when the God-Arcanists

War was happening, I really didn't feel passionately about this one way or another. However, if Deimos didn't want to harm the former god-arcanist, this worked out in my favor. I really didn't want to fight a bounty hunter who was just trying to save me and the others.

But this didn't sit well with Zahn. He grabbed my shoulder and led me a few paces away from the others. They watched from afar, most of them frowning.

"You must kill this bounty hunter," Zahn harshly whispered. "He's been asking too many questions. And if he finds out a piece of my brother's soul is chained to yours, he'll kill you both."

"Who, exactly, is this guy?" I asked, keeping my voice low.

"Lucian Nellit, the Dauntless."

Huh.

That was an impressive title, I wasn't going to lie, but that didn't scare me. First off, I had seen Deimos fight some truly spooky opponents. Secondly, I didn't want to fight, so if this man was on our side, I imagined combat could be avoided.

"Why don't *you* handle it?" I gestured to Zahn's mimic. "Why me? I'm a little busy."

"He's too powerful. I can't mimic his eldrin."

He *couldn't?*

What kind of creature was it?

I removed Zahn's hand from my shoulder. "Okay. That's unfortunate. But don't worry—everything will be fine. Actually, I have a better plan."

Zahn lifted an eyebrow and said nothing. Clearly, he thought this was going to be terrible.

"I'll leave the compound and draw him away from here, how's that?" I snapped my fingers, pretending I was coming up with this plan on the fly. "I'll go to Astra Academy, tell everyone we're fine, and then, once they call off all this bounty hunter nonsense, I'll come back."

Zahn crossed his arms.

Twice, his mimic, tilted her head back and forth. "Well... That could actually work."

I pointed to her. "See? Smart, right? So, how about you help me sneak out a window? I can probably make my way out the garden and over the compound wall."

I couldn't believe I would be doing this a third time in one day. It almost got me chuckling.

Zahn didn't seem amused, though. He mulled over my "impromptu" plan as though he hated every aspect of it. But when he returned his attention to me, his expression was softer. "Do you think it's wise, brother?"

"We shouldn't kill a god-arcanist," Deimos said through me. "Any plan that involves spilling his blood is off the table."

Crackles of power rolled down the hallway. Flashes of sparks and lightning made everything flicker. I tensed as I sensed two arcanists draw near. They both turned the corner and entered our hallway just as I turned to look.

It was Lord Oto and someone I had never seen before.

Oto seemed extremely short compared to the other man, and he walked with his cane clacking the entire way. A blue phoenix strode next to him, its heron body and grand peacock tail all a radiant sapphire color. Soot dappled the floor with each step, and the phoenix's silver eyes glittered with fierce intelligence.

Oto stroked the phoenix's head—it was obviously his eldrin.

"And here's my guests right here," Lord Oto drawled. "Just as I was telling you." He motioned with his cane. "You don't need to keep threatening me with the use of your aura. I'm a man of my word—I said I'd show you everything, and I did."

Everyone in the hallway froze.

Ashlyn and Raaza remained in the doorway that led to the stairs, Ashlyn more jittery than Raaza. Despite the fact this "Lucian the Dauntless" was imposing, I tried not to be intimidated.

Clad in leather armor so fancy it probably had its own skincare routine, Lucian looked like a warrior who maintained himself. His hair was as black as a raven, and his expression just as ominous.

Actually, his expression seemed etched in stone, as though the man rarely smiled. He was probably allergic to that. His idea of a joke was sharpening it and then stabbing someone.

And his arcanist mark...

It was a star with *nine* points, rather than one with seven. The creature wrapped around the points appeared to be a cloud, which wasn't anything I was familiar with.

In class, we had learned about *unique creatures*—like the Mother of Shapeshifters. They were mystical creatures that were different from the others because only one of them ever existed. Whenever someone bonded to them, the arcanist gained a nine-pointed star, to indicate their special bond.

Lucian was obviously bonded to one of these unique beasts.

Which meant he could have unique and powerful abilities I had never heard of.

And I didn't like that.

I wiped the sweat on my palms off on my pants. Fortunately, I still wore a cloak, and it hid all my nervous tics.

"What is he bonded with?" I whispered to Zahn.

Lord Oto and Lucian headed straight for us.

"He's bonded to *the Source of the Storm*," Zahn darkly muttered. "A creature so powerful, they say he's invincible."

CHAPTER 29

DEATH LORD OF DECEPTION

Invincible?

Deimos's thoughts were the same as my own: no arcanist was *invincible*.

Lucian strode over, walking faster than Lord Oto, and reached Zahn and me before the other man. His dark-eyed gaze was a little unsettling, especially as he examined me from head to toe without blinking.

Zahn and his mimic tensed, but they said and did nothing, other than occasionally glancing over, waiting for me to act.

"I am Lucian Nellit—inquisitor, bounty hunter, guildmaster," Lucian said matter-of-factly. "And you are?"

I straightened my posture and smiled. "I'm Gray Lexly—student, mimic arcanist, and loved by all. It's a real honor to meet one of the god-arcanists. Ex-god-arcanist? I'm not sure what term you would use." I bowed my head slightly, to show respect, even if my words were soaked in sarcasm.

Deimos didn't like that I tried to hide my nervousness with humor.

And neither did Lucian.

That man maintained his hardened expression like he would

die if he switched to another. His scrutinizing gaze went from me, to Ashlyn, to Raaza, and then over to Jacinto and Rosella.

Up close, his leather armor was mastercraft. It was darker than most, weathered from use, and clearly flexible. He carried smaller knives—more like darts—that were held in sheaths sewn straight into his armor. He had to be carrying at least ten of them, and even from here, I felt they were magical.

His boots were scuffed, though, as though he didn't care about them as much as the rest of his armor.

His skin was darkly tanned, soaked in the sun, and even when he moved his head to glance around, I could tell he was tense—coiled and waiting for someone to do something.

"Headmaster Venrover asked me to accompany his lost students back to Astra Academy," Lucian stated—once again, with the matter-of-fact precision that reminded me of a textbook. When he returned his gaze to me, lightning flashed throughout a portion of the hallway.

Lucian then pulled a piece of parchment from his belt and unrolled it, revealing a letter Headmaster Venrover's signature, along with the crest of Astra Academy, signature at the bottom. "The headmaster also asked me to figure out how his students went missing in the first place. Tell me—how is it you ended up in the Nation of Sellix, of all places?"

He rolled up his letter and tucked it away.

Everyone was dead silent. The crackle of the agitated air around us was the only noise in the whole damn compound.

I didn't dare look at the others—Lucian's gaze had me pinned down—but I heard Lord Oto and his blue phoenix casually stride up next to us.

"We were teleported," I said, half a lie and half not. "Really strange. I'm just a student, a first year, and I have *no idea* what kind of magic pulled us all the way from Astra Academy to *this* strange location. I woke up, my head blurry, and thankfully all these kind people were here to help."

I motioned to Zahn and the others.

Lucian didn't offer them a second glance. He just maintained eye contact with me.

Did he know I was lying? Maybe. But what was he going to do about it? He was here to escort me back to the Academy—the faster that happened, the better. And he didn't need to know I had been in the abyssal hells. Frankly, I didn't trust him with that kind of information. He seemed ready for a fight, and I wanted that least of all.

"And everyone is here?" Lucian asked. "Ashlyn Kross, Nini Wanderlin, and Knovak Gentz? All four students who are missing?" He turned his piercing gaze to Ashlyn and then returned it to me. "I need all four of you before we can head back to Astra Academy."

"That's good," I said. "Because we're all here and ready to go." I pointed to Ashlyn. "There's Lady Kross." Then I pointed to Raaza. "That's good ol' Knovak." And then I gestured to Rosella. "And there's Nini." I clapped my hands together twice. "We can go. Do you have a boat? Or an airship, maybe? I can't wait to speak to the headmaster. This has been an *ordeal*, let me tell you."

I couldn't tell him we had lost Nini in the abyssal hells. Well, not now. Not after I had said we teleported here. And if I had said she was missing, he was clearly going to insist on looking for her—and that was foolish. No one was going to find her until we found a way back into the abyssal hells themselves.

The air...

The lightning stopped, and it was no longer oppressive and spicy. Lucian's thunderous aura had terminated.

"See?" Lord Oto tapped his black cane on the tile of the hall. "I told you everything was fine. We haven't hurt anyone, and you can—"

"Quiet, *slumlord*," Lucian growled. "You're lucky I don't turn this whole place inside out. But I *will* be back to investigate everything in Waxing City further. You can count on that as much as the sun rising in the morning."

Lord Oto's smile went a little wider, as though he were ready for a challenge, but he said nothing.

I sort of liked Lucian a little more after that. Was he going to help the people here? Maybe he could help us gather up Raaza's mother so we could take her straight to the Academy.

Before I could voice my support, a tiny bird zipped through the air and flew straight over to Lucian. It landed on his shoulder with such speed, and such precision, it almost looked fake, like a toy on a string tugged over to its location.

It was... a white hummingbird.

Small.

Puffy.

Its eyes were glowing blue, and the tips of its minuscule feathers sparked with the small bits of lightning. It was rather adorable, though it appeared like it would zap you if you tried to touch it.

"I'm done searching the property, my arcanist," the white hummingbird said, its voice quite audible despite its size. The last syllables of its words were harsh, as though even its speech was charged with static.

"What did you find?" Lucian asked.

The hummingbird hopped across Lucian's shoulder until it was close to his ear. Then it turned its long beak and whispered.

Was that little hummingbird *the Source of the Storm*? It didn't look like Lucian's arcanist mark, which was dominated by a cloud. It barely took up any space—it could've easily hidden in a pile of pebbles.

Lucian was quiet for some time, then he returned his attention to me.

"Headmaster Venrover told me he was afraid this would happen," Lucian said.

"Afraid *what* would happen?" I lifted an eyebrow. "That

your mission would be effortless and we could all go home without any trouble?"

"That Gray Lexly would be possessed by one of the Death Lords, and he would be masquerading as an ally."

I caught my breath, but only for half a moment. "Well, I'm not *possessed* by a Death Lord."

"But you're clearly *masquerading*," Lucian said through gritted teeth. "Most of what you've said so far is a lie."

Everyone waited, the tension once again rising.

"You think I wasn't briefed on what kind of arcanists the students were?" Lucian huffed and then eyed Raaza. "Does he look like a unicorn arcanist?" He motioned to Rosella. "Is she bonded with a reaper? Your words are flimsy, and your motivations clear. You *want* to get to Astra Academy as quickly as possible."

I held up a hand. "Yeah. Absolutely. So I can explain everything to Headmaster Venrover."

"And you expect me to believe that? It's more likely you're out to harm him—the Death Lords can't be trusted."

"Whoa, whoa," I said, hesitantly scooting back. "I don't want to hurt the headmaster. And the Death Lords aren't all evil. They're, uh, misunderstood."

"Seriously?" I heard Ashlyn whisper. "That's what you went with?"

"I told you not to underestimate the god-arcanist, child," Deimos muttered through me.

The hummingbird puffed its white feathers. "I'm the Source of the Storm, and you're the darkness that creeps in the abyssal hells. My arcanist and I are here to stop you, fiend. You can either lay down your arms and surrender, or face the wrath of the Dauntless. The choice is yours."

Wow.

Even Lucian's eldrin was as no-nonsense as he was.

This was not going to end well. I had to deescalate the situation, before it turned bloody.

"*Listen,*" I said, one hand held up. "I apologize. I did lie. It was idiotic of me—and a bad habit I can't seem to shake. I don't want to fight you. I'm surrendering."

I knelt on one knee, preparing myself to be restrained. Whenever Lucian *did* bring me to the headmaster, I was certain this would all get sorted out. Clearly, even if I told the truth now, Lucian wasn't about to believe me.

"What're you doing?" Jacinto hissed. He rushed to my side, grabbed my arms, and then yanked me to my feet. "Death Lord Deimos—you should *never* kneel to the likes of this trash! He is far beneath you!"

Rosella and her kappa also leapt to my side. "Yes, we're here for you, Death Lord Deimos. He won't escape this compound— not after this disrespect."

I should've been more thoughtful with my lies—or not done them at all. All I had wanted was to leave this place as soon as possible!

"I figured this would happen," Lucian said, deadpan and set for violence.

The next thing that happened shocked me so much, I almost forgot to move.

The little hummingbird—the Source of the Storm—leapt into the side of its arcanist's neck. It drilled into Lucian's flesh, disappearing into his body, beak first, within a half second, like it was absorbed by Lucian's skin and then accepted into the muscle as though it had always belonged.

Jacinto unleashed a blast of ice. It struck Lucian, and he was forced back a step, the rime coating most of his body and armor.

Zahn stumbled backward, cursing under his breath. "We should've ended this when we had the element of surprise." His mimic, Twice, leapt off his shoulder and bubbled as she transformed into a typhoon dragon.

Which was smart.

"Twain!" I shouted.

My eldrin—who was still sitting on top of Ecrib's head—shimmered and shifted until he was *also* a typhoon dragon, my arcanist mark burning the entire time. He fumbled off Ecrib, and the two of them stood side by side, identical in every way.

I wanted the immunity to lightning, because I knew it was coming.

Then, before Lucian could recover from the ice, I reached for Vivigöl. The weapon surged to life as soon as my fingers grazed the outside. It *click-click-clicked* into its favorite shape, the trident, and I brandished it with both hands.

Jacinto held out his hand again and evoked more ice than he had before. Unfortunately, a blast of air ripped down the hallway with such ferocity, the ice evocation was thrown back at Jacinto, Rosella, and me, the harsh sting of winter cascading over us. I had to lift my arm to prevent myself from being temporarily blinded.

"It's heinous to fight the god-arcanists," Deimos said through me, his words practically venom, "but they are just human. And they make *grievous errors* just like the rest of mankind. If the Dauntless attempts to kill you—strike him down first."

The wind in the hallway took his words so fast, I almost couldn't hear them fully.

While everyone was struggling to maintain their footing, Lucian leapt away from the group. He half bent forward and crossed his arms over his chest, his face twisted in agony. The sound of wet flesh ripping was carried on the gale-force winds, and a splatter of blood whipped across the walls and floor.

White wings tore out of Lucian's back, the feathers half stained in crimson.

Avian talons jutted from Lucian's fingertips, and when he lifted his gaze, he no longer seemed in pain—he seemed excited.

"By the abyssal hells," Zahn groaned, his words hurled away by the strong wind.

Lightning crackled through the hall again, the whole area soaked in potent magic. Lucian's *aura* was filling the compound, bringing the heart of the storm straight to our doorstep. We were inside, yet it felt like the worst ocean hurricane I had ever lived through. I struggled to stay on my feet, and when Lucian jumped up, he moved with frightening speed. He twisted, landed with his boots on the ceiling, and then *shot* toward me, using the ceiling as merely a stopping point from which to get a better jumping angle.

I barely moved out of the way, half taken by the wind, and half moving because of Deimos's combat reflexes. As Lucian hit the floor, lightning exploded from him, washing over Jacinto, Rosella, Zahn, and me. It wasn't a big enough blast to hit Lord Oto and the others, but arcs of lightning flashed off the impact and hit the walls, leaving marks and holes from their sheer power.

The explosion of power didn't hurt me—thanks to the typhoon dragon magic now in my veins. It was the same for Zahn. The magic lightning washed over my body, a tingling sensation rippling across my skin.

But Rosella, her kappa, and Jacinto spasmed as though about to explode themselves. They hit the floor afterward, twitching and being dragged across the tile by the wind.

Lucian stood straight and fluttered his white wings. The blood flicked away, leaving them pristine.

"Surrender, Death Lord," he said, his voice a mix of his own and the Source of the Storm's. "Your villainy ends *today*."

CHAPTER 30

COLLATERAL DAMAGE

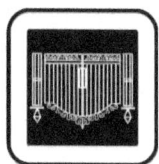

"I don't want to fight you," I repeated, shouting into the wind.

Lucian lashed out at me, swiping his talons with such speed as to catch me off guard. He cut clean into my chest, just below my throat, as I stepped backward. His talons sliced through my flesh, hot blood gushing over my white clothing. Panic and adrenaline both flooded my veins.

Lucian was fast.

I grabbed my chest, trying to stop the blood flow. If I weren't an arcanist, this would be fatal. Even as it stood, this injury was enough to slow me down, and I could still die if I was too reckless. Lucian's *opening move* had been to end my life.

What a swell guy.

When Lucian slashed again, I stepped faster, my muscles already tense, my focus solely on his movements. His expression —it was ice cold. He had the kind of hate in his eyes reserved for the worst of dastards.

Lucian truly thought me evil.

And why wouldn't he? Until a few months ago, *I* had

thought all the Death Lords were evil and just trying to get to the land of the living to eat us all—or something like that. Now that I knew everyone was in trouble, this all seemed petty. Lucian should've just taken me straight to Headmaster Venrover.

A blast of lightning struck Lucian, but he shrugged it off, clearly not affected by the magic. Typhoon dragons weren't the only things immune to that magic, it seemed. When I glanced over my shoulder, I realized the lightning had come from Twain, who was now clawing against the wind, heading in my direction.

Lucian turned his attention to my eldrin as well. I knew Lucian would lunge—I saw it in the way his body moved, how his hips turned to face a new target, and how his muscles coiled. Was that Deimos's knowledge, or my own? I didn't give a damn. I leapt with the wind and Lucian lunged at Twain.

I thrust Vivigöl, catching part of Lucian's arm, cutting a small furrow through his skin before he could reach Twain. Despite the insignificance of the strike, I felt Vivigöl pulse. It was made of abyssal coral, and it yearned to drain Lucian of his very soul. Like a leech sapping blood, if I cut him enough, my weapon would do just that.

Lucian leapt backward and then returned his hate-filled gaze to me.

"*Get out of here!*" I shouted.

I had meant that for Twain, but Raaza and Ashlyn were the ones to act on it. Ashlyn pointed to the window, and Ecrib threw his whole dragon body at the glass. It shattered, eating a path to the outside. They flung themselves through it as fast as possible.

The wind in the hallway picked up, howling with the anger clearly etched on Lucian's face. He didn't focus on the people fleeing. He just kept his sights on me.

I felt his determination in the way he met my gaze—he'd collect the others once we were done.

"This is my home!" Lord Oto yelled. "*I won't let this go unpunished.*"

His blue phoenix flapped its wings. Soot and sapphire feathers were pulled into the wind and fluttered past me.

But then came the fire. The phoenix erupted in smoke and flame, and the wind took it *everywhere.*

More panic.

More drastic thoughts. Each inhale tasted of copper.

I tugged on the thread of magic that led to the phoenix just as the flames started to wash over me. My skin burned, but only for a half a moment—as soon as the blue phoenix magic was in my body, I was no longer harmed by the heat.

My clothes, on the other hand, were mostly charred within a matter of seconds.

As a phoenix, Twain wasn't strong enough to resist the wind. He squawked and tumbled down the hallway. He wasn't burnt, which I was grateful for.

Lucian leapt back to the ceiling, moving faster than any living thing I had ever witnessed. He dodged the torrent of flame, shot across the ceiling, and then shifted the wind so the fire *whooshed* in the opposite direction. Twain came tumbling back.

Zahn, not caught in the heat, did the exact same thing I had done—his mimic shifted into a blue phoenix. Twice remained at his side, though, clinging to Zahn's body with sharp talons. Zahn didn't seem to care. He held out a hand and *added* more flames to the pyre of heat, flooding the hallway further, even aiming at the ceiling so the inferno was impossible to escape.

Lucian yelled—but it was impossible to see him. There was so much smoke, and the fire was white and red, blinding and deadly beautiful. Even though it didn't hurt me, it was still *bright*, and its illumination was filling the compound with destruction.

The wind shifted directions again.

Dagger-darts flew through the hallway, carried with the fire. Three of them pierced right through Zahn's chest and stomach like they were bullets from a well-aimed pistol.

"*Zahn*!" I shouted—Deimos shouted?

Zahn hit the floor and was dragged away by the wind, his blood burning to a crisp in the ever-growing pyre all around us.

Then pure strength filled me. It was abyssal dragon magic—Deimos hadn't wanted to do this. I felt his reticence. He hadn't wanted to consume souls from his dragon to empower me, but it was clear Deimos didn't want Zahn harmed.

One soul gave me strength.

Another healed me of my injuries.

With the third, speed became my ally.

Then more of the fire died down. Lord Oto had *also* been stabbed with the dagger-darts. He had taken four through the gut, and he was gulping down air, barely able to get his breath in this tornado.

Lucian, on the ceiling, had burns across the portions of his body not covered by his leather armor. His white wings were charred, but for some reason I didn't understand, he was becoming more... bird-like?

More feathers were sprouting from his skin, like seedlings bursting from the soil in spring. His boots were ripped open, and now his feet had the talons of a hawk. His raven hair was feathered as well, and he seemed more muscular—his physique nearly doubling.

When Lucian exhaled, smoke came out with his breath.

No.

Not smoke—it was a mist. Clouds.

Lightning crackled across his wings, and I sensed the area for Ashlyn's typhoon dragon. I needed her magic.

Twain was still in the hallway, just a few feet behind me. He was a blue phoenix, but as he ran to my side, practically hobbling, he shifted into a majestic typhoon dragon, complete with scales and fins.

Lucian pulled more of his deadly darts from the sheaths tucked in his armor. Instead of waiting for his attack, I rushed down the hall. With my increased strength, I managed to move against the wind, and when I was nearly under Lucian, I shifted Vivigöl into a sword, the gold weapon *click-click-clicking* into place as I jumped.

Lucian threw his darts as soon as I was in the air. Two sliced through my shoulders, but Deimos's magic held me together. The healing was on a whole new level, and I barely felt the sting of the metal piercing my body.

I slashed, but Lucian was faster than I anticipated. The man shot away and hit the floor with precision and grace. He flapped his mostly burnt wings, and the wind in the hallway ceased.

I landed, rolled, and then was on my feet in one fluid move. After shuddering, I turned on my heel and faced Lucian.

The man stood, his charred feathers falling from his wings. They were being replaced with new feathers—first small, but then larger, sprouting from the depths of his wings with purpose.

"Zahn?" I called out. "Are you all right?"

The man was on the floor, shaken. His mimic transformed from a blue phoenix, into a gigantic manticore, complete with leathery bat wings. Zahn couldn't seem to get the air necessary to answer, but once he had the manticore magic, his injuries healed faster.

Because manticore arcanists had improved regeneration.

Clever.

Zahn knew how to use his mimic magic to the best of its ability. When he glanced over at me, blood was trickling from his mouth and dripping onto the floor, but his irritated expression said more than his inevitable tirade ever could. He would be fine, so long as he wasn't pierced several more times.

"Aren't you gonna ask whether *I'm* alive?" Lord Oto shouted. He leaned heavily on his cane, blood splattering his shoes as he managed to stand. "*I pay you dolts*, and not even a lick of concern for my wellbeing?"

Lucian stood tall. "I knew," he whispered, more mist escaping his lips. "I knew the moment I stepped foot here, it was a den of snakes and cravens. I can't believe you were housing a Death Lord for your own personal gain. Disgusting."

I tightened my grip on Vivigöl. "It's not what you think. Let's all calm down, have a chat—you'll see. I just need to speak with Headmaster Venrover, and this whole mess will be cleared up."

As I finished my sentence, Twain bounded over, his dragon form not as swift as it would've been in the water.

"*Nothing* is getting cleared up," Lord Oto yelled. Still gripping his cane, and leaning on it to stand, he glared at me. "This lunatic is here to rip apart our whole operation. You slit his throat, or else we're all going down."

Lucian turned on his heel, facing me with a look of icy hate. "It seems your allies are more willing to speak the truth than you are."

"He's not my ally," I ground out, waving my hand in Oto's general direction. "I just met him this morning! He doesn't speak for me!"

"Ugh." Lord Oto stepped close to the shattered window. "*Yex, Wella!* Earn your damn keep and finish this!" Then he hobbled to his eldrin who was huddled on the floor. "Cielo, get them. Get them here now—you're the only one I can ever rely on."

"Of course," the phoenix said, regal and beautiful. Then it spread its wings, and flew out the window, soot dropping as it went.

Lucian rotated his shoulders and several *cracks* echoed in the hallway. More feathers sprouted from his elbows, shoulders, and even from his wrists. He was avian, and somehow the white plumes gave him a regal look, similar to a hawk.

"Call your goons," Lucian stated. "I'll deal with them all at once." Lightning surged from his wings and arced down the hall.

When it struck me, it only tingled, my magic rendering it harmless.

"I don't want to cut up your soul," I said. "But I will if you don't listen to reason. I'm not with these dirtbags. I'm Gray Lexly, a student at Astra Academy. Well, I'm also a little bit Death Lord Deimos, but honestly that's negligible."

"I can smell the abyssal dragon magic radiating from your body." Lucian spread his wings, the lightning in the air growing thicker. "You're a blight on this land. No Death Lord should be among the living—not even in part. I'm sorry you were possessed, Gray. I truly am. But I'll do whatever I have to in order to ensure the safety of everyone *not* under a Death Lord's influence."

"I saw your soul when you briefly entered the abyssal hells," Deimos said through me. "You were stubborn then, too—a soul made of tenacity, but little wisdom. Your old master would be disappointed."

That last statement seemed to shake Lucian. He tensed, the hate in his eyes replaced with uncertainty.

But it lasted only a second. Lucian shook his head, dispelling any doubts. "You can spin your lies into attractive silk, but they won't ever tempt me."

I hadn't noticed it before, but the hallway was foggier than before. The mists were gathering, and the lightning was growing stronger. It seemed the longer Lucian was merged with the Source of the Storm, the stronger he became.

Perhaps that was why some people considered him "invincible."

Two manticores and their arcanists landed just beyond the window, and I knew this was about to get out of control. Lord Oto wanted Lucian dead—but I really didn't want it to end that way.

When Lucian lowered himself into an attack stance, I knew he was going to force my hand, one way or another.

CHAPTER 31

NO MORE MERCY

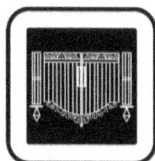

The two manticore arcanists hurried toward the shattered window—one man, one woman. They were both equally roughly equipped, with half-plate armor, each carrying a pistol and brandishing a dagger.

The man was so tall, his bald head would likely touch the ceiling in any normal house. His muscles were barely contained by his armor, which he had dyed mostly black, complementing his darker complexion.

The woman was lithe and wiry. Her brown hair, cut to her chin, hung perfectly straight, the tips of her locks honeyed, like her tanned skin. She was the opposite of the man in all regards, from her dyed white armor to her blue pants, and short stature. When she leapt over the windowsill and landed in the hallway with a bit of grace and flair, I was halfway reminded of Ashlyn.

The manticores lumbered over as well.

And while their arcanists weren't siblings, I suspected the creatures were.

Both of those monstrous creatures had black scorpion tails, leathery bat wings and the golden body of a lion, their fangs capable of crushing a man's skull. Their manes were a vibrant red, and their claws viciously sharp.

They moved forward together, like two 700-pound cats stalking their prey. They didn't have time to get into the hallway before Lucian acted, however.

A blast of stormy wind shattered three other windows, the glass spraying into the garden with enough force to slice up the male manticore arcanist, along with the two manticores themselves. The shards tore through the leathery wings of the beasts, and I assumed Lucian had done this intentionally.

Lord Oto held on to a windowsill, flames flowing off his body as his evocation was interrupted. "Wella!" He snapped his fingers at the female manticore arcanist. "*Kill him!* I'll double your pay if you bring me his head."

Wella, Oto's goon, hadn't been blasted very far. She stomped forward, her strength increased by the manticore magic in her veins.

"Yex!" Oto pointed to the male arcanist. "*You, too! Earn your keep!*"

And while Lucian's wind manipulation had knocked me back a few paces, I still had the abyssal dragon strength, thanks to Deimos. I leapt forward, Vivigöl in sword form.

I didn't have the combat experience Deimos did, so I allowed his instincts to guide me. Instead of slashing, I planted my foot and leapt into the air—just before Lucian shot himself toward the ceiling. It was as if Deimos knew, from centuries of warfare, exactly how Lucian would react to an incoming foe. I was taking action one step ahead of Lucian.

And it worked.

I slashed with Vivigöl, cutting down from Lucian's chest to his stomach. It was a shallow injury, but that didn't matter. His very soul had taken a wound, and Lucian staggered away from me, his jaw clenched, the wind slowing.

Twain roared and pounced at Lucian. His typhoon dragon

body was more suited to the water, however. He awkwardly slashed, and Lucian jumped out of his range. "Damn," Twain muttered. "I'm sorry, Gray..."

Then Wella entered the fray.

Her strength allowed her to rush forward at a scary pace. She attempted to stab Lucian straight in the chest, but the winds picked up again, causing her hand to wobble to the side. Lucian expertly sidestepped, and then slashed with both his talon-hands, cutting straight through Wella's armor.

Lucian aimed for her right shoulder and armpit.

She screamed as the talons sliced flesh. She leapt out the window, and the male manticore arcanist, Yex, rushed into the building a moment later. He shot with his pistol, but the wind around Lucian acted defensively. Whenever something was coming close, it howled in response. The bullet was whipped away and slammed ineffectively into a wall.

Lightning flashed throughout the hall and out in the courtyard, and crackling power shot at Yex and the manticores themselves.

Yex shuddered and then shook. I thought he would fall, but through sheer strength, he stayed on his feet, though he did lose his pistol. However, Yex still held his dagger at the ready.

Lucian flew out the window into the garden.

"What are you buffoons doing?" Lord Oto shouted.

Deimos's concern immediately went to his brother.

I turned and found Zahn panting. He wasn't shaken or disturbed by the fighting—no, he was calm and taking this moment to catch his own breath and recover. I hurried to his side.

"How fare you?" Deimos asked through me.

Instantly, Zahn's expression softened. "I'm fine, brother. Focus on our mutual enemy."

Before I could follow through on that request, a blast of wind brought a thick bank of clouds through the hallway. In an instant, darkness descended, all thanks to the literal storm engulfing Lord Oto's compound.

A screaming wind ripped through the property, and lightning flashed in the clouds. When the lightning came for me, my skin absorbed the energy, and it disappeared.

Zahn's mimic transformed into a typhoon dragon as well. Then he slid closer to me, his hand gripping my shoulder as tightly as Zahn could manage. Did he want me to protect him? No—he wanted Deimos to help him. And that was what Deimos wanted as well, so I obliged.

"Don't leave my side," I said, my words taken into the maelstrom.

I worried about the others, though.

And with these thick clouds, it was difficult to see.

A burst of fire lit up the hallway again. Lord Oto used his magic to burn away some of the clouds, but it wasn't enough.

"I have to do everything myself," Oto yelled.

And then the world around us filled with even *more* magic. Deimos's thoughts flooded mine. Another *aura* had been activated, this time by Lord Oto himself. Although I hadn't yet learned in class what these auras could do, Deimos already knew. His knowledge became mine, and I understood that blue phoenixes caused mass exhaustion—they heated an area so much that people couldn't bear it, and often fainted or even died, if they were left in the aura too long.

If I were a blue phoenix arcanist, I'd be immune to this. But I couldn't be two types of arcanists at once—I could either be immune to the constant lightning all around me, or the ever-growing temperature flaring throughout the compound.

For now, I stayed a typhoon dragon arcanist. The lightning would stun me otherwise. The heat would take a few minutes to cause me to faint. I had to use that time wisely.

Twain emerged from the clouds and then wrapped his dragon body protectively around me. Twice, Zahn's eldrin, did the same with him, and we were a fortified little bubble in the middle of the hurricane, but that wouldn't be enough to end this.

"Do we have a plan to slay the Source of the Storm?" Twain asked, his scales flaring.

The sounds of combat were carried on the air—everything from screams to the clang of metal. It was clear Lucian had decided to cull the battlefield, and he was using the cloud cover to help him manage the many enemies.

But I was a mimic arcanist—I could sense his magic, and I felt an invisible thread that led back to his eldrin, which was currently deep in his own body.

"I changed my mind," I said to Zahn. "Wait here."

And while I hadn't yet articulated my plan to Deimos, I felt his approval.

"Come, Twain," I shouted.

My eldrin moved with me across the hallway, and then we climbed out the window into the stormy gardens. There were bursts of lightning, the flash of fire, and even the chill sting of ice. More concerning was the *click clack* of wood.

The soul catcher and its arcanist were here. I sensed their magic as well.

All the arcanists in the whole compound had come to the eye of the storm, likely hoping to end this.

"Twain," I said, my teeth gritted.

I tugged on the thread of magic that led back to Deimos's eldrin. Twain's dragon body warped as flesh exploded outward. Shrubbery was blasted aside. Stepping stones were pulverized by his weight. Twain's rapidly growing tail lashed out, carving a line through the wall of the mansion. He grew until his head towered over the compound, casting a good portion of the garden in shadow.

His blue scales practically melted off as he became an undead monster with a slimy exterior. Twain also sprouted four more eyes, for a total of six, and he grew wings that were nothing more than tortured souls stretched taut.

For the first time in millennia, an abyssal dragon stood under the sky, a dark legend brought to life.

My arcanist mark burned as Twain finalized his horrifying form. Then my eldrin roared, his voice laced with the screams of the tormented.

"Let's end this," I said to him.

Twain nodded his draconic head, a slight smile on his rotted lips.

I shivered at the increase in power. Abyssal dragon arcanists could consume souls to add to their strength and magic, but what would happen if *I* did that? Twain had souls on his body, but those were just duplicates of ones Deimos had grafted to *his* eldrin's body. If I used a soul, would I actually gain the benefit? Or because the souls on Twain were fake, would I gain nothing?

Now was the time to experiment further. I had used "souls" when I fought Naiad, but I wasn't entirely sure the extent of the power or whether the souls used harmed Hektor. I wasn't entirely sure how any of this worked—and I doubted there was research on the matter anywhere.

With Deimos's help, I concentrated on a single soul and "absorbed" it into myself.

It was... jarring.

It felt as though someone had punched me in the gut, but the agony radiated to the tips of my limbs, and then to my mind, where it blossomed into a temporary headache. A second later, the pain was one with my body, and I had embraced it so thoroughly, I no longer felt it. But the power remained.

I had "consumed" a soul to empower myself.

The soul vanished from Twain's body—but according to Deimos's thoughts, the soul *hadn't* disappeared from Hektor's body.

Interesting.

Although the wind was howling, and branches of trees were whipping past us, I pulled myself onto Twain, climbing his decaying body, my bare feet soaking in the slime, and one falling into his ribs. While I climbed, I was getting cut up. I barely had any clothing—and no armor—and the glass fragments, bits of debris, and random magic were now taking their toll. Additionally, when the lightning crackled, it hurt me. Fortunately, abyssal dragon magic allowed me to heal faster, though I still momentarily spasmed.

Twain took the strikes of lightning with little damage. His body was giant, and his skin only flaked off where it was struck, as though it was barely hanging together in the first place.

Once I was on Twain's back and situated between his wings, Vivigöl *click-click-clicked* into the shape of the golden trident. I urged Twain forward, and he spread his vile wings. The winds were merciless, trying to rip everything off the ground and pull them into a tornado, but Twain was too large for that.

We charged forward, guided by our mimic magic, even though I couldn't see. Lucian's magic was *unique*. No other mystical creature in the area felt like his did, which made it effortless to sense.

Probably to Lucian's surprise, Twain and I emerged from the clouds right next to him. He stood at the eye of the storm, where the air was still clear, his white wings glistening, but the slash on his chest and stomach was still open. Vivigöl's soul-sucking magic would make it so those injuries would heal slower —and likely scar.

Lucian's dark eyes went wide.

"You really *are* a Death Lord," he whispered, his words whisked away by the wind.

Twain lunged, maw open, and chomped at Lucian. My eldrin managed to sink his fangs into Lucian's left arm, catching the man completely off guard. Lucian flapped his wings, and tried to flee, but he couldn't—not unless he was going to tear his arm off.

His complete lack of concentration caused his aura and manipulation to end.

The storm died, and the winds calmed.

The clouds evaporated, leaving only the heat of Lord Oto's aura.

It also left us with a massive—and destroyed—garden area, filled to the brim with arcanists who were roughed up. Two manticores, a sea serpent, a soul catcher, and all their arcanists, had been tossed around like rag dolls. Yex was in a bush, Wella slammed up against a wall. It was chaos.

Knovak and his unicorn were here, too, as though they had been attempting to enter the fray. And to my amusement, they were the first to recover, both on their feet long before the others.

Lucian held a hand up to one of Twain's eyes. He exploded with lightning, and Twain screeched. My eldrin let go of Lucian and reared back, clearly agonized. I held onto Twain as he crashed backward, smashing into a part of Lord Oto's compound.

"*Death Lord Deimos is on our side*," someone shrieked with glee.

The sea serpent, an emerald creature that resembled a gigantic eel, opened its mouth and blasted ice across the garden, freezing most of the debris in place. Then it turned its evocation onto Lucian, who shielded most of his body with his wings.

One of the manticores flapped its wings and leapt across the rime. It landed on Lucian, goring his back and ripping off feathers. The soul catcher arcanist—some thin woman with a sunken face and dark rings under her eyes—pointed. Her wooden puppet eldrin clattered over, unconcerned with the ice, and flexed its fingers. It was shaped like a spider, with the mask of a human for a "face," and at the end of its eight legs were human hands. The fingers were nothing more than knives, and the soul catcher slashed at Lucian's legs, aiming for the calves as though to hobble him.

Lord Oto's blue phoenix shot out of the building and took to the sky, a streak of blazing sapphire. Then it turned its slender head downward and washed the garden in a torrent of flame it breathed straight from its mouth. The majestic bird flew over Lucian, drowning him in fire.

When Lucian attempted to fly, Knovak held up his hand, and a blast of force knocked Lucian down. His unicorn galloped over, flashing fangs as though ready to eat the wings right off his opponent.

It was as if my presence was a rallying call.

Everyone who saw me—and thought a Death Lord was now on their side—was emboldened to attack with everything they had.

Despite taking the hits, Lucian spread his feathered wings. His physical power was enough that a single flap lifted him straight into the air. When he evoked lightning, it burst off him from the tips of his feathers, in almost all directions. It was as if he didn't have as much control of it, like a storm unleashed.

Almost everyone was struck, though a few of the smarter fighters managed to leap away.

His magic spread throughout the garden, and even washed over me, but I was able to shake it off, my muscles healing, the spasms barely lasting.

Oto's phoenix slammed into Lucian. The two tumbled to the ground. The sea serpent lunged, fangs first, and bit down on Lucian's mangled arm. One of the manticores—who hadn't been struck with lightning—flew at Lucian and slashed with its claws, cutting away portions of his upper leg.

Lucian threw the phoenix off, swiped with his talon-hands at the manticore, and even evoked more lightning at the sea serpent. The soul catcher clattered over, and Lucian managed to evoke another wave of lightning, but that caused him to ignore the other manticore. The lion-sized monstrosity lunged for Lucian and raked its claws across Lucian's feathered back.

Starling the elder unicorn raced in and slashed with his horn, Knovak using his evocation to strike at Lucian's wings, in case he should attempt to fly.

It was all happening so chaotically—so quickly. It was a dogpile to get Lucian down, to make sure he didn't create his clouds and tornado again...

Yex ran up and once again fired with his pistol. Lucian's wind manipulation didn't protect him this time. He was too distracted. The bullet tore through one of his wings. He was ragged, and swallowing air at a quick rate, clearly spent. He turned on his heel, determination in his eyes, but not in his movements.

Sluggish. Bleeding out. His gaze unfocused.

The man had fought a Death Lord and eight bloodthirsty arcanists like a champ. But I supposed that was too much for anyone, even a former god.

Then I sensed something... It was different from all my other senses. This wasn't touch, hearing, sight, taste, smell, or even magic. This was some sort of *other* sense. It was Deimos, and he was reaching out, like a mimic arcanist reaches for threads of magic. He was sensing Lucian's life force.

And it was fading.

CHAPTER 32

ESCAPE FROM WAXING CITY

I jumped off Twain—off his massive abyssal dragon form—and flew a solid twenty feet before landing in the wrecked garden. The rime underfoot was difficult to maneuver on, but I used Vivigöl like a cane rather than a trident, and dashed forward.

Right as a manticore was about to slam its fangs down on Lucian's neck, I thrust with Vivigöl and skewered the monster in the chest. The manticore roared and hobbled backward, pulling itself from the tines of my weapon. Blood splashed into the garden, and the screech of agony stopping most other people from attacking.

I rushed to Lucian's side. The man collapsed to one knee, blood weeping from every injury across his body. His wings sagged, the feathers mostly broken.

"Don't die on me," I said to him, our gazes meeting for only a moment.

A moment long enough to tell me Lucian was utterly baffled by my actions.

"What're you doing?" Yex roared. He was the tallest man I

had ever seen, and when he came stomping forward, it felt like the whole garden was shaking.

Despite that, he didn't scare me. I twirled Vivigöl in my hand and then spread my feet, putting myself in a defensive stance. Deimos's memories mingled with mine, and I saw several fights where someone angry had rushed Deimos out of nowhere.

Yex was like that.

He went straight for me, and I sidestepped, then thrust with the points of the trident. I caught Yex in the ribs, and he sucked in air through his teeth. He jumped and kicked, but I effortlessly ducked and dodged. Manticore arcanists were stronger and faster than any mortal man, but I was empowered by abyssal dragon magic.

I slammed Yex in the side of the hand with the shaft of my weapon.

The man staggered, clearly dazed for a moment.

"*Whose side are you on?*" Knovak shouted.

"My own," I yelled back. "Are you with me? Or are you with these lunatics? Because you need to make some quick decisions."

After recovering from the shock of my attack and the lightning that had been discharged, the second manticore stalked forward. Twain opened his mouth and evoked a beam of raw magic straight from his gullet. The bluish energy, so powerful I felt it from across the garden, tore through the dirt, the trees, and the stepping stones. As Twain angled his head back, the beam sliced through the building itself, cutting a clean line through a window and wall, and even through the roof.

Twain stopped his evocation, leaving a scar on the whole compound.

It seemed Twain had been aiming for the manticore, but the lion-like monster was smart enough to fly as fast as it could in the opposite direction, its golden fur puffed up in fright.

My eldrin growled, his voice echoing around us. Light

filtered through his soul-stretched wings, as they were mostly transparent, and a sickly blue hue washed over the area as he spread his wings.

"I'm taking the bounty hunter," I said, loud enough for everyone to hear me. "And I'm leaving. No one try to stop me. Or else."

"You're not going *anywhere*," Lord Oto shouted. He climbed out into the garden, fumbling over the windowsill, and then huffed as he stood straight with his cane. He pointed at Twain. "That's what I've been looking for! That's it! That's the abyssal dragon! I was promised parts of its body, and I'm not about to get gypped. I helped you all! Now you have to pay up!"

"You made a deal with *these fools*," I said as I motioned around to the arcanists in the garden. Then I pointed to myself. "You didn't make a deal with *me*. Now, do I have to repeat myself, or am I gonna have to get violent? Because no one here can stand against the might of a Death Lord."

"*I won't allow you to disrespect me in my own home!*" Lord Oto held up his hand, fire already flaring from his body, he was so enraged. He was about to evoke his magic when a bolt of lightning struck him from behind.

Oto stumbled forward, gritting his teeth as he twitched a bit. The lightning was *nowhere* near as strong as Lucian's.

The magic had come from the corner of the garden, and I spotted Ashlyn, Ecrib, Miko, and Raaza stepping out from behind an overturned bush. They were all dirty, but whole, and Ashlyn charged into the garden with her magic flashing all around her.

"Gray!"

Ashlyn ran straight to me. Her eldrin, and then Raaza and Miko, followed closely behind. As Raaza came over, he evoked *fox fire*, a type of flame illusion that could change into physical objects, but only for a short period of time. He evoked some fire and then made himself a bow, along with a single arrow. He pointed it at the nearest enemy arcanists as he made his way to my side.

Ecrib leapt to my left, and Ashlyn stood at my right, both taking defensive stances around the bleeding Lucian.

When Ashlyn glanced over, I knew what she wanted to say. *Look what you've done!* And when I narrowed my eyes in confidence, I was replying, *I got this.*

Ashlyn exhaled, her lightning crackling, her focus on the enemy arcanists now slowly inching toward us.

Twain, as an abyssal dragon, was everyone's primary focus. A manticore and the sea serpent got close, their fangs flashing. The soul catcher clattered around the edge of the garden, creeping toward us.

"Urg!" Knovak shook his head.

Then he grabbed the mane of his unicorn eldrin and hoisted himself onto the beast's back. The two galloped over to me, and they also stood at the ready.

"You somehow manage to always ruin everything," Knovak said in a harsh whisper.

Starling snorted in agreement, glowering at me when I glanced between them.

"Glad we're on the same team, too," I quipped. "You still have time to side with Lord Oto."

"If you had let them kill the bounty hunter, everything would've been good afterward," Knovak spat.

I darkly chuckled, mostly because I disagreed. I wasn't here to help these people. Right now, my goal was to help Death Lord Deimos mend the abyssal hells.

"Thank you, mimic arcanist," Deimos said through me.

"Don't mention it," I replied—talking to myself.

It was hotter than before, however, and I had almost forgotten about Lord Oto's *exhaustion aura*. He was still fighting us, and I knew I couldn't stay here.

"Twain," I shouted. "It's time to go!"

My eldrin thrashed his tail and slammed it into another wall of the compound. Lord Oto shouted curses, but he didn't move on me or order any of his goons.

"My brother," Deimos said through me.

"Zahn!" I shouted, irritated we had to deal with this.

Lucky for me, Deimos's twin ran out immediately. He climbed over some of the broken wall, and then his mimic helped him the rest of the way. Twice was still a typhoon dragon, and large enough to carry most of Zahn's weight. The two of them clambered up onto Twain.

"All our work here," I heard Zahn ground out.

But I didn't care. I hated this place.

Twain leaned in close, and I leapt to his shoulder. Ecrib, Ashlyn, Raaza, and Miko all climbed onto his massive form, each slightly disgusted by the rotting dragon flesh. And while they did that, several of the enemy mystical creatures decided to attack.

When the manticore rushed forward, I held out my hand and blasted it with raw magic evocation. The beam *tore* through the creature's chest, and the manticore crumpled to the ground. Everyone else backed away, tense and agitated.

Lord Oto's aura continued, and my head felt lighter. Twain spread his wings, flapped twice, and then as he was taking off out of the garden, he scooped Lucian up in his back claws, and then Knovak and Starling with his front claws. The unicorn neighed and thrashed, but Knovak calmed his eldrin as we took to the sky.

I was thankful Deimos's eldrin was so large. It made this flight possible.

On the flip side, I *hated* that his eldrin was so large. We flew over Waxing City, and Twain's shadow sailed over the streets like a void, calling attention to our presence in the sky. Several denizens of the city pointed up at us, some even shouting.

It would be difficult to explain this away.

My only solace came from the fact that probably no one in Waxing City knew what an abyssal dragon looked like, so they wouldn't be able to properly identify it to anyone who would care. To them, this was just a weird, terrifying dragon. Flying out of Lord Oto's compound. With half a dozen arcanists all on its back.

Hopefully it wasn't *too* out of the ordinary.

The soul-wings of Twain moaned and moved as we flew, however, and I knew that would make for an interesting story.

"Gray!" Ashlyn grabbed my shoulder, her blonde hair fluttering all around her head as we flew. "Where are we going?"

I didn't know. I hadn't thought that far ahead.

"To the docks," I said on the fly. "Hear that, Twain? We have to get to a boat. We need to leave as fast as possible."

"What about my family?" Raaza clung to Twain's rotting scales, his fingers digging into my eldrin's decaying flesh. "They're in trouble! Lord Oto... He won't forgive me for going with you."

His kitsune was tucked into his shirt, her flaming paws glowing through the fabric. "We have to help them!"

"I'll handle it," I said, mentally making a note to send Twain back to get them once we secured passage out of the city.

After just a few short minutes, Twain angled himself down toward the small docks that protruded into the ocean from the city's main street. There was only one ship anchored, and it waved a flag with a nine-pointed star with a cloud wrapped around the points.

This was Lucian's ship.

An odd vessel with a smokestack, rather than sails. That meant it was the kind of ship powered by an engine, and likely stayed close to the coast, and only ventured down rivers. I didn't care—so long as it would take us from here, I was happy.

"There!" I pointed.

Twain glanced back at me before nodding. He dove and then flapped his translucent wings in order to stop us from crashing into the docks. His massive body hit, and the wood groaned under his weight.

"I can't..." Twain growled, and his whole body bubbled underneath me.

Everyone fell onto the dock as Twain's body shriveled down into his kitten size.

Lucian collapsed into a splatter of his own blood, his own body shrinking. His wings slithered into his back, and the feathers on his arms and legs molted off. His talons shrank into his fingers, disappearing completely.

And then the Source of the Storm wiggled its way out of his neck, the little white hummingbird soaked in crimson as though it had burst from a fleshy egg.

Ashlyn and Ecrib, both athletic and agile, were on their feet and helping everyone else stand. Knovak and his unicorn were agitated, and Knovak ripped his arm out of Ashlyn's grip as soon as he stood.

Raaza and his eldrin both turned their attention to the city.

"Twain?" I hurried over and scooped my eldrin into my arms. "Are you okay?"

"It was just a lot..." He sighed and smiled up at me. "Let me catch my breath, and I'll go save Raaza's mom and sister."

"You think you can handle that?"

"I'm a powerful *mimic*, thank you very much." He waved a little paw through the air. "Did you see the way I *exploded* Lord Oto's compound? That was all me."

I smiled as I nuzzled my eldrin close. His joking put me at ease.

Then sailors ran off the nearby boat—which was named *The Elegant Rider*—and onto the dock, their attention solely focused on Lucian, who hadn't yet stood.

"The Dauntless!" one of the sailors breathed as he got close.

The Source of the Storm hopped around its arcanist. "Hurry! Hurry! Take him to safety and then hoist anchor immediately. We need to leave this place as soon as possible."

CHAPTER 33

A FRIEND'S HOUSE

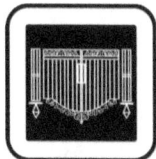

Sailors from *The Elegant Rider* hurried around us. They glanced at our arcanist marks, and mostly avoided us, but they danced to the commands issued by the Source of the Storm.

"Hurry!" the little bird shouted, its voice crackling. "Bring my arcanist to Mehdia at once!"

Men grabbed Lucian and carried him onto the ship, hustling across the gangplank as quickly as possible. They avoided meeting my gaze, and I didn't blame them.

I had *just* had an abyssal dragon as an eldrin. While they probably didn't know exactly what it was, it was still spooky.

Twain ran off down the dock, moving as swiftly as his little kitten legs would take him. I suspected he didn't want to transform just yet—so he could transform to fly Raaza's family to us and not grow too tired in the process.

Additionally, it would be much easier to explain everything to Emma and her mother as a kitten. They would listen to a mimic, and wouldn't be as frightened when he transformed into a freakish dragon that appeared to have been born in a grave.

When I headed for the gangplank, the others joined me.

Ashlyn, Raaza, and Knovak were all quick to crowd around, clearly nervous about the situation.

Zahn and his mimic were less joyful to be here.

Twice transformed back into her cat form, her pink coat striking. She leapt onto her arcanist's shoulder and glowered in my direction.

"Are we riding on *that*?" Raaza asked as he pointed to the ship.

The engine-powered vessel was definitely strange. Not many people trusted them. Several ships a while back had caught fire from mishandling, and ships that used paddles to move—like most engine-ships did—caused so much turbulence when they sailed that they eroded the banks of narrow waterways, like rivers or canals.

And because they burned fuel to move, most people saw them as nothing but *destructive*.

This ship didn't have any visible paddles, though. Just a large black smokestack sticking up near the stern. The ship was large enough to have two decks, and the captain's cabin was rather prominent. No masts for sails. No holes for oars. Just a large engine, it seemed.

However, I heard that the engines made the ships much faster than those with sails. And the sailors weren't dependent on the winds, which was a boon.

My father said they were bad omens for the future...

But we didn't have many choices. Lord Oto's goons and the cultists would surely come for us.

"Oh! The missing students!"

A woman stood at the top of the gangplank, her eyes as wide as saucers. My eyes went straight to her arcanist mark, and I squinted at the bizarre design. It was a seven-pointed star with an orb behind it.

"An enigma arcanist," Deimos said through me.

I hadn't heard of that mystical creature before.

It was—I almost laughed at my own stupid joke—*an enigma*.

The woman standing before us rubbed her hands together. She wore a simple white dress with a large black coat over top. Her boots were more sensible than fashion forward, as they were large, had noticeable grip, and were just as black as the coat.

Her brown hair was short and curly, her eyes large and watery—if they all mixed together, they'd be mud, but as it stood, she reminded me of spring.

"My name is Mehdia," she said. "I'm Lucian's daughter. I'm here to help him secure the students. That's you all, correct?"

I stepped onto the gangplank. It was sturdy, and even had guardrails to prevent people from falling. "I'm Gray Lexly, and not *all* the students who went missing are here. It's a rather complicated situation, so could we weigh anchor and maybe get out of here before all the local arcanists come to kill us?"

"Oh, my," Mehdia whispered. She held a hand up to her mouth. "I can't believe he angered a whole city yet again..."

"Your father's adherence to his principles is a constant variable in his behavioral pattern." A floating glass orb the size of a human fist hovered out from behind Mehdia's back. Its interior sparkled gray and pink, and the faint image of a library could be seen within. "This outcome does not deviate from established data," a voice echoing from the orb said.

Mehdia sighed. Then she grabbed the glass orb out of the air and cradled it like someone cradled a baby animal. "Maybe that's true, Gamma, but—"

"We need to go," I interjected. Then I hurried up the gangplank and stood directly next to the woman. She was much shorter than me. Since she was at the top of the gangplank, I hadn't noticed, but I suspected she was only five feet tall. At most.

Mehdia stared up at me. "Right. We'll weigh anchor and

start the engine, but then you must tell me everything that has happened."

Deimos's abyssal dragon magic stayed with me longer than I would've thought. The magic he provided me through our soul-link was different than the magic I gained from Twain's transformation. It seemed whenever Deimos used a soul to fuel his power, some of that fuel trickled to me—and stayed for as long as his empowerment lasted.

All my injuries had healed, and despite the immense ordeals of the past day, I still felt fresh and focused. I paced the deck of the ship, waiting for my eldrin to return, confused by the lack of concern the sailors were showing for Lucian.

Where was Twain?

I hadn't seen the Source of the Storm, either. They were all missing. Or perhaps in the captain's cabin? No one would allow me entry there.

Knovak and his elder unicorn stayed on the deck, both their attention consumed by the smokestack. White smoke puffed out the top, which was odd, because I had only ever seen black smoke from the burning of coal and coke on other vessels.

What was this ship using as fuel?

But I didn't ask, because it ultimately didn't matter. We just needed to leave.

Ashlyn and her typhoon dragon stayed close to me. They leaned against the railings of the ship, their fascination either on me, the sailors, or the underside of the vessel.

There were fin-like paddles on the underside of the ship. They moved like a fish's, powered by the engine, propelling us forward at a swift, but gentle, rate. It would've made for a fine discussion—on a different day. Maybe once we reached Astra Academy, I could speak to Lucian all about it.

Zahn spoke to a few people, and when a sailor asked for his name he replied, "I'm Temmony, a mimic arcanist in the employ of the Academy."

No one questioned that.

And I suspected he was lying because *Zahn* was wanted for murder, and for half destroying Astra Academy. It was bizarre to see him here, just standing around on the deck, staring off into the distance as though he were contemplating leaping into the waves to end it all.

"Leave him," Deimos whispered. "He won't betray me—he's simply irritated."

I huffed. "Yeah, well, he's not the greatest conversationalist anyway. He can sit and stew for a bit."

When Twain flew back to the boat, we were already several hundred feet from the docks.

He carried both Raaza's mother and Emma, but neither appeared happy or healthy. Twain flew down to the deck, his grotesque form startling all the sailors. When he got close, I feared he would shatter the deck, but he flapped his soul-bound wings and landed as gently as he could.

With one clawed foot, he set Raaza's mother on the deck.

Raaza and his kitsune ran forward to help her. "Mom! I'm here. Don't worry."

"Raaza..." she breathed, her eyes unfocused.

I suspected she had no idea she had just ridden on an abyssal dragon.

Then Emma was placed on the deck next to them. Satisfied his cargo was safely transported, Twain transformed back into his kitten form. Then he collapsed forward, a little orange puddle who obviously didn't want to move.

I went to him, scooped him into my arms, and patted his head.

The sailors continued to stare. I gave them a friendly wave. Almost collectively they shrugged and returned to their work. I supposed sailing with someone like Lucian meant they were used to the bizarre.

"Who's a good boy?" I playfully asked Twain. "You are!"

Twain growled the cutest growl imaginable. "*That's* the thanks I get?"

I chuckled. "Don't worry. They have plenty of fish here."

Twain perked up, his eyes big. "I'm so hungry. I've never been this hungry, that's how hungry I am."

The short woman, Mehdia, opened the door to the captain's cabin and stepped out. Once she spotted Raaza and his mother, she hurried across the deck. It was almost sundown, and the shadows cast were long—her shadow was taller than she was.

"Here, let me help," Mehdia said with a smile.

Her little enigma eldrin floated around behind her, its pink interior shining bright in the orange rays cast by the setting sun.

Raaza held his mother close, her feet on the deck, but clearly not supporting her weight. "She needs to lie down. Do you have another bed?"

"I have a safe place to put her." Mehdia slowed her walk once she was close. Then she pointed to the deck. Everyone stopped what they were doing—even the sailors—and focused on the deck. Those long shadows made it a little difficult to see, but *Mehdia's shadow* started moving.

I caught my breath as it grew larger and more spherical. The shadow expanded outward, like a dark pool of water growing larger with the rain.

The shadow expanded until it was under Raaza and his mother.

Then they slipped into the shadow.

And disappeared.

"What happened?" Knovak shouted.

"B-Brother?" Emma yelled.

Knovak's unicorn stomped his hooves. "*She's tricking us! Kill her!*"

"Her magic isn't used for death," Deimos said through me, somehow getting my voice to be gruffer than before. "Enigmas can create tiny worlds where they store objects—or people. They are guardians of secret places. Mysterious. Rare. Extraordinary."

Knovak glanced over, his expression still bordering on rage.

Ashlyn swallowed hard. Then she moved over to my side, avoiding the shadows as she went, and placed a hand on my shoulder. "What kind of magics does that mystical creature have?"

"My eldrin creates a home," Mehdia said as she held up both her hands, trying to pantomime what she was saying. "It's like a house, but it doesn't exist anywhere but inside my shadow. While people are within it, they're comforted by the magic that makes the place."

The shadows on the deck shrank and returned to their normal form.

Raaza and his mother were nowhere to be seen.

"But *where* are they?" Knovak demanded.

Mehdia motioned to the air around us. "In... a pocket."

"A pocket space is a magical anomaly that is not bound by the normal laws of the universe." The little glass orb, the enigma, swirled around its arcanist, glittering as it went. It spoke like an otherworldly *thing*, barely human, even if it was using our words. "The conditions within a pocket space can be precisely calibrated for the optimal healing processes."

"Gamma is correct." When Mehdia smiled, she was warm and bright. "I used my magic to craft a little home so I can help people recover from long adventures. My father always needs time to rest, so, you understand."

Ashlyn nodded once. Then she gave me a sidelong glance. "And I thought *I* was too attached to my dad," she whispered under her breath.

"Adding comfort and compassion to her parental unit's life isn't the only reason for my arcanist's decisions," Gamma said, matter-of-factly, as it floated around. "It is pertinent to note that Mehdia also wishes to impress a particular male individual, commonly referred to as a *crush*."

I snorted back a laugh.

Ashlyn shook her head.

Mehdia grabbed her enigma and shoved it deep into her black coat. Her face was as red as the setting sun. "You don't need to listen to my eldrin. All you need to know is that *everyone is okay*. I have things under control. I'm a professional arcanist, almost a master arcanist, and I've done this for several years now. Everyone *will* recover."

"Really?" Emma, the ten-year-old girl, took a brave step forward, even though she was clearly terrified. "They'll be okay?"

"Would you like to see your mother?" Mehdia motioned to the shadows. "I can take you all into the pocket space for a short period of time. It might be a little cramped with everyone... And you might have to leave the larger eldrin here."

I exchanged glances with Knovak and Ashlyn.

Zahn turned, sneered, and then intentionally glanced away. He clearly had no intent of taking a peek at the little enigma's magical abilities.

"I want to see my mom," Emma said, her voice small.

Mehdia nodded. "Very well. Don't be scared."

Her shadow stretched out once again. It became darker, and pooled out across the entire deck. A few of the sailors hurried away from it, still tending to their duties, just mindful of where they stepped.

When the darkness reached my feet, I tensed. What was this going to feel like? Would it hurt? Mehdia had said this space would be small. Would we be hurt entering, or standing around inside it? Did it have air?

"You won't be harmed," Deimos said through me, almost in a reassuring tone.

"You got my back, Dee?" I playfully asked. "You're looking out for me?"

The Death Lord didn't answer. I could tell I irritated him.

But I couldn't think about that for long. Ashlyn grabbed my hand as the two of us sank into the depths. I met her gaze, realizing she was a little startled by the transition. We were engulfed by the shadow, its cold presence comforting, like it was gently lowering us to the deck below.

But when the shadows lifted, we weren't on the boat anymore.

We...

We were in some sort of paradise.

It was a house—but it wasn't *built*, it was *grown*. The walls were lush oak trees, their trunks wide and ancient, their bark creased deep by the weather over the centuries. Each branch was woven with the next to create definable walls, and floor, and even the furniture. They were smooth where they needed to be a seat, and rough underfoot, to prevent slipping.

This house was both mystical and alive.

The canopy above formed the roof, a living mosaic of green, where light filtered through in dappled patterns, casting an ever-changing tapestry of shadows and luminescence within. The air was alive with the scent of sap and earth.

Emma, Ashlyn, Knovak, Mehdia, Gamma, Twain, and I all stood in a sitting room. Well, Gamma floated, but still. Multiple chairs and the large table could accommodate four, maybe five people, so it was feeling rather cramped.

Large-leafed vines grew on the walls in some places, creating little pictures, decorating the space with vibrance. There was a long hallway, a kitchen with a brass teapot on a stove, and even several windows, though the blinds were all drawn.

"What is this?" Knovak asked. He stumbled around, trying to glance at everything all at once. He shielded his eyes from the light streaming down through the leaves.

"I told you," Mehdia said. "This is my little pocket space. As an enigma arcanist, I have control here."

"What, exactly, do you evoke?" I asked as I marveled at the way the roots formed into the feet of the chairs.

"I evoke the *gateways*. Mine looks like a pool of shadow, but Gamma tells me other enigmas create different-looking portal types."

"And what does your magic manipulate?"

I sounded like a student going through a checklist, but in all fairness, I was a student. I didn't mind asking questions, because I hadn't even known this type of mystical creature existed until right now.

"I manipulate pocket spaces," Mehdia said with a nervous laugh. She waved her hand, and the tree walls shifted with her will. Branches appeared, and then cups emerged from the bark, like fish rising to the surface of water, and each cup was filled with piping hot tea.

"I can create anything here," Mehdia said. She pointed to the hallway, and then to two doors made of twisted leaves and bark. "I placed my father in that room, and the ill woman and her son in the other."

Emma's eyes were wide, her mouth hanging open. It was clear the little girl had never seen anything so magical before. She said nothing, just observed, taking in every little detail.

"You can make this space into anything?" Knovak stepped away from us until his back hit the living wall of tree trunks. "So... So... you could turn this all into lava and kill us? Is that it?"

The panic in his voice was unnerving. Did he really think Mehdia had brought us here to kill us? Knovak was already sweating, and his arcanist star, which still looked as though it had melted, suddenly appeared more like it would slide right off his face.

Mehdia held up both hands. "O-Oh, no! Please don't panic. I wouldn't hurt you."

"Even if she attempted to harm us, the change is gradual," Deimos said through me. "And harming the arcanist, or the environment too thoroughly, will cause us to be expelled."

"That is one hundred percent correct," Gamma chimed in, almost cheerily.

Ashlyn—who still held my hand—leaned in closer to me. "You can make this environment look like anything? What if you wanted... to make it seem like we were underwater? But not *actually* underwater?"

Mehdia nodded. "I could do that. Um, the real benefit comes in altering the very fundamental nature of the space, though. You see these trees? It wasn't just an aesthetic choice. I made it so that things grow faster here. I slightly changed a fundamental aspect of reality, if that makes sense... I mean, I can't make *huge* changes, only small ones. And it's reflected in the environment."

"Wow..."

Ashlyn released my hand, and I watched her slowly meander her way around the sitting room. Twain gave me an odd glance from the floor, and I waved away his look. I wasn't in the mood for teasing.

As Mehdia motioned to the hall and guided Emma, Ashlyn, and Knovak to the closest room, I stayed behind.

"Why do you know so much about enigmas?" I whispered.

"These mystical creatures... Their magic has similar properties to the Twilight Gate. They make gateways to new worlds."

"Can we use one to help restore the abyssal hells?" I asked, my excitement mounting.

Twain glanced up at me, his large ears perked. He was curious, too, it seemed.

"My brother already investigated the matter. While they are similar, they don't make gateways to the hells—only their own tiny realms. This place you stand in, much like the abyssal hells, has properties unlike normal reality. That is how they are similar."

"So we *can't* use an enigma to fix the Twilight Gate? Or maybe make a new one?"

Deimos growled, and my throat hurt from the effort. "According to my brother, they are not strong enough."

I rubbed my chin as I pondered the problem. I hadn't known creatures like enigmas existed in the world. Perhaps, if we found other creatures like this, or maybe other creatures that empowered other magics, we could cobble together a solution.

I shook my head.

This was a problem for someone like Zahn, though. I wasn't an expert on magical item creation—I wasn't even a second-year student at Astra Academy. If I wanted solutions to complicated problems, I either needed a new angle no one had tried before, or masters of magic far outside of my capabilities.

"What're we going to do, Gray?" Twain asked.

After a long sigh, I motioned to the hallway. "I need to think about it. Let's join the others."

We headed down the hallway, and Mehdia stepped out of the first room, followed closely by her enigma. She smiled at me, so short, and somewhat adorable, as though she was much happier here in this small, living house than out on the deck of the ship.

"Oh, um, student... Gray? Was it? You can stay here for a little while, but then you need to return to the surface. We're taking a river into the Argo Empire."

"Why?" I asked.

"My father has many friends, and one of them is Lord Dodger. He will make sure my father is healed—along with everyone else who is considered a good friend."

Lord Dodger?

"Wait, isn't that Nasbit's family name?" Twain asked. "If we go to see his family, I'm sure they'll help us get back to Astra Academy in no time."

CHAPTER 34

RIVER NIGHT

"But before we reach Lord Dodger, I need to ask you something," Mehdia said.

I lifted an eyebrow. "Sure."

"Well, I can tell through *context* that you're obviously not a Death Lord." Mehdia chuckled, half-nervous and half like she had told an inside joke and found it really amusing. "My father said there was a chance you would be possessed by Death Lord Deimos, but the fact you brought him back to the boat—and then went out of your way to save a sickly woman and a small child—I think it's clear you're not *evil*."

"Tell that to Lucian," I said, rather serious in tone. "I didn't explain myself well, and things sort of spiraled out of control. Lucian won't believe a word I say."

Mehdia, still chuckling, said, "My father doesn't believe a lot of things. He's rather *adamant* that scoundrels will use lies as much as a soldier will their weapon, so he often closes his ears, to the point we run into a lot of problems."

"But he'll listen to you, right?"

Mehdia slowly nodded, her smile wavering. "I... *will*... speak to my father, but I have a few more questions."

"Hit me."

Twain rubbed up against my legs, his expression set in stony determination. Gamma, on the other hand, orbited its arcanist, glittering as it went.

"Mimic arcanists can only mimic creatures who are nearby." Mehdia eyed me. There was no question there, but her tone made it seem like there was.

Then she was quiet. Silence stretched between us, and then it dawned on me. She was confused—Twain had shifted into an abyssal dragon, *implying* that a *real* abyssal dragon was nearby. Which would be both terrifying and dangerous. Perhaps a *real* Death Lord was nearby, and she wanted to tell Lucian all about it.

"Through a bizarre series of events, I have a fragment of a soul trapped within me," I said, careful with my words. "And that soul gives me access to an abyssal dragon. It isn't nearby. It's still in the abyssal hells. I'm not a Death Lord—even if I have some Death Lord powers."

"Oh, whew."

Mehdia's laughter returned and became genuine. She made a playful motion of wiping away sweat from her forehead. It was rather... awkward. But cute?

"I'm so glad we cleared that up," Mehdia said.

"You believe me?"

Twain tilted his head. "You seem a lot more reasonable than your father."

"In my little pocket space here, I can sense things better." Mehdia tapped her fingertips together. "I know. From the way you breathe. Move. Your heartbeat. You're not lying. You're just as relieved as I am—and that's a good sign. I'm so glad you're not our enemy."

"Oh, I wanted to ask you... What do enigma arcanists augment? I mean, forgive me, I know I must sound like a know-nothing nincompoop, but I *am* still a student, and I've never seen a mystical creature like yours before."

Mehdia smiled brightly. "Oh, I love it when people ask me about Gamma."

"That is accurate," her enigma stated. "She has informed one hundred and seventy-two individuals about my powers, and only forty-three of them prompted the conversation by inquiring ahead of time."

"Enigmas and their arcanists prevent teleportation," Mehdia said matter-of-factly. "They can also shunt people back through portals, or prevent them from being forcefully teleported. Enigmas are like magical gatekeepers, keeping people where they belong. At least, that's how I like to think about it."

"Interesting..." I whispered.

When I stared at Gamma, the little glass orb reminded me of a pearl. I wondered if enigmas somehow came from the abyssal hells, or if they were made of the same material as the Twilight Gate.

That would be interesting indeed.

"Well, thank you," I said to Mehdia. "I appreciate you taking the time to answer all my questions."

"And thank you *so much* for bringing my father back to me."

Mehdia actually bowed to me, rather formally, which left me feeling a little nervous. The only reason her father had gotten hurt was because of me, so I didn't think I deserved to be thanked.

I stepped away from her and shrugged. "Eh. It's fine. I'm just glad he and his hummingbird didn't kill me."

"What?" Twain leapt from the root-twisted floor up to my shoulder. He perched himself gracefully and sniffed my cheek. "You think a little bird is going to kill you? Never."

"*Little?*"

The door to Lucian's room was open just a tiny bit, but the gap was large enough for the Source of the Storm to fly through. The pure white hummingbird flitted into the hallway and then zoomed around my head, its wings beating so furiously that I couldn't see them individually, just as a blur around its body.

"I'm not *little*! The nerve!" The Source of the Storm darted around my head and then poked at me with its beak, jabbing my ear and then my scalp.

"Ow, ow," I said as I waved my arms, trying to shoo it away.

Twain puffed up his orange fur and swiped with his claws, trying to catch the Source of the Storm as it flitted about.

"You're right," Twain said. "You're not little, you're *tiny!*"

The Source of the Storm puffed itself up, matching Twain's angry posture with its own floofy feathers. "The audacity! The rudeness! This is why felines are the worst! *The absolute worst!* They don't follow the rules! They just do whatever they want!"

"Now, now," I said in a playfully scolding tone. "That's not —*ow, ow!* Stop that! I didn't insult you!"

The Source of the Storm jabbed me over and over. "You're that rude cat's arcanist! You're just like him, no doubt. Ill-mannered!"

This creature didn't have the right name. It shouldn't be the *Source of the Storm*, it should be *No Calm, All Riot*. It was completely unhinged, and just as oddly stubborn as Lucian. I hadn't done anything wrong, and it was already out to peck my face off.

But then Deimos's reflexes and instincts kicked in. As the hummingbird was flying around the side of my head, I took advantage of the fact that it couldn't see my hand for half a second and grabbed the bird as it rounded the bend near my ear.

It made a *peep* as I gripped it tight, but not powerfully enough to actually hurt it.

"Okay, now you need to calm yourself," I muttered. "Take a tiny breath and—"

The little monster evoked lightning from its wings, zapping my hand so thoroughly I yelled and dropped it.

"Oh my goodness," Mehdia said. She leapt forward, grabbed

the Source of the Storm as it flew from my grasp and then held it close.

"Unhand me!" the hummingbird chirped.

"Gray?" Ashlyn charged out of the other room and ran to my side. "Are you okay?"

I shook out my hand and then shrugged. "I was almost killed by nature's punch line, but I'll be fine."

The hummingbird snuggled into Mehdia's hands and then stuck its long tongue out at me.

Ashlyn touched my shoulder, then grabbed my hand and examined the palm. When she met my eyes again, I already knew what she was thinking. She was upset I had been mean to the little bird—but she hadn't seen what an awful monster it had been.

"The bird was being mean to me," I said with a playful pout.

Twain nodded. "It was. I can vouch for that."

"I apologize for my father's eldrin," Mehdia stated. "He's a handful sometimes."

Just like Lucian.

"It's fine." Then I shrugged. "I'll just exit your little space here and head up to the deck. Let me know when we reach Lord Dodger's abode."

I stood on the deck of *The Elegant Rider* as the moon rose in the night sky, and the stars came out to greet it. Part of me expected to see Lord Oto, with his blue phoenix, chasing us down the river, but I never caught sight of them, not with my eyes or my ability to sense magic.

Instead, our engine-powered ship swam against the stream, heading into the Argo Empire on a river that was so wide, it was almost difficult to see the shore. The fin-shaped paddles under the ship's hull were gentle enough that it didn't disturb the water much, and the banks of the river weren't destroyed by this new engine technology.

I wondered if my father would think that was a *good omen*.

Twain sat on the railing next to me. His large ears caught the wind and fluttered about. He actually had to keep them down if he wanted to relax, and I chuckled when his whiskers wiggled so much he frowned.

What was Sorin up to, I wondered?

Was he still at Astra Academy?

I hadn't been away too long, but apparently, I had disappeared so thoroughly, the headmaster hired a bounty hunter to bring me home.

Sorin and I...

Had never been apart from each other quite like this. I didn't know where he was... and he didn't know where I was.

It made my chest ache.

But then I took a deep breath, and kept my gaze to the stars. It wouldn't be long now, and I'd see him again. He was fine. Of course he was fine. Why wouldn't he be fine?

"This must be how you felt when you were separated from Zahn," I whispered.

Twain glanced over and eyed me. "You talk to Deimos a lot, ya know."

"It is rather irritating," Deimos said through me.

I chuckled, amused by his constant grumpiness. At some level, he enjoyed seeing the world around me. I felt it. He paid attention when I went someplace new, and when I was engaging in conversation.

"I've been away from Zahn for centuries," Deimos said. "I rarely feel the agony anymore... Except that night, not too long ago, when I entered your Academy. I saw Zahn then. Saw him with my own eyes. And since then, it's been difficult. We had been so close to achieving all our goals, and finally reuniting in the land of the living."

Zahn had been *insanely happy* to see his brother.

He had also been *insanely murderous*, but that was another matter. At some level, I felt like Zahn was getting so desperate to see Deimos he would kill himself just to do it. But perhaps I was being too morbid.

Zahn hadn't spoken to me this whole trip, yet here he was with us.

Would he accompany me back to Astra Academy? Headmaster Venrover wouldn't suffer his presence, that much I knew.

"I hope you and your brother are reunited soon," Deimos said, softer this time.

"That's uncharacteristically nice of you," I quipped.

Twain huffed. "Right? I didn't know Death Lords could be sappy. We've been a bad influence on him."

Deimos's irritation spiked, and I issued a groan on his behalf.

I was about to laugh when I heard whispered words carried by the evening winds. Tearing my gaze away from the sky, I glanced around. There was a single sailor tending to the cleaning, but other than that, I was alone. Large eldrin slept in the hold while everyone else had gone into Mehdia's pocket-space, since she could use her manipulation to change all the rooms in her "tree" house to make comfortable bedrooms.

"You really think it was worth it?" someone asked, their voice louder than before.

Where had it come from?

I glanced over at the captain's cabin. Two individuals were standing on top of the cabin, though it was difficult to see. However, when they spoke next, I recognized them. Raaza and Knovak.

"I thought the abyssal hells were dangerous?" Raaza asked.

"They are, but if you want power and magic, you have to be willing to face danger," Knovak responded, his tone haughty.

I walked across the deck, and Twain chased after me. When I

reached the captain's cabin, I spotted a ladder and quickly ascended to the roof. Knovak and Raaza had stopped their conversation the second I touched the first rung, and were quiet until I was fully standing on the upper deck.

Miko was here, too, her little fox feet glowing in the darkness.

But Knovak's unicorn wasn't here. The horse-sized beast was down in the hold.

"Good evening, gentlemen," I said as I sauntered over. Then I nodded to Miko. "And lady, of course."

She twitched her nose.

Twain leapt up the ladder and then lifted his head high as he strode next to me. Was he mimicking me? Sometimes he was too adorable.

"Get out of here, Gray," Knovak stated. "This conversation isn't for you."

"*Not for me*?" I held my cloak tight around my shoulders, trying to protect myself from the chill of night. "Are you having a secret conversation about all the things you're going to do for my birthday party?"

Knovak glared at me as though he'd love to see me fall off the side of the boat.

Raaza, on the other hand, chuckled.

Some people still enjoyed sarcasm.

But then Raaza stopped, and he looked me straight in the face. "Gray…" He didn't follow that up with anything, but his tone was heavy. I could practically taste the regret on the air.

"It's okay," I said.

He didn't need to apologize to me. I probably would've done something similar in his shoes.

"Next time, you should kill anyone who threatens your blood," Deimos said through me.

Raaza rolled his eyes. "Yeah, well, it's easy for *you* to say. You have all this power, and a magical weapon, and an abyssal dragon."

"That's why you're not allowed in this conversation," Knovak interjected. He stomped forward, his eyes yellowish in the moonlight. Normally he was a plain boy with blondish-brown hair, and no notable features—the plainest of plain—but tonight he just seemed...

Sickly.

"I don't follow you," I said. "Why am I not allowed?"

"Because we were talking about how to go about getting power." Knovak turned so most of his back faced me. "What would you know? Of course you'd recommend *killing people* who threaten your family—you have the power to do that. But Raaza didn't."

"Well, that was Deimos's advice," I said with a shrug. "And in case you weren't aware, he really likes *death*."

It was Twain's turn to chuckle, but he tried to stifle it before it became audible.

"But even if I didn't have all this power, I'd still have told someone my family was in danger." I glanced over at Raaza, and then returned my attention to Knovak. "People like Lucian are eager to bust into someone's house and punch everyone in the throat with the power of justice."

Again, Twain was laughing.

I loved my eldrin.

"I told people," Raaza stated. "But no one wanted to fight against Lord Oto."

"Clearly, you didn't speak of your plight to Lucian," I quipped. But then I offered a second shrug. "Did you tell Headmaster Venrover?"

Raaza threw both his hands up in the air. "I was sent to the school to help the Followers of Death Lord Deimos. I didn't want to risk my enrollment by telling him that! Getting accepted into Astra Academy was the *best thing that ever happened to me*. I figured, if I just got strong enough on my own, I could handle my own damn problems, and then I could be free—along with my family."

Miko puffed up her fur and held her head high. "And we're still going to do so, my arcanist! I told you. I'm really strong. And the more you train, the better we'll become."

"You would've lost your family if Gray hadn't intervened," Knovak snapped, his voice half a growl. "*Training* is never going to make you as powerful as a Death Lord. You need to find *other* ways to improve yourself. Trinkets. Artifacts. Runes across your body."

Knovak stopped talking and then grazed his fingers over his melted arcanist mark.

"Or eating fruit from the abyssal hells," Knovak whispered, his gaze losing focus as his thoughts roamed. Then he snapped his attention back to Raaza. "If you're not willing to take the next steps to make yourself strong, you're *always* going to have to rely on others."

I stepped closer, practically shoving my way between Knovak and Raaza. "There's nothing wrong with depending on others," I said as firmly as possible without sounding angry. "Nations don't hire one arcanist for their military—they have several who all work together for a greater goal. It's like that for plenty of things in life."

Knovak sneered as he stepped away from me. "You don't know what you're talking about, Gray. I didn't become powerful listening to *you*. I became powerful doing what I knew would work." Knovak glared at Raaza. "Just remember that when some *other* powerful arcanist has you under his thumb because you were too weak to do anything about it."

Then Knovak stormed across the cabin and leapt off the side, not even bothering to use the ladder.

I didn't like his attitude. It seemed out of character for him. Too dark. Too forceful. Had he always been like this, and he had just been hiding it? Or was this all happening because of the fruit he had eaten in the abyssal hells?

Honestly, I was worried about him.

"I really appreciate you helping my mother and sister," Raaza whispered.

I glanced over. "Oh. Don't worry about it. Hopefully once we land, some healers can help your mother. And if they need payment or something, I'm sure we'll figure something out."

"Because I should learn to depend on others?" Raaza lifted an eyebrow.

I smacked his shoulder. "Something like that." Then I looked him hard in the eye. "Just don't turn out like Knovak, all right? Promise me that."

"Oh, you have my promise." Raaza frowned. "He... reminds me a bit of Lord Oto right now, honestly. And I told myself I'd never be like that man. Not now, not ever."

CHAPTER 35

ELOPED

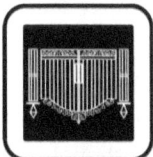

The *Elegant Rider* smoothly sailed into a city I had never heard of.

It was called *Orlindis*, and apparently it was some sort of artist's paradise. I leaned on the railing of the ship, waiting for this wonderland of creativity to come into the sight, just because I couldn't believe a city for artists even existed.

What did they do all day?

Twain was asleep in one of my arms, his purring loud enough that it made me smile. I stroked his warm orange fur while keeping my gaze straight ahead.

The water around the ship moved, and I glanced down to find Ecrib swimming in the river. His beautiful blue scales practically blended with the liquid around him.

"Ashlyn in there with you?" I asked, lifting an eyebrow.

"She's napping," Ecrib said.

I patted Twain again. "Ashlyn and my eldrin are a lot alike."

"Ha!" Ecrib huffed. Then he lifted his head high out of the river and spat water at me. I leaned away, and it splattered across the deck. "My arcanist is way more likeable than your kitten."

Twain yawned, stretched his paws until his claws stuck all

the way out, and then stared up at me with a groggy expression. "Are you talkin' about me? While I'm sleepin' right here? Rude."

Ecrib shot another stream of water. I sidestepped that one, too, but I took note that it was aimed straight at Twain.

"Double rude," Twain playfully said.

I was about to add another quip when the city of Orlindis came into view.

Houses and stores were built on both sides of the shimmering river, each one made of white birchwood with glittering blue windows, as though the glass were made of clear aquamarine. The glass only partially reflected the light, which was what caused the *glitter* effect. The small bits that were reflected danced across the grass, roads, and walls of the nearby buildings.

It was as if the whole city was glowing.

The river, acting as Orlindis's lifeblood, flowed quietly, allowing the city to have a tranquil atmosphere. And as we traveled deeper, the vibrancy of life here was unmistakable. Verdant plants adorned every balcony, windowsill, and rooftop, their lush foliage spilling over the edges in a controlled manner.

Nothing was *overgrown*. It was artistically cut to make it seem *alive*.

It was as if nature itself had taken up the brush and palette, adding vibrant splashes of color to this white and blue canvas of a town.

"Do you smell all this, Gray?" Twain leapt to my shoulder and sniffed the air with enthusiasm.

The air was perfumed with the scent of blooming flowers and fresh foliage. It wasn't overpowering, but it was unique and difficult to ignore now that it was washing over me.

"Sorin would love this city," I said—the first conclusion that came to my mind.

"Oh, yes! Your brother would love this place." Twain continued to sniff. "I bet he would make, like, a poem about it.

In this city of white and green, so clean, even the pigeons strut about, snobbishly preen! Something like that."

I chuckled. "Yeah, something like that indeed."

I missed my brother. Which was silly—we hadn't even been apart that long. But still. Why was I visiting a city meant for artists *without* him? Sorin would cut off his left hand to live here.

As our boat drew closer to the dock, I smiled to myself. Someone, somewhere, was playing a lute, and the notes danced on the wind. This place really did feel like an artist's paradise.

"Finally," Ecrib said. But then he lifted his head again, his scales flared. "Wait..."

"What's wrong?" I asked.

Then I searched for magical threads and quickly gathered the answer myself. There was another typhoon dragon here—one much stronger than Ecrib. Two of them, actually. How many typhoon dragons could fit into such a small area? There was also a leviathan nearby, which was unusual. How many leviathans were seen in rivers? I heard they never left the safety of their salt water, but I supposed weirder things had happened.

As *The Elegant Rider* pulled into the river dock, the ship's handful of sailors tied everything off.

Mehdia, Ashlyn, Raaza, and Knovak all came topside and stood on the deck, either having walked up from the hold, or appearing from a shadow portal Mehdia had created. Thankfully, we had all ditched our cult attire and were now wearing sailing gear. Thick pants, loose shirts, and thin coats all around—it wasn't fancy, but at least I had sturdy boots again.

Well, I had kept my cloak. It was beautifully white, and soft to the touch. Why wouldn't I keep it?

Starling, Miko, and Gamma were also in attendance. Miko playfully swiped at Gamma as the little orb sailed by. Starling, on the other hand...

Wasn't cute at all.

Had he grown more muscles since last I looked at him?

The muscled unicorn moved across the deck with the gait of a predator. I had seen large draft horses in the past, but Starling was starting to put them to shame.

But the ship rocked, drawing my attention back to the immediate. I glanced over the railing of the ship and spotted something monstrous rising from the river waters.

It was a humongous typhoon dragon—one I had met before. This was Ashlyn's father's eldrin, Enki.

The dragon was a creature of the water, covered in fins and spines. His feet were webbed, and his scales were every color of water, from the deepest blue to the slightly aqua-white of seafoam. He was long, and slender, but still powerful and agile. The crest of fins on his head was a marvel, and once the upper half of his body was above the water, he roared.

People in the city of Orlindis panicked and ran for the buildings. Several doors were slammed and curtains pulled over the glittering windows.

"What is the meaning of this?" Mehdia asked as she rushed to the boat's railing.

"Oh, no." The color drained from Ashlyn's face.

"I think Archduke Septimus Kross is here," I said, sarcastically casual. "But that's just a guess, since the man is reserved and *definitely* doesn't just announce his presence wherever he goes."

Knovak glanced up to stare at the mighty typhoon dragon looming over the bow of our ship. "The Kross family has always been insufferable."

Ashlyn shot him a sidelong glance, but Knovak didn't apologize for his statement.

As our ship lowered the gangplank, a man came walking down the dock.

If there was ever someone who had a *condescending walk*, it was Septimus Kross. The archduke just had a special way of walking that conveyed all his disappointment in every step. And today was a special day, because his expression was so severely angry, I'd be surprised if he ever smiled again.

"Oh, *this* guy," Twain whispered.

Archduke Kross's typhoon dragon arcanist mark was strikingly evident, especially since the man wore his blond hair so short. He kept the sides shaved, and the top was neatly combed back, and still rather short itself. His skin was fair, but the mark —the seven-pointed star with a massive typhoon dragon wrapped throughout it—was dark, that was how deep it marked his flesh.

His eyes, a piercing blue, held the depth and allure of the most vibrant turquoise waters—more so than even the river we sat upon.

Archduke Kross came to a halt at the end of the gangplank.

"*Ashlyn*," he called out.

The archduke wore a beautiful silk outfit that moved with the wind. A white shirt, black pants, and a deep red cloak all came together to give him an elegant—and regal—appearance. I felt a little embarrassed because I wasn't wearing my ridiculously expensive cult attire anymore, but at least I still had the cloak, which I could use to hide my scruffy hand-me-down sailor outfit.

Archduke Kross also sported a short beard. However, its light blond color rendered it nearly imperceptible, blending subtly with the contours of his face—and his frown.

Ashlyn hurried to the gangplank.

As she went, Mehdia said, "I'll be taking my father and your friend to Lord Dodger's estate. I'm certain my father will want to—"

But Ashlyn didn't say anything or even acknowledge her statements. Ashlyn headed down the gangplank as quickly as she could, straight to her own father.

"—escort you back to Astra Academy," Mehdia lamely

continued, her own tone indicating she knew she was being ignored.

"We really appreciate that," I said as I headed over to the gangplank myself. "But that's Ashlyn's dad, and I think she needs to have a chat with him first. Once we've wrapped up all our personal business, we'll definitely head back to the Academy. With the Dauntless, of course."

Mehdia nervously chuckled. "Oh, good."

I headed down to the dock, but neither Raaza nor Knovak followed.

And now that I thought about it, I hadn't seen Zahn all morning. Would he be joining us? I was starting to think the man would never reveal himself now that we were back in proper civilization. I felt Deimos's concern through our connection, so I made a mental note to seek Zahn out before we headed to the Academy.

But all those thoughts ended when I reached the bottom of the gangplank.

Archduke Kross's complexion was now a shade of tomato. He wasn't shouting—I had figured someone with that amount of red would be yelling so loud, the people in the neighboring nation would hear—but instead, it was worse. He was whispering.

"I cannot believe what you have done to this family's reputation," he said, every word an even deeper level of seething than the last.

Ashlyn stepped closer to her father. "I swear to you, Father, I can explain everything."

As she spoke, Ecrib dragged himself out of the river and climbed onto the dock to be next to his arcanist. The massive typhoon dragon, the archduke's eldrin, moved closer, disturbing the water so much it splashed up onto the boat, the dock, and even portions of the city's riverfront.

"I already know what happened," Archduke Kross said. He

glared at me as I walked over, and I stopped a few feet behind Ashlyn.

"You... *know* what happened?" Ashlyn asked, her eyebrows knitted.

"Oh, yes. I knew the moment you disappeared from the Astra Academy celebrations—especially after you implored me to make this *foozler* your fiancé."

Foozler?

That was a new word I had never heard. I kinda liked it.

"You *ran off with him*," Archduke Kross said, his volume now rising with every word. "You eloped! And you did so in such dramatic fashion that *everyone* knows of your deed. That's all they speak of! How my daughter disrespected me, left a party where *everyone was in attendance*, and made such a scene that it'll never be forgotten!"

"F-Father," Ashlyn said, trying to raise her voice to match his, but failing to do so. "We didn't—"

"Don't you understand this *boy* has nothing but a prurient interest in you? Don't you realize how you've sullied yourself? *Sullied our family's good name?*"

Prurient was a new word, too.

This man was on a roll.

But while I was willing to let him scream himself into a much-needed nap time, that was clearly not how Ashlyn felt. When I glanced over, she was wringing her hands, her shoulders bunched at her neck. She looked on the verge of crying—I had never seen her quite this distraught before.

"*Do you want everyone to think you're a harlot?*" the archduke asked. "Because that's what you've done."

I grabbed Vivigöl from my person and it *click-click-clicked* as it transformed from a piece of jewelry to a full-blown sword with a dark gold blade. Twain leapt from my shoulder, and in one quick swipe, I slashed through a portion of the dock right in front of Archduke Kross, leaving a gouge so thorough, I could see the river through it.

Archduke Kross stopped talking. He didn't flinch, he didn't yell, and he didn't back away—he glowered at me, icy hate in his gaze.

"I think it's Ashlyn's turn to speak," I said, calm but clear.

Ashlyn took a deep breath.

But she didn't say anything.

I turned slightly to meet her gaze, and the look she gave me said everything. Ashlyn hated we were doing this in public. When I glanced around, I realized everyone *was* watching. Raaza, Knovak, Mehdia—the denizens of Orlindis. Even the lute music had stopped, so I assumed the musicians were getting in on this drama.

I suspected Archduke Kross wanted everyone to hear him yelling at his daughter, so he could say, beyond a shadow of a doubt, that he obviously hadn't approved of her actions. But he was just embarrassing Ashlyn, and himself.

And it was upsetting her.

So it had to stop.

"Why don't we go have a family discussion *indoors*?" I asked, trying not to be sardonic, but failing. "I think it deserves a little bit of privacy."

CHAPTER 36

A REAL MARRIAGE

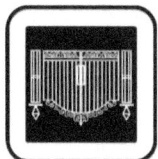

The insides of the buildings were more impressive than their outsides. While the buildings were all made of white birch on the outside, the interior was mostly red oak, bricks, and iron. It was like the building had flesh on the inside, and the wood was stained with blood. It was beautiful, but in a haunting way.

Or maybe that was Death Lord Deimos's influence on me. I doubted I would've thought of red wood as bloodstained six months ago.

This whole town almost reminded me of the abyssal hells. It had an aesthetic that was both mystical and deep.

After I had transformed Vivigöl back into jewelry, we had entered some sort of inn nearly in the heart of town. When I sensed for magic now, I felt dozens of threads, some of which I didn't recognize. However, I smiled when I felt a stone golem and a coatl. Were Nasbit and Phila here?

Not only did I miss my brother, but I missed Astra Academy as well. If Nasbit and Phila *were* here, I would love to see them, even for just a moment.

Ashlyn, Ecrib, Twain, and I stood in the lobby, admiring the large fireplace. It was currently empty, but it was still large enough to fit ten people, so it was impressive even when not in use. Twain leapt to the mantel and walked across it. Ecrib sniffed at the bricks, his scales flaring.

Archduke Kross and another arcanist were also here in the lobby, though they stood on the other side of the room, near the largest window.

I recognized the person next to the archduke—it was Valo, the leviathan arcanist. He had a last name, but I didn't care to remember it. He was just *Valo* to me, his name so repulsive to say, it felt more like a curse word I would fling at my enemies.

"You're making a fool of yourself," Deimos whispered through me.

I rolled my eyes—seemingly at myself—and replied in a quiet voice, "I've met this man before. He's insufferable, and just wants a young wife to look good in front of others. He doesn't care about Ashlyn, and he certainly doesn't deserve my respect."

"You don't show someone respect as a reflection of *their* character—you do it because it's a reflection of *your* character. Maintain your composure, and you will have the upper hand in any conversation you take place in."

I wanted to reply with a quip, but I didn't have one, so I remained silent.

Archduke Kross turned to face us. There was at least twenty feet of empty space between his location and our location, but he didn't seem interested in closing that gap.

"I've rented this building for a few days," he stated. Then he swept a hand to the side, gesturing to mortals who wandered around cleaning. "These are all individuals in the employ of House Kross. This is the most private space we could gather in all Orlindis."

I hadn't even noticed the individuals dusting and mopping. Was the inn not clean enough for the mighty archduke? Seemed so.

"I've invited Valo Fitzroy here because this concerns him," Archduke Kross stated. "As he is Ashlyn's fiancé, he has a say in the ultimate outcome of this matter."

Oh, right.

Fitzroy was Valo's family name.

Everything about the man was insufferable.

"Your pettiness is a weakness," Deimos whispered.

"What's *your* advice?" I quickly, and quietly, asked. "*Kill them all?* Just stay silent and let me handle this."

"You never listen when I advise you to slay someone. If you had, Valo wouldn't even be here."

That was a good point. But I couldn't time travel, so this whole conversation was moot.

Ashlyn gently took my elbow, and I stopped thinking about Deimos altogether. She seemed more herself now—more confident and self-assured. She stood tall as she said, "Gray and I didn't elope, Father. We were attacked by a Death Lord and drawn into the abyssal hells. That's why you couldn't track us."

"*That's* the explanation you're offering?" Valo interjected.

He had a lot of striking similarities to both Ashlyn and Archduke Kross. His hair was a noticeable blond, his complexion moderately fair, and he wore an expensive outfit made of fitted silk. His shirt, vest, and long pants were probably from the same place the archduke got all his clothing.

But Valo had muddy brown eyes that seemed on the verge of tears. Nothing like Ashlyn's or her father's.

Lastly, Valo's eldrin wasn't here. Leviathans were large, so it was probably in the river, along with Archduke Kross's typhoon dragon, but I was still surprised. Valo's eldrin was still young, after all.

"Ashlyn spoke the truth," I said, also cutting into the conversation.

"So you were both whisked away to the abyssal hells for a week?" Valo huffed out a laugh, and then did it a second time, only louder. "Do you hear this, Septimus? That man is a terrible influence on your daughter. They're weaving lies—and not even *good* lies."

I was about to make a sarcastic joke at Valo's expense. I wanted to—I wanted to be so petty, and irritate him so much he stormed from the room. But Deimos's advice lingered in mind. He was right. I should maintain my composure. I was in the right, I was telling the truth, and I knew Valo was trash.

There was no reason to throw verbal jabs. He was already hilariously wrong about everything.

"I was in the abyssal hells," Ashlyn firmly stated. "If it weren't for my magic, we would've died. I gave people the ability to breathe underwater, and we had to navigate our way through the first abyss in order to flee the clutches of the other Death Lords."

She said every word as though she had mentally practiced and prepared.

The archduke crossed his arms over his chest. "That's impossible."

"*It isn't*, and I have dire news. The abyssal hells are in turmoil, and we need to speak with Headmaster Venrover at once."

I nodded along with her words. That was true. We needed everyone to know.

Ecrib walked over, his claws clicking across the wood floor. "My arcanist is correct. We witnessed several of the Death Lords fighting. They're doing terrible things in the realm of the dead, and if we don't act, the world as we know it may be in grave danger."

"Meow, that's right," Twain said, probably more as a joke, but I appreciated him chiming in.

"Do you have any proof?" Archduke Kross asked, his tone now all business. "Objects you stole from the hells? An entrance we can use to go back?"

Ashlyn took in a deep breath, but then hesitated. We didn't have a way back, and we hadn't brought anything *specifically* hells-related, even if we had a few minor things that would be ridiculous to deny. Knovak's arcanist mark and elder eldrin were a lot of proof, and the necklace I wore was from someone who was supposedly dead.

What else did we have?

Because none of those things were *definitive.*

"The moment you and *the boy* disappeared from the Astra Academy celebrations, the rumors spread like wildfire," the archduke stated. "Everyone knew you fancied him. Everyone knew he was vying for my approval. And when I didn't give it to you—*the both of you vanished.* As far as every other noble house is concerned, there was no need for an investigation, because the writing was on the wall."

Everyone was silent.

He was probably right. It looked suspicious. The easiest explanation was that Ashlyn and I had eloped. I understood.

"Unless you have solid proof," Archduke Kross continued, "it will be beyond difficult to wash this stain off our family name."

"Father…" Ashlyn muttered.

"I *hope* you're not lying to me, because this explanation is better than the one where you're spreading your legs for the men in your class."

"*What was that?*" I shouted—and also laughed, because I couldn't believe what I was hearing. It probably came across as threatening, especially as I took two steps forward. "Ashlyn is trying to tell you the truth, and with every breath you take, word you form, you belittle her further and further like this is all some sort of sick game for you. *What kind of father does that to his own daughter?*"

I was yelling, and I half expected Deimos to say I should keep my composure, but that wasn't the case. Deep in my thoughts, he told me—*Disregard my earlier advice. There is no need for civility here.* Deimos didn't like Septimus Kross— probably because Deimos didn't appreciate *any* fathers who disrespected their children. Deimos was ready to solve this with violence.

I supposed fighting would solve some problems, but only temporarily. And Ashlyn had made it clear to me that she still loved her family—she didn't want me to bury them all.

But this had to stop.

Archduke Kross didn't have to insult Ashlyn with every other word. He was just being a passive-aggressive windbag.

"*You shouldn't even be here,*" Valo shouted back, his volume on par with mine. "I heard about your attempts to take my bride —you're just a power-hungry lowborn trying to sleep your way into a noble family!"

"You know what would get all the other noble houses to shut up? *If I threw you both a beating and left with Ashlyn.*" I pointed at Valo and then to Ashlyn's father—both of whom looked completely taken aback. "Don't. Insult her. Any further. You can either speak to her like the fully grown woman and arcanist she is, or I'll start to make good on my threats. The choice is yours."

I wasn't entirely certain if Ashlyn wanted me to stand up for her, but she didn't protest when I made my statement. And when I glanced over my shoulder, to make sure I wasn't doing something she would hate me for, I spotted the slightest hint of a smile.

I got the feeling not a lot of people stood in her corner. Most people probably sided with her father in these kinds of arguments.

But I wasn't most people.

Archduke Kross laughed. It was a kind of forced and dramatic laugh, like this was a stage play and this was his part to take center stage. He stepped forward, so he was a bit closer to me.

"You? Threaten *me*?" He shook his head. "Do you even know who you're talking to, boy? I've fought in wars, slain dozens of arcanists, and weathered the kind of hurricanes you've only ever seen in your nightmares. If this were to come down to a fight, I'd break every bone in your body."

"You may test that assumption at your convenience," I said in a calm and icy tone.

It wasn't just me. It was also Deimos.

We both wanted to kick this man in the teeth. No one spoke to Ashlyn like she was some kind of whore—not while I still took breath, anyway.

"Gray." Ashlyn walked over and placed a hand on my shoulder. "It's okay. I really appreciate you doing this, but I think my father will listen to reason."

Valo also moved forward—all four of us were now in the middle of the lobby, only a few feet away from each other.

"No, I think Septimus would do right in this situation if he put the boy in his place," Valo stated. "Clearly, the little first-year student thinks too highly of himself. He's not worthy of Ashlyn's hand, and he's certainly not worthy of the Kross name."

"You could always challenge me yourself," I said under my breath, glaring at the man.

Ashlyn stepped between us all. "Stop." Then she turned to face me with a frown. "I don't want you to hurt my father. Please, Gray, let's just do this civilly."

"You don't want *him* to hurt *me*?" Archduke Kross asked, indignant. He sounded as though he would start choking on his own laughter. He was both incredulous and enraged, and it made for an amusing moment where he couldn't even find the right words. "My own daughter? *Doubting me*?"

"You don't understand," Ashlyn said, facing her father.

"Gray helped us escape the abyssal hells. He's not a normal mimic arcanist. He has—"

"I don't care if he marched across all the deserts on Vardin. He's still just a man, and I won't tolerate his insults."

"*Gray has the power of a Death Lord himself,*" Ashlyn shouted—straight at her father. Which was likely the first time that had ever happened. "Listen to me for once, Father. This is different!"

After her loud statements, no one said a word.

Technically, I didn't want that to get out, but I supposed too many people were learning about it to keep it hidden forever. Now all the nobility would know. And soon, so would everyone else.

That was fine. I felt Deimos's acceptance—and something else. He seemed resigned, which was an odd emotion to have. But I couldn't ask him about it, because we were in the middle of a heated argument with Ashlyn's family.

"Mimic arcanists just *copy* whatever arcanist they're facing," Valo said as though he were giving us a lecture. "If a mimic arcanist fights you, it's like facing a mirror in terms of magic— but not in skill. Whoever is the more adept fighter would win if it came to blows."

Ashlyn dragged a hand down her face, her cheeks red with anger. "I'm not... I'm not saying he's mimicking the magic of a Death Lord. I'm saying Gray has *all* the abilities of one. The combat prowess, the knowledge. *Please*. We can just talk this over. I don't want to see my father hurt."

It seemed Archduke Kross really didn't like someone pleading on his behalf. His face was scarlet all over again, his livid expression contorting his whole face with rage lines. Sparks of lightning flickered all around us, and it almost felt like the Source of the Storm's thundering aura.

"Are you saying Gray has been consumed by the abyssal hells themselves?" Valo asked. "He's an evil lord of death? Is that it?"

If Ashlyn had been allowed to strangle Valo, I suspected she would have. She took a deep breath before saying, "I'm saying Gray is himself. He's just extremely skilled for someone of his youth."

Valo opened his mouth, but Ashlyn held up her hand. Then Ecrib stomped over and flashed his fangs, growling at Valo until he closed his mouth.

"We didn't elope," Ashlyn stated. "Gray saved us all. He's brave, he's charming, and he stands beside his friends and family to the bitter end. Frankly, it is embarrassing that my own father thought I had run off, when *my whole life* I have done nothing but a-attempt to prove myself to... to..."

Her lip quavered, and her words began to fail her.

But I understood.

I placed a hand on her shoulder and looked her dead in the eyes. I *would* be there for her. And if she didn't want to have this conversation, I'd tell her father to take a slow boat ride home.

Despite all that, Ashlyn steadied herself again with another deep breath. All the water in her eyes vanished, replaced by iron determination and cold anger.

"You wanted me to get good marks from tutors? So I did. You wanted me to get accepted into Astra Academy? I did that, too. You wanted me to learn to fight? I'm one of the best of my age. I accomplished every goal I set my mind to."

"Ashlyn," the archduke muttered, but Ashlyn silenced him with a wave of her hand.

"When we were in the abyssal hells, I thought—*if I just give this my all, we'll make it out of here.* But the only goal I can't ever seem to achieve, no matter how hard I try, is... Well, *it's making you happy.* You're *never* happy, Father. *Never.* So if you're not going to be happy, maybe *I* should just be happy instead."

Ashlyn grabbed my arm.

I tried not to blush, but I hadn't been expecting her sudden display of affection.

A nervous chuckle escaped me for half a second. Then I quelled all that and stood a little straighter.

Perhaps fighting our way out of the abyssal hells had done Ashlyn's self-confidence a lot of good. She had refused to fight her father when we were celebrating at Astra Academy. Now she was ready to speak her mind, even if it was obviously difficult for her.

"You already have my brother," Ashlyn said. "He's perfect, isn't he? You don't also need to control everything about me."

"Are you serious?" Valo interjected.

He stomped around the lobby for a second, clearly flabbergasted. If I could have gotten a painting to immortalize his expression on canvas, I would have. He was so childishly distraught, it was hilarious.

"*This* boy makes you happy?" Valo motioned a hand up and down. "He's a lowborn gibface who barely understands etiquette or honor! He's nowhere near as handsome as I am, and even his *kitten eldrin* is an embarrassment to look at."

"Hey!" Twain shouted from the fireplace. His ears flattened against his skull. He leapt off the bricks and dashed to my side. With one graceful bound, he landed on my shoulder, his orange fur puffed to the maximum. "A snob like you isn't even *worthy* of talking to my arcanist! Back off, or else I'll make your face just as ugly as your insides!"

It seemed like everyone wanted to get into a fight, despite how hard Ashlyn was working to prevent it.

"By the stars," Ashlyn groaned. She rubbed her temples and then shook her head. "Gray is—"

I grabbed her hand. She stopped talking. Everyone turned to me, both the archduke and Valo with pure disgust.

But I wanted to say something.

"Ashlyn has all these goals she wants to conquer," I said, mostly speaking to her, but halfway speaking to the whole room. "But for most of my life, I never had any real goals. I wanted to be an arcanist, sure, but that was just to get to Astra Academy. I'm supposed to pick a vocation at the end of my studies, but even that I have no strong preferences about—whatever role I'm in, I'll be fine. And if I switch trades or professions, I'm certain I'll do well in those, too."

That was all true. I could be happy flitting from one thing to another, and none of the skills or trades offered by Astra Academy even really appealed to me.

"However," I said, my voice becoming softer, "the moment I laid eyes on Ashlyn, there were no other options for me—there weren't even any doubts. My soul is that of a wanderer, but my heart knows its true destination."

Ashlyn's face reddened. She tightened her grip on my hand, and I returned the gesture.

The others were listening, but I barely paid them any mind.

"Even if I had a thousand lifetimes, my heart would never grow bored," I said,

"my heart will never venture down another path. I'll be with Ashlyn, or I'll be forever alone. This is my declaration, my vow, my eternal promise." Then I turned to face the archduke. "And I'm not making it to *you*. I'm making it to *her*."

Silence descended over the room once again.

And while I meant what I said, they weren't entirely my words. It was as if... Deimos's memories were becoming one with mine. I felt like I had said this to someone before, a long time ago.

I ignored that feeling and instead focused on the immediate.

It was still true. My heart only wanted to love one person in a deep and romantic way. And it wouldn't settle, or search for something better—it had found its other half, and there was nothing else I could do about it.

The creak of a door startled everyone. We all turned, practically in unison.

Two individuals stepped into the lobby from the deeper part

of the inn. It was a woman and a young man, both of whom were so lovely and perfect they could've come straight from an oil painting of royalty.

"Mother?" Ashlyn asked, half gasping. "Brother?"

Oh.

The Kross family was here. And since we had all been yelling, I was certain Ashlyn's mother and brother had heard every word and every threat as though they had been in the lobby beside us.

Lovely.

CHAPTER 37

A REAL TEST

I knew now where Ashlyn had gotten all her good looks.

Ashlyn's mother had a slender build, yet she moved with confidence and grace, as though she had once been a dancer. Her hair, a shade of dusty oak, was pulled back in a practical yet elegant knot, revealing the sharp intelligence in her deep-set eyes, a striking shade of hazel that seemed to flicker when her gaze met mine.

Runes glittered on the side of her neck, both sandstone tan and aquamarine, as though she were wearing necklaces of pure power. They were just as beautiful as she was, their design playful yet elegant, done in tight swirls from her shoulders up to her jaw.

"Gray," Ashlyn whispered. "This is my mother, Kaitlyn Kross, Grand Artificer at the Elliot Library, and a master minerva owl arcanist."

Sure enough, when I glanced up at the woman's forehead, I caught sight of the seven-pointed star with the image of an owl woven among the points.

Kaitlyn? I had also discovered a hint as to where Ashlyn got her name.

Ashlyn's mother strode over to the archduke. Her attire was a blend of functionality and sophistication—a tailored jacket of deep burgundy, over a blouse of soft ivory. Her hands, deft and assured, bore the subtle stains of ink, as though she had just been penning something before she had arrived.

"We heard everything," Kaitlyn said, confirming my fears. "I thought you said you would handle this with *care*, Septimus."

A minerva owl flew through the open door and glided around the lobby. It had the large body of a barn owl, with the large feathers of a horned owl, along with the copper armor of a small soldier. The armor itself was only on the creature's chest and along its spine, blending into its feathers as though grown from its very flesh.

The owl's striking yellow eyes were practically glowing, and they reminded me of the gazes the Death Lords had.

The owl circled once and then elegantly landed on the mantel of the fireplace, perched precisely on the edge.

"This debate has spread to the people of Orlindis," the minerva owl stated, her voice rich and lyrical. "They speak of the Kross family as though it were in turmoil."

From what I could remember in class, minerva owls evoked wind, and augmented things to temporarily weigh less. It was why they could wear armor, even as small birds. What did they manipulate? Was it also wind? They were fast moving creatures with a tendency for trickery, that much I knew for certain.

Kaitlyn turned to her daughter. The fine lines at the corners of her eyes spoke of years spent in studious dedication—not in laughter, nor in happiness.

"I'm sorry," Kaitlyn said. "I knew you weren't ready to venture out into the world. I should've kept you closer and simply paid tutors until you were mentally well enough to handle reality."

Wow.

And here I had thought Ashlyn's mother would be kinder, but that was probably me being foolish.

Before Ashlyn or I could say anything, her brother sauntered over. Instead of taking his place by the archduke or his wife, the man went straight to Ashlyn.

And this whole family had enough confidence to fuel an army.

Ashlyn's brother made his way over as though he owned the place. His hair, the same golden blond as his father's, was tousled to look messy, but it clearly wasn't. His eyes, a vibrant blue, scanned me from head to toe with an inquisitive gaze, missing nothing.

"This is my brother," Ashlyn whispered. "Evander Kross."

Though still rather youthful, there was a budding sharpness to Evander's features that hinted at the handsome man he would become, a subtle echo of his father's refined physique. He was also a man of appearances, and his outfit said as much. Evander was dressed less formally than Kaitlyn, in a shirt of soft blue that brought out the color of his eyes, and trousers that, while neat, allowed him the freedom to move in unexpected ways.

But it was his arcanist mark I cared about the most. He had the same design as Ashlyn and her father—a typhoon dragon.

It really ran in the family, it seemed.

Instead of speaking to Ashlyn, however, Evander kept his sights on me.

"I heard your declaration of love," he said. "Mother and I were just beyond the door when you started your serenade. We didn't want to interrupt, but perhaps we should've saved you the embarrassment."

I couldn't stop myself from smiling. This man was fixing to get his face punched in.

Deep in my soul, I hoped this came to a fight. Deimos wanted it, too, even if he had originally advised me to show respect. Since clearly everyone here wasn't concerned with whether they angered me or Ashlyn, I wasn't going to be concerned if I broke their noses.

"Dear sister," Evander said as he glanced away from me. "What were you—"

"Whoa, whoa." I stepped between him and Ashlyn. "Who do you think you're talking to? Because I've known you for a grand total of five seconds, and I can guarantee no one wants to speak with you."

"*Gray*," Ashlyn hissed through clenched teeth.

I didn't look back at her. If I did, I'd see her anger and shame at the situation, but I wasn't about to let *everyone* in her family waltz in here and insult her before we came to a conclusion.

It took Evander a *split second* to realize I had been insulting him, which really betrayed a lot about his character. He wasn't slow, or dim—he had just wildly underestimated me. Evander hadn't thought I would open our meeting with an insult, probably because he was far too used to people licking his boots.

"If you and your mother heard everything, then you must know Ashlyn and I escaped the abyssal hells together," I said, staring Evander in the eyes. "That's the kind of adventure where you learn who you can really trust in life—and I learned Ashlyn has more bravery and integrity than a room full of knights. So *of course* I had to declare my love for her. That's what you do when you find someone as amazing as Ashlyn—not that *you* would understand."

Despite the fact that we were in a large and spacious lobby, Valo weaseled himself ever closer, huffing the whole time. "Ashlyn's *true fiancé* is *right here*."

"End this charade," Kaitlyn said, holding her husband's arm. "Please, Septimus. I don't want any further shame. Lord Dodger is certain to know of our quarreling."

Archduke Kross turned to his wife. He held her hand and grazed her knuckles with his thumb. "Kait—we should consider the possibility they're telling the truth. It changes the whole situation."

"How so?"

"If our daughter is a hero who ventured into the abyssal hells, it is quite the accomplishment."

Kaitlyn replied with a curt and dignified nod.

"Let me handle it, my love."

Ashlyn's mother kissed the archduke on the jaw and then sighed. "So be it. But end this embarrassment, Septimus. It hurts my heart to hear the rumors day in and day out."

Archduke Kross faced me. "Were you truly in the abyssal hells?"

I nodded once. "That's right."

"And you have the battle prowess of a Death Lord?"

"Also correct."

"Then we should take a walk outside, where I will test your claims for myself."

Evander smoothed his coat and then took his place at his father's side. He was almost identical to his father once they were close enough to compare. No wonder the archduke favored him so much—it was like paying compliments to a mirror.

"Father, allow me to do this for you," Evander said.

I motioned over to Ashlyn's fiancé. "Why not Valo? He looks like the kind of man who could easily test my claims."

Valo had this disgusting slippery expression, like he wanted to glare and curse my name, but he knew he couldn't be so cowardly. His lips curled upward in an unnatural smile, but before he could choke out an acceptance, Kaitlyn shook her head.

"No, Valo is still a young arcanist," she said. "He hasn't all the skills yet to make such a determination."

It was nice to know she was condescending to *everyone*, not just Ashlyn.

Archduke Kross patted his son on the shoulder. "We shall do

this together. After all, if Gray is as skilled as a Death Lord, two typhoon dragon arcanists are no match. He should be plenty fine."

"Just add everyone," I said with a sarcastic shrug. "Hear that, Valo? You're back in the game. Lady Kross, why not join in? Four on one, that's fine. I'm fine. Everything is fine."

Kaitlyn narrowed her beautiful hazel eyes. "I earned the title of *grand artificer* through years of magical research. I will observe your powers from afar, have no doubt of that."

And despite the fact I had called him out twice, Valo remained silent. A pity.

I wasn't entirely sure how Archduke Kross wanted to test my skills, but the way he moved told me he wanted to see my *battle prowess* up close. He had been so enraged when Ashlyn doubted him that it felt like he wanted to earn his daughter's respect back—by showing her how fearsome he truly was.

That was fine.

"Occasionally, fools will only listen to power," Deimos whispered.

I chuckled as Archduke Kross and his son made their way to the other side of the lobby and then exited onto the clean streets of Orlindis. Twain purred, his whole body practically shaking on my shoulder.

"Are we going to do this?" he asked, his whiskers tickling my cheek.

"Sure are," I said.

Ashlyn held my elbow, preventing me from exiting the inn. When I glanced over, she frowned.

"Don't actually hurt them," she whispered.

"If they attack me, I might hurt them." Then I smirked. "But I won't do anything that'll have a lasting effect."

"Promise?"

I nodded.

Twain nodded as well. "I'll just give them *little* scratches."

He placed a forepaw on his chest. "You have my word as a mimic."

Ashlyn smiled. "Thank you, Twain."

Ecrib snorted. "You should be careful. Enki is a powerful typhoon dragon, and Ashlyn's brother is bonded to Ezran, a dragon who has had several years to mature."

"My mimic is just as good as any of them," I said in a playful tone. "Remember? It's a little mirror battle. You don't have to worry about me."

Ecrib snorted.

He *was* worried about me.

I was almost touched.

"I'll be watching from the sidelines as well," Valo announced.

I wasn't entirely sure who cared about where he would be—because not even Kaitlyn seemed concerned about his plan. Ashlyn's mother smoothly walked across the lobby and headed outside, away from us. She didn't say anything to me, or to Ashlyn, and she certainly didn't glance back at Valo.

Her minerva owl flew off with her, exiting the inn at the same time with a smooth and easy glide.

After a long, and awkward, moment, Valo hurried to go join them, leaving Ashlyn, Twain, Ecrib, and myself alone in the inn front room.

Even the servants had vanished, though I didn't know when they had gone.

"Gray," Ashlyn said to me, her voice soft.

I waved my hand through the air. "I already said I wouldn't hurt them too bad."

"That's not what I was going to say."

I lifted an eyebrow.

She stepped close to me. Then Ashlyn wrapped her arms around my body. When our bodies pressed together, I took note of every little feeling, every soft movement, every subtle shift.

Ashlyn placed her forehead on my chest. "Did you really mean all those things you said?"

"About how no one would ever want to speak to your brother?" I quipped. "Oh, yes. Definitely."

She snorted back a laugh. Then Ashlyn tightened her grip on me. "I meant... about how you felt. And that you think I'm amazing."

"I've told you that you're amazing dozens of times." I returned her embrace and held back a laugh. "How many more times do I have to tell you before you believe me?"

"I don't... I don't know. I might never believe it."

I leaned against her, smelling her hair, enjoying every moment. "Then I guess I'll just have to say it forever."

"Do you think I should just go outside and tell my family to leave us alone?" she whispered into my chest. "Do you think it would be better if we actually eloped? And never returned to them?"

"You say the word, and I'll do that right now," I said. "But I was doing this for you." I closed my eyes and sighed. "I thought you wanted your family's approval—and you wanted them to allow us to wed? Because, let's be serious, they're never going to *like* me. Not after today. But they might respect the fact I have power, and that I'm devoted to you."

Ashlyn chuckled. She held me even tighter than before. "You honestly think you can prove to them you have the skills of a Death Lord? In a single friendly duel?"

"Definitely," Deimos said.

CHAPTER 38

A REAL FIGHT

I exited the inn along with Ashlyn and our eldrin. The streets of Orlindis were carefully crafted with beads of blue glass mixed between the other stones. When the sunlight hit the walkways just right, they shone like water. As I walked away from the inn, I even felt like I was gliding over a beautiful sheet of blue ice, and I was both impressed and sad Sorin wasn't here to see this.

Surprisingly, Archduke Kross and his family weren't waiting directly outside. They were down the road a way, at the large market square, with several of their house's retainers scurrying all around them, like ants massing over a piece of bread left on the ground.

When Ashlyn and I approached, I noticed the Kross family ushered all the Orlindis citizens away from the square to clear out a space. The baffled denizens of this beautiful town stood around in small groups in the alleyways and roads, looking on with frowns and crossed arms. The Kross family had also brought weapons—the archduke held a polearm, and his son had a two-handed sword.

"What's going on here?" someone on the road asked.

"We should inform Lord Dodger at once," another whispered in response.

I walked by without answering, wondering if the Kross family was just in love with drama—they seemed to create it wherever they went.

The archduke's polearm was a long shaft with a sword-like blade at the end, all done in silver and black, with the moon and stars carved into the side of the weapon. It had to be seven feet long, at least.

Evander had a sword made of the same type of material, and designed with the exact same care.

Neither compared to Vivigöl, so I didn't know what they thought they were doing. Perhaps the weapons were also magical items? If that was the case, Twain could theoretically transform into them, though I had never actually had Twain do that before. My eldrin didn't like the idea of being an inanimate object.

"What kind of weapon is your father holding?" I asked Ashlyn.

Before she could respond, Deimos replied for her. "It's a glaive. A type of weapon favored by infantry who wished to fight mounted opponents, or mounted knights who desire a weapon they can use while in the saddle."

Ashlyn nodded. "My father fought in several smaller wars when he was younger, and *his* father was the Marshall of the Southern Seas, who taught him all about combat with a glaive."

"Do you know how to wield a glaive?" I whispered.

"I'm a master of every weapon," Deimos muttered.

I rolled my eyes. "I'm certain I could find a rare and bizarre weapon you're not a master of."

"*Tsk.*" Deimos's irritation filled my thoughts. "You won't find it in the *glaive*, one of the most common weapons known to infantry."

Ashlyn eyed me and then half chuckled. "Is the Death Lord with you at all times?"

"It's not bad unless he gets grumpy," I quipped. "Deimos, do you know anything useful about glaives?"

"Much like a trident, it is a weapon that is best used to keep opponents at a distance. Up close, it's more difficult to maneuver. If the girl's father wishes to challenge you to a bout of skill, stay close to him at all times."

I motioned to Ashlyn, and then to myself. "See, he's great. Dee just gets a little upset whenever I make jokes."

Ashlyn slowly nodded, as though weighing some unknown fact, and then coming to the conclusion everything was okay.

Twain hopped around at my feet as I made my way into the center of the city's market square. Ashlyn and Ecrib walked over to Kaitlyn, who stood away from the city's citizens. Her owl sat perched on the nearby rooftop, its polished armor contrasting nicely with the white birch of the building.

Valo was only ten feet away, standing stiff and sneering.

I wondered what he thought about all this, but only because it would be hilarious to hear his innermost thoughts on this event.

Once I was in front of Archduke Kross, I stopped and waited. How did he want to go about proving I was a Death Lord? I could have Twain transform into an abyssal dragon—but that wouldn't be as much fun as making everyone answer for how they treated Ashlyn. I hoped the archduke would suggest we spar, even for just a moment.

The archduke snapped his fingers, and the mortals in his employ ran over with a second glaive. They attempted to present it to me.

Archduke Kross *did* want to have a little test of skill with a weapon. That made me smile. I waved away his weapon and instead grabbed Vivigöl. It transformed as I pulled it from my body, and once it was done *clicking*, Vivigöl was a glaive that matched the archduke's.

Well, it didn't *completely* match. Vivigöl was still sickly golden because it was a weapon made of pure abyssal coral.

"What is that?" Evander asked, incredulous.

"*Vivigöl, Silencer of the Damned*," I said. "A weapon crafted by Death Lord Deimos himself."

"You were just *wearing* a weapon crafted by a Death Lord? What a preposterous tale."

"Do you want to hold it?" I asked, holding the weapon out for him to take.

Evander hesitated.

Which was good, because if he touched the weapon, it would start draining his soul. It seemed only abyssal dragon arcanists could touch and hold the coral that grew in the abyssal hells. Well, perhaps *any* arcanists who were death-dealers. Nini and her reaper weren't affected by the bizarre fatal properties of the hells, so perhaps reaper arcanists could touch this as well, though I wasn't about to start testing any theories.

"Don't taunt us with games," Archduke Kross said.

I lowered my hand and then shrugged. "So? What's the test? You just want to spar really quick? Because Death Lord Deimos is a master of all weapons—which means I am, too."

"Then I would love for you to prove that," Archduke Kross stated.

"Perfect." I stood across from him and spread my feet to take up a combat stance. "I'm *so* ready for this."

And while I had never fought with a glaive in my life, I allowed Deimos's training and instincts to guide my handling of the weapon. With my dominant hand, I grabbed the rear end of the staff, and with my left hand, I held the middle. Both thumbs pointed forward, and I kept the tip of the blade closer to the ground.

Archduke Kross watched me, his face natural and betraying

nothing. Then he grabbed his silk shirt, and quickly tugged it off his body. I was shocked to see he was rather muscled, but also more shocked to see the glittering runes that covered most of his skin. They were bright red and swirled, and in the vague shape of serpentine dragons.

When the archduke held his weapon, it was different from how I held mine.

He had his dominant hand on the end, and his other hand in the middle, but his thumbs were pointed at each other.

"It's a defensive stance," Deimos whispered through me. "Easier to block incoming attacks and then counter."

"Is he more skilled than you are?" I asked.

"This *child* doesn't understand that true skill with a weapon can only be purchased in blood."

"Or by accidentally inheriting it from a Death Lord," I quipped.

I felt Deimos's amusement at that comment, and I smiled.

"Don't look so confident," Archduke Kross snapped. "Come. Show me your combat skill, and then we can move on to the magical. I want to assess all your knowledge and all your supposed capabilities."

"I'll wait for you right over here," Twain said. He hopped a good twenty feet away and then took a seat. People pointed at him, but Twain didn't pay them any attention.

With a chuckle, I stepped forward and then swung upward, the tip of the glaive aimed at the man's face. Despite the fact that I had attacked without much warning, Archduke Kross easily blocked with the shaft of his weapon, the loud *clang* of metal on abyssal coral echoing around the city square.

Gasps rang out from the crowd. Several citizens ran off, as though they couldn't believe this was happening. It was a city of artists, after all. I supposed not too many people came here to have impromptu sparring matches.

Archduke Kross didn't seem to care. He took a step backward and waited.

I stepped forward and swung upward again, this time a little more forcefully than before. As if this was a duel on repeat, the archduke blocked a second time.

When I stepped forward a *third* time, Archduke Kross spun to the side, and then swung wide with his weapon, aiming for my guts. If I had slashed upward, like the two times previous, he would've cut open my stomach and allowed everyone to get a good view of my breakfast.

But that wasn't what I did.

I switched my grip, so my thumbs were both pointed away from the blade, and then lunged forward, so I was closer. The archduke hit me with the shaft of his glaive, but I *thrust* forward, stabbing at his ribs, but missing only slightly because Archduke Kross was agile enough to react in the middle of the attack.

He quickly stepped to the side, and my blade sliced him across the ribs, carving a bloody furrow beneath his glittering red runes.

He gritted his teeth and leapt away from me, scarlet blood dripping across the beautiful city square.

"By the stars!" someone shouted.

Gasps and whispering filled the whole area. Kaitlyn's eyes were so large I noticed them from across the square.

"Are you okay, Father?" Evander asked.

I stood straight and adjusted my grip on Vivigöl back to how it had been before.

Archduke Kross placed a hand on his injury. He took a deep breath, but he didn't look like he was in much pain. His wife hurried to his side, and she shook her head.

The two had a whispered conversation before Kaitlyn placed her hand on the wound. The tan rune markings on her neck glowed, and when she removed her hand, the injury was gone.

She had some sort of healing enchantment, it seemed.

"Minerva owls don't have healing magics," Deimos stated.

"Ever since we started harvesting occult ore, wealthy arcanists have taken to giving themselves all sorts of useful runes," I muttered. "Don't you remember? We learned about that in class."

"Don't talk like we're in the same class, *boy*," Deimos growled. "I have little use for—"

But he cut himself off.

Once Archduke Kross and Kaitlyn were done speaking, they separated. Kaitlyn returned to her position on the sidelines, and the archduke returned his attention to me.

"Deimos?" I whispered, too soft for anyone else to hear.

But he didn't reply.

His thoughts were... jumbled. Panicked.

I didn't like that. Was something wrong?

"You said you were a master of all weapons?" Archduke Kross asked.

I sighed and then nodded. "That's right."

"My son has long studied the art of swordsmanship."

Evander stepped forward. He held his two-handed sword with quite a bit of finesse, even though it was a larger weapon. The blade was nearly three feet in length.

I tightened my grip on Vivigöl, and it clicked as it transformed into a nearly identical two-handed sword. My guard had three spikes that flared out on either side, making it seem a little deadlier than Evander's.

Evander held his sword low.

Without Deimos's commentary, I wasn't entirely certain if this was a defensive or offensive stance. Despite that, I held my weapon close and my body practically moved on its own as I widened my stance and readied myself. I decided I'd let Evander make the first move.

"I don't believe you have the power of a Death Lord," Evander stated. "Even if you've allied with one, and have his knowledge—it's not the same. You're still a mimic arcanist, and mimics are good at only one thing. Pretending."

I was pretty good at pretending, actually. Evander wasn't wrong about that.

But that didn't matter.

He could throw insults at me all day. At least he wasn't insulting Ashlyn.

"I've studied the sword with three masters," Evander said. He slowly began to circle me. "And I bested them all."

"Okay," I replied.

"I learned magic from the Marshall of the Southern Seas, and I graduated from Astra Academy at the top of my class. My father taught me the ways of combat, and the rigors of war. Even if you have the skill you speak of, and you were in the abyssal hells, one trying experience does not make you great."

"Are you going somewhere with this?" I muttered.

Evander frowned and narrowed his eyes. "I think you're unworthy of my sister's hand. You wouldn't just be part of our family—you'd be part of *history*. The Kross family is made up of nothing but *exceptional* individuals who influence all the world with their magic, skill, and leadership."

"And *Valo* is worthy of all that?" I snorted back a laugh. "I'm not bothered by your insults because I've seen the individuals you praise. You have no idea who will make history."

Evander smirked.

Then he rushed forward. He slashed downward with his heavy weapon. I pivoted to the side, half deflecting his blow with the side of my sword. The resulting *clang* was quieter than when I fought the archduke, but the blow had been heavier. My arm hurt afterward. I had to step away and rotate my shoulder.

I had all of Deimos's skill, but not his muscles.

I really needed to work on that.

Evander rushed at me again, and I easily deflected his strike. Another clang, but my shoulder hurt even more afterward. I backed up further this time, my thoughts filled with potential strategies. Deimos would know what to do, but since he was preoccupied, I'd just have to think of something.

Evander liked heavy hits, so perhaps speed was the only suitable counter.

I was prepared to do just that when a white-hot pain bloomed across my chest. I groaned as I doubled over, the agony terrible. The crowd around us shouted things, but I couldn't hear the words.

Blood dripped from my clothes.

What had happened?

I glanced down. My clothes were undamaged, but they were soaked in crimson. When I pulled my shirt forward, I realized I had a large gouge in my flesh. It wasn't a sword wound—it was something else.

"What the?" I muttered to myself.

"Gray?" My eldrin ran straight to my side. "What's wrong?"

"*What happened*?" Ashlyn called from the sidelines.

I shook my head and closed my eyes.

Last time, when I had concentrated, I had managed to see through Deimos's eyes. I tried focusing on him, because that was the only explanation. Something was wrong *on his end*. Not mine.

It was difficult to focus when my chest burned, but I managed to push away everything else.

Deimos...

He stood somewhere in the abyssal hells. It was raining. Beads of cold water pelted him at a fearsome rate. A castle made of black bone, twisted metal, and crystal windows was in the distance, visible even through the horrible weather.

Around the castle was a wasteland of desert. The monsoon's worth of water didn't seem to change that, either. The rain hit the sand and then was soaked away, disappearing as though the desert could never be quenched.

The beating of wings caught my attention. It was louder than the downpour.

Deimos glanced up, and I saw Xuandi, the elder phoenix dragon.

That disgusting monstrosity of feathers and scales slowly lowered himself onto the sand before Deimos. He was gigantic, and loomed over the desert, his red feathers soaked in the waters of the abyss. His sickly yellow scales matched the sickly yellow of leathery portions of his wings. He was a freakish mix of bird, bat, and lizard, his talon-claws so large, they could pierce the hull of a ship and sink it.

"You are a fool for venturing out of the safety of the Requiem Throne," Xuandi said, his voice half a growl and half a laugh. "You will be eradicated, Deimos, son of a whore, death of a king, ruler of nothing."

Xuandi was so huge, his booming voice caused the desert to tremble.

"Once you perish, no one will remember the phoenix dragons even existed," Deimos said. "I'll make sure not even the abyssal hells remember your foul kind trod these lands."

"You have already lost, Death Lord. My magic is sapping your strength, and your soul is shattered—you won't be able to recover. Soon, you will slumber, and then I will consume your flesh. Done are your days as ruler in the abyssal hells."

Then someone shook me.

Not Deimos—they shook *me*.

I opened my eyes and took a deep breath.

"Gray?"

Ashlyn held my shoulder, her blue eyes searching mine. I had to gulp down another breath, but then I nodded. "Yeah?"

"What's wrong? You've been standing here for a few minutes."

"I..."

Ashlyn placed her hand on the bloodied portion of my shirt. "What is this? My brother never touched you."

"I need a little break," I said, loud enough for the others to hear. "I'll just take a few minutes."

"You're leaving?" Evander stood straighter and lowered his blade. "How cowardly. Or is sparring with *two* arcanists just *too* much? I thought you had come of age, and were an adult. Now I see we've all misjudged you."

"He didn't even really fight either of you," Valo called out from the sidelines. "He made a grand show of his skill and he hit Septimus once, probably through sheer luck, and now he wants to quit."

Ashlyn shook her head. "Something is wrong. This is more important than Gray proving himself to the family."

But no one replied to that. They probably all thought *this* was the most important thing happening. That was fine. We could do this. I just had to do it quick, so I could return my focus to Deimos.

I met Ashlyn's gaze, and in a couple of seconds, I conveyed to her that I was fine, and I'd handle this. Her expression told me she was concerned but accepting. She released my shoulder and then returned to her mother's side. Kaitlyn nodded approvingly to her daughter.

"Okay, listen up," I said, announcing it to everyone here. "I'm getting real bored of all this. How about the two of you—and Valo as well, if his testicles have finally dropped—just come at me with everything you've got? Magic, weapons, whatever. I don't care."

"You want us to fight you?" Archduke Kross asked. "At the same time?"

"Yeah, that's what I said." I rolled my hand, trying to get him to hurry. "C'mon, now. I don't have all day."

Evander scoffed. "Is this a duel to the death? A proper *magi cross?*"

"If you manage to harm me twice, even just drawing a slight amount of blood, I lose." I pointed to Evander. "And if I draw blood twice on any of you, then you have to step out of the fight. Whoever is left standing wins this *fun little sparring match*. No deaths. No permanent damage. Just skill and magic—so you can make all your assessments at once."

Archduke Kross tightened his grip on his glaive. "And you think you can win?"

"I know I can," I stated. "Because I've got the power of a Death Lord on my side. I mean, if you people would clean out your ears, we wouldn't be in this situation—because you would know I am too powerful to defeat, and that Ashlyn doesn't approve of your constant condescension. And if you knew both of those things, you would've been a better family for her, and we wouldn't be fighting in the middle of Orlindis."

"What a pompous buffoon," Evander ground out.

I shrugged. "But instead, here we are. You calling me names and not listening." I transformed Vivigöl into a sleeker, smaller sword. "Well? Let's do this."

But as I made that statement, another unexpected lance of agony went through my left arm. Blood wept from a new injury, splattering on the road, and my heart rate accelerated.

"Are you... falling apart?" Evander asked.

"Maybe," I playfully said, shrugging. "Should be easier for the two of you, right? The faster you win, the faster I can get out of your life—so come at me with everything you've got."

CHAPTER 39

A WINNING STRATEGY

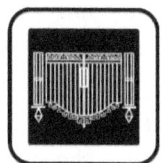

A rchduke Kross took hold of his glaive, and then lightning rippled across his body. His magical power was so controlled, it slid from his hands and coursed over the length of his weapon. The crackle of the lightning, and the intense flashes it sent across the square, frightened more of the Orlindis citizenry. Another group fled, clearly fearing for their safety.

Evander, not to be outdone, apparently, did the same trick. Lightning erupted across his body and arced along the edge of his blade. His was less powerful—I suspected because he was younger, or perhaps because he hadn't developed it as much.

Magic was akin to a muscle, after all, and if you didn't work on it, your powers would shrivel a bit.

I took a deep breath and tugged on the thread of magic leading to Ecrib.

My eldrin transformed from an orange cat into a typhoon dragon, my arcanist mark burning as it happened. But now I would at least be immune to the lightning...

Archduke Kross smiled.

I had a feeling that if Deimos were paying attention, he

would tell me the archduke was up to something. So, I kept Deimos's imaginary advice in mind as I focused on my plan to win this bout.

Deimos gave me skills—but I didn't need his help for the strategy.

Evander and his father exchanged glances. Then Evander lunged first.

The man came for me and slashed with his thicker and heavier sword. I deflected the blow, and his lightning hopped from the metal of his blade to the abyssal coral of Vivigöl. And since the coral was so much like metal, it was just as conductive —the lightning lanced down the blade and then hit my hand.

Thankfully, because I was immune, it just tingled. No harm done.

But I suddenly realized they had an extremely effective tactic for fighting people with metal weapons. Their magic would act as both offense and defense—disarming their opponents if they were shocked badly enough. And they didn't even have to evoke much. They were allowing their weapons to act as a mini trap.

Clever.

Archduke Kross dashed around us. He was trying to come at me from behind.

Evander swung down with his sword, and I jumped out of the way just in time. Then I moved, trying to keep both of them in front of me, but I knew I was too slow.

The archduke slashed wide with his glaive.

I moved away, just barely, and then transformed Vivigöl into a chain whip. Deimos's favorite weapon.

Before Archduke Kross could recover from the gigantic swing, I lashed my whip straight at his face. Under normal circumstances, I had no idea how to use a whip in the heat of battle. Thankfully, Deimos was more than a master of the exotic weapon, and the tip of the chain weapon slashed Archduke Kross clean across the face.

He hadn't been expecting that.

Evander shouted and then swung at my back. I barely managed to throw myself on the ground to avoid the blade. Then I rolled to the side and leapt to my feet.

Evander swung again while I was recovering. I backed away, leapt, and continued to stumble, never fully regaining my footing. Evander pressured me. He kept swinging, his lightning becoming more furious, the power crackling, the arcs becoming bigger.

Some of the lightning shot off his body and struck a nearby building. It shattered one of the beautiful blue windows, and the glass went everywhere.

"Stop running, *coward*," Evander shouted.

"Top of your class, master sword fighter, *still struggling*," I taunted, still moving.

The pure rage in Evander's expression was priceless. He chased me like a man possessed—he wasn't one to keep his cool. It would hinder him.

Unfortunately, the lightning evocation that typhoon dragons gave me would do nothing against Evander. So instead, I cracked the chain whip close to his feet. Evander dodged away, and that gave me enough time to get my footing.

Once settled, I cracked the chain whip again, striking Evander on the arm. He cursed and moved even *further* away, his arm bleeding worse than mine.

Archduke Kross, also bleeding from a wound to the forehead, turned to me with an icy glare.

Then he held up a hand.

At first, I wasn't concerned, because I knew his lightning couldn't affect me, but then the red runes across his body started glowing.

"Oh, curse the abyssal hells," I whispered.

I tugged on the magical thread that led to Kaitlyn's minerva owl.

A torrent of red-hot fire shot from his hand. Archduke Kross had given himself access to some powerful fire, it seemed.

Using the minerva owl wind evocation, I blasted away most of the heat. Then I leapt into the air. Wind manipulation wasn't new to me—Phila's coatl had the same abilities—and I used the much older, and more refined, owl magic to help me sail a good fifteen feet up and then drop to the center of the square. The wind padded my fall, and I landed standing up, having taken no damage.

When Evander came for me this time, he swung with his sword, but I had to dodge. I couldn't block with my blade, or else I'd be struck by the lightning and likely incapacitated.

I would lose immediately.

I managed to put a good ten feet between me and Evander, and fifty feet from me and the archduke, but that was when another cut appeared on my body. Blood wept from a slash across the back of my left hand.

What was Deimos doing?

Then both Evander and Archduke Kross started evoking bolts of lightning.

One flew straight at my chest, but I leaned out of the way. I blasted wind around the square as two more bolts came at me. They weren't literally as fast as normal lightning, but they were unnerving. I had to fully concentrate to move out of the way. I had Twain transform back into a typhoon dragon just as the next two evocations hit me. The magic tingled through my body, doing no harm, but then Archduke Kross erupted with more fire.

I backed away, had Twain transform back into the minerva owl, and then shifted Vivigöl from a whip into a lance.

With all my wind magic, and ability to make things weigh less, I threw Vivigöl like a dart straight at Evander. The lance *might've* skewered him through the chest, but he was a skilled fighter. Evander tried to deflect the blow with his sword. But the lance still slid off the edge of the blade and cut him along the side.

Unfortunately, the wound I gave him was from a weapon made of abyssal coral. It was obvious his strength had been sapped.

Two injuries.

Evander was out.

And I hadn't even used any abyssal dragon magic. It was the ace up my sleeve, but I didn't want to resort to it. At what point did I prove *myself* worthy and not just proving that Deimos was a fearsome foe? If I relied mostly on my own tricks, and my mimic magic, and only some of Deimos's combat prowess—which I was starting to learn regardless—I could at least say this was my victory.

"Evander!" Kaitlyn shouted, slow to understand what had happened.

The man shook his head and quickly walked out of the city square, his gait long, his steps heavy. His mother rushed to him to heal the injury, but he waved her away.

"You're amazing, Gray!" Ashlyn called from the sidelines.

My chest and mind both felt lighter when I glanced over in her direction. Her smile—I was glad she was here.

"Even if you have the abilities of a Death Lord, I won't let you win," Archduke Kross said, drawing me back to the fight.

"You just hate me that much, huh?" I asked, chuckling.

"My children are the future—they deserve everything, and will get everything, and I won't let them ruin their lives." The archduke moved to the center of the city square.

"*Valo* is going to give Ashlyn everything? Don't make me laugh."

Archduke Kross smirked. "*Valo* will never hurt my daughter because he'll never defy me. He'll be loyal to House Kross—he owes our house everything. But *you*..." The man met my gaze and glared. Like with his daughter, I could read his every emotion in his expression. "You just do whatever you want. And I can't have that."

It was clearer to me now why Ashlyn's father acted the way he did. He wanted to give Ashlyn a husband like a parent gives a child a dog. He wanted to pick out the perfect dog, and he probably honestly wanted Ashlyn to love the dog, but the plan was to just keep it as a *pet*.

Because that was safe.

And perhaps, like how *my* father had never wanted Sorin or me to leave our home, Archduke Kross was just overly concerned. He wanted to control everything, because that was the only way to make sure everything would work out in the Kross family's favor.

"I'm sorry, old man," I said to the archduke. "But I'm going to win—and everyone is going to know it."

"We'll see," he confidently replied.

I didn't have Vivigöl. It sat on the ground, now in trident form, which was what it usually transformed into whenever I left it alone for too long.

The archduke clenched his fists. His red runes sparkled, and his lightning played across his skin, glowing brighter and crackling louder. The people of Orlindis hurried away, their frightened gasps barely audible over the growing firestorm before me.

Even Kaitlyn, Evander, Ashlyn, Valo and my eldrin all backed out of the city's square, hiding in the alleyway for cover.

I had Twain transform into Ecrib, so I wouldn't be harmed by the lightning. Then I prepared to dodge, but I quickly understood that was a terrible tactic.

Archduke Kross *exploded* his magic outward like an ever-growing bubble. There was no dodging. No evading. No using the wind to help me leap. The wave of damage washed over me, and I had to use my arm to shield my eyes as I was blown back by the attack.

The flames burned parts of my clothing, and all of my left arm, and most of my left side, which I had faced toward the blast. The attack was powerful, fueled by the archduke himself, and even scorched the city square. The lightning shattered windows, the flames leapt to the birchwood building, and the whole area was basically trashed in that single attack.

Despite the fact that I was still smoking, and clearly injured, I just laughed. "That only counts as one hit!"

And while I sounded haughty and arrogant, and still full of confidence, on the inside, I was panicking. He *would* win if he did that a second time.

Archduke Kross's attack had engulfed the city's square and nothing else. None of the citizens were hurt, and even though the façades of the nearby buildings were charred and ruined, they could be repaired. Plus, the archduke was a typhoon dragon arcanist. He could manipulate great amounts of water to douse all these flames.

I could transform Twain into an abyssal dragon and gain the speed and power to run out of the blast radius.

But I didn't want to use the abyssal dragon magic.

I wanted to use *my* wits—*my* magic.

Archduke Kross smirked. He didn't even reply to my taunt; he just gathered his magic again, his runes sparkling, his lightning growing brighter.

He was so good at his typhoon dragon magic, when he evoked it, all the magic came out as a perfect sphere around him, which was impressive, but not undefeatable.

I searched with my mimic magic, and tugged on Mehdia's eldrin. Her enigma... My arcanist mark burned, and right as Archduke Kross exploded his magic a second time, I evoked a portal right under my feet.

Unfortunately, I had never used enigma magic before.

The portal opened, like a thick shadow becoming a chasm

that I just *fell* into, but once on the other side, I didn't know what to do.

I had escaped Archduke Kross's attack, but now I was floating in a pure white void. It felt as though I were underwater, lazily drifting in fresh water that had no current. There was no air. Nothing to touch. It was bright, and I saw myself, but that was it.

My heart beat hard against my ribs as my lungs quickly began to burn. Could I die in the little pocket space I had created?

I shook the thought from my head. I had used *dream manipulation* before, when I used Professor Helmith's magic. I had crafted landscapes and realms—I could do it here. I just needed to concentrate.

With my eyes open, I imagined air. Magic flowed through my body, and I remembered the time I manipulated water with Ashlyn's help. How magic moved from my body to the environment.

Sure enough, the enigma magic worked. I manipulated the pocket space, and air swirled around me. I was no longer in a white void of water—I felt as though I were drifting through the sky, lightweight and free.

I took a deep breath.

Everything was fine.

With a smile, I relaxed and gave myself a little time to heal my injuries. Deimos hadn't been injured again, and I wondered if he was still fighting Xuandi.

"Deimos?" I whispered.

But he didn't answer.

As soon as I defeated Archduke Kross, I would go to him in the abyssal hells—well, at least my *consciousness* would go. My body would remain here.

"Okay," I said as I slapped my cheek a couple times. "Time to do this."

I held out my hand, and evoked the portal once more. This was probably the weirdest evocation I had ever used, since it seemed to just create a little gateway wherever I wanted, but I liked it. With barely any movement, I fell through the shadowy portal and found myself, once again, standing in Orlindis.

The city square was more busted up than ever. The nearby buildings were glowing with embers and fire, the stones and glass underfoot were black, and ash danced on the wind. The smell of static hung heavy.

"*Show yourself!*" Archduke Kross shouted. "Stop hiding and *finish this!*"

I stood only fifteen feet from him, but his back was turned to me. He was glancing around, staring at the stones where I had vanished. He probably wasn't familiar with enigma arcanists, since they were so rare and so bizarre.

I quietly picked up Vivigöl.

The citizens of Orlindis were hiding, but several watched from the streets that connected to the square, pointing and gasping. Ashlyn and the others widened their eyes when they spotted me. My disappearance had clearly been a shock for everyone.

Although my arm was burnt, and throbbing in pain, I turned on my heel. My chest was bloody, and also stung, but I hadn't felt much of that during the fight. My mind had been too focused, my blood too cold, to notice any agony.

Now, after having taken a momentary break, I felt it more, but that wasn't going to stop me.

I lunged.

"Father!" Evander shouted from the alleyway.

If he hadn't said anything, I would've gotten my second strike on Archduke Kross square in the back. Instead, the archduke turned at the last moment.

Vivigöl, as a trident, was held with both my hands, much like I had wielded the glaive. In that split second, where we were only feet from each other, Archduke Kross looked both shocked and frightened.

He hadn't expected this.

And I could've thrust the tines of Vivigöl straight into his face, but I altered my aim at just the last moment. I cut his jaw, cheek, and ear with one brutal lancing attack. His blood speckled the scorched stones behind him, crimson on only one of Vivigöl's tines.

I stood in that position for a moment. Archduke Kross didn't move, even though he had been injured. He didn't cry out in pain—his gaze remained firmly fixed on me.

I had already struck him with my chain whip, and the injury was still on his forehead and across one eyebrow, but now more of his face matched.

"I win," I whispered.

Then I carefully pulled Vivigöl back and away from the archduke.

He grazed his hand over the half of his face cut up by my assaults, his touch unsteady. "What is this?" he asked. "The cuts... burn."

"Sorry. Vivigöl is made of abyssal coral. You're going to feel the injury for a while."

He'd probably even scar, which was damn near unheard of for arcanists. But I still had scars from when Deimos had attacked me, so it would probably happen.

That was fine.

Now Archduke Kross would remember this sparring match for the rest of his life.

"Gray!"

Both Twain and Ashlyn ran out into the square to be with me. Well, Twain didn't run. He floated along as a glass orb sparkling with magical energy. He was a little enigma who looked identical to Gamma.

Ashlyn threw her arms around me. Twain bumped into me

as a little glass ball, hugging me as best he could, given his new form.

I hugged Ashlyn back, but I still felt oddly drained from the fight. Was it the pain? Or the stress of trying to outmaneuver two other highly skilled fighters? I didn't know.

"See, Father?" Ashlyn broke our embrace and then wheeled on the archduke. "I told you the truth. Gray and I were in the abyssal hells, and Gray has the power of Deimos himself. We didn't elope, and now everyone knows."

She motioned to the crowds around us.

I was surprised to see Knovak and Raaza among the people on the edge of the city square. A figure who resembled Zahn was also there, but I couldn't get a good look at him.

"I'm going to marry Gray," Ashlyn proclaimed, loud enough for the whole city.

Murmurs flew around us.

"Did she say *Gray*?" a woman asked.

"Like the color?" a man added.

"What a strange name."

Archduke Kross kept his hand over most of his injuries, even as he glowered down at his daughter. "He isn't right for the Kross family."

"Then I'm *leaving* the Kross family," Ashlyn shouted. She grabbed my injured arm, which was honestly painful, but I gritted back the flaring agony as she jerked me closer. "I'm never enough. Now Gray is never enough? I don't want this anymore, Father!"

"I'm not going to disown you," the archduke shouted right back.

"I don't need your permission—I'll do it myself!"

Ashlyn's mother dashed over to the archduke, her minerva owl flying over with her. She touched Archduke Kross's face with the tips of her fingers, and the tannish runes on Kaitlyn's neck glowed again. The injuries were mended—before everyone's eyes—but just as I had suspected, white lines remained under the blood smears.

"Ashlyn," her mother said. "I think we should talk about this later tonight, once everyone has had a chance to calm down." Then Kaitlyn gestured to the destruction around us. "We'll speak to Lord Dodger, have this repaired, and then discuss your betrothal. Is that acceptable?"

She spoke with a false calm, and I knew she was angry, but the woman clearly prioritized civility. It was rather classless to argue personal matters in the middle of town. It was pretty classless destroying the nearby buildings, now that I thought about it, but at least the Kross family would fix all that.

Still—if I lived here, I'd be angry.

As I thought about that, blood dripped from my left hand. I glanced down, and my palm had a cut across it.

"*Gray*?" Ashlyn turned to me. "Gray, what is it?"

"Well..." I rubbed the side of my face. "I think something is wrong with Deimos."

Twain's orb shape morphed. He became a kitten, still in midair, and then fell to the road. He landed on his feet, of course, but then stared up at me in concern. "What's happening?"

Kaitlyn moved forward. She held out a hand. "Let me."

She touched my shoulder, and I felt her healing, but I closed my eyes halfway through.

I needed to see what was happening to Deimos.

CHAPTER 40

REVERSE HELP

When I opened my eyes, I was back with Death Lord Deimos.

It was still raining. His thoughts told me we were in the third abyss, deep below the Twilight Gate, and far from anything I had seen while I had been in the abyssal hells.

Xuandi the phoenix dragon was in the sky, and Deimos stood in the strange desert. Deimos's bone-and-twisted-metal armor was soaked by the downpour—and his own blood.

"Deimos," I said through him. "What's happening?"

He grunted as he stumbled backward, his limbs heavy. After wiping the water from his brow, he said, "Xuandi is here to take my life."

"Where's your eldrin? Where is Hektor?"

"I sent him to the Spire of the Gods."

From Deimos's memories I understood it was a location in the abyssal hells where the souls of god-arcanists resided. I didn't understand *why* Deimos would send his eldrin there, but at least I understood it was a place.

"What're you doing?" I asked, his voice strange to my ears. It was odd talking with someone else's mouth.

Deimos kept his gaze upward. The dark figure of Xuandi circled closer. "I left the sanctuary of the Requiem Throne to meet with the reaper arcanist."

"Nini?" I half gasped. "She's okay? You're helping her?"

"She's lost."

"She... lost? What does that mean?"

Deimos didn't reply. Instead, he fell to one knee, the sand under him giving out slightly, his armor sinking a few inches. When he took a deep breath, I felt the lance of pain.

"Deimos?" I asked. "What's happening?"

Xuandi roared. Then the massive dragon dove through the air, faster than the rain, his claw-talons outstretched in front of him. Deimos watched, his breathing ragged, and when the beast was close, he held up his right hand and evoked a beam of raw magic.

It...

Wasn't as powerful as normal.

The beam pierced a hole in Xuandi, but the phoenix dragon got close with his wicked talons. In one powerful attack, Xuandi swiped and struck Deimos across the shoulder. Deimos's armor protected him somewhat, but the metal bent, cutting into his flesh. He was knocked backward by the attack, and almost collapsed into the sand.

Xuandi flapped his wings, the powerful beast kicking up sand that mixed with the rain. Then the dragon went higher and higher, until he could circle again.

"He's killing you?" I asked.

Deimos exhaled. "My soul is shattered, and I can't seem to heal properly. Phoenix dragons can drain the life out of nearby people, and his magic has soaked this whole area."

"What're you going to do about it?"

"If I can make it... to the Requiem Throne... Xuandi won't be able to hurt me."

Deimos pointed into the distance, where the castle was

positioned. It wasn't too far, but at the rate Deimos was moving, he would surely die.

"Why aren't you running there?" I asked.

Deimos glanced up. Xuandi hadn't flown far. The massive abomination of a dragon kept his eyes on Deimos at all times, tightly circling like a vulture over carrion.

"It cannot be helped," Deimos whispered. "Phoenix dragon magic..."

And I knew he was telling the truth. I felt Deimos's exhaustion, even from my own body in the living realm.

"Is there some way I can help?" I asked. "Can I repair your soul? Or just, I dunno, give it energy? I'm grasping at straws here, but you get the picture."

Deimos darkly chuckled. He kept his attention on Xuandi, but his thoughts became scattered. Was he trying to think of a solution? Or just imagining things right before he passed out?

"If I died, you'd be free of me," he said. "You should hope I perish here."

"I already told you I'm going to help. Don't doubt me now. Tell me what I need to do. You can trust me."

Deimos clenched his jaw. His sight was unfocused. He seemed resistant, but then he sighed and let some of his frustrations go.

"I need to rest," Deimos whispered. "You can... take control..."

"Of what? *Your body?*"

He didn't answer. Instead, he collapsed forward onto both knees now. Xuandi noticed. The monster sharply turned in the air, preparing for his final dive.

How I was supposed to control Deimos? He had taken me over for a short time because a fragment of his soul was in my body. Why could I now see through him? And why was my body taking damage when *he* was taking damage?

My thoughts quickly went to the moment in my dream.

His body had been melting—our arms stuck together.

His soul was melding with mine, like two pieces of metal placed in the same hot furnace. I supposed, at some level, souls weren't supposed to mingle like this. That was why I felt Deimos's emotions, and knew things he knew, and why we could speak through each other.

We were connected probably more than any arcanists before.

I tried to move his body.

Deimos didn't resist.

I stood, and when I did, it felt like slipping on warm clothes in the morning, as though I hadn't been able to influence him before, but now that he wasn't resisting, I had the ability to move him.

"Deimos," I whispered.

Xuandi dove.

The rain made it difficult to stare straight up at him, but I didn't care. I held up my hand. I had used abyssal dragon magic several times now—but this was different. The moment I evoked the raw magic, it flowed straight out of me, more powerful than I had ever felt before.

The raw magic was bluish white, and it lit up the storm like a thunderstorm.

I sliced Xuandi's leg, and the monster must've known something had changed, because he veered to the side and quickly flapped his wings, returning to the sky.

I took a step forward. Deimos's body was larger than mine. He was taller, wider, and his muscle mass significantly more... *there*. I rotated my shoulders, and the injuries across his body seemed to stitch themselves together a little faster now. Deimos's abyssal dragon magic was taking effect more than before.

"What's going on?" I asked.

I was asking that a lot lately.

"Without a complete soul, my body was dying," Deimos

replied. "Now that you've assumed control, the flow of magic is no longer interrupted."

I was thankful Deimos had answers, but a little disturbed by the information. How badly was Deimos's soul shattered, anyway? And was it too late to release his fragment so he could completely heal?

But we didn't have time to discuss all that. Xuandi was still in the sky.

I ran.

Despite the fact Deimos's armor was full plate and heavy, I didn't find it difficult to move. Even though I was running on sand, which was much harder to get footing on, I still managed to run at a decent pace.

Xuandi roared again, his frustration evident.

He probably didn't understand why Death Lord Deimos suddenly had a second wind.

As I hurried toward the Requiem Throne, the phoenix dragon pursued me. When I heard the beat of wings, and saw the embers in the air, I stopped and turned. Xuandi growled as he evoked flames so hot and bright, they turned the rain into steam.

I waved my hand. Well, *Deimos* waved his own hand, but still. He used his manipulation, and the sand around my feet leapt up like a wall, taking the brunt of the attack. The fire died across the granules.

Then Xuandi took back to the sky. He was almost untouchable there, unless I wanted to evoke raw magic until I was exhausted.

"You can manipulate sand?" I asked.

Deimos huffed. "Death Lords manipulate *souls*. This desert here is made of soul fragments that have hardened with time."

When I glanced around, and saw the dark dunes and the vast empty area, my heart hurt. How many people had died to create this? But I shook away the morbid thoughts and continued to the Requiem Throne.

I ran, faster than before, power flowing into me from a spent soul. Deimos must've used his abyssal dragon ability to empower me.

It wasn't long before I came to the black-and-bone gates of the castle.

And it was unlike anything I had ever seen. The gates were twisted together, made of spines. The structure wasn't any architecture I recognized. The roofs at the top of the towers were bulbous, and at their base were jagged bone fragments, as if they were growing out of the castle itself.

The crystal-clear windows were nothing more than slits, but there were several bell towers, black flowers around the outside, and redwood door handles on everything.

"The Requiem Throne is sacred," Deimos whispered.

I pushed open the gate. It made no noise, but two of the bells sounded.

Ding, ding.

The rain ceased.

Just... all at once.

It had been raining. Now it wasn't. It was that fast.

Xuandi screeched, and then turned his attention higher. He flapped his wings, sailing off now that he wouldn't be able to harm Deimos. I didn't know why the Requiem Throne was so sacred, but clearly not even the powerful phoenix dragon would step foot here.

"Why did you go out looking for Nini?" I asked.

It would've made more sense for him to wait.

Deimos didn't reply. His thoughts betrayed him, though.

He was concerned for her. He had given her directions on how to make it to this castle, and how to navigate the rest of the hells, but once she left his side, he hadn't heard from her.

I walked through the black-flower garden that surrounded the strange castle, my attention on the front door.

With a chuckle, I said, "It amuses me that you're concerned about her."

"Oh?" Deimos's sarcasm was thick. "Here to mock me, are you?"

"No. It's just—you're a *Death* Lord. I just thought you loved death more than anything." When I reached the front door, I stopped. It was eleven feet tall, and for some reason, it unnerved me.

"It has been... too long... since I interacted with people," Deimos muttered. After a short sigh, he continued, "You may think me weak—because *I* think I'm growing weak—but it bothered me to think she might perish, and I would be alone here once more."

That struck me as deeply sad.

I grabbed the door handle, my thoughts a mix of feelings. Deimos didn't want Nini to die just because he didn't want to be alone? Then again, he had been so close to escaping the abyssal hells... If I hadn't stopped him, he wouldn't be here.

"You have me," I playfully stated.

"Heh."

But Deimos didn't say anything else. He seemed reassured by that statement, though.

"I'm going to go," I muttered. "When I'm seeing things through your eyes, my body isn't moving in the realm of the living. I think... it's because my soul isn't in pieces. I can only be in one place at a time."

"You could learn to astral project, and then this wouldn't be a problem."

I rolled my eyes. "Yeah, well, next time I want to feel like a tall, buff man, I'll swing by again to sail your body around the land of the dead. We'll make it a weekend thing. Vacations for everyone."

"I don't understand your humor," Deimos replied, deadpan.

I chuckled at my own joke. "I'll be back. Don't get yourself killed in the meantime."

When I opened my eyes, I was lying on a comfortable bed.

At first, I had déjà vu of Lord Oto's compound. Was I back there? I sat up, panicked, but quickly came to the conclusion I wasn't back in the man's clutches. Instead, I was in a room with lush red carpets, brick walls, and a beautiful blue-glass window.

Orlindis.

I was in a room with multiple beds, all lined against one wall.

My bed was the closest to the window and the farthest from the door. On the next bed over to me sat a beautiful woman with a bright smile. She had the blankets up to her waist, and her lush black hair spilled down to her hips.

When she glanced over, her smile somehow widened.

"Oh, you're awake," she breathed.

I nodded once. I didn't feel ill—I had just been visiting the abyssal hells.

"Yeah, finally ready to start the day," I playfully said.

"It's almost dinner."

I pushed the blankets off my body and swung my legs over the side of the bed. "Perfect timing. I'm starved." But a knot formed in my gut when I glanced around and found the rest of the room empty. Where was Twain? Where was Ashlyn?

"Before you go," the woman murmured, "I wanted to thank you."

"Me?"

I stood from the bed. I wore a clean pair of pants and a silk tunic. When I grabbed at my neck, I realized I still had the necklace Everett had given me, but not Vivigöl. My concerns were mounting, even if this seemed like a quiet infirmary. I tucked the necklace under my tunic, fearful I would lose it again.

"Raaza told me you are the one who brought me here." The woman bowed her head. "Thank you so much."

"Raaza did?" I glanced over. "You're his mother?"

She nodded once.

Wow. The difference in her appearance was night and day. She had been half a corpse before—now she seemed young and vibrant. What had happened? How had they healed her?

"He told me you are a student in his class." Raaza's mother rubbed at her eyes. They were glassy. "I'm so lucky to have a boy like Raaza. Thank you so much for being a good friend. For helping him. I'm f-forever in your debt."

"Don't." I waved away her comments. "Raaza was the one risking everything to make sure you and your daughter were okay. I just... helped him with the last little bit."

The door to the room slammed open.

I tensed in place, and Raaza's mother practically leapt out of bed in fright. At first, I thought we were under attack, but once a single man stepped into the room, and no one else, I calmed down a bit.

He was a large man in a black outfit. He wore a long coat that went to his ankles, rough pants, shirt, thick boots—and they were all made of leather, cotton, or dark iron plating. His shoulders, legs, and forearms were protected, and when he strode into the room, it was with the confidence of a killer.

The man had coppery hair, and equally copper stubble, which shone in the light streaming through the window. He had an intense expression, and his eyes immediately snapped to my arcanist mark. He caught his breath, but then when he looked at the rest of me, disappointment flooded him.

The man frowned, his expression so sunken, he seemed dead inside.

"Damn," he muttered. Then he dug his fingers into his scalp as he combed back his hair.

He seemed... distraught.

"Who are you?" I asked. "Is everything okay?"

The man closed his eyes. He took in even breaths, as if he had to force himself to breathe. He didn't seem well. Perhaps that was why he was in an infirmary. His arcanist mark was a seven-pointed star with a lion-shaped creature woven throughout the points.

"It doesn't matter," the man finally said. "I heard there was a mimic arcanist fighting in town, and... I got my hopes up. Like an idiot." He turned and walked straight out of the infirmary. "Forget I was even here." He slammed the door as he left.

"Wow," Raaza's mother said. "He was so handsome."

I shrugged. "I've only got eyes for my lady." I gave her a smile. "I'm glad you're doing better, by the way. I'm, uh, going to go and find my eldrin—and the rest of my friends."

"I believe they're at Lord Dodger's summer home."

Oh?

"Thank you." I headed for the door, and found a pair of boots. After slipping them on, I said, "And make sure not to get sick in the future, all right? We can't have Raaza put in any more sticky situations."

CHAPTER 41

ALMOST HOME

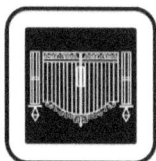

The moment I exited the infirmary, I spotted Raaza. He was waiting with his hands in his coat pockets, his black hair waving in the wind. When I walked over, he turned to me with a smile that matched his mother's.

"Oh, you're finally back with us." Raaza patted my shoulder. "I was getting worried."

"Where is everyone?" I asked.

Twain came running around the corner of the white birch building as fast as his little orange legs would carry him. "Gray! Gray!" He leapt onto my shoulder as soon as he could, gracefully landing with unparalleled skill. "I'm so happy you're awake! I was about to get water to splash you good."

Twain purred as he rubbed against the side of my face.

I scratched his back, smiling the entire time. "I'm happy to see you, too."

Miko came bounding around the corner as well. Had they been playing together?

The little kitsune went straight to her arcanist's feet. She nuzzled the side of Raaza's leg. "Are we going to head over to Lord Dodger's as well?" Miko asked.

Raaza scooped her up into his arms. "You better believe it."

"Excellent!"

Together, we headed down the road. Stoneworkers and carpenters were already hard at work at rebuilding the city's market square, because as we walked, I saw dozens of men with horses and carts hauling away charred birchwood and shattered glass.

A few of them even gave me odd glances.

It was half my fault.

I nervously waved to them.

As we rounded a corner, and headed onto the largest road in Orlindis, I spotted a man in a hood. A kitsune stood at his feet—a kitsune identical to Miko. Instantly, I knew it was Zahn. Was he hiding in plain sight?

"One moment, Raaza," I muttered. "I need to speak with someone."

"I'll wait here." He knelt and petted his eldrin. "But don't go getting yourself whisked away to the abyssal hells."

I pointed at him and forced a laugh. Then I headed over to Zahn. He wore the thickest cloak, and the heaviest hood I had seen in a long time. It was so bright in Orlindis that even now, when it was almost dusk, everything seemed beautiful. There was no reason to wear a hood, yet here Zahn was, looking as suspicious as he could.

"Do you *want* people to question whether you belong here?" I asked as I strode up to him.

Twain rested on my shoulder and twitched his ears. "You remind me of those beggars I'd see at port."

Zahn pulled his hood back just enough for me to see him scowling. "Hilarious. Truly."

"What're you doing?"

"I'm leaving," he stated. "I've heard from several people in town that Headmaster Venrover will be heading here with his husband and sister."

"*The headmaster is married?*" I thought for a long moment, trying to remember if he had ever mentioned that in my presence. "Wow. He's kind of a secretive man."

"I'm certain you've met his husband," Zahn stated. "The man never leaves his side. The two are basically together at all points during the day."

I thought back to the many times I had been with Headmaster Venrover. Most of the time, he seemed alone—but then I remembered the wendigo arcanist. "Wait, the headmaster is married to his assassin?"

"Did you just say his *assassin*?" Zahn snorted and laughed at the same time. "I supposed that's an accurate word, yes. Or perhaps his *sea bandit*. The headmaster and the man are quite inseparable."

"Well, whatever, I'm just glad Headmaster Venrover is headed here. The sooner I can speak with him, the better."

Zahn frowned. "I can't face the headmaster, so I will be off. If you need me, I'll be in Bizfile, a town not far from Astra Academy. They supply Venrover with iron and other materials whenever he expands the grounds, and they have nullstone in such quantities that I can hide from his ability to search for me."

"Right." I then snapped my fingers and pointed. "Wait. Do you know anything about enigmas?"

"I do."

"Really?" I lifted both eyebrows. "I had never heard of them."

"Only one is born every thousand years," Zahn said matter-of-factly. "They have a fable birth, in the middle of nowhere, far from civilization. I've only ever met one other enigma arcanist, and it was brief."

"Do you think... their weird powers could help us? In some way? Ya know." I lowered my voice and leaned in close. "To get to the abyssal hells? I have this feeling they're related to the Twilight Gate. It's just a hunch, though."

Zahn's tone changed in an instant. "You've seen the Twilight Gate?"

I nodded. "I can see things through Deimos's eyes. He showed it to me."

"You can?" His hopeful tone just kept getting higher. "Is that right, brother?"

"The child is correct," Deimos said through me. "But I don't know if an enigma can help us."

"I'll research it right away." Zahn turned to his kitsune. "Come, Twice. This is a promising lead. Something we can work with."

Twice nodded and then playfully hopped around Zahn's feet. "Yes, of course, of course."

"What about Lord Oto and the other cultists?" I glanced around. "They're not here, are they?"

"No, but some will join me in Bizfile. Not Lord Oto—not unless he manages to figure out where I'm going. If the man isn't providing us with funds, I have no more use for him." Zahn sighed. "I never much cared for his ways, but it was nice to have a patron who sheltered us completely."

I pointed at him. "Do you think the Kross family has the resources to help find a way into the abyssal hells?"

"They do, but I doubt they would allocate any to the likes of *me*."

I said nothing, but my mind was now filled with possibilities. What if I got the Kross family to help me get into the abyssal hells? Then I could help Deimos set everything right. It wasn't the best plan, but at least it was a *real* plan.

"Gray?" Raaza called out. "It's getting dark!"

He was right. The sun was on its way down, the last of its light casting long shadows across the picturesque city. The windows continued to glitter blue, and the white of the buildings gave the whole area a feeling of warmth, even as the night descended.

"I'll speak to you later," I said. "Deimos? You want to say anything before we part?"

"It won't be much longer yet, brother," Deimos said through me.

That seemed to really cheer up Zahn. He genuinely smiled, and then pulled his hood most of the way over his face. "Goodbye, Gray."

I was a little sad to see him go, if only because his departure depressed Deimos. Feeling almost everything Deimos did was tiring.

After a long exhale, I returned to Raaza, and as a group, we continued through the city. At first, I thought it might be difficult to find Lord Dodger's estate because all the buildings were crafted from the exact same materials, and almost appeared identical from the outside.

However, all my worries were dispelled when we came close to the river.

There was a building that was halfway built on land, and halfway in the water. It was a palace of sorts, with its own tiny dock, and its own grand ballroom. Raaza and I approached the front double doors, and they opened the moment we got close. Two doormen had opened them and bowed as we entered.

"The Dodger family is considerably wealthy, I see," Raaza muttered, his eyes wide.

"You haven't been here yet?" I asked as I glanced around.

"No. I was visiting with my mother, and I figured I would just wait for you to wake up. Everyone else went ahead, and I kinda wish I had, too, now that I've seen the place."

I half laughed. "Thanks."

"I'm just messing with you."

"You're expected in the courtyard," one of the doormen stated. "Please continue forward and exit through the glass doors."

I nodded, and then headed in the direction the man had indicated.

As we strolled through the opulent corridor, I realized we were surrounded by dozens of artworks that breathed life into legends, each one more colorful than the last.

The walls themselves were murals, hosting a myriad of creatures that frolicked in painted woods and soared through stonework skies. One piece of art depicted a rainbow phoenix ablaze with the fiery kiss of rebirth, giving life to multiple individuals who had seemingly died on a beach.

In another art piece, there was a unicorn, pure and poised, its horn a spiral of glittering power, seemingly dispelling poison. Drifting from frame to frame, I spotted a king basilisk with eyes like polished obsidian, its gaze frozen in stone.

I thought king basilisks were dangerous and violent, but the art depicted it as soft and caring as it held a dozen little baby basilisks in its claws.

The plaque underneath the artwork read: *Compassion. Without it, we make the world a crueler place.*

Sculptures of fairies peeked from alcoves, which was a cute detail I hadn't been expecting.

What a weird home.

"Are you seeing this, Gray?" Raaza elbowed me and then pointed up. "This place is wild."

Most of the ceilings were domes, each one painted with a dozen ethereal whelks intermingled with the stars. Some of the constellations had the appearance of creatures as well. A giant wolf, a long serpent, a majestic four-winged bird—so many things to see that I couldn't make sense of it all before we reached the glass doors.

"I like this place," I said, turning my attention to Raaza.

He shrugged. "I don't know… Anything that reminds me of Lord Oto makes me uncomfortable. I don't like it here."

"Fair." I opened the glass door that led to the courtyard. "I guess you'll just have to be a successful adventurer."

Once we stepped outside, I realized this was some sort of gathering. There were firepits with meat smoking, and several dozen servants all carrying trays of drinks. The laughter and music were louder than I had been expecting, and it filled me with life and cheer almost immediately.

Enclosed by the high, vine-draped walls, this courtyard was the perfect place to have a party. At its center, a griffin fountain carved from marble cascaded water from the open jaws of the mystical creature. The griffin's wings arched over the basin, as if in mid-flight, and the droplets that fell from its beak caught the fading sunlight, scattering rainbows that danced like tiny sprites across the cobblestone.

Someone strode straight over to Raaza and me, as though they had been waiting.

It was Lucian.

I stood a little straighter as he approached, his nine-point star arcanist mark unique here at this party. His eldrin, the Source of the Storm, sat on his shoulder. The cute little white hummingbird was rather fluffed. Was it full?

"Gray Lexly?" Lucian asked. "I would like to formally apologize for my attack. I should've exercised more patience."

Then he waited.

Lucian didn't say anything else. I glanced over at Raaza—the other man shrugged.

Then I returned my gaze to Lucian. "Don't worry about it."

Lucian always had an intense expression, and right now was no different. He stepped closer and lowered his voice. "My daughter explained everything, but you should keep in mind that even she is concerned by your mental state."

"Why is that?"

"You talk to yourself often. And since your headmaster

questions whether you'll maintain your own identity, just know… that I'll always have my eye on you."

I choked out a laugh. "Fair."

Lucian forced a smile, slightly bowed his head. "I will be escorting you back to Astra Academy once your headmaster is prepared to leave."

"Are we going tonight?"

"I believe the current plan is to leave after your wedding."

My thoughts ground to an absolute halt. I had to process the sentence for a few moments, wondering if I had heard him correctly.

Raaza spoke before I could. "You're getting married?"

"Hopefully it's to Ashlyn?" Twain asked with a tilt of his head. "Because this is going to be *really* awkward if it's someone else."

Lucian shook his head. "I didn't bother to ask who you were marrying, because I simply don't care." Then he stopped, and somehow frowned deeper. "Unless you're talking about my daughter." Lucian glared at me. "Don't even *look* at Mehdia if you know what's good for you."

I lifted both hands. "Whoa, whoa. Not me. I'm not that kind of man. It's Ashlyn or no one."

"Hm." Lucian patted his tiny eldrin. "Good." Then he turned on his heel. "Then you will see me once again when we're preparing to depart. Stay out of trouble until then. No one appreciated your stunt out in the city, but everyone understands it was the archduke's fault—but you've been formally warned now."

I nodded as he left. Lucian immediately crossed the lush and palatial courtyard until he reached a servant holding some drinks, and then grabbed two. He wandered off into the crowds of people, never once glancing back at me.

He recovered rather fast.

And even though he had almost died, the man was ready to get right back into a fight.

I wondered if that kind of confidence came from the fact that he used to be a god-arcanist.

Raaza tugged the sleeve of my tunic. "Look over there. It's Nasbit and Phila."

"Really?" I had wanted to see them ever since arriving in Orlindis. "Let's say hello. Then I need to find my future wife—we have some things to discuss."

CHAPTER 42

THE REAL TOMORROW

Nasbit and Phila sat at a table under a gigantic sun umbrella. It was evening now, and the sunlight gone, but the points of the umbrella were all glowing. Small nets that held one or two glowstones were tied to the umbrella's points, giving it both a mystical and romantic feel.

Once he spotted us, Nasbit waved Raaza and me over.

I had to navigate my way through the guests and servants. The energy of the party was reaching new heights, and I heard laughter and loud talking from every direction. The smell of beef and root vegetables cooking replaced all other scents.

"Gray!" Nasbit said as I approached. "Oh, thank the good winds the rumors were *not* true."

He was a round man with a round face and perfectly slicked-back brown hair. His complexion seemed paler than normal, as though he hadn't gotten out in the sun much, but his arcanist mark was more prominent than ever. It was a seven-pointed star with a golem between the points.

Tonight, Nasbit wore an outfit of white and blue, which made him seem very regal. He even wore a little hat with a feather, which reminded me a bit of Knovak.

"What were the rumors about me?" I asked.

"Everyone said you ran off and eloped with Ashlyn Kross," Nasbit immediately replied. "*Everyone.*"

Phila leaned forward and smiled. She was a tall girl with long strawberry blonde hair that went all the way to her waist. Her cute heart-shaped face was made even more adorable when she grinned from ear to ear. "I just heard from Archduke Kross himself that you were taken against your will, but that you and Ashlyn fought your way back to us. And through all those trials and tribulations, you fell deeply in love!"

"Archduke Kross said that?" I asked, dumbfounded.

Phila nodded.

Her arcanist mark was a seven-pointed star with a coatl—a snake with feathered wings. I didn't see either of their eldrin here, but I understood why. This courtyard was only so big, and most eldrin were inside or on the sidelines. Having a horse-sized creature lumbering about could make things awkward, after all.

However, Phila had some of her eldrin with her. She wore a white dress with feathers around the shoulders—rainbow colors, clearly taken straight from her eldrin. It gave her a striking appearance, different than anyone in attendance.

"The archduke announced your marriage on the morrow," Nasbit said. "Congratulations, Gray. Joining House Kross is a huge honor."

"Wait, did you just say *on the morrow?*" My stomach twisted in both delight and pure bewilderment. "As in—tomorrow? Not some other day in the future? Just... tomorrow? Not a fake tomorrow?"

Nasbit poked the tips of his fingers together. "Oh. Yes. I did mean the *real* tomorrow. But by the sound of your voice, I take it this comes as a surprise. Which is—how do I say this?—very awkward."

"I don't think it's awkward at all," Phila said. She stood from her chair and leapt to my side. "Aren't you excited? To be married so soon after becoming an adult?"

"I suppose…" It was difficult to put my feelings into words. Was Ashlyn fine with this?

I would turn sixteen in a few weeks. Most mortals married soon after fifteen, but arcanists could theoretically live forever, if they didn't die. They aged differently. Zahn was a good example —that man was actually ancient, but he didn't look his age at all.

"I'm worried Ashlyn's father is pressuring her to do this," I finally said. "I don't see eye to eye with the man on a lot of issues, and neither does Ashlyn, so this might be a problem."

Phila giggled. "Oh, we heard all about your sparring match in the city! Archduke Kross said you wanted to gallantly prove yourself to the family."

Interesting. I wouldn't have described it quite like that, but I supposed I was happy the archduke was saying positive things about me.

"I think marrying early is for the best," Nasbit chimed in. "That way, you won't be distracted by gorgeous ladies as you enter your second year at Astra Academy. A-And, also, you won't have to compete with anyone over someone's affection. I think that would be wonderful."

His mention of the Academy got me nervous. Would I have time for that if I was going to help Deimos? On the other hand, I had no way to get back to the abyssal hells, currently. Perhaps it would be best if I left the Academy and focused purely on returning.

"What's wrong, Gray?" Phila asked. "You look unhappy. Which is odd, considering all the amazing things you've done lately."

"Did the archduke mention Ashlyn, Knovak, Nini, and I were all in the abyssal hells?"

Phila and Nasbit both sucked in air and widened their eyes. Which was all the answer I was looking for. The archduke *hadn't* mentioned the most interesting part, probably to keep his story simple. He wasn't lying when he said we had gone on an adventure, after all.

"Oh, that's why the headmaster couldn't locate you." Nasbit leapt from his chair. "Gray—you were *truly* in the abyssal hells?"

I nodded. "Yeah. And I discovered it's really messed up and needs to be corrected. Or else."

"Or else what?" Phila whispered.

"We could all die," Twain interjected. "The realm of the dead will implode, and all will be consumed in darkness and magical destruction. Or something like that, I don't think I got all the details."

Even Raaza, who had been entirely too quiet this whole conversation, faced me with color draining from his face. He exchanged nervous glances with Nasbit and Phila, and the three of them came to some sort of quiet agreement.

"What are you planning to do?" Raaza asked.

"I need to speak with the headmaster." I sighed. "I might have to leave the Academy. Handle this on my own."

"I'll go with you," Raaza immediately stated.

I lifted an eyebrow. "What? Why? You want to fight a Death Lord that badly? Or maybe you're just done with living?"

"You saved my mother *and* my sister." Raaza stared me dead in the eyes. "I owe you a great deal, Gray. Whatever happens, I'll be there."

The way he said that made me think of my brother. I wished Sorin were here. I wished *he* were the one saying that to me. If we went into the abyssal hells together, I was certain we'd eventually ride out as heroes.

But still—it was nice of him.

"Thank you, Raaza," I said. "I appreciate that you have my back."

"Can I have some time to think about whether I want to help?" Nasbit sheepishly asked. "I mean, I don't know if I want to leave Astra Academy. And—let's be truthful—you probably don't need help from someone like me. I'm not..."

"Oh, pish-posh, Naz!" Phila walked around the table and grabbed one of Nasbit's arms with both of hers. His face was red as Phila continued with, "Our whole class has been plagued by the ills of the abyssal hells since we started. We can't abandon Gray, or Ashlyn, his soon-to-be wife. What if they need us?"

"Uh..." Nasbit gulped down air. "Well, but I'm not *the best* at anything."

"Nonsense! You're so good at research and reading. I couldn't imagine going on an adventure without you."

"Ph-Phila, let's be reasonable. Surely, if Gray is going to venture into the abyssal hells, he wouldn't take random students from Astra Academy. He would take someone like Lucian the Dauntless, or Atty the Phoenix Master, or the Warlord of Magic, or my father—or even my uncles. People who are, well, *heroes of legend*. I'm not... I'm not that."

Phila mulled over his statements. She then nodded. "You do make a good point." She poked him in the chest with a slender finger. "But if adventure calls, you need to promise me you *aren't* going to ignore her."

Nasbit frowned. "Do I... Do I have to?"

Raaza laughed at that, and I was tempted to chuckle myself, but my mind was still on the headmaster. What was I going to do about this? It didn't matter if I had a whole army of arcanists at my back if I didn't have a way to get back into the abyssal hells.

"Gray," Phila said. She tilted her head, much like a cat. "Do you still have the occult ore I gave you?"

I nodded. "Well, it should be in the dorm at Astra Academy. I didn't move it from there."

"Perhaps you should enchant yourself soon. It seems... you might need it."

The way Phila's voice lowered when she said the last bit

made me worried. She wasn't *wrong*. I would need it. Perhaps I could ask the Mother of Shapeshifters and her arcanist to enchant me, so my mimic magic would be stronger. That would probably be the most advantageous use of Phila's gift.

"Thank you," I said to her. Then I glanced around to everyone. "I really appreciate you all." I felt corny saying that, but I meant it. They all seemed to care about me.

"Do you want to eat something with us?" Phila motioned to the table.

"Headmaster Venrover is here, right?" I asked.

Both Nasbit and Phila nodded.

"Then I'm going to find him. I'll be back once we've spoken."

I turned and headed away from the romantically lit table, Twain still on my shoulder. Raaza and his eldrin stayed behind, eager to speak to the others. While I made my way back across the courtyard, my thoughts also drifted to Ashlyn.

Why would the archduke plan a wedding for us so quickly? What was the purpose? To dispel rumors of us eloping?

I just had to find out.

CHAPTER 43

LORD DODGER

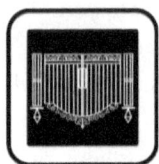

The celebration in the courtyard was so cheery and festive, it was difficult not to smile. Twain stayed on my shoulder, sniffing at the air, licking his lips whenever we traveled through a gust of food smells.

"What do you think the purpose of this gathering is?" Twain asked.

I shook my head. "I don't know. Maybe they're all just happy Headmaster Venrover is visiting."

"Oh, yeah. That could be it."

As I made my way through a throng of guests, I noticed there was a younger man attempting to juggle several empty glasses. A crowd had gathered to watch his attempt. He threw four into the air, but when they came down, he just pinwheeled his arms and failed to catch anything. The glasses broke on the ground, and everyone laughed so loud it could be heard halfway across Orlindis.

"That was silly," Twain said.

"They're drunk," Deimos muttered through me.

I stutter-stepped and almost crashed into someone. After I corrected course and apologized, I hurried toward the glass doors and whispered, "Deimos? Are you okay? Shouldn't you be resting?"

"I *am* resting."

Deimos still seemed weaker, but I was glad the Requiem Throne kept him safe. Was his soul just impervious to harm while he was there?

"Enjoying the party?" I asked.

I had expected him to be irritated, but his emotions turned melancholy. He didn't reply to my question, but I knew the answer.

"What about Nini?" I asked.

Twain's ears twitched. "I hope you have good news, Death Lord."

"She remains lost in the abyssal hells," Deimos stated. "And since I can't leave the castle, I suspect she'll remain that way."

That was the piece of information I dreaded telling my brother about the most. He was going to be so upset, especially since I didn't have a solution for him. What if Nini died in the abyssal hells? What would I say to him?

Before I made it back indoors, I spotted a smaller group of individuals all gathered around another sun umbrella covered in glowstones. Among the group was a blond-haired individual, so I veered toward them, hoping it was my favorite member of the Kross family.

When I got closer, I spotted Evander. He was far from my favorite, so I started to turn away, until I noticed another arcanist in the group.

This arcanist had a seven-pointed star with the picture of a cape and mace woven throughout the points. It reminded me of my brother's knightmare, so I stopped and stared, my attention on the nearby shadows. They moved and flickered at the edges, and I knew in my heart a knightmare was here.

"Is that a *mimic* arcanist?" the knightmare arcanist asked.

The man wore interesting clothing—a black coat with white

fur on the collar, and several silver necklaces. His gloves had metal on the knuckles, and his belt was thicker and meant for carrying heavy pouches and weapons.

His white pants and black boots were also quite striking. No one else at this party had anything quite like it.

He motioned me over.

"I'm talking to you, mimic arcanist," the man said. "Come over here. I have a few questions for you."

Reluctantly, I made my way to his group. The instant I joined them, Evander frowned. The man held a delicate glass of wine with only three fingers, and I wondered if I should also be drinking.

"Where did you get your mimic?" the knightmare arcanist asked.

"Hello, nice to meet you," I sarcastically replied. "I'm Gray Lexly. What's your name?"

The man huffed out a laugh, and several people around us all joined in. "What? Your parents teach you never to speak to strangers?" The man placed a hand on his bare chest. "I'm Lord Dodger, the owner of this fine estate. My friends just call me Dodger—and since you're here, I'm going to count you among them."

"*You're* Lord Dodger?" I asked.

He was both casual and intimidating. The man wasn't like anyone else here, and definitely held himself with the kind of confidence only a real warrior had.

"I am," Dodger said. "Most people recognize me once I'm merged with my knightmare, but since tonight is one for celebrations, I decided to go as just myself."

"You're related to Nasbit?" Twain asked. "You don't look anything alike."

Dodger shrugged. "I'm his loveable uncle. Well, one of them, at least." He smoothed his shirt. "I'm certain Naz doesn't talk about me much, but I used to watch him when he was younger.

Naz is a smart kid. Timid, though. I hope Astra Academy has been beating that out of him. My sister and Naz's father were always too doting..."

"Nasbit talks about his uncles pretty frequently," I muttered.

"Does he? Well, he's got plenty. Me and Lynus, and also Everett Junior. Well, technically they're not all Naz's blood relatives—they're just related by title. It's the legal equivalent of pretending."

"Pretending?" Evander asked with a sneer.

I chuckled. "What are you talking about? How are people related by title?"

Dodger waggled a finger. "Don't you know? After the God-Arcanist's War, there were a lot of wayward orphans. One of the god-arcanists—the bonded with the typhon beast—went around saving children who were on the brink of starvation. I was one of them, along with my sister, and we are technically nobility." Dodger shrugged. "So our *new parents* and siblings became part of our family, not the other way around."

"Is that how that works?" Twain asked.

Dodge waved away the comment. "Like I said—it's legal pretending."

"Aren't all the god-arcanists nobles?" I asked.

"Most of the god-arcanists weren't noble, actually, and no one wanted to confer a title to the typhon beast god-arcanist. He used to be a dread pirate, or so the stories say. No titles for that man, but he was absorbed into the Dodger family."

Just like I would be marrying into the Kross family.

I crossed my arms and exhaled. I needed to pay more attention in history class. Even though all the god-creatures were dead, it was probably still important for me to know who *used* to be a god-arcanist. Deimos seemed to think it was important, at least.

"The Dodger house is more of a family garden than a family tree," Dodger quipped.

Several people chuckled at the joke.

But as they giggled, my thoughts circled back to the mention of *Everett*. I reached into my tunic and pulled out the necklace with the pendant. Was Dodger the man Everett wanted me to give the pendant to? He was a member of Everett's family at the very least.

"Here," I said, handing over the necklace. "I was told to give this to you."

Dodger took the necklace from me. At first, there was no reaction, but the moment he flipped the pendant over in his hands, he stiffened and didn't move. He stared at the words for a prolonged moment, not even breathing.

"I have to go," Dodger whispered.

"What?" I held up a hand. "I haven't even told you how—"

Before I could protest further, the man stepped backward and fell into the darkness—slipping into the shadows as though they were liquid and just *slithering* away as an inky puddle. I had seen my brother do that several times, so it didn't surprise me, but several individuals in the courtyard pointed and gasped.

Shadow-stepping wasn't extremely common, it seemed.

And that was it? I didn't even get a chance to explain everything I saw about Everett. Although, I wasn't entirely sure *how* to explain the situation. Everett was still alive—that much I still needed to tell him.

Hopefully I'd see him again.

But the instant Dodger had disappeared, Evander moved closer to me. Music continued to play, and servants came by offering drinks, all of them cheery.

"My sister should be inside," Evander stated.

"Really?" I gave him an odd glance. "Where?"

"In the kitchen or the dining room. She and my father were

having a long discussion. I left them there to join the festivities."
Evander motioned to the people around the courtyard.

He didn't seem angry. I had expected a lot of rage from him.

"I'm going to go see her," I said.

Evander lifted his wineglass to bid me farewell. But I couldn't just leave it at that. I motioned him away from the group, and he stepped closer to me so we could have a mild amount of privacy.

I looked him dead in the eyes. "You're not upset?"

"About what?" Evander sipped his drink. "Our little bout? Oh, no. My father asked Lord Dodger to have this gathering so he could spread the word about the whole event, and how you fought for your love of my sister. As far as most people know, it was a noble bout in the streets of Orlindis where you showed off your skills and helped us to evaluate them. The good name of House Kross is being repaired as we speak."

"And you're okay with that?"

Evander lifted an eyebrow. "If I got angry with you at this party, it would *undo* all my father's work. So—no. I'm not angry. You proved your worth. Congratulations."

Oh.

He had to play the part, and he was willing to do that. His real feelings on the matter remained buried.

"Just so you know, I meant what I said about Ashlyn," I said.

Evander frowned. "That's fine. She's always been a little behind, ever since she was sickly as a child. I figured my sister would ultimately pick someone like you to wed."

"What's that supposed to mean?"

"It's much easier to impress a lowborn arcanist who came from a tiny island. Even my father knew—why do you think he picked someone as soft in the head as Valo to be with my sister?" Again, Evander lifted a glass. "And with that, I'll be going. I think it's important that everyone get a chance to ask questions about our bout, so I can clear things up for everyone."

I watched him go, half tempted to make him regret those words.

Twain clung a little tighter to my shoulder. "You have to practice to be that insufferable." He narrowed his eyes as he glanced over. "Are you sure you want to take the last name *Kross*? Seems like you could do better than these arcanists."

I patted his head. "It's fine."

"If you kill one of them, they'll think twice before opening their mouths around you," Deimos muttered.

I rolled my eyes. "I'm starting to think you're right."

Twain chuckled. "Could you imagine? I think Ashlyn would be sad, though."

With that, I knew I had to speak with her. I quickly went to the glass doors, and then into the summer home. While I wasn't entirely sure where the kitchen was, it wouldn't be difficult to find. The home was so open, it made exploring rather easy.

After checking a few rooms, and an empty closet, I finally pushed open a door and found myself in a gigantic kitchen, complete with five brick stoves and a pantry the size of my father's house.

And there, leaning on the counter, was my future wife.

CHAPTER 44

ABYSSAL SENTRIES

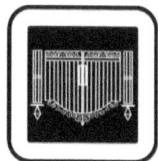

Ashlyn stood straight as I entered the massive kitchen. My boots clicked on the stone floor as I made my way over, each step echoing in the empty space around us. The stoves had been used hours ago, but it was still warm here. Ashlyn's face was flushed, but she was still the most beautiful arcanist in all of Astra Academy.

Ecrib was here, which came as a surprise. He was panting, similar to a dog, clearly upset by the heat in the kitchen. He sucked in a breath and stood tall on his four legs as I approached, the fins on his head flared to give him even more height.

"Ashlyn," I said.

"Gray," she replied. Then she motioned to a far counter. Something long was wrapped in blankets and just waiting, like a present. "I made sure no one touched Vivigöl."

"Really?" I walked over, threw off the blankets, and then admired my golden weapon. After I grazed my fingers along the staff of the trident, I transformed it back into an object I could wear around my shoulders and neck.

It felt good to have Vivigöl again.

Then I turned around to face Ashlyn.

"Did you hear I'm getting married tomorrow?" I playfully asked as I tapped my chin. "That came as a shock. I thought people were involved in the planning of their own wedding, but perhaps I'm the exception."

Ashlyn lifted an eyebrow, her stare telling me *she* had picked the date.

I walked close and stopped only a foot from her. "You're okay with this?"

"I'm the one who insisted we marry as soon as possible," she said.

I held my breath as I processed the new information. Was this bad news? No. I wanted to marry her—but it did feel *odd*.

"Is there a reason you set it for tomorrow?" I asked.

Ashlyn stepped close, smiled, and then shrugged. "I'm just excited to marry you."

"Oh, I understand—I'd be excited to marry me, too," I quipped.

She choked out a laugh, clearly caught off guard by my joke. But then her serious expression returned, and she stared up at me with no mirth in her eyes. "You were pulled into the abyssal hells by Death Lord Naiad without any warning. And then you almost died in the abyssal hells, trying to get out."

I didn't reply.

Those were all facts.

"And you talk to Death Lord Deimos all the time," Ashlyn whispered. Her blue eyes searched mine. "Sometimes you seem different. Sometimes... I think something has happened to you that can never be undone."

Her words sank into my thoughts like rocks in a pond. She wasn't wrong.

I just hadn't thought about the situation from her perspective.

Ashlyn touched my chest with both her hands. "I'm really

afraid," she said, her voice almost inaudible, "that you're going to disappear one day. Either physically or... mentally."

I grabbed both her wrists and held tight for just a moment. Once I fully absorbed what she was saying, I asked, "So you want to get married right away? Just in case I *poof* out of your life?"

Ashlyn only answered me with a nod.

Damn.

That was a good reason. I hadn't been expecting that.

"My father was against the idea, but my mother thought it was prudent." Ashlyn placed her forehead on my chest. "She said it would quell all the rumors about us eloping."

"I see."

Ashlyn pushed away from me, her stance stiff. "You don't want to? Is that it? After *everything,* you don't want to be wed?"

Her eldrin stepped closer, his nostrils flaring. He practically loomed over the both of us. Twain just gave him an icy glare.

"It's not that I don't *want* to," I said, holding up both my hands. "But *tomorrow* is really short notice. It's not even proper. I mean, on the Isle of Haylin, you're supposed to get your newly betrothed a bouquet of honeysuckles, and then there's an exchange of gifts." I pantomimed the whole thing with my hands. "And we've done none of that."

"Is it really necessary?"

"No, but having my twin brother in attendance is," I stated. Then I motioned to the empty kitchen. "And he's not here." I stepped closer to her. "Look, I want to marry you. Let's just do it in a few weeks—on my birthday, let's say. So I have time to prepare. And speak to Sorin—and my parents. I know *your family* is very important, but *my family* should also be taken into consideration. Just a little."

"What if you're consumed by the abyssal hells before then?" Ecrib asked, his voice practically a growl.

I shrugged. "I'll try *really* hard not to be abducted."

Ashlyn chuckled while she rolled her eyes. "I think you struggle to take things seriously."

"I just prefer levity when things get too dour," I stated.

"Aren't you worried, though? About your connection with a Death Lord? I'm really afraid I'm going to lose you, and that I won't be able to do anything about it."

After a long exhale, I said, "I'm a little worried. Deimos and I can feel emotions through one another, and it's already gotten awkward more than once." I smirked as I gave her a playful and knowing glance.

Ashlyn couldn't stifle her laugh. "Gray... You're the only one who can make me laugh even when I'm angry."

"But you have to admit my plan to wait for the wedding is better." When I smiled, Ashlyn smiled back.

"Fine," she said, crossing her arms. "You're right. This is a better plan. I'm sorry I didn't take your family into consideration." Ashlyn's expression softened. "And, Gray, I just... As long as we're married, I'll feel better about the future. More certain. I want to be by your side if... something happens."

Everyone was concerned about me lately.

I supposed I didn't blame them.

I wrapped my arms around Ashlyn and hugged her. Twain started purring, and I thought about taking him off my shoulder, but I decided to let him stay.

What if Ashlyn and Ecrib were right? What if I just disappeared again? Perhaps it was better to just enjoy my time while I had it. I might never get this chance again.

I stayed with Ashlyn for a few hours before venturing out of the kitchen to find Headmaster Venrover. It was quieter now, and my thoughts less jumbled. I appreciated Ashlyn sticking close, and now that I wasn't so worried, I used my mimic magic to sense what was around me.

And it was effortless to sense the headmaster's sphinx. And just as Zahn had said, there was a thread of magic that led back to a wendigo, who belonged to Headmaster Venrover's assassin. They were here at the estate, deeper in the home.

As Ashlyn and I walked down a long corridor, she grabbed my hand and held it. I tightened my fingers around hers as I continued to sense other magics. When I felt a knightmare, my heart raced—was Sorin here?—but I quickly calmed myself when I realized it was Lord Dodger.

I also sensed a unicorn near the headmaster, and I knew Knovak had to be with the man. Was he explaining what had happened to him in the abyssal hells? Perhaps Headmaster Venrover would have a solution to his problem.

Ecrib stomped alongside us, and sniffed the air. Twain remained perched on my shoulder, almost as if he refused to ever leave that spot. He really was getting bigger, though. It was getting harder to turn my head with his furry orange body pressed against my cheek.

"You know where we're going?" Ashlyn asked.

I led her down the next hall and nodded. "Yeah. I can sense them with my magic."

Ashlyn lifted an eyebrow. "I've been here several times. I bet they're in the main dining room. Everyone conducts all their business there."

"Oh," I said, faux impressed. "You mean you've been in such a fancy building before? So extraordinary!"

She rolled her eyes and squeezed my hand. "You better not act like this during the wedding."

I replied with a fake salute. "I will be on my best behavior."

But just as Ashlyn had predicted, we came to a door that led straight into a gigantic dining room. It was the type of room that was built long, with windows dotting two walls, and a table that stretched the full length. At least forty chairs were around the banquet table, each cushioned and plush. Fresh flowers in vases were placed every five seats, giving color to the otherwise plain white and red decorations.

Headmaster Venrover stood at the end of the table. I didn't see Fain, his assassin, but I knew he was close. Knovak, on the other hand, was difficult to miss. He was back to wearing extravagant clothing, only this time it reminded me of Dodger.

Knovak had a black coat with a white fur collar, and a hunting cap with a feather that hid most of his distorted arcanist mark.

His expression...

He looked displeased.

Beyond one of the beautiful blue windows was Starling, his unicorn. The stallion walked through the garden, never once leaning over to eat the grass or touch the leaves on the bushes. He kept his gaze on the dining room, an unnerving intensity about him.

"Gray Lexly," the headmaster said once he spotted me. "And Ashlyn Kross. I'm so glad to see you're both safe."

He walked around the end of the table and strode halfway down the long room before stopping.

Headmaster Venrover wore his long, inky hair in a ponytail at the base of his neck. He wore long blue and white robes that almost dragged along the floor but instead grazed the top of the dining room rug, perfectly tailored for his height. Everything about the man was ethereal, soft, and somehow a mix of feminine and masculine.

His arcanist mark, with the seven-pointed star and a sphinx, seemed more noticeable today.

His eldrin wasn't here, however. I wondered why.

"Your classmate told me all about your time in the abyssal

hells," Headmaster Venrover said. "It's unfortunate, but everyone now seems to know of your venture."

"Why is that unfortunate?" I asked.

"You should know more than anyone. There are plenty of unsavory people who want to get into the hells, and none of them for honorable reasons."

The cultists of Death Lord Naiad had wanted to kill me, that was true. And people like Lord Oto, who thought they could steal chunks of an abyssal dragon for their own use in item creation, certainly wanted to find a way into the abyssal hells.

"Did Knovak tell you about what was wrong in the abyssal hells?" I stepped around the table and walked over to the headmaster, lowering my voice as I went. "About how everything is messed up? How Death Lord Naiad has a bunch of Death Lord souls on her dragon, empowering her? And how Death Lord Kallikore is amassing an army of elder creatures? And how Death Lord Umbriel is looking to find the Oblivion Gate?"

I just... rattled off all the information I had gathered. I trusted Headmaster Venrover. Since everyone knew everything else anyway, why not just get the information out there?

"Death Lord Deimos believes that if the abyssal hells aren't fixed soon, or if the other Death Lords aren't stopped, terrible things will happen."

Headmaster Venrover nodded once. His expressions were so difficult to read. I didn't know if he was angry or concerned or confused. He just stared at me, his dark eyes searching mine.

"Do you have a way back to the abyssal hells?" he finally asked.

I shook my head. "N-No. But I know someone who is searching for a way."

"Zahn?"

I held my breath. Then I glanced over at Knovak, who met my gaze only briefly before staring at the window at his bizarre unicorn eldrin.

"Well, maybe," I finally replied.

"I wouldn't trust his methods," the headmaster said. "But thankfully, the news of your adventure has spurred many of my old friends to help."

Ashlyn walked around the table. "What're we going to do?" She strode to my side and stood close, practically shoulder to shoulder with me.

"Since you've been away, I made changes to Astra Academy," Headmaster Venrover said. "I secured most of the lands, and made it impossible to move in or out of the grounds without specific trinkets. And I've hired the best of the best researchers to help with our knowledge of the abyssal hells. If everything is as bad as you and Knovak make it sound, I think we should prepare."

"What do you mean?" I asked.

Twain nodded. "Yeah. Who is preparing?"

"Normally, students at the academy go through one year of general studies and then pick a specialization. Knights, artificers, mystic guardians, cultivators, or viziers—but I've convinced some master arcanists that perhaps we should be training individuals to deal with threats of an abyssal nature."

The headmaster slowly panned his gaze over to Knovak's unicorn. The beast still haunted the garden, looming over the flowers, and staring with an unblinking gaze.

I shuddered and then glanced away. "What's your plan, then?"

"Since I have so many people volunteering to learn about the hells, I was planning on adding a new course of study—one I would call the *abyssal sentinels*. The focus of the classes would be to prepare to enter the abyssal hells, or to prepare for... if something escaped."

Abyssal sentinels?

That was an interesting profession to pursue.

"You're going to train arcanists on how to deal with threats from the abyssal hells?" I asked, shocked.

Headmaster Venrover nodded. "I do believe knowledge is power. Well, to a certain extent. We still need to be able to neutralize a threat, should it occur."

"Who's going to teach these classes?" Ashlyn asked. "And who can join them? Anyone?"

The headmaster nervously chuckled. "Currently, I was going to allow arcanists from outside the Academy to join the studies. And I was hoping the people who were trapped in the abyssal hells might share all the knowledge they gathered, so that the realm of the dead is no surprise to our sentinels."

So, the headmaster wanted *us* to explain to a class what to expect. And he wanted even more powerful arcanists to learn, so that we could amass our *own* army of people to fight against the threat of the Death Lords.

"And you're going to find a way back to the abyssal hells?" I asked.

Headmaster Venrover nodded. "That was my plan, yes. Once we have a way to deal with this, I was hoping we would. Waiting will only cause things to become worse."

Our first year at the Academy was basically over. If I did as Headmaster Venrover wanted, I would join his abyssal sentinel studies, and help other arcanists learn more about the abyssal hells until we could find a way back there.

That wasn't a bad plan. We could learn more about the hells before plunging back in.

But was it the *best* plan? I didn't know. Deimos's thoughts on the matter seemed split. If Astra Academy was helping me, and gathering all the best arcanists for the task, it seemed like the correct move.

"I don't know how much time we have," I whispered.

Headmaster Venrover nodded. "Probably not much, given

the circumstances." His tone hadn't changed, even if his words were dire. The headmaster had an odd way of conducting himself, but at least I knew he was aware of all the dangers that waited on the horizon.

The door to the dining room slammed open.

Everyone flinched, and Knovak jumped from his chair, his eyes wide.

We all glanced over and found a man breathing heavy in the doorway. I recognized him, only because of his coppery hair and impressive physique. He was the man who had busted into the infirmary. And now that I got a better look at him, I understood he was part of Dodger's family. He was wearing the same black leather style as the rest of the house.

"Where is he?" the man asked, rage in his voice, even if his volume was low.

Everyone exchanged quiet glances.

Who was he looking for?

"Lynus?" Headmaster Venrover asked. "You seem... less stable than normal. Is everything well?"

The man—Lynus, I supposed—faced the headmaster with a look that could kill. He held up the necklace I had given Dodger.

"Where is he?" Lynus took a deep breath. "I need to have a word."

A lion walked into the dining room after Lynus.

No.

Not a normal lion.

This was a *nemean* lion. It was a giant cat with metallic steel-like fur. Spikes grew in clumps and had hook tips all across its muscled body. Its mane, claws, and fangs, were razor-sharp, but despite it appearing like metal, and clanking across the floor as though it were, its body moved like a living creature. The lion was sleek, powerful, and bold.

I had never seen a nemean lion up close. I had only seen

drawings in my class books, or heard stories from Professor Helmith.

Seeing one up close was terrifying. It had to be several tons worth of weight, and it looked deadly.

Supposedly nemean lions were impossible to kill in battle. That was myth, really, but I could see why it had started.

"My arcanist?" the lion asked.

"Find him, Vaysil," Lynus commanded. "Where is he?"

The lion turned his golden eyes to me. Vaysil's nostrils flared, and then he glared. "There, my arcanist," the lion said with a metallic edge to his words.

Lynus grabbed the side of the banquet table and then *shoved* it out of the way, flipping it in the process and slamming it onto its side. The table was massive, but nemean lion arcanists all had phenomenal amounts of personal strength.

The chairs were crushed under the table, and the clatter and destruction echoed throughout the dining room.

I stood rooted in place as Lynus stormed over to me.

He grabbed the collar of my coat and twisted his fingers into the fabric, practically choking me as he lifted me from the floor to get me closer to his eye level. I hadn't realized he was a few inches taller than me when we were in the infirmary—now it was *very* apparent.

Twain hissed, but somehow managed to stay on my shoulder, even though he wasn't graceful about it. He was clinging to my clothing for dear life, his fur on end, his ears laid back.

"*Lynus,*" Headmaster Venrover snapped.

"What're you doing?" Ashlyn shouted.

She and Ecrib both crackled with electricity, but before they could attack, Lynus held up the necklace.

"Did you bring this here? *Where did you get it?*"

This man was completely irrational. I had no idea who he

was, or why he was so angry, but he had to know Everett, or else why would he be swinging around his pendant everywhere?

"Did one of those Death Lord Naiad worshippers have it?" Lynus asked. "Were they carrying it around like some sort of damn trophy? *Answer me.* I'm gonna run their insides over the walls to paint this whole house in crimson."

I grabbed his wrist and managed to pull myself up to take a decent breath. "Everett gave it to me. He told me to give it to his family—and to tell them he misses them and loves them."

I wished Dodger had stuck around long enough for me to have relayed *that* part of the message.

Lynus dropped me.

He just...

Unceremoniously dropped me.

I landed on my feet and stumbled backward, caught off guard. Ashlyn was right there by my side, helping me get my balance. I smiled at her, and she held me close.

Lynus didn't say anything for a long moment.

"I told you," Headmaster Venrover whispered. "My students were dragged into the abyssal hells. The unicorn, and now this pendant, are definitive proof it happened."

But still, Lynus didn't answer.

His nemean lion strode over, the *clink* of each step a reminder of his power.

"My arcanist?" Vaysil asked. "What should we do?"

Once Lynus managed to gather his composure, he exhaled and then stared at me. "His soul gave you this?"

"No," I said. "It was him. He was... I mean, he wasn't *well*. He's really sick, but he's alive in the abyssal hells, fighting against the Death Lords."

Headmaster Venrover's eyebrows went to his hairline. When he glanced over at Lynus, it was still with the same shocked and worried expression.

"He's in the abyssal hells?" Lynus repeated, icy and quiet.

"Yes," I hesitantly replied.

The man clenched his fists. Blood dripped from the wrinkles in his palms. "Adelgis—you said you were looking for a way into the hells, didn't you?"

"I did," the headmaster replied.

"Then I don't care what it costs, or what we have to do. I'm going to make sure we get there and bring Everett home. Sooner, rather than later."

Chapter 45

Nini In The Abyssal Hells

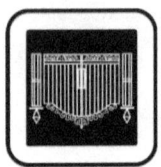

While Gray and the others were in the abyssal hells, Nini went to fight with Death Lord Kallikore in the hopes of distracting him and his eldrin long enough for everyone to escape.

This is what happened.

Nini's Perspective—

T needed to help my friends. I couldn't be scared. I couldn't question myself.

C'mon, Nini! Pull yourself together.

"*Do not fret, my arcanist,*" Waste said, not aloud, but straight to my thoughts. "*Focus. The enemy is near.*"

Being merged with Waste always felt *powerful* and *right*, but now that the fragments of souls coursed through his fabric and chains, it was different. The surge of purpose, and the increase in my physical prowess, gave me confidence unlike any before. And Waste's thoughts wove into my own, like he wasn't just clothing, but bits of myself that seeped into my skin and latched on to my veins.

We moved through the roots of the *Wraithborne Orchard*. It reminded me of the treehouse in Astra Academy—trees so large, their very roots were gigantic structures. The golden chains that hung from my cloak—Waste's cloak?—acted as limbs. I used them to grab a hold of branch-like appendages jutting from the massive roots. Then I swung from one to another, at least a hundred feet from the water, sailing through the bizarre and freakish environment.

The lanterns hanging from my chains bothered me.

They reminded me of the night... I had killed my brother.

I shook that thought away.

Below me was a swamp of souls. Dark water that rippled, even when nothing touched it. The ground was made of black and white stones, some of which were in the shape of faces. Their expressions ranged, but I tried not to look at them. Waste was under the impression they were all the powerful emotions people had when they were suddenly killed.

The scarlet sky—if you can call it a sky—had a haze of gray clouds that I sailed through. Death Lord Deimos was below me, riding his gargantuan abyssal dragon, Hektor. The Death Lord said we needed to stop Death Lord Kallikore and the elder phoenix dragon, Xuandi. While the fabric of my new being said that was heinous, I knew, intellectually, that we were siding with Deimos.

"*Fighting a Death Lord is a terrible act,*" Waste telepathically said, our minds as one. "*But the Death Lords were the ones who first broke this sacred rule. They are attacking us, not the other way around.*"

I gripped my scythe firmly with both hands. It was so much more beautiful now. Golden, like the chains. Silver, like my favorite metal. And rubies littered it in strange places, like glittering blood splatters turned into gemstones.

This weapon would be my tool.

I had to stop Death Lord Kallikore and Xuandi from reaching the others. We had to fend him off so we could all return to the realm of the living. Knovak and Ashlyn would die if they stayed here too long... and we never should've come here in the first place.

Deimos and I were high up—he flew, I swung using my chains—and it was easy to spot our target.

"Prepare yourself, Reaper Girl," Deimos called out.

I nodded to him, my heart pounding. Waste's presence calmed me, and despite my fear of the abyssal hells in general, I was able to push my dread to the side.

Xuandi, the mighty phoenix dragon, dove through the sky and nearly collided with me and Deimos.

He was so massive!

My chains rattled, and as Xuandi rushed by, his tail smashed the root I had been holding on to. Little wisps of souls cried out and faded into the gray clouds and scarlet skies.

Then I tumbled downward, my chain-limbs reaching out for anything to grab hold of. My chains latched on to a weak and twisted branch growing from the root. It wasn't enough, so with the blade of the scythe, I cut myself down my arm, my blood weeping from my shallow injury.

I splattered some on the root and then allowed more of it to fall to the stones below. Waste infused me with power and confidence.

I had seen Sorin shadow-step several times. He slipped into the darkness and emerged elsewhere, seemingly within seconds. I could do the same. I could.

Just with blood.

Reapers could blood-step. It was more limiting than shadow-stepping, since blood wasn't *everywhere*, but it was more of a teleporting ability. I had attempted it before, but Sorin was always mad at me. He never wanted me to hurt myself—to use my own blood—and it wasn't like people were bleeding all the time in Astra Academy, so my practice had been limited.

"We can do this," Waste and I said together. "Focus."

I swung into the blood splatter, hitting the droplets of red with my boots first. Augmentation magic was still new to me, and it took Waste's added concentration for me to slip into the red vital fluid.

It was like...

A small Gate of Crossing. I slipped into the blood, felt its heat, and its life source, and then traveled through to my other blood splatter far below. I couldn't breathe as I traveled, but I didn't care—I had been holding my breath the entire way.

When I stepped out, I half splashed through my own blood and then straightened my posture.

Xuandi came crashing into the soul-infested water.

His large mouth, with two rows of fangs, flashed before me. They were as gold as abyssal coral, and I had to leap away. Xuandi was so massive, he could easily gulp me down in a single bite.

The phoenix dragon's wings were a beautiful mix of crimson feathers and leathery, amber skin. Xuandi's body, covered from head to talons in scales and feathers, was the perfect blend of phoenix and dragon.

When Xuandi turned his yellow eyes to face me, I held firm. He had a mane of souls—all around his neck and flaring around his head. It was an affront to nature. That was what Waste thought—no elder creature should truly exist. Eating souls was a crime.

An unforgivable crime.

"Reaper arcanist," Xuandi said, his voice reverberating through my bones. "Your tricks won't save you this time."

Death Lord Deimos and Hektor landed in the mire water not far from me. Deimos hadn't yet fully recovered, but he didn't let it show. His bone armor was shattered in a few places, and yet, he held himself as though nothing were wrong.

"Xuandi," Deimos growled. "Your kind isn't allowed here. *You belong to the oblivion.*"

The phoenix dragon roared.

And then, Death Lord Kallikore and his eldrin joined the fray.

They sloshed through the mire toward us, both as confident as Deimos. Kallikore's abyssal dragon was disgusting, though. More so than normal. It was a sad creature without wings—its back oozed fluids, nothing more than a tangled mess of injuries. If it were bleeding, I could've used that to my advantage, but it wasn't. The abyssal dragons were filled with a disgusting goo-like gore that seemed to be made of souls, flesh matter, and pure magic.

The dragon's six eyes glanced at both me and Deimos, and then the dragon flashed its fangs. "*Let's take this Death Lord's power for our own.*"

Kallikore was some sort of mix...

Half-man, half-elder creature.

He was taller than most, but like a tree. Gaunt. Wiry. Thin and disgusting. He had dark tanned skin and black hair that rivaled the night. His eyes were a pale and sickly yellow. Disturbing to look at, and almost difficult to see, as they blended with the white.

And he had wings. Not any wings—the ghostly wings of his eldrin. He had hacked away at his abyssal dragon and somehow removed the soul-made wings of the beast and grafted them to his own back. What was Kallikore trying to do? Become an elder creature himself?

Disgusting.

"What're you doing here, Deimos?" Kallikore asked, his pale eyes looking him over. "You knew as soon as you stepped foot in the first abyss, we would all know. Yet you did it anyway. What is here that is worth your soul?"

I widened my stance and readied my scythe. It was me, Deimos, and Hektor versus Kallikore, Xuandi, and the mutilated abyssal dragon. While we were numerically evenly matched, that couldn't be said in terms of power. Kallikore had strength on his side—strength stolen from souls.

"There are humans here." Xuandi's scales flared, and he spread his wings, casting a dark shadow over the mire. "Creatures that are alive. Deimos has found a way to summon them. *The veil between the worlds is unraveling.* Use his blood to grease the wheels of destiny—let us escape this place *today*."

A surge of power came over the first abyss. While I wasn't certain what was happening, Waste seemed to have a good idea.

"*Xuandi has the ability to create an aura...*" Waste's inner voice was filled with awe. "*Normally, only mystical creatures who are bonded can achieve such a feat.*"

Elder creatures were different, it seemed. They weren't bonded to anyone, but several souls were "bonded" to them.

Xuandi took a deep breath, embers sparking in the depths of his gullet, and I took a step back, surprised. Wasn't he afraid of dying? To kill a reaper arcanist meant to suffer the *King's Revenge*—an automatic death sentence.

Deimos held up his hand and evoked a beam of raw magic. It sliced right through Xuandi's throat, and flames erupted from the new hole in the side of his neck. Xuandi screamed, and more fire blasted from his mouth.

Using my chains, I quickly pulled my body out of the way of the inferno. Seeing my opportunity, I threw my scythe. Normally, I'd be too weak to throw a weapon that size with any effect, but together with Waste, I was capable of great things.

My scythe hit blade-first at the base of Xuandi's neck. Blood gushed from the injury, but it was tainted with something blue.

Kallikore and his dragon evoked their magic. I dodged aside, but it wasn't necessary. They weren't aiming for me—they wanted Deimos.

Again, with the aid of my chains, I pulled myself forward, entering the fray much faster than if I were going by foot.

Xuandi's blood spoke to me. I waved my hand, and the gallons that had gushed from his injuries were mine to control. I formed them into hellish knives and flung them upward, into Xuandi's body.

The phoenix dragon lunged forward without warning. One of his talons was nearly the size of my whole body. Fortunately, I blood-stepped away, diving into his vital fluid and emerging behind him.

But then his tail thrashed, and caught me off guard. I was hit, stunned, and slammed into a root, my body aching so much, I couldn't take in a breath. I slid into the shallow waters of the mire, trying to pull myself together.

"You can do it," Waste whispered to me.

Or perhaps I whispered to myself.

Deimos, Kallikore, and their dragons were locked in a fight. My vision blurred as I spotted Deimos outmaneuvering Kallikore. It was like... Deimos was just a better fighter...

Xuandi whipped around, his eyes searching for me. When he spotted me, I noticed my scythe was still lodged in his collarbone. The dragon charged for me. My chains pulled me into a standing position just as the monster was about to crunch me with his gold teeth.

The hole in his neck—given to him by Deimos—was already almost healed. The soul mane was using withered arms to patch up the injuries, and every second, a few faded away. When Xuandi inhaled, I used one of my chains to grab the shaft of my scythe and yank it free.

Xuandi exhaled a torrent of fire.

I tried to dodge, but the flames managed to engulf part of my left arm and leg. Waste's cloak caught fire, and everything hurt—the sheer heat charred some of my skin, and left my reaper's body scorched.

I yelled out, and Deimos must've heard because a beam of raw magic pierced Xuandi's chest a moment later. The phoenix dragon stumbled forward, more blood gushing across the rocks and into the mire water.

The ray of magic had certainly cut through Xuandi's heart.

Why wasn't this beast dead?

But still, the dragon managed to lift his head. With each breath, more embers filled the air. It was getting hotter and hotter.

"You'll never kill me," Xuandi said with a growl. "I am immortal. *Phoenix dragons cannot die.*"

He had been afraid of attacking me before...

Could it be his aura? Was his aura so powerful, it kept him alive, even through fatal injuries? It had to be.

I needed...

I needed to end that somehow.

With my breath held, I waved my hand and attempted to manipulate the dragon's blood. It seemed my magic had a difficult time taking hold of someone's blood while it coursed through their veins—as though their being, their soul, or the fabric of their body, kept my magic at bay—but the moment it left them, it was mine.

I crystalized the blood gushing from Xuandi and turned it into deadly needles that pointed inward. I stabbed at the dragon with his own blood, and the monster roared.

Xuandi staggered backward, growling and breathing deep. It was difficult for him to move now.

My power...

It was so much more now that my chains had so many links. They were souls, and technically there were souls all around me...

In a desperate bid to gain more power, I slashed with my scythe at the water, at the roots—at anything I could reach. I stabbed at the bizarre tree, and then swung hard enough to crack a stone face.

That gave me one more link.

And my arcanist mark glowed with power. Waste transformed—the blue magic spilling from the folds of his cloak, wrapping around me like a shell. I saw the lanterns, and the fire, that had taken my brother's life.

They scared me so much.

Two more lanterns sprouted on Waste's chains, and a mask fell over my face. I was more powerful than ever before, my deep connection with my reaper undeniable.

Waste had achieved his true form. He was complete.

When I waved my hand, blood tore out of Xuandi and flew to me. The dragon screamed. I had never felt this way before, where every fiber of my being felt alive and rejuvenated.

"You're a stain on the world," Waste and I said as one. "And a stain like you will never take my life."

"*Enough*," Kallikore roared. "We should take this fight to someplace proper."

Then the ground beneath us shook. My control over Xuandi's blood left me.

"What's going on?" Waste and I asked as one.

A crack opened beneath my feet as a small portion of the first abyss was torn asunder. Water rushed down, as though being drained. The ground unraveled slightly, the whole area screeching with agony. Motes of light, grasping root hands, and fireflies all acted erratically. The fireflies shot off into the distance by the dozens, and the hands shrank into the roots, disappearing. The motes wafted into the air, never to be seen again.

I fell.

It was as if the first abyss was crumbling into the second. Or perhaps, just a small segment. Did the Death Lords have that kind of power?

Xuandi shouted. He almost tumbled down with me. Instead, the massive dragon clung to the edges of the crack, his blood showering around me.

I fell into the darkness. I couldn't see a thing, but the sensation of free fall never let me.

"*Stay strong, my arcanist,*" Waste telepathically said.

Then someone grabbed my arm.

"Don't let go," they commanded.

Deimos.

I held on to his hand, and the Death Lord yanked me through the void. I was lifted up, and up. Unable to see, I just held on. He was so powerful—more than even Waste—and my chains wrapped around his body for added protection.

When we finally stopped moving, I was standing on something. Despite my newfound true form magic, I felt drained. I stumbled, and then fell onto my knees. But I never released Deimos's hand. My legs hurt—was this stone?—and then I heard Deimos mutter something else.

"How do you fare?" he asked, his tone demanding.

I rubbed my eyes under my new mask and blinked. But I saw nothing. My vision remained black. "I think I'm okay, but... My eyes... They hurt. I can't see anything, Death Lord."

For a long moment, Deimos didn't speak. Then he squeezed my hand, and helped me to my feet.

"I have you," he said. "You needn't worry, Reaper Girl. Losing your sight is quite normal when you travel from the first abyss down to the second. Those who are still alive must pay the price for venturing too deep into the realm of the dead."

My heart hammered. I touched the mask over my face, wondering what I would do with my life if I was blind forever.

"Losing your eyesight is normal?" I asked.

"Yes. All those who are alive will lose their sight if they travel from the first abyss to the second. You will lose your ability to smell if you venture to the third abyss. You will lose your ability to hear if you travel to the fourth. And if you make it to the fifth, you will have lost your ability to taste."

My throat felt dry. "You never lose your sense of touch?"

"Up until you die—and then you lose everything."

Tears welled in my useless eyes, and Waste's inner voice comforted me. *"Never fret, my arcanist. There are ways to restore your lost senses."*

As if answering Waste's inner voice, Deimos continued with, "There are fountains in the second abyss that will restore your lost eyesight." He released my hand, but then held onto my shoulder.

He was...

Shaking.

Was something wrong?

He did seem weaker than before. But I couldn't see.

"This place is a labyrinth," Deimos said. "But there are fountains littered all throughout. If you drink the water at the fountain—and *only* the fountain—you will regain your sight."

"O-Okay," Waste and I whispered. "Will you take us to one?"

"I can't." Even Deimos's voice was weaker.

The smell of his blood filled the air.

"Kallikore will come here. He wanted to rip a hole straight to the fifth abyss, but his mastery of his magic isn't greater than mine. I stopped him, and brought us here, but he still gives chase. I need to return to the Requiem Throne."

"How will I make it to the fountains, then?"

The thought of getting lost in a labyrinth frightened me. What if more elder creatures were waiting?

What if...

What if I found the soul of my brother? What if he wanted revenge?

I didn't want to be here.

"Normally you would use bells to guide you through the labyrinth, but I know the route by heart." Deimos took a deep breath, and then he whispered, "Follow my instructions. Take the first right three times, the third right once, the first left once, the tenth right once, the second left, and then continue for some time, curving with the walls, until you reach a fountain."

His directions rattled around my dazed mind, but Waste seemed to grasp them with perfect clarity.

"We won't get lost," Waste and I said as one.

Deimos exhaled. "Then once you've healed yourself, come to the third abyss and find the Requiem Throne. I will be waiting."

Find it?

But I...

Blood splattered on the floor. I heard every drop, and felt their hot power.

"I need to rest," Deimos muttered with a grunt.

Where was his eldrin?

I nodded. "I'll make it back to you. I promise."

"Good. Then I'll await your arrival."

And with that... Deimos vanished. He left me alone, at the edge of the massive labyrinth.

Without my eyesight.

If only Sorin were here. He would make things better. He was so kind and honest and brave—I would've given anything to have him at my side.

But if I ever wanted to see him again, I needed to follow Deimos's instructions... And I needed to make it out of the abyssal hells.

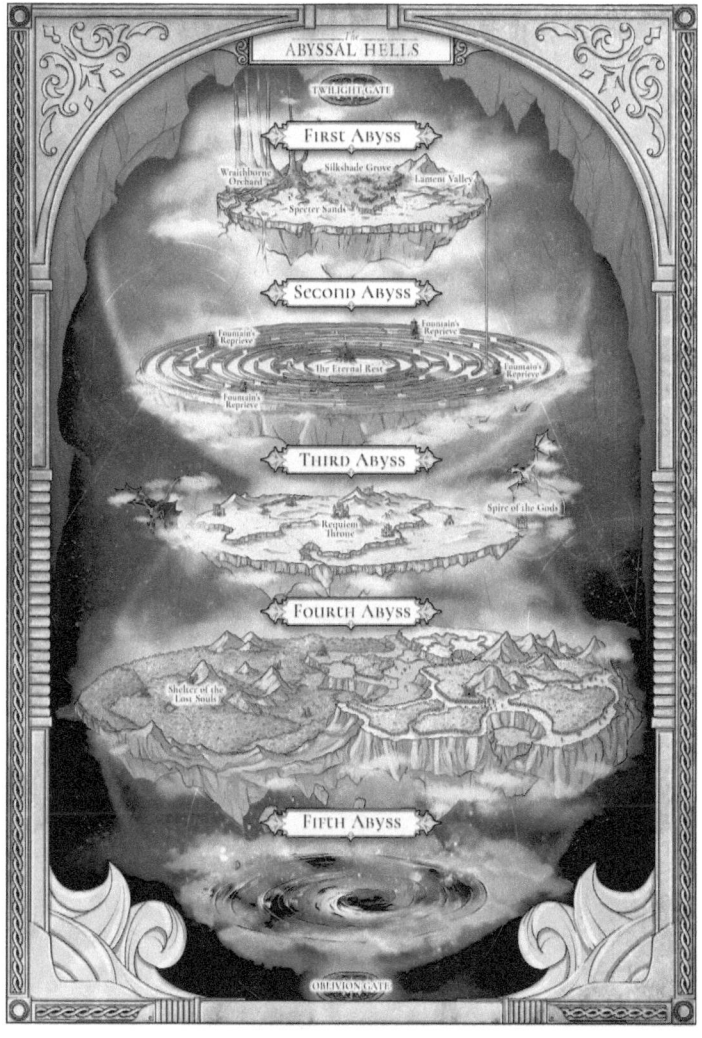

THANK YOU SO MUCH FOR READING!

Please consider leaving a review—any and all feedback is much appreciated!

Gray's story continues in *Labyrinth Arcanist*!

To find out more about Shami Stovall and Astra Academy, take a look at her website:
https://sastovallauthor.com/newsletter/

To help Shami Stovall (and see advanced chapters ahead of time) take a look at her Patreon:
https://www.patreon.com/shamistovall

Want more arcanist novels? Good news! <u>The Frith Chronicles</u> is where is all started! Join Volke and the Frith Guild as they travel the world.

ABOUT THE AUTHOR

Shami Stovall is a multi-award-winning author of fantasy and science fiction. Before that, she taught history and criminal law at the college level and loved every second. When she's not reading fascinating articles and books about ancient China or the Byzantine Empire, Stovall can be found playing way too many video games, especially RPGs and tactics simulators.

Shami loves John, reading, video games, and writing about herself in the third person.

If you want to contact her, you can do so at the following locations:

Website: https://sastovallauthor.com
Email: s.adelle.s@gmail.com

facebook.com/SAStovall
x.com/GameOverStation